THE SECRET OF
THE CATHARS

The Languedoc Trilogy -
Volume 1

AMR (Adventure, Mystery,
Romance)
Series No 4

Michael Hillier

To my late wife Sue.

Inspiration, researcher, critic, editor and best friend

Author and professional editor and critic **Caroline Smailes** made the following comments about **The Secret of the Cathars:-**

I have thoroughly enjoyed reading this

The standard of writing is very high

The narrative is strong and well structured

It is impossible to resist the comparison to Dan Brown

If you want to know more about Michael Hillier's writing visit the website:

www.mikehillier.com

Author's Note

For those unaware of the history of the Cathars, I provide the following brief note:-

The Cathars were a mediaeval heretic sect living in Languedoc, which is the region around Carcassonne in Southern France at the Mediterranean end of the Pyrenees. In the twelfth century the Languedoc was ruled by the Count of Toulouse who was theoretically vassal to the King of France. But, in practice, the region was a semi-independent buffer state between France, the kingdom of Aragon in Northern Spain and Aquitaine which was under the control of the English crown. A variety of cultural influences (including Islam) had centred on the area and this had resulted in the Languedoc becoming one of the most civilised regions of mediaeval Europe – the land of the troubadours; the centre of knightly conduct; the home of individual liberty.

The official religion of Languedoc was Roman Catholic Christianity, as it was of the neighbouring states. However the influence of the Church of Rome was weak and generally unpopular. Many of the clergy were either idle or absent. Under these conditions the Cathar heresy developed and became so strong that it began to supplant the official religion. It was tolerated, if not actually encouraged, by successive Counts of Toulouse. Rome could not allow this situation to continue and in 1208 Pope Innocent III declared the holy war against the Cathars which has since become known as the Albigensian Crusade – the only ever crusade against a Christian population.

For reasons mainly of territorial expansion, the French king, Philip II, accepted nominal leadership of the Crusade after initial hesitation. However it was his liege, Simon de Montfort, who led the campaign until his death in 1218. Gradually the superior forces of France and her allies overcame Cathar resistance until they were driven back into the spectacular mountain-top eyrie of Montségur. After a siege of the castle lasting nearly ten months, the final two hundred *perfecti* (senior adherents of the sect) surrendered on the first of March, 1244.

The terms of the surrender were unusual in that the occupants of the fortress were allowed to remain there for a further two weeks, before they had to give themselves up to abjure their heretical beliefs or be burned as heretics. Towards the end of this period they carried out some kind of religious festival, the details of which have not been recorded, before they marched out to their mass incineration. They also left behind four of their number who escaped down the sheer cliffs on the north east side of the castle the following night with the "treasure of the Cathars". Neither the four men nor the treasure were ever discovered.

Coincidentally, legend has it that the same region was a stronghold of the Order of the Knights Templar. The Templars were an international body whose headquarters was later based in Paris. However at least one Cathar was a Grand Master of the Order. The castle of le Bézu is marked on maps as "Chateau des Templiers". Sixty-three years after the Cathars surrendered, all the Templars in France were arrested by the orders of King Philip IV (*Philippe le Bel*) on Friday thirteenth October 1307. The king, as well as believing they had become too strong for him to manage, also wanted to seize their immense wealth. However in this he was unsuccessful. The Templar treasure was either spirited away by sea (nobody knows where) or else carefully hidden and, despite imprisoning and torturing their leaders, it was never recovered.

Furthermore, the southern capital of the Visigoth empire was located at Rhedae, a city of 20,000 inhabitants in the fifth century, and it was rumoured that they brought their treasures here after sacking Rome in AD 410. Rhedae, occupying an undulating plateau just to the south of the present-day village of Rennes-le-Chateau and overlooked by le Bezu fortress, was wiped off the map during the twelfth and thirteenth centuries.

Thus the region is deep in fascinating history and legend.

1

Philip Sinclair entered the building from the gloomy London street and looked at the list of companies on the notice board in the unmanned reception hall. Half-way down was the name he wanted – Smythe and Baker, Solicitors – fourth floor.

He sighed. He'd had enough of lawyers in the last few months. Now he wondered what this lot wanted. His mind went back to the telephone call he'd received just a few days ago.

"Ah, Mr Sinclair - at last! I've been trying to contact you for several weeks." There was an accusing note in the voice. "The woman at the address we had for you said that nobody of your name lived there, even though your name was down against the number in the telephone directory."

"Oh, that would be my mother-in-law – er – my ex-mother-in-law. She's been trying to pretend that I didn't exist for some time."

"Yes - well." The throat was cleared. "My name is Baker. It's important that I see you as soon as possible, Mr Sinclair. Can you come to my office?"

Now here he was, somewhat unwillingly, clutching his recently received copy of the Decree Absolute and wondering what on earth still had to be cleared up about this messy divorce.

He went over to the lifts. A sign said that one was temporarily out of use. He pressed the button to summon the other one, but it seemed to be obstinately stuck at the seventh floor. So, after a couple of minutes, he gave up waiting and unwillingly started to climb the stairs.

He wasn't looking forward to another session of legal complaints and advice. One thing he was certain about – they wouldn't be able to get much more out of him. By now he had little left in the way of personal savings. That had all been gobbled up by his rapacious mother-in-law or the various lawyers she had employed to ensure that her dear little

Madeline received every last pound and item of property that she could get.

He didn't really blame Madeline. She just carried on with her merry round of parties and shopping and more parties, somehow managing to consume the majority of two decent salaries in the process. Occasionally, she had slipped into the odd male bed to relieve the boredom of being married to Philip. It was when he committed the sin of deciding that he'd finally had enough that mother-in-law had taken over.

Puffing more than he should, he reached the fourth floor. Straight in front of him was an obscured glass door with 'Smythe and Baker – Solicitors' inscribed on it in bold gilt letters. After a slight hesitation, he raised his hand and pressed the buzzer. Various noises emitted from the grille below the button but nothing else happened.

After about half a minute, a metallic female voice said, "Please press the buzzer again and the lock will release for fifteen seconds. Just push the door open and walk in."

He obediently did as he was instructed and found he had entered a rather expensive-looking reception area. It reinforced his nasty feeling that this interview was going to cost him a lot of money.

The unsmiling, carefully-groomed young lady behind the reception desk paused from her important work to look up at him. "The entry system is standard," she said, and Philip noticed the metallic tone was missing.

"Really? Oh, sorry." He restrained himself from adding, "I would have hated to make you get up and walk ten feet to open the door," in case the sarcasm might cost him more money.

"Please take a seat."

He obediently sat on the edge of the nearest chair and waited patiently, hoping to be economical. After a few minutes, the receptionist broke off from her important work and picked up the phone. There was a pause before she said, "James? Mr Sinclair has arrived." She replaced the phone and looked at Philip. "He will be with you as soon as he's free."

The words were hardly out of her mouth when a short, middle-aged, balding man bounded out of one of the glass doors. He had a round, pink face and wore half-moon spectacles.

"Welcome, Mr Sinclair." He held his hand straight out in front of him to be shaken. His smile seemed to be genuine. Philip found himself liking the man. He hoped he wasn't going to be too expensive.

"Come into my office."

Philip followed him out of the ultra-modern reception area into a typically old-fashioned lawyer's office. All the walls, except where there were windows or doors, were covered from floor to ceiling with deep shelves. And all the shelves seemed to be stacked high with dusty old books or bundles of papers tied up with pink ribbon.

"Please take a seat." Baker removed two files from a chair and made a show of dusting off the seat. Then he went round to the far side of his desk.

"Now, what did I want to talk to you about?" He shuffled through the stacks of paper on his desk until he found the file he wanted, already waiting on his blotter. "Ah, yes." He picked up the file and took his seat.

After opening it and studying the first sheet of paper he resumed. "Ha-hmm. I apologise but, before I talk to you about this matter, I need you to provide proof of identity. Do you have one of those new-fangled photo driving licences?"

Philip took out his wallet and extracted the seven-year-old piece of plastic, which he passed to the solicitor. Baker studied both the back and front of it carefully. He squinted at the photo through his glasses. Then he gazed across the desk at Philip with his disconcertingly pale blue eyes.

"Yes," he said at last, "I think that will do." He handed back the card. "Well, Mr Sinclair, my name is James Baker. I am dealing with the estate of Mrs Marie Sinclair."

"Her estate? Do you mean grandmother's dead?"

Baker lowered his head. "I'm afraid so. Three weeks ago. It's taken me that long to find you."

"Oh, dear. Poor old gran. I feel awful. I should have been there."

The solicitor leaned forward. "I don't know that you would have been able to help. I understand her death came quite suddenly."

Philip sighed. "I'm afraid I've been so wrapped up in my own problems that I haven't been in touch with her recently. I should have thought more about her."

"Well." Baker smiled sympathetically. "I hadn't seen anything of her myself for more than a year. She came to visit me here, soon after your father died, to alter her Will in your favour. That was in January of last year. Even then, at the age of ninety-two, she was still a doughty old lady."

"How did she die?"

"I understand it was a heart attack. She had a mild one at home and was admitted to hospital in Yeovil. A few hours later she had a second, more serious one. It was that which killed her."

"Has the funeral taken place?"

Baker nodded. "Last Thursday in Templecombe. I did attend to represent you."

"Thank you."

"She has been buried in the local churchyard. A headstone has been erected near the tower, in case you wish to visit some time."

Philip smiled. Perhaps he'd have time to do that now.

"While I was there," continued Baker, "I was given a bag containing her keys and some of her personal possessions which I have here for you. An unsealed letter, addressed to you, was in the bag. I hope you don't mind, but I took the liberty of reading it in case there was anything important that I should deal with." The man looked embarrassed. "You see, I didn't know when I would be able to get hold of you."

He laid the file back on the blotter and took out the envelope which he handed across the desk to Philip. "The contents are quite unusual."

Philip lifted the flap of the envelope and took out two sheets of paper which were filled with writing in his grandmother's small neat hand. He could almost hear her old but decisive voice as he started to read:-

Dear Philip,

Since the death of your father, you are now the last of the Sinclairs – a family name which goes back nearly a thousand years. Although I was disappointed to hear of your divorce from Madeline, I must confess I was not surprised. Those university romances which take place in that cloistered setting often do not last. I suppose twelve years is quite a long time in this modern world. And I hope the divorce will give you an opportunity to meet a young woman who will be able to give you children to continue the Sinclair line.

By the time you read this, you will probably be aware that I have named you as my heir. You may not be enthusiastic about inheriting the large old house in Templecombe, which has been the home of the Sinclairs since they came from France more than seven centuries ago. However, I ask you not to sell the place, even if you can't bring yourself to live in it.

You will find there is a substantial sum of money left to you, even after paying death duties. I am happy that you should do with this as you please, but I ask you to promise me to spend some of it on a task which I wish to set for you.

Some time ago, I discovered some interesting documents in the loft which go back to the building of the house by Phillipe de Saint Claire. He was a Cathar perfectus who escaped from the fall of Montségur in 1244. Among the other papers, there was a journal written by Phillipe about his experiences. It was written in the language of old Occitan – the common language in the South of France in those days. It took me many years of study before I was able to translate it. You will find my translation in the drawer beside my bed and I ask you to read it.

When you do, you will see that it describes Phillipe's escape with part of 'The Secret Treasure of the Cathars' tied to his back and how he hid it in a castle in the Pyrenees called le Bézu. The task I now set you is to go to this castle, do your best to attempt to find the hiding-place he describes and, if possible, try to recover it for the Sinclair family as your legitimate inheritance.

11

Of course, I appreciate that French officialdom or the owners of the castle may prevent you from taking possession of it. However, I would expect you to do your best to find out what the secret is and to publicise it for the wider information of mankind.

May I wish you the best of luck with this task and the full enjoyment of your inheritance in the future.

Philip put down the letter and looked across at James Baker who smiled and raised his eyebrows.

"I told you it was unusual."

Philip grinned. "She doesn't ask much, does she?"

"I don't know about that. It's a perfectly practical task. I understand that you no longer have any family ties to prevent you from going to France."

"But I've got no idea how long it will take."

"It's only a long day's drive from the channel ports. Surely you can take a fortnight's holiday to visit the place. That should give you an idea of the size of the problem."

"And I don't know what it would cost."

Baker leaned forward. "I don't think the question of money should be a problem. I've done a quick assessment of your grandmother's assets and, after all expenses and death duties are paid, I estimate the estate will be worth well over a hundred thousand pounds. That's not including the house in Templecombe."

Philip whistled. "A hundred thousand pounds? I'm going to get that much?"

The solicitor nodded.

"And I came here expecting to have to pay *you* money."

"How nice it is," said James Baker, "to be the bearer of good tidings."

Philip took a deep breath. "Well," he said, "at the weekend I'd better go down to Templecombe and look for this journal. Perhaps it will give me some idea of the problems I'm likely to encounter."

"I have the keys here." Baker rose and went to the corner of the room where a dark blue duffle bag lay. He picked it up and passed it to the young man. "The keys are in there, together with various other personal items and several hundred pounds in cash. Your grandmother seemed to want to be well provided for when she went into hospital. Of course it is all yours."

"Once I've found out something about this place - le Bézu, I'll have to talk to my employers about a holiday. I must say I feel I could do with one."

"I could let you have an initial cheque for ten thousand, after I obtain probate – probably in about two weeks."

"Ten thousand pounds?"

Baker nodded. "That's right. I would have to hang on to the rest until I've settled all the bills and paid the Inland Revenue – say two to three months."

"So I could arrange for my holiday to start in about three weeks?"

"That seems perfectly possible. Leave me your home address and up-to-date telephone numbers and I will contact you when I've got the cheque ready."

"One thing I need to check," said Philip, "is the exact date when my gran died."

He left James Baker with the delightful information that Marie Sinclair had died two days after the Decree Absolute was issued. That meant his ex-mother-in-law wouldn't be able to sink her claws into any of his inheritance. She would be furious.

In the smart reception lobby, he scandalised the receptionist by blowing her a kiss as he went out. On the landing outside he found that the lift was waiting for him with the doors wide open. As he left the building the sun came out to brighten the dull London street.

2

André Jolyon pulled the Land Cruiser into the lay-by and switched off the engine.

"This is as close as we're going to get."

Jacqueline climbed down from the passenger seat and walked round to the front of the vehicle, her slim body moving easily. She rested one hand on the warm bonnet and gazed up at the small part she could see of the ruins of the chateau, clinging to the series of precipitous rocky peaks which projected from the forested slopes.

André leaned on the steering wheel and watched her. A teasing wind was blowing a veil of titian hair across her cheek and partly obscuring the beautiful, almost purple eyes which had captivated her TV audiences. He had admitted to himself a while ago that he was in love with her. He certainly didn't want to be anywhere else but in her company. He knew his devotion was a waste of effort. The emotion wasn't returned. Jacqueline Blontard was already the most famous archaeologist in France and, as far as he knew, she had reached the age of thirty-two without losing her heart to anybody. With a sigh, he pushed open the door and joined her in front of the vehicle.

"There it is then, Jo." She linked her arm through his. "Not much to see, is there?"

"Is it worth all the effort?" As far as he knew she had been camping outside the Department of Ancient Monuments for nearly a year to get permission to excavate at this location. But he didn't understand why it was so important to her.

"We won't know until we get up there and start clearing away more than five hundred years of vegetation and detritus." She turned and grinned at him in that heart-stopping way that had made her such a hit on television. "Come on. Let's go up and have a look around."

She set off with long, energetic strides along the overgrown path that led up the hill. He followed close behind her ready, as always, to help her if she got into difficulties. They passed a small sign which informed the few members of the public who got this far that they were approaching the ruined Cathar stronghold of le Bézu.

Jolyon always made sure he was ready when she needed him. He realised that to her he was just her special assistant - part minder, part enabler, part enforcer, part organiser – but he would never be any more. He performed all of his duties to her complete satisfaction. His reward, as well as sharing a part of the funds and the reflected glow she attracted, was the occasional night in her bed and the knowledge that she looked on him as her best friend and support. And he had decided to accept that was as far as their personal relationship would ever progress. He would have to keep his love to himself.

They didn't talk much on the ascent. Instead, they kept their breath to cope with the steepness of the path and the irregular rough stretches of scrambling over rocks.

"You will have to warn all the helpers to be careful of the rough terrain," she observed as they struggled over one particularly difficult section. "We can't afford to have any accidents."

"I've chosen three guys for the start who also have experience of rock-climbing. I've warned them that the site is very rugged. That's really whetted their appetites. They have promised me that they've all got suitable kit."

"I know I can always rely on you to think of these things, Jo."

The comment was unnecessary. They both knew that he wouldn't let her start any kind of archaeological exploration without proper preparations being made. It was his particular talent. She had found this out when he was seconded to her by the Louvre for her first television series *The Archaeological Treasures of the Louvre*. That series had been so successful that it had made Jacqueline Blontard a household name throughout the French-speaking world. She had refused to let Jolyon go back to his old job and had insisted that he accompany her on all her subsequent digs. She had appointed him as her technical director on the second record-breaking series, *Napoleon's*

Archaeological Adventures in Egypt. Now it was unthinkable to each of them that they should start a new project without the other.

When they had scrambled up the slope and finally reached the remains of the eastern entrance to the castle, they climbed over a rough cattle fence, scrambled up the remains of a low wall and found themselves on a small level terrace where, they paused to catch their breath. Even though they hadn't yet climbed to the top of the chateau, they could see the views were magnificent.

"Wow! Look at that."

Jolyon looked down where she was pointing. Carved rather crudely into the large stone step at her feet was an equal-armed cross with forked ends held within a circle - the symbol of the Knights Templar. André felt a tingle run down his spine.

"Do you think it's genuine?"

She shrugged. "It hardly matters, does it?" She looked at him seriously. "I have every reason to believe there is a lot more evidence here of both the Templars and their predecessors – the Cathars."

"Ah." He grimaced. "Sounds like your old uncle talking."

"I'm serious, Jo. Nobody else may have believed him. But he told me enough when I was a youngster for me to be confident his research notes weren't a tissue of lies."

André kept silent. So this was why she had chosen le Bézu. He knew Jacqueline still believed old Albert Blontard had been badly treated by the academic world when he published his ground-breaking exposure of the end of the Cathars. The problem was that the old boy had failed to come up with enough supporting evidence to back up his astonishing claims. He had been ridiculed by his contemporaries and had never been able to get the funding to continue his work. Jolyon swallowed. It looked as though Jackie was hoping to find evidence to support his claims. She was very sensitive about this subject. He would have to be careful in his choice of comments to avoid upsetting her.

He looked round at the scene. The weather wasn't particularly fine today and there were great banks of cloud hiding the high Pyrenees to the south. Those were being driven along by a strong westerly wind. The nearer, lower mountains were clad almost to their peaks in dark forest but, as they looked away to the northwest, the sun suddenly came out and lit up the village of Rennes-le-Chateau, about six kilometres away. Jacqueline pointed towards the main centre of fascination with the local legends for the last one hundred and fifty years.

"That's where the famous cleric, Bérenger Saunière, lived in the late nineteenth century."

"Do you mean the poor parish priest who became fabulously wealthy but nobody knows how?"

"That's it. And the area between here and the village was once the city of Rhedae, capital of the Visigoth empire."

"My God, that must have been a big place."

She nodded. "Twenty thousand inhabitants, one of the largest cities in France a thousand years ago until it was laid waste by Simon de Montfort in the Albigensian Crusade."

Jolyon looked around him at the remains of the chateau. It was difficult to make out much of the original construction. The mountain itself was spectacular enough. The series of giant rocky teeth which climbed into the low cloud were impossible to scale without full rock-climbing kit. The walls which once linked them into an impregnable stronghold had now mainly crumbled away or been robbed for use in later buildings in the neighbourhood. What remained around the bottom of the sheer rocks was now shrouded in dense undergrowth. The effect was awe-inspiring.

"I bet this fortress was a sight in those days."

"It certainly was," she agreed. "On the north side of the ridge there's a sheer drop of more than thirty metres. The guys working on that side will have to wear safety harnesses."

He turned and faced her. "This is going to be totally different from our normal excavations, Jackie. The site is going to be very difficult to explore. Why are you doing it? What are we looking for?"

"Anything." She had the grace to look slightly embarrassed. "I want to prove some points. I believe we will find the evidence here."

17

She hurried on when he pulled a face.

"Jo – before Uncle Albert committed suicide, he made a Will leaving me all his papers. He had nothing else to leave. Every franc he possessed had been invested in his search for the Cathar remains. He had nothing left but those papers."

"And you want to carry on his work."

"Not exactly. During the last fifteen years, whenever I could find the time, I have been working through his notes. They took up seven filing cabinets, so it wasn't quick. However, I think I've picked up enough to convince me that the answer is here under our feet."

"You believe this castle is the hiding-place of the Cathar treasure?"

"I wouldn't go so far as to say that. I'm looking for facts. All I know up to now about le Bézu is that the chateau was confiscated from the Cathars by Simon de Montfort. Later it was awarded to Pierre de Voisins in 1231."

"I've not heard of him before. Who's this chap de Voisins?"

"He was a very interesting character. You'll know that the Albigensian Crusade was led by Simon de Montfort. Pierre de Voisins was one of his lieutenants. Some time after de Montfort's death, he seems to have decided to withdraw from the Crusade and retire to le Bézu."

"Are you hoping to find out more about him by excavating here?"

She shook her head. "De Voisins is only peripheral to what I'm looking for. Uncle's files contained Occitan documents with references to him. My reading of those notes suggests de Voisins had a change of heart in later life and became sympathetic to the Cathar cause. In fact, it is possible that le Bézu may have become a haven for some of the Cathars escaping from Montségur."

Jolyon looked puzzled. "It doesn't seem much of a basis for a major excavation."

"Come off it, André." Her face was flushed with enthusiasm as she looked up at him. "We know that only four Cathar *perfecti* escaped from Montségur and they were recorded as taking 'The Treasure of the Cathars' with them. Le Bézu is not much more than a long day's walk through the mountains from Montségur. I have been unable to find records of any other safe havens in the area. The Cathar escapers and their treasure have never been found. Can you think of a more likely place for them to have come than here?"

"But wouldn't they have been pursued by the French?"

"Yes – sooner or later. However, suppose de Voisins was willing to shelter them, being secretly sympathetic to the Cathar cause. All he needed to say was that he hadn't seen the escapers. Nobody would have been likely to argue with *him*." She swept her arm round, indicating the whole site. "If they didn't accept his word, it would have resulted in another twelve-month siege of a powerful and easily-defended castle. In addition, the French would have assumed that de Voisins was an enemy of the Cathars, so they would have been much more likely to accept his word and look elsewhere."

"OK, Jackie." He grinned. "I can see *you're* convinced. Who am I to argue?"

She tossed her head angrily. "In any case it fits in with the rest of the research I've been doing about the Albigensian Crusade and its aftermath. So I want to check it out."

"I still think it's hardly enough to justify a whole summer's excavations in a remote spot like this." He hesitated. "Are you sure you are being professional about this?" That was as far as he dared to go in arguing with her.

Jacqueline stared into the distance, her eyes misting over. "Maybe I'm not. But I still can't forget the stories my uncle used to tell me when I was a little girl. He swore they were true, Jo."

André wasn't so sure, but he decided not to confront her further on that topic.

"So how did you sell it to the backers?"

She shrugged. "I didn't have to sell it to them. After the success of the last two series, they were desperate to get me started on a new one. I only had to point to the spectacular nature of the site and the huge interest in the Cathars which there is throughout France, to get their backing. Once we've got something to show them we'll have the television crews down here. That's another reason why we have to get the site safely roped up."

"Huh. That's *if* we've got something to show them."

Jacqueline looked at him sharply. There was more than a hint of aggression in her reply. "It's not like you to be negative, Jo. It's normally me who's holding *you* back."

"I just don't want you to slip up, Jackie. Your career has been all success so far. I don't want this one to be a flop." He grinned, trying to mollify her. "Of course, I'm partly thinking of myself as well as you."

"It won't be a flop." She linked her arm through his in the way she had of persuading him. "Even if we don't find anything, we've still got a damn good story to tell. Don't worry, Jo. Have I ever let you down?"

"No, you haven't." He admitted. "OK. I accept the Cathars are your new fixation."

"Remember, Jo - this was a very murky period in French history. Languedoc wasn't a full part of a united France in those days. The Albigensian Crusade was a particularly bloody affair. I believe the French have to face up to this old skeleton in their cupboard. But – much more than that – it also involves the very truth about the origins of Christianity. That's what will sell the series all over the world."

Jolyon was starting to feel a bit worried about that. Publicity was a two-edged sword. He could see that there might be a lot of opposition from very influential groups in the government and the Roman Catholic Church. Was that what was niggling at the back of his mind? He hadn't got any other good reason for doubting her. In fact, he didn't know why he wasn't happy about this new project. Perhaps it was the strange sensation of remoteness which the site encouraged. But it wouldn't be any good trying to put her off without a very good reason. Jackie could be extremely obstinate at times. So he decided to ignore his doubts. He shook his head and turned away, looking up the ridge towards the highest peak.

"So – what are we looking for then?"

"I won't know precisely until we start digging. Look, Jo - this is a wild, untamed site. It's more than four hundred years

20

since anybody was here except the odd casual tourist. I doubt whether anyone has ever properly explored it in a structured way. We're going to clear the site section by section, photograph it, measure and draw it on the computer in three dimensions, investigate any anomalies or potential hiding places. Then we'll go on from there."

"Are you expecting to find anything valuable?"

She shrugged again. "I don't know. The castle is known as the fortress of the Templars. As well as the Cathar connection, there have been vague local rumours for centuries about treasure being hidden round here. But I discount those."

"You're doing this for research?"

"That's right. Even if we don't find anything specific, we'll still be able to produce a detailed survey of a former Cathar stronghold. It will form a novel and effective backdrop to the Albigensian series." She turned and grinned at him. "And can you think of a better place to spend a summer's excavation?"

The cheekiness of her expression made him laugh. She suddenly seemed half her real age. He felt as though he was confronting a naughty schoolgirl.

"Oh - I'm not complaining." In truth, he had to admit he would probably enjoy the next few months here with Jackie and a few other archaeologists and students. "What I don't understand is how you managed to get permission. They're pretty tough on licences in this area."

"Ah. There I was just a little bit crafty," she said. "When I first submitted the application to excavate at Rennes-le-Chateau, I knew I didn't stand a chance of receiving a licence. All the publicity of the last thirty years, combined with the huge pressure brought by the Church, has ensured that the place is shut up like a prison. If a person so much as carries a spade up the main street of Rennes-le-Chateau he is likely to be arrested. So I knew I'd never get permission there. The place is shut down tight. But, with my television backers, Jo, I pack a lot of punch nowadays."

"You can say that again. Half of France would be howling for their blood if they seemed to be treating you unfairly."

"They were frightened I'd make a big fuss if I didn't get some sort of go-ahead. They kept putting me off for about six months, until they knew they were going to have to give me an answer one way or the other. Then I pretended that I'd got tired of waiting and banged in an alternative application to work here." She laughed outright. "They were so relieved that they gave me the licence straight away without putting any conditions on it."

"You never were interested in Rennes?"

"Of course not. That place was cleaned out more than a century ago. On the other hand, this is one of the few Cathar strongholds which weren't razed to the ground in the wake of the Albigensian Crusade. I hope we'll find some interesting remains here - that is providing Saunière didn't pillage this site in his forays into the countryside around the area."

She rested a hand on his shoulder. "The other good thing, Jo, is that nobody knows that we are here so far. Of course, I expect someone will start asking where we've disappeared to in due course. And, in a few months, some hungry news-hound will track us down, but I'm counting on getting most of the season's work completed before we're troubled by treasure seekers and all the other characters who'll be poking around as soon as they find out what we're doing."

Jolyon frowned. "I hope you're right. But let's get practical." He looked along the ridge, running irregularly for more than two hundred and fifty metres, and broken up into several sections by the rugged terrain. "This is a big, irregular site. So where do you want us to start?"

"It might as well be at this eastern end. The first thing you'll need to do is get your guys to carefully rope off a secure working area. And I don't want anyone scrambling around outside the safe zones. It's too dangerous." She prodded him in the chest. "And that includes you, André Jolyon. I know what you're like."

He smiled lopsidedly. "OK. You're the boss. Gaston Lesmoines and the other two rock-climbers you took on are turning up on Monday. Their first job will be to fix anchors and safety ropes. Will that satisfy you?"

22

"Just remember you've promised." Her eyes were suddenly serious. "You're too valuable to me to take any silly risks."

"Of course I promise. Do you want to explore any further today?"

"No. I think it's too dangerous until we've got the ropes firmly fixed all the way along both sides of the ridge." She wagged a finger at him. "I tell you I don't want any accidents. We'll go back to the hotel in Quillan now and start to plan our campaign."

Without further hesitation, she set off back down the rough path towards the car. He watched her trim, lithe figure as she sprang over the boulders. Perhaps she was right. Perhaps the next few months would be fun. And it would be good for a change to be away from all the publicity which usually hounded Jacqueline Blontard nowadays.

He followed her more slowly, deep in thought.

3

The magnificent timber gates of the Bishop's Palace were firmly closed. The big man with the fair crew-cut hair style lifted a large fist and hammered upon them. He paused to listen as the echoes rattled along the street. He counted to twenty then raised his hand to strike again. As he did so, the door began to move. It swung back with a grinding sound, and he saw a short, tonsured monk standing in the gap before him. The fellow lifted his head in silent attention but his eyes avoided the big man's.

"My name is Jean-Luc Lerenard. I have an appointment with Monsignor Clemente Galbaccino."

The silent priest lowered his head and moved to close the door, but Lerenard had his foot in the gap before it shut. He leaned against the door and it opened with little resistance.

"I will wait inside."

The monk raised no objection. He stood aside as the big man entered, then closed the door behind the new arrival and dropped the securing latch, before padding away down the short, arched corridor to the sunlit cloister beyond. Feeling that he had made his point, Jean-Luc let him go. He stood patiently and studied his surroundings. Although he would not have admitted it if questioned, he was impressed by the ancient, nearly blackened stonework, the peaceful silence which reigned in this haven from the violent life that he knew, and the almost tangible atmosphere of unchanging faith which seemed to reach back over centuries.

It was several minutes before the cleric returned. He stood just inside the archway leading to the quad and said in a high, piping voice, "Please to come this way."

Lerenard followed him across the sun-patched quadrangle, along a paved corridor and up two flights of stone steps to a half-open landing. The monk stopped in front of an old timber door, knocked, paused and knocked again. Then he opened it without audible invitation. He stood aside to allow Jean-Luc to enter and closed the door quietly behind the big man.

Across the room in a sunny bay window sat a man dressed in a plain charcoal grey suit. The cardinal had his back to him and was bent over a desk, apparently reading some book or document which couldn't be seen from the other side of the room. It wasn't a usual side of Lerenard's character to remain quiet and let others dictate to him, but on this occasion he held his peace and waited for the cardinal to speak.

After a long two minutes, the man raised his head from what he was studying and swivelled in his chair to face the room. Galbaccino had a round, pink visage topped by thinning white hair. Jean-Luc knew him to be well over seventy years of age, yet the man looked no more than fifty. Presumably that was the benefit of a lifetime of self-denial.

"You are Jean-Luc Lerenard?"

"Yes."

"I was pleased with the way you handled the release of Father Juan and the ten members of his flock in Medellin."

"It was only eight." Jean-Luc straightened his back and looked straight at the old man. "I regret that the five *terroristas* died in the fight."

"Only the evil ones died," said the cardinal, "and that could not be avoided."

Lerenard kept silent. He knew he did not need to comment further.

"We have another task for you." Galbaccino paused a moment. "It is a far more delicate task."

The old man stared deep into Jean-Luc's eyes. It was surprising how his look could penetrate – seemingly to the centre of the big man's soul.

"And no-one is to die this time." The cardinal sighed. "Unless it is unavoidable."

Galbaccino pointed a finger at him. "If that should happen it is essential that the death must appear to be an accident. Do you understand?"

"Yes."

Lerenard waited for the rest of the instructions.

25

The nasty part of business concluded, the cardinal seemed more at ease. "Informers at the Department of Ancient Monuments tell us that a licence has recently been issued to the famous woman archaeologist, Jacqueline Blontard, to excavate in the ruins of a castle called Bézu, which is somewhere south of Carcassonne. They advise us that they had little choice. She has very powerful people supporting her application, including the President, and there seemed no good reason why they could dare to refuse." He smiled mirthlessly at Lerenard. "Nevertheless, we are concerned that this Blontard woman may know more than she has divulged to the authorities about Bézu castle. She had already indicated sympathy for the heretic Cathar cause and her late uncle was a well-known adherent. You will not understand the threat the Cathars used to pose to the true Church. However, that threat is by no means as dead as most people would like to believe."

Galbaccino breathed deeply several times. Then he again looked straight at Lerenard.

"We wish to find out what Mademoiselle Blontard is doing at le Bézu. Is there some new information which she knows? We want you to contrive to get close to her. If she - shall we say – unearths anything, we wish to know about it before she is able to release the information to the general public." He sat back in his chair. "We think that may not be difficult, because she will want to keep any finds under wraps – I believe that is the term - until it can be released as part of the television series which she will inevitably produce after the excavation is completed. Do you understand me?"

Lerenard's mind was already focussing on how he could begin to perform this most complex task. The first problem was solved for him by the cardinal's next remark.

"We think we could find a way to introduce you into her team as an archaeologist. You would need a quick training course in archaeology."

"I certainly would."

"That can be arranged. The Abbé Dugard is himself a famed excavator of ancient remains. He can train you in the techniques of excavation and in classification of the type of finds you are likely to encounter at Bézu."

"That sounds suitable."

"He is currently excavating at Prouille monastery which is about fifty kilometres from Bézu. We will place you there as his personal assistant for a few weeks until the time is suitable to introduce you to Mademoiselle Blontard. You will start on Monday."

"As you wish."

"It only remains for me to inform you of the terms of payment." Galbaccino paused for effect. "When you report to Abbé Dugard, we will put a quarter of a million euros into your account at the Bank of Zurich. Of course your expenses during training will be paid by us."

Lerenard was impressed. That was twice what he had been paid for the job in Medellin. And this time there was to be no killing and the messy disposal of bodies.

The prelate was still speaking. "Providing that all the instructions you are given during the digging season are carried out satisfactorily, you will be paid a similar amount when the excavating licence ends in September. Furthermore, providing nothing is revealed which might embarrass the Church in the television series which will follow in the autumn, an additional one million euros will be paid to you."

Jean-Luc suddenly found it difficult to breathe. This was real personal wealth. This meant the end of travelling the world as a mercenary.

Galbaccino raised a finger. "That might require you to remove secretly and pass to us – or even destroy – certain evidence which may be turned up by the Blontard excavations. Do you understand?"

"I understand completely."

"Good." A pause. "I presume the terms are acceptable to you."

"Yes."

The cardinal nodded. "It will be essential that you keep us fully informed of Blontard's progress. We shall require a report from you twice a week. These should be made to an individual who will contact you and give you the password "Cathar". Instructions to you will be channelled through him. A mobile telephone with a barred number will be provided to you which you should carry with you at all times and should only be used for this one purpose." A brief pause. "Is everything clear to you?"

Lerenard bowed slightly. "It is, your eminence." He could now contemplate a comfortable retirement. There would be no more dirty jobs after this one.

Galbaccino lifted an unsealed envelope from the desk beside him and held it out. "These are your directions for contacting Dugard. There is also a sum to cover expenses until you meet him."

The big man took the envelope, raised the flap and looked inside. There was a plain sheet of paper with a few typed instructions on it and five five-hundred euro notes. He slipped the envelope into his inside pocket. As he looked up, he saw that the cardinal had already turned back to the document he was reading in the window.

"Thank you, monsignor."

There was no reply. He turned to leave and saw that the door was already open and the little bald-headed monk was standing there, waiting to escort him from the august presence.

4

At the weekend, Philip went down to inspect his inheritance. Although the old house stood no more than ten yards from the road, it was hidden out of sight behind several large trees and shrubs, giving it an air of secrecy. He had to put a considerable effort into pushing the gates open due to the mass of weeds and fallen leaves that had collected behind them. Was it really only four weeks since his grandmother had left the place?

He drove in to the paved area and parked in front of the two-storey stone building that had been built sideways on to the road. The ancient masonry seemed to glower down challengingly at him. He had never really liked the place. Even when his parents had taken him there as a lad on visits, it had always been a relief to get out and walk on the hills above the small town. He supposed he would now have to engage a local estate agent to arrange for the place to be cleaned up and maybe he would then be able to let it.

Philip pushed the key he had received from James Baker into the lock. Somewhat to his surprise it turned easily, and the door swung open to admit him into a small lobby with an umbrella stand in the corner. Beyond this was the gloomy hall. He pressed the switch and some pale lights came on. It was a relief to know the electricity was still connected. He knew where he was going.

With a certain degree of trepidation, he mounted the stairs to the first floor. He remembered his gran's room had been the one in the corner of the house nearest to the road. It was a large room. When he entered, he was immediately assailed by the scent of lavender. It reminded him again of the perfume she had trailed behind her everywhere she went. He crossed to the bed and opened the drawer in the bedside table.

From it he drew out three large, unsealed envelopes. He inspected her neat writing on the covers. The second one was entitled "Journal of Phillipe de Saint Claire - Translation". He returned the other two envelopes to the drawer for later inspection and turned his attention to this one. He found it contained a hard cover exercise book with the same title on a label in the top right hand corner. He opened it to reveal it was full of the old lady's small neat handwriting. He started to read:-

This is the journal of the experiences of Phillipe de Saint Claire set down in this Christian year of one thousand two hundred and forty-four in the settlement known as the Coombe of the Templars in the Shire of Somerset in the Country of Wessex in the Kingdom of England.

My beginnings were in the City of Carcassonne in the land of the Langue d'Oc which is now taken into the kingdom of France since the Christian year of one thousand two hundred and eighteen. My father was Edmund de Saint Claire, a burger of Carcassonne and owing fealty to his lord, Raymond-Roger de Trencavel, Viscount of Béziers and Carcassonne. I know that my father is now dead, perished in the burning at Montségur on the sixteenth of March of this year, being an adherent to the true Cathar faith. His death is a great sadness to me who am now left alone in the world, although I know that he has passed to a greater life in the arms of the good god in heaven.

The tale of my experiences starts on the eve of the sixteenth of March when I was accepted into our faith as a perfectus although I had not been through the proper training and the consolamentum which is usual before such a high honour can be bestowed upon an adherent. However the convocation of perfecti gathered in our stronghold at Montségur had decreed that my elevation was recognised in the eyes of god because of the necessity for some strong young perfecti to be in place to carry forward the tenets of our faith.

I knew on the day in question that I was very young to be given this honour and I wasn't sure whether I would always be able to carry out to the full the responsibilities which it bestowed upon me. For it had been vouchsafed to me that it was to be the duty of myself and of three other strong young perfecti to escape down the North precipice from our stronghold. We were to be carrying certain important objects tied to our backs, the contents of which are to remain unknown to us. Carrying these, we were urged to make our way speedily away from Montségur and to find places of extreme safety which have been nominated to us to leave the objects hidden so that they cannot be found by the emissaries of Rome.

We were told that the guards surrounding the stronghold had been well paid to ignore our passage. Yet we could not risk that all of us could be taken captive at one stroke. Therefore we were to separate completely from each other and to have no contact, the one with the others.

I was personally advised that I was to make my way by diverse paths towards the elevated and remote stronghold called le Bézu where its Lord, who is called Pierre de Voisins, is believed to be sympathetic to the cause of the Cathars while at the same time being a former lieutenant of the dreadful and dreaded Simon de Montfort, one time leader of the oppressors of the Cathars. I am told that this Pierre de Voisins has vouchsafed to my leaders that he will secretly help me to hide my precious burden and then aid my escape from the French before I can be captured and tortured to give up the secret of the hiding-place.

This is the journal of my experiences on the sixteenth of March one thousand two hundred and forty-four.

In the very early hours of the day and long before dawn we escaped from the castle on ropes of woven fabric. It was a fearsome experience. The ropes were not long enough or strong enough to let us down the whole height of the rock-face and a fifth perfectus had to come with us to hold the ropes. He had to climb down the whole way with his hands. He would be captured, tried and put to death by burning but, as he knew nothing of our orders, so he would not be able to give us away even if he were to weaken under torture, which he had sworn he would not do.

The secrets of the Cathars were concealed in wax-sealed tubes of bamboo which were tied to our backs. They were not

31

heavy but they were long and made our movements difficult, especially when we were climbing down the cliffs. We did not know what was in the tubes. However we knew it could not be anything big or heavy. It certainly could not have been treasure or gold.

I was the second perfectus to reach the valley. The first of my colleagues had already disappeared and, in any case, I did not wish to make contact with any one of the others. My orders were to go south for the first part of my journey, so I immediately set off in a loop round the east side of the mountain, keeping well away from the positions where I had been advised there were guards who were supposed to be securing the castle against the escape of the Cathars. I saw no-one, nor did I expect to since we had also been promised that the guards had been well paid to keep clear of our path.

The night was very dark with clouds obscuring any moonlight and it was necessary to proceed slowly. However it was important that I should be well clear of the besiegers before daylight exposed my progress.

I travelled up the course of the small river known locally as the Lassate which led in the direction of the Peak of Saint Barthélemy. Sometimes I was able to walk along the banks of the river, but much of the time I had to follow the bed of the stream itself, stumbling over rocks and into deep pools. I often fell and I was fearful that the precious tubes on my back might be damaged even though I had been assured they were well sealed in waxed linen with the joints double-waxed. So, when I was confident that I was more than a league from the castle and knew I was well clear of the besiegers on the south side, I decided to rest up until day-break in a small cave near a water-fall.

When the dawn came I was feeling very cold and stiff and immediately decided to proceed upon my way before my body might become disabled by aches and shivers. It now being light, I could move apace and made better progress, gradually climbing out of the forest and on to the mountainside.

I directed my steps towards a col in the ridge ahead which was to the east of the twin peaks which form St Barthélemy and

32

I achieved the summit just as the sun arose, lighting up the morning clouds. I was greatly warmed and heartened by the sight. In my innocence I felt as though the good God in heaven had blessed me and was with me in my endeavours.

I crossed the col and started down towards the valley of the Hersa river. As I made my way with care through the undergrowth, I espied a peasant leading his goats to spring pasture. I approached him and made the secret sign of the Cathars to him but he understood me not. However I ascertained that the few words he had were only of the Occitan which is the language of our supporters and therefore that he could tell the French nothing of my presence or direction. As a result I persuaded him, not without some difficulty, to take me to his hut and provide me with some basic sustenance for which I paid him two sous from the purse-full at my belt which I had been given for this purpose. I think it was the first time that he had seen coinage, although he was aware of its usage, for he became very excited and spent a long time turning it over and over in his hands and inspecting both sides most carefully.

I was also able to partly dry my clothes over his very smoky fire. Therefore I set out again after about a half an hour both in greater comfort and with the worst of my hunger quelled. Now I was heading mainly east above the Hersa river. I regret to say that the early morning sun had by now disappeared behind low clouds coming from the west and after a further hour it began to rain. Thus I was made to pay for my temerity in pausing to satisfy my own comforts instead of hastening to achieve completion of the task which I had been set. I learned from this experience never again to allow my thoughts of personal comfort to delay me from my endeavours until they were brought to fruition.

After about two hours I saw that the river was approaching a deep narrow gorge between the hills. The cloud had lowered itself upon the mountain-tops and the place looked most forbidding. I went towards the gorge with some trepidation, being fearful that I might not be able to get through to achieve my goal. However, as I came near to the mouth of this entrance to Hades, I beheld a path, steep but clear, which ascended to the right – that is in the direction of the east.

Although I was still plagued by the steady rain I felt almost as though I had been rescued. Therefore I made my way up this path and within the hour I found myself crossing another col and beginning the descent towards a third river which miraculously disappeared as I approached it into the mouth of a deep cave.

I decided to avoid this defile and kept to the high ground above the departing river, heading generally a little north of east. After a further hour of open mountainside I came to a small hamlet which I discovered glorified in the name of Bel-Caire which means beautiful stone. I thought this was something of a misnomer for it was a rather ugly little settlement, although I was not unwise enough to say so to its inhabitants.

In this place I was able to purchase some food for a further five sous. This consisted of coarse bread, goat's cheese and two green apples. However, having learned from my mistake in the morning, I did not linger to consume it but continued with the food in my pocket, eating it as I walked. I had also felt uncomfortable while I was in Bel-Caire, as though the inhabitants were regarding the tubes on my back and wondering what was in them. So I left the hamlet with many a backward glance to check that I was not followed.

It was approaching noon as I came out on to an open plateau which was perhaps two leagues in length and nearly half of that in width. Here my prudence in continuing on my way was rewarded by the rain easing to almost nothing and the cloud lifting to improve my visibility. Away to my right, that is to say to the south, I could now see a series of moderately high peaks, the furthest of which were topped with snow.

My clothes had begun to dry and I was feeling almost cheerful as I stepped out, following whichever tracks appeared to lead in my chosen direction to the east and covering the ground quite speedily. After about a further two and a half hours I came to the end of the plateau and found a way leading down through the forest towards a large valley below.

34

From time to time I was able to glimpse parts of a large settlement crowned by a substantial castle. I was somewhat afeared when I approached this centre of habitation for I knew I would be at a greater risk of discovery among so many people. However it was important to me that I should obtain directions to lead me to the castle of le Bézu which I knew to be somewhere further to the east of my present position.

Here again I was in luck when I espied a fortified farmstead on a rise above the town. I thought there was a good possibility that a place such as this might be occupied by sympathisers. So I strode up to the gates and knocked boldly. This time my secret Cathar code-words were met with the correct response and I knew it signified that I was among friends. The gates were opened to me and I was welcomed in, albeit with some reserve, as is customary among sympathisers with the true faith in these hard times.

It turned out that the family occupying this bastion were called de la Tour-Cuillanais and that they claimed to be well-regarded in the locality. As I had suspected they told me the township below was known as Cuillan. I realised that this meant that I was within three leagues of my objective.

I explained to Senor de la Tour that I wished to get to le Bézu as soon as I might. However he pointed out that it could not be achieved on that day during daylight hours. He told me that the path up to the castle could be hazardous by night, He also pointed out to me that many brigands lurked around Cuillan as around most large towns in the Languedoc in these lawless times. With my precious burden I might well attract the attention of such men. He promised that he would provide me with a guide and protector on the morrow who would get me to my destination in the forenoon. This I accepted since I realised that it would not in any case help my mission to try to gain access to Pierre de Voisins in the middle of the night.

Senor de la Tour was also kind enough to offer me a bed for the night and a clean night-shirt while my clothes were being dried by the courtyard fire. He even allowed me a private room where I might barricade myself in for the night with my precious burden. So, giving many thanks to the good God for *guiding me to this hospitable place, I accepted his offer and spent a most comfortable night, being greatly tired from lack of sleep and my great exertions.*

When I awoke I was briefly worried lest I had slept too deeply and too long and that others might have invaded my privacy unwelcomed. However I soon saw that I had no cause for disquiet. After breaking my fast with my kind host, who would accept no payment for the food or for the bed where I had spent the night, I set off, guided by one of his manservants.

We skirted the township of Cuillan, waded across the lively river Aud at a ford known to my guide, and ascended a steep hill to a view-point whence we could look down on the castle of Cuillan at no great distance. It was a somewhat minor stronghold and I knew that it had never been besieged. It was still early and there were few folk abroad.

So we set out on the final two leagues to my destination. I was partially lame in my left foot after my exertions of the previous day and was unable to make progress as speedily as I would have wished. However I was cheered by seeing the sun rise over the mountains to herald in a splendid day and, when it was pointed out to me by my guide, to light up the southern walls of the great castle of le Bézu, perched like a row of eagles on the ridge above us. I was mightily impressed by its location. It did not have the sheer soaring cliffs of Montségur but relied more for defence on the complete absence of any means of mounting an attack on it from any direction, being obscurely located on rocky outcrops in the midst of deep forests.

Because of the precipitous nature of the path, it was another hour before I was standing before the great entrance gateway at the east end of the castle. We had seen no person on our walk except a cowherd in the distance. Having delivered me to my destination, my guide left me with a courteous word and a pat on the shoulder. So I mounted the last few steps to halloa at the gate.

A short time later I was ushered directly into the presence of none other than the said Lord de Voisins himself by his sheriff. It seemed, by the great blessing of the Almighty, that I had arrived at this stronghold only one day before he would be leaving to present himself to King Louis Capet of France who is now his liege lord.

As soon as we were alone in his chamber I handed over my instructions from the convocation and explained the purpose of my visit.

By chance, Philip looked at his watch at this moment and was astonished to find that it was already early evening. So he took the envelopes with him to a local hotel which he had booked earlier. There he dined and spent the night sleeping deeply and dreaming of the rugged mountain ranges of the Languedoc.

5

Charles Robert briskly walked the short distance from the Ministry of Culture to the elegant old apartment building in the Rue Cambriet. He nodded to Bernard, the concierge, as he passed the ground floor office with its little glass window.

"Bonsoir monsieur." The man knew him well enough to be familiar.

Nevertheless, Charles decided he should check again with the *Président* whether the concierge could be trusted not to talk to his friends. It was important that no word of his visit should get back to the Ministry. However, for now that wasn't important. He was late responding to the summons.

He ignored the ancient, wheezing lift and mounted the stairs two at a time to the third floor. Charles had always kept himself fit and was hardly puffing as he paused outside the door to the Council Chamber, which was covered with maroon padded fabric. He smiled briefly to himself as he regarded the slightly absurd bravado in the choice of colour. He took the cane from its holder, tapped sharply four times on the push-plate, then once more to activate the release. He pushed the door half open and went inside, pausing to look around the room before he advanced to the table.

The walls were covered from the floor to a metre below the high ceiling with rich mahogany panelling, with the exception of the four three-quarter height double windows whose shutters were folded back to allow the last of the evening sun to filter in. The large, almost square table with the white recessed baize top that stood in the middle of the deep-pile ruby carpet was also of mahogany. Two long red runners were laid at right angles across it. They crossed in the centre and the ends fell smoothly over the specially designed recesses in the middle of each side. The concealed lighting below the carved and dentillated cornice, which ran around the perimeter of the ceiling, cast a warm glow to augment the sunset.

However, the atmosphere in the room was far from cordial. There were only three other people present. The matter which had arisen was too urgent to allow time to summon the whole council of fourteen, more than half of whom would have had to fly in to Paris from around Europe and the Middle East.

Monsieur le Président sat in his usual place in the centre seat at the far end of the table. He was now a very old man, probably in his early nineties, but still in possession of all his mental faculties. He was much diminished in stature from the hundred-and-ninety-centimetre, ninety-five kilo giant he had once been and his back was seriously bent. But between the hollow cheeks and beneath the nearly bald scalp with its ridiculous single wisp of silver hair, the dark eyes still glinted ferociously.

To his left sat Marcus Heilburg, the Grand Treasurer. Heilburg was a man whom it was easy to overlook and even easier to forget when the eyes had passed on to the president. However, with the advancing years of the man in charge, the main reins of power now rested in Heilburg's hands. He was the only full-time member of the Council of Preceptories and all the information passed through his small office on the floor above. He was on first-name terms with most of the nominal leaders of Europe. His seldom-stated views were listened to with care by most of those with real power. The great wealth of the council which he was able to wield at short notice gave him immense influence with Europe's decision makers.

Charles did not personally know the third man, seated opposite the president at the foot of the table. He was young and slight of build. From this he guessed the fellow to be the agent who had been referred to by Marcus as Armand – one of the facilitators used by the council when it was necessary for their presence to take a physical form, underlining their influence with action. He was rumoured to be the son of one of the council members, fanatically loyal and trained to be deadly when required. However, his withdrawn yet pleasant personality made it possible for him to melt into the background when necessary. Nevertheless, Robert was surprised that such a man had been admitted to the council chamber. It underlined the urgency of the meeting.

"Sit down, Charles." The president's voice was barely above a whisper.

Robert sat in his usual place, three down on the side facing the window. He looked at the old man and prepared for his condemnation.

"We are here to discuss the Blontard situation," murmured the president unnecessarily. "We are disappointed that it took nearly three weeks to become aware of what is happening."

Robert cleared his throat. "The decision to grant the licence was taken with some haste by the Chief Secretary. Unusually he did it alone without consulting me. I had been seconded to Brussels for a month. My assistant, who would normally have alerted me to any new developments, was accompanying me. I regret that I took a weekend's holiday before I returned to the office. Of course I alerted you to the problem this morning as soon as the relevance of this decision became clear."

"Hmm." No further condemnation was necessary. It would be a black mark on Robert's record, possibly barring his elevation to the highest positions on the council in the years to come. "Meanwhile the lady in question is already on location."

Robert bowed his head in acquiescence.

"This Blontard woman – is she related to the late Albert Blontard?"

"She is his niece," Heilburg interrupted.

"What is her attitude to his suicide?"

"That is unknown. She has said nothing about it. However it is notable that. now she has gained some influence with her successful television series, she should decide to stray on to the same territory in which he used to be so interested. She probably has access to the information her uncle built up during his lifetime of investigating our organisation. She will almost certainly be motivated to expose anything related to his death. All our careful repairs to our reputation over the last five years may be at risk."

There was a long silence while those round the table digested the import of his comments. Robert wondered whether

Heilburg had gone too far in mentioning his fears in front of young Armand, who was not a council member. However, a glance at the other faces reassured him that his imprudence was not seen as a problem by his superior.

Marcus Heilburg spoke again. "It is important that we understand her motivation."

"That is why young Séjour is here," said the president. "You have already briefed him?"

Heilburg nodded.

The old man looked down the table to the fellow. "Do you have a proposed course of action?"

Armand looked up and Robert noticed that his previously soft blue-grey eyes had hardened to the colour of steel. "Yes, Monsieur le Président. I have access to a young woman who I can trust absolutely. I propose that she and I should act as a recently-married couple on a touring holiday. We will book in at the hotel in Quillan where the archaeologists are staying. We will appear to be fascinated by the activities of Blontard's group. We may even volunteer to join them as amateur assistants. I believe that archaeologists never have enough assistants. We will report to the grand treasurer on our progress and receive his instructions on what further action it is necessary to take."

The president turned to his left. "Are you happy with this?"

"With respect, Claude." Heilburg's lack of formality betrayed his anxiety. "I think we should have a council member on station locally."

The old man nodded. "I agree." His gaze swivelled to Robert. "It will have to be you, Charles."

"I am not sure I can take the time, Président. You know I have only just returned from Brussels. The Chief Secretary wants to see me on Wednesday to receive my report and he will require me to take early action on it. This is a matter of importance to France."

"But this is *more* important," said Heilburg.

"I am sure that France can wait." The president turned to his left. "We can arrange this, can we not, Marcus?"

The grand treasurer nodded.

"Very well. It will be your opportunity to redeem yourself, Charles."

Robert observed his career prospects in government receding. However he knew where his personal priorities lay. He looked down at the table, the square cross reminding him of his duty. "As you say, Monsieur le Président."

The grand treasurer slid a slim file across the table towards him and Charles Robert reached out and picked it up. He opened the file, which contained a brochure for a hotel in Foix. Pinned to the cover was confirmation of his booking of a room for one month starting from the following evening. Charles noted that it was a single room. This was clearly a duty without any pleasure. There was also a further sheet of paper with the mobile phone number of Armand and an instruction to ring the young man at a specific time each day. Marcus Heilburg was always thorough.

Charles realised that this was his dismissal. He rose, bowed slowly to the president and went out through the heavy panelled door, faced with the maroon baize on the outside. He knew he was not required to listen to the briefing given to Armand. In any case, he would need to make his peace with his long-suffering wife before he set off south only a few days after his return from Brussels.

6

It was a wet night in Marseilles. The back streets off the Quai de la Joliette were almost deserted – just the odd rat picking through the refuse in the gutters, the occasional cat tiptoeing round the puddles, irritably twitching raindrops from its ears. In the alley, grandly named the Rue de Printemps, there were two exceptions. A small, weasel-faced crook, hunch-backed against the rain, had a firm hold on the sleeve of a tall middle-aged individual who was sheltering beneath a large black umbrella as he was led up the alley.

The tall man picked his way through the soggy garbage with almost as much care as the cat. He had a look of extreme distaste on his aquiline features, and the way in which he held back from his guide suggested that he would have his slightly worn suit dry-cleaned as soon as he returned to decent society.

The crook stopped beside an old oak door which was in better condition than most of the others in the alley and tapped twice. The two men stood in the steady downpour, waiting for a response, unaware that they were being carefully examined through a night-light peephole in the door.

After half a minute the door was opened by a great, violent-looking beast of a man with a clean-shaven scalp. He stood slightly aside to give them a narrow corridor of entry. The umbrella was collapsed and the two entered. The door was immediately closed and bolted behind them and they were led down a passage into a rear room which was warm and well lit.

In this room two men sat opposite each other at a table on the far wall from the fire. The one facing them was shortish and stout with a generous head of ginger hair and similar clusters for eyebrows and moustache. What one could see of his arms was carpeted with a thick mat of sandy down which extended along the backs of his hands into sprouts at his knuckles. He scowled at the new arrivals.

Weasel-face spoke up. "This is the bloke I told you about, Henri."

"Go upstairs, Mickey."

The little man departed with alacrity.

There was a long pause while the ginger-headed man inspected his guest closely. At last he stood up and extended a hairy hand. "I am Henri Montluçon. I hear you've been asking around for me."

"You are a member of *La Force Marseillaise?*"

"Yes."

"Then that is correct." The accent was cultured – almost grand.

Montluçon shrugged. "So – who are you?"

"You may call me Alain Hébert."

"And what's your real name?"

"At present I wish to keep that to myself."

There was silence while this was digested. Montluçon glanced uncertainly at the other man at the table. At last he said, "All right. You can sit down." He indicated the third chair with its back to the fire and resumed his own seat.

Hébert carefully leaned his folded umbrella in the corner near the door and took the offered seat between the two gangsters. Now he could look at the face of the other man, the back of whose nearly-bald head had been the only feature which was previously visible to him. What he saw made his blood go cold, although he suppressed any reaction from showing on his face.

A dreadful wound down the whole of the right side of the man's face had removed the eye and the skin now sank into the hollow socket. The cheek-bone had been cloven in two and an attempt to repair it had been botched. The corner of the mouth had been drawn down to the broken jaw-bone which had been untidily wired together to allow the man to eat, and which now gave a permanently mournful twist on that side to the otherwise savage face. The long, irregular scar glared bright pink in the pale face. It was at least a half a centimetre wide. Glancing quickly at it, careful not to stare, Hébert calculated that the wound was less than six months old.

It was Montluçon who spoke. "What did you want to say to me?"

The incomer paused for a few moments to gather his thoughts. He decided there was no point in fencing with these people.

"Have you heard of the treasure of the Templars?"

"Maybe."

"The Templars were an order of warrior monks in the Middle Ages. They had become extremely rich. The French king of the day wanted their treasure. So he outlawed the order, captured and tortured their leaders, and took hold of their property." He paused for dramatic effect. "The Templars in France were liquidated."

"What does that mean to us?"

"Despite his efforts, the king failed to find the extensive Treasure of the Templars."

Montluçon wriggled on his seat, waiting for the silence to end. At last he enquired, "So?"

"So – I know the location of the treasure which King Phillipe le Bel failed to find."

The scarred man took a dribbling breath – the first sound he had made. But once again it was ginger who spoke. "Why do you come to see us about it? Why don't you collect it yourself and make a killing?"

Hébert permitted himself a slight smile. "The size of the treasure is too huge for me to handle on my own. I need assistance."

"But why us?"

"I believe that you have an organisation which could solve a problem of this size." He shrugged at the man's enquiring look. "It is not only a question of removing the treasure from its hiding place. There are also many valuable artefacts which will have to be disposed of privately to rich collectors around the world. I can advise on the likely value and the possible purchasers but, in my position, I cannot be the man who makes the contacts. Then there is the probability of government – er – let us call it 'intervention' to be avoided. It requires your sort of organisation to handle that problem."

45

"So?" The ginger features twisted. "Just how big is this treasure?"

"Nobody knows with any accuracy. I have not yet actually seen the treasure myself and I cannot put a value on it or any part of it. However, the latest estimates of scholars who have been researching the subject calculate the market value is likely to be somewhere between one billion and five billion euros."

There was another drooling intake of breath from Hébert's right, but he didn't look at the man.

"Five *billion*?" Montluçon sat back in his chair and the expression on his face was almost laughable as his brain slowly worked out what that sum would actually mean to their organisation. "Did I hear you say five *billion*?"

"That's right. But that is only a guess. It may be much more."

"And how much of the five billion would you expect to give us?"

"You can have it all except for one tenth of the proceeds, which I would want to be deposited anonymously in my family trust, in return for my leading you to the treasure and advising you of the way for you to get the most money for disposing of it."

"We would get nine tenths of five billion?"

"Of course, it may not be worth that much."

Montluçon nodded. "It may be only one billion. In that case our share would be at least nine hundred million."

"I believe so."

There was a long pause while the two members of La Force worked out just what that amount of money would mean to their organisation and to them personally.

At last the ginger-haired man said. "But how do we know what you are telling us is right? How do we know the whole thing isn't just a great big con?"

Hébert reached inside his jacket pocket and brought out a folded A4 sheet of paper. He opened it and glanced at it briefly. Then he handed it across the table. "Here is a list of eight people and organisations who can verify each point of what I have told you – except of course the location of the treasure. I expect you to be completely satisfied by their replies to your enquiries within two weeks. However, please withhold my name when your representatives approach them – even though they would not recognise it."

"You say these guys don't know where the treasure is hidden?"

"No. Only I know that."

"How do you know it?"

There was a long pause while Hébert prepared his story. At last he said, "My great uncle died five years ago. He was a Roman Catholic bishop. He was confessor to a priest who had himself heard the last confession of a woman called Marie Denarnaud. She was the former housekeeper – some say the mistress - of a famous priest called Bérenger Saunière who apparently gave her the secret. She was the one who knew the location of the treasure. My great uncle passed on to me the information which she gave him on her death-bed, when he knew he was about to die himself. He believed that such information should not be allowed to die with him."

"He died five years ago?"

"It has taken me that long to check out all the details."

"So – where is this treasure?"

Hébert permitted himself a smile. "I am keeping that information to myself until we have an agreement."

There followed a further long silence while this was digested. After a short while Alain Hébert added, "In case there is any misunderstanding between us, I should perhaps mention that my lawyer has a letter informing him that I am meeting you tonight. It is attached to a sealed envelope. I apologise for the fact that the letter instructs him that I shall telephone him before ten o'clock tomorrow morning. If I do not do so, he is to open the envelope and release the information it contains to the authorities." He smiled without embarrassment. "You will therefore be able to understand that I have thought this whole business through very carefully. I believe in preparing for all eventualities."

Montluçon pulled a face. "Not very trusting, are you?"

47

"We don't know each other well enough for trust – yet."
Hébert reached inside his pocket and brought out another sheet
of paper which he handed over without inspection. "This is how
to contact me. When you have checked out my information, and
if you decide you want to deal with me, you can get in touch,
giving me a point of contact. If I do not hear from you within
two weeks, I will assume you are not interested and I will
approach another party."

"Who?"

"That is my personal information." Hébert leaned forward.
"Look, Monsieur Montluçon, I want you to realise that I have
been planning this business for five years. I do not intend to
risk failure at this late stage by saying too much to anybody. If
you decide to go with me, the care I have taken in keeping each
stage of my planning secret will be an added protection for you
and for your organisation. Do you understand me?"

Ginger glanced at scar-face and Alain Hébert detected the
briefest of nods from him. Montluçon took a breath. "OK. I
understand. I expect the same secrecy from you about our
organisation."

"Of course. Do you accept my proposed time-scale of two
weeks?"

Although he was careful not to watch the exchange between
the other two, Hébert detected that Montluçon was being
authorised by scar-face to agree.

"Yes – accepted."

"Thank you, gentlemen." Hébert rose to his feet and walked
to the door to retrieve his umbrella. "I look forward to hearing
from you before the twelfth of April. No doubt your goon will
see me out."

He opened the door and left.

7

It was more than a week before Philip had another opportunity to continue reading the journal of his ancestor. It took him a couple of days to check through the contents of the house. He found very little of interest to him. His grandmother seemed to have led a minimalist existence during the last few years of her life and the duffle bag easily contained the few items he deemed it worth keeping. However, there were a lot of things which he had to dispose of. He also made an attempt to tidy up the worst of the mess in the garden. After that he went in search of a local estate agent.

The man seemed doubtful about whether he could find a tenant willing to pay a decent rent for the large old house, but agreed he would do his best. He said he would also engage a cleaner and a gardener to tidy the place up. With that, Philip left the man the keys so that he could earn his percentage. Then he returned to catch up on lost time at his work in London.

The three envelopes containing the original of the journal and his grandmother's notes and translation were put in the bottom of the bag and there he found them the following Sunday evening, when he had the time to sort through the contents. He picked up the exercise book, quickly found the place where he had finished reading the previous weekend and continued:-

Journal of my experiences at the Chateau of le Bézu on the seventeenth to the twentieth of March one thousand two hundred and forty-four.

My lord Pierre de Voisins received me with great politeness although I fancy he was cautious about showing me too much favour or giving me too much help in case others should get to hear of his actions and it might therefore reflect badly on him with his new French masters. He explained to me that he was

49

setting out on the following day to travel by way of Béziers and Lyons to Paris to kneel before King Louis and that he had many preparations to make before he left. Therefore he was unable to be of personal assistance to me.

However he told me he would put me in the hands of one of his kinsmen who he would instruct to help me in any way that I wished. He assured me that this person, whom he named as Raymonde de Puyvert, was totally loyal to the Cause and that I could rely on him in all things. He said that he would also instruct the said Raymonde to look after me while he was away. I took the message from this that he did not wish to be made aware of what arrangements I intended to make for disposal of the tubes of bamboo. In fact he handed my instructions from the convocation back to me and told me to deal only with the said Raymonde from then on.

He then called his steward back into his presence and instructed the man to arrange food and a separate chamber for me to rest in until such time as Raymonde should wait upon me. He bade me farewell and wished me God's blessing in my future endeavours. So I left the presence of my lord Pierre de Voisins and I did not see him again.

It was late in the day when a young man knocked at my chamber door and I admitted him. We exchanged signs which convinced me that he was sympathetic to the Cause. He announced himself as Raymonde de Puyvert and I inspected him closely. He was a personable man, just a little older and two fingers shorter than myself. He had a ready smile and a co-operative personality. From our initial conversation it appeared that he had been told very little by his kinsman of my mission, except that it was important to the Cause and was to be carried out in the greatest secrecy. For this reason he advised me that, because it was late in the day, we should therefore do nothing until the morrow. This would be after the great majority of the household of his uncle, Pierre de Voisins, with nearly all his servants and his armed retainers should have left the castle. He said that there would then only be left behind a cook, a handful of armed men and a sergeant at arms charged with the securing of the castle. These men were aware of our presence but had been told to ignore us except to provide us with food and assistance when we requested it.

I found I was enjoying a great fellow feeling with Raymonde and willingly fell in with his advice. Thus it was a little before noon on the eighteenth of March that I admitted my friend again. He brought a repast for us to share and as we ate I advised him of my requirements. I indicated the bamboo tubes, of which there were five. I told him that I knew nothing of their contents, which was near to the truth. I told him also that these were to be hidden in a location which was to be known only to the two of us and that this location was not to be vouchsafed to any person except to one nominated by the convocation of perfecti of the Cathars. I told him that my instructions then said that I was to attempt to escape from any hue and cry which might follow the fall of Montségur and to place myself where I could keep the location of the treasure of the Cathars secret, until such time as the Cause might call upon me to deliver it up to them again. Raymonde said he fully understood what I was telling him and willingly swore an oath to me that he would tell no-one of the knowledge which I was placing in his hands, even under pressure of torture.

Raymonde had previously been given some small idea of my need to find a secret hiding place. He told me that as a result he had thought carefully during the last day and night about where such a suitable location might be found. He had spent several hours exploring the furthermost extents of the castle and had located a deep store room which he would show me and which he believed would satisfy my requirements. I responded that I would wish to view his proposed hiding place as soon as possible.

Thus we agreed to go to inspect this room straight away and, having carefully locked my chamber to temporarily secure the bamboo tubes and, having armed ourselves with tallow candles to enable us to see our way in the depths of the castle, I accompanied him as he directed. He took me through the silent, unoccupied buildings to the far end of the castle from the gatehouse and down a narrow stairway, at the bottom of which was a door into a small room. Raymonde explained that,

51

because the room was so isolated, it was hardly ever used for any purpose. Indeed I was able to see that it was unoccupied at that time by any goods save two opened, empty and unused barrels in one corner. I also noted that the room was dry, which I judged to be important.

I therefore confirmed to him that the room appeared to be suitable. I pointed out to Raymonde that the door was unbarred and he said that a lock could be arranged to seal it from casual entry. However I feared that such a lock could be picked or broken and that any device of that sort could not be relied upon. I looked carefully around the room. The wall facing the door was extremely solid and Raymonde confirmed that as far as he knew it was the outside wall of the castle which was almost certainly at least ten cubits thick in this area, as was the wall just to the left of the door from the staircase. The wall beside the staircase had been hewn from the bed-rock and was built in large rough stones above the descent of the stairs. The fourth wall was also mainly cut from the living rock as was a part of the floor. The exception was the top corner (about one quarter of the whole wall) which had been constructed from close-jointed random stonework. Being aware of the importance of maintaining the utmost security for the hiding place, I decided that we should see if we could secrete the bamboo tubes in the space behind this wall.

With a degree of reluctance Raymonde accepted my request to take down that part of the wall to discover if this would provide a suitable hiding place for the treasure. He offered to bring two or three of the castle's defenders to break down the wall. However I said to him that, for reasons of secrecy, only he and I must do this work and that I hoped it would be necessary to remove no more than a very few stones to make a sufficient access to the hiding place. With no great enthusiasm he agreed and set out to find suitable tools for the task.

While he was gone I took my tallow wick close to the walls and gave the whole room a further careful inspection. However I could not find any other comparable location for my cache. I upturned the barrels and moved them into a position below the wall. When I stood on them my head was just brushing the beams of the floor above. This meant that I could easily reach the part of the wall I required. However I could see that the stones had been tightly fitted together and would not be removed easily.

Raymonde returned after about a half of an hour with a large cooper's mallet, some iron picks and a kind of mattock. We closed the door behind us for privacy, put our tallows on the floor and began to break down the wall. We worked turn and turn about for a quarter of an hour each, standing on the barrels and each handing down any stones removed to the other below. It was a very long task to loosen the first large stone in the wall. Raymonde finally achieved this after about two hours and passed it to me, handling the heavy boulder with some difficulty. Thereafter the stones could be released more readily and, by the end of the day, we had removed enough of them to provide a sufficient void to contain the bamboo containers which were each about two cubits in length.

The removal of the stones had revealed a shallow cave behind the wall which was only about a cubit and a half deep and perhaps four cubits in height and six cubits in width which would have been approximately suitable to shelter a grown man on his knees. It appeared that this cave, which was a mere hollowing of the rock face, had been judged by the original builders of the castle to have no useful purpose. As a consequence it had been walled up with surplus stone when the place was constructed. However the recess was dry and still had the remains of some desiccated vegetation in it. So I judged it to be a satisfactory and secure place for the secreting of the treasure and I communicated such to my colleague Raymonde.

It being late in the day and the two of us feeling extremely tired from our long and violent exertions, we decided to leave the walling up of the bamboo tubes until the following day. So we retired to my chamber and Raymonde brought us a repast to keep our spirits up before I locked the door and we slept.

The next morning we were up at an early hour. With Raymonde leading the way to ensure that we were not surprised and discovered, I carried the precious treasure to the store-room. Fortunately we encountered no other person in our path. We closed the door behind us and secreted the tubes in the shallow cave we had found, laying them on a bed of small stones in case any moisture should enter the cave, so that it could drain away without damaging or penetrating the tubes, which in any case were wrapped and waxed and sealed as I have previously described.

We then rebuilt the wall from the larger stones we had removed. This took the two of us a long time, particularly to firmly hammer the stones below the timber floor of the room above back into place. This floor of course formed the ceiling of our store room. We also pressed in a number of small stones between the large ones, using the mallet and the mattock to force them tight. By the time we had carefully finished reconstructing the whole of the wall in this way I felt assured that it would withstand the passage of time and would only be removed by the purposeful action of men who might wish to demolish it. I was hopeful that in such a remote location it would not be discovered except by persons directed to it by the Convocation of perfecti.

I accentuated strongly to Raymonde how important it was that no unauthorised person should suspect that the wall contained a hiding place. Using the barrels therefore, we removed almost all the resulting rubble from the floor of the room and distributed it in one of the courtyards of the castle, returning with soil which we rubbed into the face of the wall and spread about the floor to attempt to disguise our activities of the last two days. Thus, weary from all our unaccustomed labours, we repaired to my chamber, ate a hearty meal and collapsed into our truckle beds.

When we awoke next morning it was to receive the alarming news that a messenger had arrived bearing tidings of the tragic happenings at Montségur. The man told us that all the remaining Cathar occupants of the castle, being more than two hundred souls, had marched out together to surrender their persons to the French besiegers. They had then been invited to forswear their heresy as the Church of Rome described it. Not one of them had weakened and all had continued to swear their belief in the Cathar faith. As a result they had all been herded into a large timber stockade filled with firewood well soaked in animal fat. This had been set alight and every last one of them had died on that dreadful pyre, suffering terrible torment, and even then none had recanted in order to survive. Then the French seneschal, Hugues des Arcis declared that the Cathar faith was at an end and that any remaining adherents to the faith were to be sought out and burned at the stake.

Although I had been expecting it, this came as terrible news to me. I was now finally aware that all my family and friends at Montségur had been utterly destroyed. In addition it was clear to me that my own life was under threat. I would not allow myself to recant my Cathar beliefs, especially as my parents had shown themselves willing to suffer an awful death, rather than turn their backs on their true religion. To do so would mean that I would certainly enter the permanent hell of the evil god. In addition I was perhaps the only one other than my friend Raymonde who knew of the location of the secrets of the Cathars, and who could help to lead the true believers in the right direction, if our religion should survive and once again flower in this imperfect world.

Thus I, a mere lad of sixteen years, but a perfectus of the Cathar faith, was faced with a dreadful dilemma. I expected that some of the besiegers of Montségur, being cleverer than most and becoming aware that four of us had escaped the funeral pyre of the Cathars, would set up a hue and cry to discover our whereabouts and recover the Secrets. Therefore, reflecting upon my position, I decided that it was my duty to escape my pursuers. It took me some time to come to this decision for I did not wish to do this merely to save my own skin. However, after discussing it with Raymonde, we decided that, having done all we possibly could to hide the secrets entrusted to me, I should leave this place at the earliest opportunity. Raymonde promised me his full support until I had got clean away from pursuit. Therefore we gathered together our few belongings and enough food for three days and hurried away from the castle of le Bézu without a backward glance.

Philip suddenly realised that he was struggling to keep his eyes open, despite the fascination which the tale had for him. He leafed through the closely-written exercise book and could see that there was still a lot to read. So he decided to call it a day. He tucked the book back into the duffle bag and went to bed.

8

Jacqueline called a progress meeting after they had been on site for a week. She, André Jolyon and Gaston Lesmoins, leader of the three rock climbers, met in her room at the hotel after dinner. They chose her room because it was the biggest.

Jackie sat on her stool with her back to the dressing-table. André lounged on the bed, trying to look as though he frequently occupied it. But the short, stocky Gaston chose to remain standing.

"OK." She kicked off. "I'm quite pleased with progress. We've got safety ropes fixed all along both sides of the chateau from the eastern to the western extremities. So, as long as we are all sensible and wear harnesses clipped on to the ropes, we can approach all sections of the site without danger. We've cleared most of the area around the eastern gateway of surface vegetation, and Jo has marked out three areas where exploration can commence. So we can start proper excavation on Monday."

André interrupted. "But we'll need to be careful, Jackie. Disposal of soil will be a problem because of the steeply sloping site, so we'll have to go slowly at the start. I've set up a tent on the eastern terrace with a couple of trestle tables for stacking finds until the proper timber sectional shed arrives. I think Marie and her assistant are due to arrive at the end of the month to do the sorting and cleaning of finds, aren't they?"

"That's right."

"We'll need the hut before then. Until that comes I think the five of us will be able to cope with the dig. After that we will need to bring in more helpers."

Gaston puffed out his chest and cleared his throat. "I've got to tell you – I'm sorry, but my guys aren't keen on digging."

"What do you mean?"

"Well, they've said to me that when they came on this job they were promised that they would be climbing over the remains of the castle, setting up ropes and clearing vegetable growth from the cliffs and walls."

"They've been doing that," said Jolyon. "Now we start the dig proper."

Gaston grinned awkwardly. "They've told me – to use their own words - they don't want to be bloody labourers."

"Aren't they interested in what's under the ground?"

"Sorry, Jo." He shrugged. "They don't seem to have the treasure hunter's urge. You've got to remember - they're used to scrambling up sheer cliffs in the mountains. They're open-air men. You can understand that they don't want to spend their time down in holes in the ground."

"Well, I'm sorry too, Gaston, but they've got to accept that a lot of archaeology consists of the boring bits of scratching around in the ground, hoping to come up with finds. And, in any case, it's not all boring. The first trench will be in the entrance gateway. We should find all sorts of things there, being the discards of more than five centuries in the Middle Ages."

Jacqueline observed that Gaston's face was set in an obstinate frown, so she interrupted. "Can't we pick up a couple of local helpers for the digging, Jo, and let Gaston's guys continue stripping vegetation from the rest of the castle?"

"You told me, Jackie, that you didn't want us to make our presence too obvious. Nothing would shout more loudly to the world about what we're doing than people seeing the whole of the castle remains emerge from its five-hundred-year-old disguise."

She had to nod agreement.

Gaston looked from her to Jolyon and found no support. "I'm afraid they're adamant," he said. "If they can't be allowed to continue up on the cliffs, I think they'll want to be off."

"Hang on. You signed a contract," Jolyon reminded him.

"I accept my personal responsibility. Of course I'll stay on as I promised. But the other two want out. I'm afraid I'm going to have to let them go."

Jacqueline looked at him suspiciously. "Why have they decided that they've lost interest in the project after just one week on site, Gaston? They haven't even dug a spade into the ground yet. How do they know they don't like the work?"

"Well," he looked uncomfortable, "they also say that they don't like being ordered around like students. They're not schoolboys any more. They like to make their own decisions."

Jolyon bristled. "I'm sorry too, Gaston, but this is a scientific expedition. Everything has to be done to a set routine. Therefore they've got to go where I tell them and do what I tell them. We can't have everybody going off and doing whatever they feel like doing. The result would be chaos and the whole purpose of the investigation and the subsequent reports and documentaries would be thrown into doubt. I'm afraid I can't allow that."

Gaston was silent in the face of Jolyon's outburst. Jackie agreed that André was quite correct in insisting that everything was done in a strict, recorded manner. But she was aware that he could behave a bit like a sergeant major at times. She could understand that his attitude might jar with free-thinking individuals like rock climbers.

"The other thing," continued Jolyon, "is that everything seemed perfectly OK until your two guys decided to take that day out in Foix last Thursday. I admit I bawled them out for that – which I was entitled to do. They didn't like it, of course. But I noticed they were perfectly happy until after that visit. It seemed to be the Foix trip that changed their attitude. I want to know just what happened on that visit to Foix."

Jacqueline looked at him suspiciously. "What's this, Gaston? I don't know anything about any visit to Foix."

"It was the day you flew back to Paris, Jackie," said Jolyon. "You said we could take it easy that day. So these three lads decided to take a trip to Foix."

"You mean you went as well, Gaston?"

He nodded, shifting his weight from one foot to the other in embarrassment.

"Why choose Foix?"

Gaston shrugged. "We'd never been there. We fancied a look around."

"But why Foix? It's some distance away. And it's not the most interesting place in the world for three young guys."

"Jean-Claude suggested it. Apparently he knew somebody who'd told him it was a good place to visit."

"Jean-Claude? He's the short, slim one – is that right?"

"That's right," said Jolyon.

"So *was* it a good place to visit?"

Gaston frowned. "We didn't get there until nearly one o'clock. So we decided to go into a bar and have a drink."

"Where did you go after that?"

"We stayed in the bar."

"What – all day?"

"Yes – for a couple of hours anyway. We had something to eat and a couple more drinks."

"And was that all? You didn't go for a look around?"

"No."

"Even though you'd been told it was a good place to look round?"

He looked guilty as he shook his head. His truculent attitude had evaporated.

Jacqueline was suspicious of Gaston's manner. She noticed he could hardly meet her eyes. "Did you come across anybody you knew while you were there? Did you talk to anyone?"

"Well," he admitted, "we did get chatting to a couple of guys."

"What did you say to them?" Jolyon jumped in. "Did they ask you what you were doing? Did you tell them anything about what we're doing here?"

"We may have said something."

"You know you were supposed to keep quiet about what we're doing here. You signed an agreement which said that you wouldn't tell anybody about what we were doing here without our prior authorisation."

Gaston shook his head. "We didn't say anything about what we were doing. In fact it was the other guys who raised the subject."

"What do you mean by that?" asked Jackie. "What exactly did they say?"

"I don't remember the exact words."

"How did this happen?"

He just shrugged again.

Jacqueline stood up, crossed over to him and looked straight into his eyes. "I think you'd better tell us the whole story, Gaston. First of all – the three of you were having a drink. Were you at the bar?"

"No, we were sitting at a table in the corner."

"And what happened? Did these guys approach you or did you invite them over?"

"They were sitting at the next table. I forget how it happened exactly. I think Jean-Claude was saying that he wasn't very happy with the work, when one of the blokes leaned over and asked if we were the guys working on le Bézu."

"He asked you that straight out?"

"I think so – yes."

"Bloody hell!" Jolyon burst out. He was on his feet now. "So much for secrecy! And they know all about it fifty kilometres away in Foix after we've only been on site a week."

Jacqueline laid a hand on Jolyon's arm to restrain him. To have a shouting match wouldn't help anyone. But she continued to Gaston. "Had you mentioned the name – le Bézu - in your conversation?"

"I dunno." Gaston shrugged. "We might have done."

"So what did you say to them?"

"I didn't say anything - but Jean-Claude did confirm this was where we were working. They wanted to know if we'd found anything."

"And what did you say to that?"

"Jean-Claude, or it might have been Willem, said that it was early days and we'd only been clearing the undergrowth. He said he reckoned it would be a long time before we found anything."

"Did you tell them anything else?"

Gaston shook his head. "I don't think so."

"How long did this conversation go on for?"

"Oh – only a short time."

"Do you think they were quizzing you to find out as much as they could about what we were doing?"

"I don't think so." He cast around for justification. "It wasn't a question and answer session. I think it was only casual conversation."

Jacqueline frowned. "And did they give you a contact phone number or anything like that? Did they ask you to give them any information in the future?"

"No, of course not."

"Did they try to get you to do anything for them while you were working here?"

"Certainly not."

"So there's no way you're likely to see them again?"

"I don't think so."

"What do you mean?" demanded Jolyon aggressively. "Why don't you *think* so? Why don't you *know* so?"

Gaston looked extremely uncomfortable. "Well, I wasn't there all the time. I wanted to get some cigarettes and they didn't have my brand in the bar. So I left them talking while I went up the street."

"How long were you gone for?"

"I suppose for ten minutes, quarter of an hour." He shook his head. "It took me some time to find a shop stocking my brand."

Jackie and André looked at each other. Jolyon pulled a face but said nothing. She turned back to the climber, suddenly aware that she was several centimetres taller than he was.

"All right, Gaston," she said quietly. "I agree that we'd better let Jean-Claude and Willem go. I think it should be as soon as possible. Can you arrange it for first thing in the morning?"

"I'll see to it," he said.

"And Gaston – will you please emphasise to them that they are not to say anything to anybody about what we're doing here? That also goes for you, Gaston. Will you promise me that you won't say anything in future, without first checking with me?"

He hung his head. "You can rely on me," he mumbled.

"All right. You'd better go and speak to the other two."

Gaston turned and left the room, closing the door quietly behind him. When he had gone there was silence for a couple of minutes.

Jackie turned to her colleague. "Well – what do you think?"

"I don't like it."

"They can't have told these other guys very much. There's not much to tell at this stage."

"I agree," said Jolyon, "but what worries me is that they were approached at all – and in Foix of all places. If it was down the road in Quillan or maybe in Cuiza it would have been less surprising. There's bound to be some local interest in what's going on up here. But Foix is a long way away. It looks to me as if some sort of arrangement was made by Jean-Claude to meet up with those other guys."

"You don't think it was just chance?"

"I certainly do *not*. Besides, why should the two guys decide to leave the dig after just a short, innocent meeting with some blokes they'd never seen before?"

"Do you think something more important was said while Gaston was conveniently out of the way?"

"Either that, or Gaston's giving us a pack of lies."

Jacqueline shook her head. "I don't think Gaston's that bad. He didn't *have* to tell us *anything*. He could have just said they had a drink and walked round the town and never met anyone. I think he was genuinely embarrassed by what happened."

"The other thing I don't understand is why Jean-Claude and Willem should decide to pack in working here immediately after they'd met those guys in Foix. If somebody was trying to use them to gain information, you'd have thought they'd have offered them money or some other sort of inducement to stay."

"Perhaps we're seeing some sort of conspiracy where there's nothing, Jo. Perhaps the two guys had already decided they wanted out and the meeting in Foix was an irrelevance. You can see it happening. I guess there was an argument going on between Gaston and the other two which they didn't feel able to have here, where we might hear them."

"Mmm – maybe."

"I think that's what occurred. Voices were probably raised. The blokes at the next table would have wondered what the argument was about. Perhaps they heard the name le Bézu and it caught their interest. They might have known about the place and were intrigued to hear it was being discussed. It's a remote location with an unusual name. Such things can happen."

Jolyon was clearly unhappy with her suggested solution, but she poked him in the chest.

"Don't worry, Jo. Only you and I, my agent Bernard and Alain Gisours at TV France know what we're looking for. We haven't even told Gaston what the real object of the expedition is. It can't have got out to the general public."

"I suppose you're right." He shrugged his shoulders. "But I do think we need to be more careful with our recruitment of staff in future."

"What do you mean?"

"You're too trusting, Jackie. You'll take on anybody who turns up and asks for a job. I think in the future we should only take on people who come from sources we can trust and we need to check them out before taking them on."

"What about students?"

He pulled a face. "I think students are a bit risky. Besides which, they're not going to become available after their exams for at least another two months. The alternative is a few local people who, as far as we can tell, are unlikely to have been got at by anybody who might want to find out our real reasons for being here."

She smiled at his seriousness. "OK, Jo. I'll leave you to do the recruitment in future. So – what are we going to do about replacing Willem and Jean-Claude?"

"Let's leave it for a few days. We don't really need any more rock climbers at present. Just the three of us can start the trench by the main entrance without outside help. So let's see how it goes for the next couple of weeks."

Jackie nodded. "I agree that's sensible. There's no point in committing ourselves to the excavation too heavily, until we've got more idea of the layout of the place. Then we can plan our strategy more fully and recruit the labour force we need at that time."

So no more was said about the staff problems. But André Jolyon was a worried man as he returned to his room.

9

Abbé Dugard looked up from his trench and straightened his back, massaging the muscles as he breathed in deeply. His eye fell on Jean-Luc Lerenard who was still working hard, less than three metres from him.

Bertrand Dugard couldn't fault the fellow's industry. He slaved away for twelve hours every day, scraping with trowel and knife, brushing furiously with his five-centimetre paint brush and enthusiastically pushing the barrows of spoil to the tip. Jean-Luc's fault was that he tended to rush at his finds, desperate to uncover the mediaeval corpses in his trench. This led him to ignore the little finds in the overburden on top of the skeletons – the small, decomposed remains of shrouds and coffins; the indications of disintegrated lesser grave-goods tossed in after the burials; the tell-tale signs of grave robbing which might have occurred soon after internment. These were the faults which marked him out as a treasure-seeking amateur. It was this weakness in his technique which would betray him to his future employers.

Bertrand's gaze wandered over the private archaeological excavations which he was conducting in the ancient monks' graveyard in a part of the garden near the monastery. He appreciated that his exploration of Dominican remains might appear a rather dry subject to many people. However, he was uncovering unique evidence about the behaviour and lifestyle of the early years of the brotherhood which he personally was finding fascinating. When he published his results he was confident it would completely change the way the public perceived the followers of Saint Dominic. And he knew that this changed perception was going to be difficult for the Roman Catholic Church to swallow. In fact, he might not be allowed to publish at all. And if he went ahead without consent, he knew it wouldn't do his pension prospects any good.

He shook his head. His immediate problem was to turn this mature trainee into an apparent archaeologist and he only had two weeks left in which to do it. He laboriously hauled his seventy-two-year-old frame out of the trench and strolled over to watch Lerenard at work. The big man was applying himself so enthusiastically to his task that it was a couple of minutes before he noticed the Abbé standing above him.

"Is it all right?" he asked.

"Mmm." The old man's nod of assent was short of a full endorsement.

"I find it frustrating to have to go back and check through each container-full of material for finds I might have missed," admitted Lerenard.

Bertrand bent down to examine the finds tray. The contents were reassuringly varied. "Well, you seem to have learnt pretty well what the items are that you're looking for," he grudgingly attested.

Jean-Luc's chest swelled with pride. He was aware of the compliment that he was being paid by this kindly old man who was thought of as a great expert by the Catholic intelligentsia.

"And you've worked very hard," continued Dugard. "I've never known anybody who applied themselves as you do. I think you could become a success at almost anything that you fully put your mind to." He sighed. "Unfortunately, I only had four short weeks to turn you into an archaeologist and that is nowhere near enough time, even though you are only specialising in the mediaeval period.

"I've been reading every night," assured the big man. "And I've been making a lot of notes to ensure I absorb it all. I have a good understanding now of seven of the twelve books which you have given me. I'm now concentrating on the rest. You'll be able to question me on them before I complete my training."

The Abbé nodded. "I'm sure you'll be almost word perfect. In fact, I wonder when you find time to sleep. I hope you realise you are trying to compress a three-year degree course and five years' practical experience into less than a month. I confess the very thought of it exhausts me. I don't know why you do it."

67

However of course he did know. The instruction to train this man had come from on high. And there were things he had noticed about Monsieur Lerenard which made his blood run cold – the way he had broken those bricks to get them into a waste bucket; his habit of disposing of unwelcome insects between his finger and thumb; the look which shaded his eyes when the Abbé pointed out to him that he had made a mistake in his understanding of an instruction. Bertrand had never met a trained killer, so he did not know exactly what they were like, but he suspected that Jean-Luc Lerenard might be one. However, his telephone call to the cardinal last week to voice his misgivings about the man, had elicited the promise that Jacqueline Blontard had nothing to fear from him.

"It's important that I can obtain a position on the excavations at le Bézu," said Jean-Luc as though he was reading the Abbé's mind in his uncanny and slightly frightening way. "I believe that Jacqueline Blontard is the gateway to the future for me."

Dugard knew the man was lying, but he had to go along with the deception. "That was the object of your coming here?" he asked "- to get a place with Mademoiselle Blontard?"

"I hope so. I do very much hope so."

"But," said the Abbé, "I do not know her well. She came to work with me some years ago in the holidays from her studies. It is true that I was able to teach her a certain amount. However, she has now moved far beyond my humble field of endeavour. I don't believe a recommendation from me would necessarily ensure you a place on her team."

"That won't be necessary." Lerenard smiled his bleak smile that made Dugard shiver. "I hope the recommendation to employ me will come from higher up. I only request that, if she contacts you to ask for a reference, you say that I have worked satisfactorily for you. I do not ask you to lie for me. You do not have to say how long you have known me. All I want you to say is that I have some knowledge of the mediaeval period. You need say no more than that."

"Hmm."

Seeing his doubts, the big man continued, "As I say - I do not ask you to tell lies. But I request that you do *not* tell her how little experience I have had." He looked straight at the Abbé with his frosty grey eyes. "I will try to make up with industry for my lack of experience. I will not let you down."

Jean-Luc paused and, when Dugard did not respond, he prompted, "Will you do that for me?"

There was no apparent threat in the man's tone. However, in view of the orders he had received from above, Bertrand knew he had no choice. At last he said, "I do not know why you wish to get a post with Jacqueline Blontard and I do not wish to know." He paused, then nodded. "I will give you the reference you ask for." He raised a hand. "But I must have an undertaking from you. Will you promise me, that if you get a place with her, no harm will come to her from your hand? I cannot be a party to any violence or to putting the lady in danger."

"I will give you that promise freely," said the big man. "In fact I can assure you that it will be my intention, when I work for her, to do all in my power to protect and care for Mademoiselle Blontard."

He paused and the Abbé waited for his next comment with some trepidation.

"It is my task to see that the excavations at le Bézu come to a satisfactory conclusion for everybody."

For some reason Bertrand Dugard did not feel reassured by Lerenard's promises. However he couldn't call the fellow a liar and he realised that it wasn't really the big man's fault. He could see better than Lerenard that they were both only performing tasks allotted to them by higher authorities.

"Very well," he said as he turned away. "We had better continue our training with our fullest application so that there is no reason for me to lie when I give you your reference."

However, he felt severe misgivings about the task he had been given. And if he had seen the look which the big man directed at his back as he returned to his trench, he would have felt even more disquiet.

10

It was an advantage for Philip that he worked in the history research department at the university. He had some questions to ask, raised by his reading of his grandmother's manuscript. Mediaeval history wasn't his speciality. However, he had a chat with a colleague who was able to tell him a great deal about the Albigensian crusade. In a couple of hours, he felt he had picked up a lot of background information about the Cathars and their oppressors. His friend was very intrigued about the direction of his questioning, but he put the chap off for now, promising him the full story in due course, if there was one.

A couple of evenings later he pulled his grandmother's exercise book out of the duffle bag and found the place he had marked, to continue the story:-

Being how I escaped the search for the perfecti who had survived the massacre at Montségur in the spring of the year of one thousand two hundred and forty-four.

Before Raymonde de Puyvert and I fled from the castle at le Bézu, we considered carefully which direction we should take. It was unthinkable to go north into the heart of the Languedoc which was now totally occupied by the French. Raymonde suggested, and I agreed, that it would be best in any circumstances for us to direct ourselves towards the sea, where it might be possible to find a ship to take us to some safe shore which was beyond pursuit. This was closest in the east. However to go in that direction would require us to cross an area of the country which was still heavily occupied by the enemy and would involve us in great risk.

There was a problem if we chose to go west in an attempt to reach the lands controlled by the English. We could at least have hopes that they would be sympathetic to our cause. However, to get there, it would mean that we had first to pass close to Montségur where the hue and cry would be greatest. Therefore we decided the only practical course was to cross the high mountains to the south and enter the lands of the King of Aragon, who we believed was still sympathetic to members of the Cathar faith.

We knew it would be necessary to find a guide to lead us over the paths which crossed the mountains, some of which were still covered with the remains of the winter snows. However I had a generous purse of denarii and sous provided to me by the now destroyed credentes of Montségur. Therefore I did not doubt that we would be able to find a suitable person to lead us over the Pyrenees into Spain.

We decided to avoid the town of Cuillan which we feared might already have been reached by the hue and cry. So we took the track through the hamlet of Saint Julia and up to the col known locally as the place where the wild cherries grew. Continuing south we avoided the great citadel of Puylaurens, keeping to the woods on the other side of the river. Then we proceeded up the valley and continued to the Col d'Aussieres in the Escales range of lesser mountains. Here we experienced our first snow but it was not very deep. We then made our way down towards the springs at Molitge, finding ourselves a night's lodgings at the house of a peasant about half a league from the town.

We had made about eight leagues in all during that first day and were therefore most weary. However we took turns to stay on watch during the night, to ensure that the peasant and his woman did not attempt to give our position away to earn themselves more money than we were paying for the night's food and lodgings. As a consequence, we were up and away before dawn when the sky was just turning light.

The peasant whose shelter we had hired over-night had volunteered to show us the way into Spain in order to earn himself more denarii. He claimed to have carried out such commissions before. We were suspicious of whether he really had the knowledge necessary to discharge this duty, but felt we had nothing to lose by taking him with us, since he said he

71

accepted that he would not receive payment until we arrived at the first habitation in Aragon.

Thus we spent most of the day skirting the massive peak of Canigou and climbing up through the valley of the stream known locally as the Rotjer until, ascending out of the valley, we were confronted for the first time by a range of high mountains all covered in snow which we knew we had to cross to achieve our goal. It being late in the day, we decided to rest for the night in a shepherd's hut of rough stone with a roof of pine branches. Since it wasn't raining, we felt we would be dry enough for the night. We were carrying sufficient food on our backs for two more nights and we were able to light a fire in the corner of the building for warmth.

The next morning Raymonde complained of feeling unwell. He had pains in his chest and was finding breathing difficult – a problem which I believe can be experienced by many people in the high mountains if they attempt to exercise their bodies too greatly. For myself, being younger, I was still feeling quite well and wished to push on towards our destination. I understood the border with Aragon was only four or five leagues distant and could easily be achieved in the day, notwithstanding the fact that much of the way would be up steep snow slopes. Faced with my enthusiasm, Raymonde assured me that he was well enough to accompany me. It was therefore my intemperate nature that was the cause of the tragedy which later befell us.

With little thought of the possible consequences, we set out on the start of our climb. Within a short distance we encountered deep snow. We were heading for a high col between two peaks and had probably therefore chosen to follow a shallow valley where the snow was deepest. However I had no intention of turning back. I insisted that the peasant, whose name was Guillaume, should take the lead on this part of the mission since he claimed to know where he was going, although I was now even more doubtful of that fact.

As we climbed, it began to snow and the visibility became very bad. Guillaume desired to return but I believed we were within a quarter of a league of the top. In any case I was *uncertain that we could find our way back the way we had come. Although he was flagging badly, Raymonde foolishly supported me in my wish to proceed. Thus we continued towards disaster.*

When we drew near to the top the way became much steeper. There was a lot of projecting rock which was slippery with ice and with deep crevasses of snow in between. Guillaume said we would not reach the top this way in these conditions. I accused him of losing his way and leading us astray. He replied, in his rough patois, that it was impossible for anyone to find their way in such conditions. He said he would go no further and demanded his payment now unless we agreed to go back and wait for the weather to improve. When I persisted, his mood became ugly. I could see in any case that Raymonde could go no further. So, in great frustration, I was forced to agree to return.

As we set off back down the mountain, Guillaume was once again leading. Raymonde went next with me following in the rear. The terrain was extremely difficult. Our hands and feet were very cold from the snow and ice. Raymonde said he had lost the sense of feeling in his legs. Suddenly he slipped and fell on to his back. Because of the steepness of the slope he started sliding ever faster, bumping over rocks and flying through the air in places and landing with a crash on the icy surface until he came up with an awful impact against a large rock.

I hastened as speedily as I could to his side but the sight when I got there was enough to make the heart quail. His body was bent backwards around the sharp rock at an impossible angle and I was certain that he had broken many bones. His face was smeared with blood which was welling from his mouth. That made me believe he had also damaged some of his internal organs, perhaps even his heart or lungs. He was breathing very slowly and was deeply unconscious.

Despite my experience of seeing many men killed during the siege of Montségur, I had never been called upon to attempt to repair such damage to a man's body. In the last few days I had come to love Raymonde as if he had been one of my family. I desperately wanted to be able to treat his injuries. However I doubted if I could do anything to save him.

I knew the most important thing at that moment was to get his body off this mountainside and into the protection of a building where it could be warmed. At the same time I must try very hard not to cause him any more hurt than he had suffered already. I looked to Guillaume, who was standing nearby, for assistance but he simply shrugged and said, "That one is dead." But I could not accept that. I made the man unpack his back coverings and I did the same myself. With those materials I was able to fashion a layer of fabric on which we carefully laid the poor broken figure of Raymonde. Then we set off, slowly guiding his body down the slope which was at least getting less steep now.

After about an hour the snow was thinning and we reasoned that we were coming down into the valley we had left that morning. In a while I espied the shepherd's hut where we had spent the night. It was about half a league further down the valley. The snow soon ran out as we made for it. We were going to have to carry Raymonde the rest of the way. I looked at the rough terrain and my heart failed me. I knew we would never make it.

Guillaume was bent over Raymonde. "He is certainly dead," he said.

I went to inspect the body of my companion. He had turned a sort of pale grey except for the clot of blood which had frozen in his mouth. I knew then that Guillaume spoke correctly. I felt for a pulse on his wrists and at his neck and there was no sign of life. So I wept for the last man in the whole of the Languedoc whom I could call a friend. I knew then that I was alone in the world.

We laid the body out straight on a level patch of ground. We then collected a number of stones with which we covered the body and put further stones to each side to form a christian cross. To us Cathars the burial of the body is not important because the spirit of the dead person is now with the good God. However I was not quite sure that Raymonde was a full Cathar and I did know that he had not received the consolamentum.

Guillaume then told me that he would go no further. He said he wished to return home and asked to be paid the money we had promised him. I reminded him that he had agreed he would only receive his money when we had reached our destination in Aragon. He was inclined to dispute the matter but I offered him a half of the sum promised for bringing me thus far. When he was still prepared to argue, although I was severely lacking in self-confidence, I put my hand on my sword hilt and made it clear that I would offer no more. So he accepted my decision with a show of churlishness.

We then returned as far as the shepherd's hut and I made him leave me with all the remaining food and equipment before I paid him off. I sat and watched his departure down the valley with a heavy heart. I knew that I was now totally dependent on my own resources. It was early in the afternoon. The weather, though clearing somewhat, was still cold and misty. The visibility was less than half a league. Therefore I judged that it was hopeless to try and make another attempt on my own at crossing the mountain range, which had so disastrously defeated us in the morning. I realised I would just have to sit and wait for an improvement in the weather.

I checked through the food and other supplies which I had with me. I divided the food into four portions, one of which I ate that afternoon. I kept another portion for breaking my fast the following morning. Then I bundled up the rest together with such items of equipment as I judged I would have need of on my journey and strapped it together ready to hoist on to my back. Then I built up the fire, wrapped myself in my rugs and prepared for a long rest. I had decided to abandon my bed on the morrow and not rest again until I reached a safe haven well inside the country of Aragon, even if I should perish in the attempt.

Having made this decision, I slept the night through and awoke to a bright, clear day with a visibility which stretched for several leagues. That made me condemn myself further, for I knew that if I had agreed to wait on the previous day until the weather was favourable I did not doubt that Raymonde would have still been alive. I have carried the burden of that knowledge with me for the remainder of my life.

I hastily consumed my breakfast, hoisted the baggage I was intending to carry on to my back and left the remainder as a gift to the first shepherd who should reach this hut with his spring herds. As I climbed out of the valley, I came into the bright sunshine which exposed fully the path I should be taking. The snow was still deep but I was able to make good progress and, in a little under two hours, I was at the place where Raymonde had fallen yesterday. I then proceeded with greater care and it took me another hour of scrambling over icy rocks to reach the summit of the col.

Now I beheld a magnificent panorama that was laid out before me. About two leagues away I could see another range of lesser mountains. They were still topped with snow, but the whiteness did not extend far into the valleys. Beyond them I could see the green forests of Aragon – the beginning of my destination.

I was careful as I descended into the next valley, being only too aware of the disaster which might befall me if I slipped badly. I did lose my footing on two occasions but was able to recover without serious inconvenience. Then, after about half an hour, I left the snow behind and was able to pick my way with more confidence through the low undergrowth which clad the landscape at this altitude.

By the middle of the day I had crossed the lower range of mountains and was descending into a forest of thin pine trees. From now on my way was much easier, following the course of a tumbling stream which in the fullness of time became a small river. The weather was fine and the sunshine warming after the cold of the mountains. I was able to converse with the few humans I met in a kind of halting patois which was composed of many words which were similar to Occitan. Thus I was able to purchase food and lodging.

The next day I set off in clear weather over the last of the mountains and, after four days walking, I came to the great city of Barcelona which was then home to the court of Aragon. There I felt I was able to disclose my identity to the court

76

chamberlain whom I met, but not of course my object. Instead I gave him the tale that I was escaping from the wrath of the French and that I wished to obtain a passage by sea to England. I found the chamberlain most helpful and, after an interval of two weeks, one of his staff introduced me to the captain of a ship making for Lisbon. There I was able to transfer to an English ship and I landed in the port of London on the first day of September in the same year of one thousand two hundred and forty-four.

I had been given the names of two people whom I might contact for assistance if I should reach England. I met the first, a lawyer named Henry Bradburn, in his dwelling in a special court in London which was called the Inner Temple. His manner was dry and less hospitable than I had hoped and I feared I would get little assistance from him. He confirmed, when I asked, that news had reached London of the destruction of the Cathar cause at Montségur and other locations thereafter. He seemed to think that I should give great thanks to God for my deliverance from the French 'crusaders'. As far as he was aware, I was the only human being to escape the hue and cry which had followed the fall of Montségur.

He also had knowledge of the other person whom I had been told I might contact – a gentleman by the name of Gérard de Molay. Apparently that man now resided in a small town in the West of England which was called Coombe Temple. Mr Bradburn thought that my best course was to travel to that place and seek out the said Gérard, who was the person most likely to be able to help me. Mr Bradburn said he would give me a sealed letter to hand to de Molay.

Therefore I travelled west and met Monsieur de Molay on a day in late September when the leaves of the great trees in the valley above Coombe Temple were starting to turn to gold. Gérard revealed that he was a supporter of the Cathars who had escaped from France when he saw that our cause had become hopeless. He had been able to transfer some of his substantial wealth through his connection with the Knights Templar and had used a part of this to obtain possession of a portion of land in the area. Because of his support for the cause he was prepared to sell me, for a very modest sum which I could pay him over the next few years, a section of that land where I might build a house and grow sufficient food to sustain me until such time as I might be contacted by an emissary from the Cathar convocation. With the blessing of the good God, I was able to make a success of this enterprise and am now accounted to be a wealthy man with a wife and three growing sons.

As my life moves towards its close, I have never received any approach from anybody in the Languedoc and I fear that I never shall. All the information we have received from France is that the Cathar faith is utterly destroyed. So I believe that I should set down my experiences of what occurred in the month of March in the year of one thousand two hundred and forty-four in case the treasure of the Cathars should ever be sought by my successors or by members of my faith. This I now do as correctly and fully as I am able to remember some forty years after the actual events took place.

I commend this account to the true God whose teachings I have always followed.

11

Armand Séjour tossed the two suitcases on to the double bed and kicked the door to room 203 closed. The Hotel du Chateau didn't run to porters and he had been forced to carry the bags up himself. He doubted that he would have been able to charge his employers for the tip in any case, so nothing had been lost.

He admitted that he didn't really mind the small additional labour. His own suitcase was quite modest, but Jeanette's great wheeled thing must have weighed well over twenty kilos. If the lovely girl had one small fault it was her desire to carry a full wardrobe of her clothes with her on her travels. However, to be fair, he had warned her that he was expecting them to stay in Quillan for up to a month.

He turned to survey her. She was not tall – perhaps twenty centimetres shorter than himself. Her figure was very shapely but only a little overweight; her fair hair fluffed out around her head; her face was pretty with deep brown eyes. And she dressed to show off her body. In fact, he had wondered whether she was too pretty, too spectacularly attractive for the task he had in mind. However, her other advantages outweighed the small one of appearance. She had already shown her willingness to play the role of his young wife to the full. With a secret smile he acknowledged that the job he had been given might turn out to be a very pleasant experience. After all, a man had to take advantage of the opportunities which were handed to him in life.

"We have about half an hour to unpack and shower." He told her. "I want us to be the first in the restaurant for dinner so that we can get a corner table. I think you should wear something that would make a man interested in you, without displaying too much of your sexy figure."

He couldn't resist reaching out and cupping one of her ripe breasts in his right hand – a gesture almost of possession. But he stepped back and raised a finger in caution as she responded by moving towards him. The job had to come first.

"I'm sorry, Jeanette, I shouldn't have done that. We haven't got time for pleasure now. That will have to wait until later."

She pouted but turned obediently away and began to unpack. It had been made very clear to her when she was offered the walking holiday in the Pyrenees that there were business priorities. Armand hadn't specified exactly what they were, but she knew that these came before pleasure.

"So what exactly are we supposed to do at dinner?" she asked as she began to hang up her bewildering display of tops, skirts and dresses that looked likely to fill by themselves the modest wardrobe which the hotel provided in a standard double room like this one.

"Well, as I told you, we will position ourselves in a corner where we can see everything that's going on and where the others can see us. Of course we will chat to each other about our plans."

Her eyes sparkled. "I'll enjoy that."

"I mean about our holiday plans - where we're going to walk, what we're going to see. The conversation must not become intimate. We can talk about the journey from Paris, of course, and our plans for exploring the countryside of the region. Have you read the guide book I gave you?"

"Mmm – but it's all about history and castles and abbeys and other ancient sites. There doesn't seem to be anything in it about shopping centres and entertainments."

"That's just the sort of philistine comment I'd expect from a Parisian *poule*." He chuckled. "My darling, this area doesn't have any shopping centres. You would have to go at least to Toulouse to find anything that calls itself a department store."

She pulled a face as he continued, "If anybody comes into the dining room and greets us, we respond with a smile, but we don't say too much."

"What if they ask why we're here?"

"You can let me answer that. If you need to say anything, it will be simply that we're on a walking holiday, exploring the area, and that we're using Quillan as our base."

"What – for four weeks?"

"We'll just say for a week or two to start with. If people ask later why we're staying on so long, we can say it's because we like the area and its history so much. I hope by then we'll have made some progress with the archaeologists."

"Will you point them out to me?"

"I only know Jacqueline Blontard from her television appearances. We'll just have to assume that the people with her are her colleagues."

"What do we say to them?"

"I think the best thing is for you to act a little bit shy and I'll do most of the talking. I chose you because I know you're a good actress."

She pouted. "I thought you chose me because you liked me."

"Of course I did. But don't get me wrong, Jeanette. We're here on business. I would have selected somebody I couldn't stand the sight of, if I thought she would play the part better." He allowed himself to come up behind her and reach round to fondle her magnificent breasts again. "I'm very lucky to have found somebody who's both clever and sexy. It makes my job a lot more fun."

As she turned to respond he stepped hastily away and began to unzip his own bag.

"Mind you, nothing may happen this evening. The archaeologists may eat somewhere else. Or they may be working hard and come back for their meal much later and we can hardly sit in the restaurant all evening. We may even find we're all on our own at dinner." He grinned at her in a way that made her heart skip. "In that case we'll be able to come to bed a bit earlier."

"Well," she said, trying to keep her voice light, "let us hope that dinner is going to be very boring."

Something about Armand turned her on. She didn't know what it was. Perhaps it was his decisiveness, his readiness to take immediate action in response to something happening, his single-minded drive to attain his ends. But there was also something about Armand's obsession with the task in hand that was slightly frightening. She always felt, when she was with him, that something dangerous was about to happen. It was part of his delicious excitement.

"If we don't have an opportunity to talk to them this evening," he went on, "then we will have to hope that the good weather continues. I want to find somewhere tomorrow where I can observe through the binoculars what is going on at this chateau of le Bézu. You borrowed some old walking boots, didn't you?"

She tossed her head. "Just as you instructed."

I want us to look as though we're experienced walkers. Perhaps we'd better spend a couple of days getting ourselves fit before we approach le Bézu. I don't want them seeing through our disguise." He straightened up. "Now, if you've finished your unpacking, you'd better have your shower before we go down to dinner."

When he came out of the shower himself twenty minutes later, he noticed with approval that she had put on a tee-shirt which hugged her figure nicely. It had a modest neckline, but the beaded decoration gave it a slightly dressy appearance – just the right touch for dinner. Her make up was careful and not overdone. Her black skirt and patent high-heels with the fishnet tights gave her quite a classy look. He told her how impressed he was.

"You can show me when you take them off later," she grinned.

As he put on his open-necked white shirt and dark slacks he thought he was going to enjoy the next few days before the serious work began. He decided that Monsieur Charles Robert could wait a while before he made his first telephone report.

It was late when they finally got to bed. The evening had been an unqualified success. There were only three archaeologists present at dinner, but they had been in a good mood. The two men, who were called André Jolyon and Gaston Lesmoins (Armand always made a point of getting the names right in the early stages of a relationship), had been a little reserved at first. However Jacqueline Blontard, the famous archaeologist, had been in sparkling form and had seemed to take to them straight away.

Armand saw immediately that she had real charisma. She had been full of stories about events on her previous expeditions. He had been careful to watch videos of her two TV series and was genuinely interested in the work she did. His admiration wasn't false, so he was soon accepted as a friend when he started asking intelligent questions.

"How long does it take to make a series?"

"Well, the actual recording is only a few weeks. But the cameramen will have spent quite a while on site before the recording starts. And of course, before the technicians arrive there will probably have been months of excavations, recording finds, research into sources. The whole thing can take well over a year." She smiled her captivating smile. "I've been working full-time on this one since last September and I'd been thinking about it for a couple of years before that. I've even started some preparatory work on my next project, which won't start until the summer of next year."

"What's that going to be about?" asked Jeanette, anxious not to be ignored.

"Ah – I'm keeping that to myself." Armand noticed that just a touch of asperity had crept into Jackie's voice. "Besides, a lot will depend on the success of this series."

"You must realise," interrupted Jolyon, "that Jacqueline is contracted to TV France. They insist on the highest confidentiality."

"What do you mean – contracted to them?"

"That means they pay her a nice retainer and that gives them first refusal on all her plans."

Jeanette's question was all innocence. "Are you contracted to them as well?"

"I'm part of Jackie's team, so I make my own arrangements with her." It seemed that Jolyon's appreciation of Jeanette's voluptuous curves prevented him from objecting to her questions.

Armand decided to change the subject. "I'd really like to see what you're doing up at this chateau where you're excavating. Are we permitted to come up there?"

"Of course you are," Jackie said. "Just let me know when you're planning to visit and I'll make sure I'm there to give you a guided tour."

He noticed a slight frown from Jolyon, as though the guy thought his boss was being too generous. "There isn't a lot to see yet," he pointed out. "We've only just started on site."

"But I expect it will be very interesting to hear you talk about the history and the setting, with all your knowledge." Armand decided to ignore Jolyon's objections. "And I've always been interested in archaeological excavations and the special techniques you use."

Jackie drained her glass. "It would give me great pleasure to show you what we do", she enthused. "Come up tomorrow morning, if you like. Your wife would be welcome as well."

"We'll do that. Can I get you another drink? What about you, André? Gaston?"

It was the start of a jolly evening. Before the end, Armand and his 'wife' had been offered the opportunity of spending time with and learning from the famous archaeologist. Everybody was on first name terms. André had unbent enough to give Jeanette a hug and a tender goodnight kiss. Even the taciturn Gaston was telling slightly crude jokes. Armand felt he had successfully carried out the first stage of his assignment.

Furthermore, the excessive amount of wine they had both consumed meant that he took much longer than he had expected to strip the clothes from the delicious curves of Jeanette's body when they retired to the bedroom.

12

Alain Hébert had taken a six-month lease on a holiday cottage on the outskirts of Rennes-les-Bains under his assumed name. He drove there in the small Citroen which had been contract-hired by a friend for the same period. He spent the first week calling into local shops and bars and chatting with anyone who would listen to him, in order to establish his credentials.

He was letting it be known that he was a writer, researching the history of the Knights Templar in the region, with the intention of publishing a book on the subject in the next two years. He was enjoying a summer sabbatical from his job as a lecturer at one of the Paris universities. It was a story which had some approximation to the truth. He had postcards printed, inviting anybody with suitable information to contact him. He felt this story would give him sufficient justification for taking walks around the area and especially up to the castle at le Bézu.

Back in Marseilles, *La Force* had taken less than a week to come back and tell him they had accepted his proposal. Already they were preparing the distribution system. They showed him the warehouse on the outskirts of the city where they would store the treasure. The premises were previously used as the base for a business providing spare parts for car repairs all over Southern France. All sizes of vehicles had delivered and collected goods at the warehouse. They could reverse vans inside, close the doors and leave them there overnight for loading and unloading. Because the car parts were valuable, the building was already surrounded by high fences and protected by a sophisticated security system. *La Force* was constructing an additional inside wall which would partition off part of the warehouse to provide a very safe store that nobody would suspect might hold a treasure of unique value. They had also shown him examples of forged paperwork to export items all over the world from the criminal-infested docks of Marseilles.

He had been impressed by their efficiency, although he still had the feeling that Montluçon was only a front man.

In return for their efforts, he had given them further evidence of his knowledge of mediaeval artefacts, their valuation and potential markets for the items of treasure that he expected to find. He believed he had convinced them they would be wise to honour their agreement with him, because the ten percent of the proceeds that he received would be more than recovered as a result of his specialist knowledge. Without releasing the exact location of the treasure, he had told them of his plans to spend the summer in Rennes-les-Bains.

All that remained after that, was to arrange a suitable means of communication between Montluçon and himself. He had rejected their first proposal of the weasel-faced Mickey who had been his original, distasteful contact with their organisation. He pointed out that so obvious a petty crook would be an uncomfortable giveaway in an upper-middle-class area like Rennes-les-Bains. So they came back to him two days later with a much better contact – a journalist named César Renoir. They told him that Renoir would contact him some time after his arrival at Rennes.

He had been sitting outside his rented cottage three days after taking up residence and enjoying the evening sun when he first saw a tall woman striding up the road towards him. He guessed she was in her early forties. She was slim and looked fit for her age. She was dressed in a grey linen shirt and dark blue, tight-fitting jeans. Her dark hair was drawn back in a tight ponytail and she wore very little make-up. However, she was a striking woman.

She stopped in front of him and appraised him carefully.

"Alain Hébert?" she asked.

"Yes."

"I am César Renoir." She held out her hand.

He rose in surprise and took it. The handshake she gave him was firm.

"I was expecting a man," he confessed.

"I know. The Christian name fools most people. When my father gave me the name, I think it was because he was disappointed I wasn't a boy. But I've been able to live up to it since – in my way."

"Your father?"

"I believe you have already met him. He was that pathetic wreck you saw in Marseilles with half his face cut away. Camille Renoir used to be a force to be reckoned with, but now he hides behind a self-important heap of crap called Montluçon."

Alain decided not to commit himself to a comment at this stage. Instead he rose, offered his chair to her and went into the cottage to get another one for himself.

"Would you like a glass of wine?"

She accepted, and he opened a bottle and brought two glasses which he set on a small table between them. They sat in almost companionable silence for a short while, looking at the view and sipping their drinks.

After a few minutes she turned to him. "You've only just arrived from Paris?"

"Three days ago."

"I've been here nearly a week. I'm doing a series of articles for '*l'Observateur*' on Cathar castles. I understand they intend to bring out a guide book later. It has given me a chance to look around."

"That seems a good idea."

"I've already visited four of the chateaux. I've been to see a nearby one today - one that nobody seems to know anything about – I suppose because it's in a remote location. It's called le Bézu."

"Really?" He was aware of a quickening of his pulse and hoped it didn't show on his face.

"Yes. It's already swarming with archaeologists." She had an infectious grin. "Well – three actually."

"Oh, my god!" He couldn't prevent the exclamation slipping out. "What are they doing there?"

"I don't know – looking for some ancient remains of the Cathars, I believe. What do archaeologists ever look for? Old bones and pottery, it seems to me. But they've got a famous woman with them. Ever heard of Jacqueline Blontard?"

87

"The one who did the television series?"

"That's the one. Well, she's leading this dig so I should think it's reckoned to be quite important. I expect it'll be her next series." César suddenly caught the expression on his face. "Are you worried about archaeologists being here?"

"Not the archaeologists. But I don't particularly welcome the prospect of television crews swarming all over the area."

She laughed. "Don't worry. There are no television cameras around – at least, not yet. And they're not interested in the Templars. They told me the tales linking le Bézu to the Templars are purest myth."

"Who told you I was interested in the Templars?"

"My father, of course." It seemed to him that there was a slight withdrawal of the good humour he had previously enjoyed. "You must understand, monsieur, that I am his closest confidante since my mother died. You don't have any need to worry. I know how to keep a secret." She tossed her hair back. "*Mon dieu*, I've been told enough in my time."

He ignored her attempts to reassure him. For now he was more interested in what was going on at le Bézu. "How long are they going to be there?" he asked, trying to sound casual.

"I don't know. The whole summer, I expect. These archaeologists do things by the season, don't they? I can tell you they're not likely to be gone in a fortnight." She looked at him carefully. "Why? Is it important?"

He didn't know her well enough yet to trust her, so he shook his head, trying to suggest it was irrelevant. "It's just interesting when other researchers coincidentally turn up in the same area. But you say they're only looking for Cathar remains?"

"So they tell me. Mind you, I haven't got really close to any of the archaeologists yet."

"Are they on the site all the time?"

"Most days, I think. I understand they're staying at a hotel in Quillan. That's on the Limoux to Axat road."

He made a decision. "I think we ought to find out some more about what they're doing – how big an area they're excavating; how long they are likely to be there – that sort of thing."

She looked at him quizzically but didn't question his interest, "I could drop in to the hotel for a drink one night, if you want me to."

Hébert nodded. "That might be useful."

"My cover would be perfect for quizzing them about what they're doing - all back-up research for my series. I may even get myself invited up to inspect the dig."

"That would be good. If you do visit the castle I would like to come with you."

"It's quite a scramble getting up to the castle. It's on a very high ridge. Probably there used to be steps but they've disappeared now. I believe there are some ropes to hang on to, but the climb is quite demanding."

"I shall be quite all right, thank you," he said stiffly, suddenly aware of his age.

There was an uncomfortable silence while he searched for a way to change the conversation. At last he said, "Forgive me, but you don't seem the same type of person as Montluçon or Mickey whatever-he's-called."

"I should hope not," she burst out. "When I was growing up, I believe I was a bit of a wild kid in the streets of Marseilles. But then my father decided he wanted me to be properly educated. So when I was ten, he sent me to a convent school to turn me into a lady." She shuddered. "Oh, I hated the discipline that those nuns imposed on me. But I admit they taught me how to behave. Then I went to university in Toulouse to complete my education. It was the university which made me what I am." She put her head on one side. "I *am* a real journalist, you know."

"I don't doubt it."

"So I won't have any problems convincing people that I have a genuine right to be here. My current employment will also enable me to go just about anywhere without raising suspicions." She looked at him sceptically. "What about you? Don't you think you stick out like a sore thumb?"

"I don't have any problems." Slightly nettled, he told her about his cover researching the Templars. "Like you, the story is close enough to the truth to stand close scrutiny. If anybody is suspicious enough to check with Paris they'll be told the same story there."

She pondered it for a while, her head on one side. "Yes," she concluded. "I think you'll do."

"In fact," he added, "the two of us fit together well. Nobody would think it suspicious if we met up from time to time to compare notes. It's just the kind of thing that two researchers into similar projects might do."

Her smile made her look attractive. "Why not? Were you thinking of offering to take me to dinner tonight?"

"I would very much like to do that. Where are you staying?"

They exchanged addresses and mobile phone numbers and arranged to meet later. When she rose and left, Alain watched her depart down the road with her long, easy stride and found he was looking forward to the evening ahead with a cheerfulness which he hadn't felt for a long time.

13

Jacqueline shook her head. "We will have been on site a month next week, Jo, and our progress is painfully slow. I'm going to have to put in a report to the sponsors in a few days. I don't think they're going to be very happy."

She and André Jolyon were standing just outside the eastern gateway to the chateau. They were looking down into the large trench which had been opened up between the remains of the entrance piers. It was about two metres wide by four metres long and a metre and a half deep. The evening was drawing in and the site was deserted.

Supervision of the excavation works was being carried out in André's usual professional style. Everything about what they were doing was correct. The sides of the trench were held back by stout planking and strutting. In the bottom of the trench was a broad strip of irregular rough stonework. This was the base of the old castle retaining wall. Jackie had been able to date it as originally Roman with later Visigoth strengthening. And in the last two days they had reached bedrock. It was clear that they weren't going to get any more out of this trench.

"Our progress *has* been disappointing," Jolyon admitted. "I'm still furious with those two climbers who packed up and left us without a decent excuse."

She wrinkled her nose. "Gaston seemed to think they were just bored with the work we were asking them to do."

"Well, I don't agree. I think they'd been got at. They seemed perfectly happy until they took that day off and went into Foix for a drink. When they came back, they suddenly decided they didn't want to continue." He scowled at her. "Jackie – I think somebody's got it in for us."

"Who, for goodness sake?"

"I don't know. I've just got this nasty feeling that somebody is peering over our shoulder, waiting for us to trip up."

She laughed. "You've been like this ever since we started here, Jo. I've never known you react like this before. Is it because you're worried that I'm opening a can of worms by going back over the work that my uncle did?"

"Perhaps it is partly that. But, be warned. I think something nasty is going on out there." He shook his head and changed the subject. "I tell you what – I'm going to be a lot more careful about who I allow on the site in future."

"At least Gaston seems reliable. All we need are some decent lads to back him up and then we'll start to make progress."

"It's been slow, hard work with just the three of us. And there have been precious few useful finds to keep up our enthusiasm. It seems as though nothing's happened at this castle for the last seven hundred years."

"You're right," she agreed. "Most of the masonry has been robbed for later buildings. The remainder has just gently collapsed and been filled with soil around the rubble."

"And it'll take us several days to backfill this trench, during which time we won't be able to work anywhere else."

She took his arm. "Don't worry about that. Now we must hire some local labourers to do the backfilling, while we move on. Of course you must photograph everything before we do that. We've already decided on the next location. I hope this new area will prove to be part of the main residential section of the castle. But it's going to be a much larger job than this trench in the gateway. We're still going to need more help. It is a pity that it's too early to recruit some students."

"What about that young couple staying at the hotel?"

"Do you mean Armand and Jeanette?"

"That's right. They seem to be quite keen on finding out about the history of the place and they say they're staying here for a month." He grinned. "I must say *she's* got a fantastic figure."

"Not necessarily an important qualification for a digger."

"I accept that. But they do seem very anxious to please."

"Are you sure it's their technical capabilities that you're interested in?"

"Well, we've had several pleasant evenings in the bar with them. At least we know what we'll be taking on."

She considered the suggestion. "I suppose Armand would be a good guy to get on our side. But somehow Jeanette doesn't seem quite right. She's too much of a city girl. I can't imagine her liking the idea of getting her hands dirty."

"I didn't think of her as a digger," admitted Jolyon. "Marie Blande joins us to start cleaning and cataloguing finds on Monday, doesn't she? Perhaps Jeanette can help her while Armand does the digging." He shrugged. "In any case, there's no reason why we can't ask them. They can only say no."

"OK." She smiled. "You can ask your little Paris *poule*."

"I'm pretty sure Armand would like to have a go at digging. He's been up here almost every day - checking on progress and looking at what we've dug up. I'd say we'll have a definite recruit there."

"But we'll need more people than Armand."

"Maybe. But the trenches won't be very deep up in the residential area. There's much less accumulated soil. It's going to be mainly a question of moving fallen masonry and the local labourers can do that under our supervision." He had a sudden thought. "There will also be plenty of photography. Maybe Jeanette would be good with a camera."

"All right. I've already agreed. You can ask them if they want to join us – only at the usual student rates though."

"I don't think that will be a problem." André raised a cautionary finger. "First, I'll get them both checked out by Paris. I think it's essential to do that with all future recruits."

"How long will that take?"

"No more than twenty-four hours. I'll ring up as soon as we get back to the hotel."

"I don't see why there should be any problems."

"No, but we have to be careful." He straightened up. "I'll also put the word out for some labourers to help with the humping and pushing barrows to do the back-filling. I expect you'll want to keep an eye on those guys to make sure there aren't any finds in the spoil heaps which we might have missed."

"I'm not too worried about that," she said. "I can't believe there's anything important in that pile of rubble."

Jolyon took a satisfied breath. "In that case we'll abandon this trench as of now, if you agree. Gaston will be delighted. It's been a real struggle to keep him digging. He doesn't like being 'down in a hole below ground' as he puts it. I've been promising him some better action in the near future."

"He's not really a cerebral archaeologist."

"No, but tomorrow we'll start to clear the residential area. That's what he's been waiting for. It will be easiest if we start from the top and work down."

She put her head on one side. "Be careful, Jo. It's exposed up there."

"We've got it all safely roped up."

"I know. But make sure that everybody's wearing safety harnesses and see that they're properly clipped on all the time – both of you. I don't want any free climbing just to reach something that you couldn't get to when you were connected to a safety rope."

"Don't worry. We'll be careful. And don't forget this is Gaston's special area of expertise. It's what we hired him for, if you remember."

"It's not Gaston I'm worried about. I know that he can look after himself. It's you that I'm not so sure about. You know that these series of ours wouldn't be the same without you in the background. I rely on you far too much."

"I've said I'll be careful." He patted her shoulder. "Wait until I tell Gaston about the new plans. He'll be delighted to be up in the fresh air again. Mind you - so will I."

She smiled at his sudden new-found enthusiasm.

"I suggest, Jackie, that we start at the eastern end first. That area's mainly masked by trees so it's unlikely to excite too much comment from the locals. We'll do a stretch about fifty metres long by ten metres wide, then work our way down from the ridge in parallel strips. Within a few days, we should have the labourers available to help with moving the larger rocks and accretions of rubble."

She was carried along by his enthusiasm as he chattered. This was the excited young André as she remembered him. He'd been getting more dismal and morose as the entrance trench went deeper without any significant finds. Now he was being released on to the main site.

"I've also been intending to talk to you about that journalist who showed up the other day," said Jackie. "What was she called? César something – unusual name."

"I know who you mean. She left me her card. I have it here somewhere." He scrabbled around in his various pockets and produced it after a prolonged search. He peered at it. "Here we are – César Renoir."

"That's it."

"A Lyons address and phone number."

"Do you think she's likely to go public about our excavations here?"

He shook his head. "Not according to what she told me. She didn't seem that interested in what we were actually doing. She claims she's a freelance. She's got this job for the summer. She's producing a guide book about the more obscure Cathar castles. She says her research has turned up precious little about le Bézu – just a few historical references and several local legends about the place. She seemed to be saying that she'd be grateful for any information we could give her."

"Who are her employers?"

"According to this it's the Languedoc newspaper group in Toulouse. They seem to have given her a free hand to go wherever she fancies."

"She should have plenty of locations to look at. There must be dozens of Cathar strongholds in the area."

"That's right." He stood back and folded his arms. "When I told her that whatever we found would be published later in the year, it seemed to satisfy her. She didn't hang around asking lots of questions. I think she regarded it as lucky that we might be able to give her some additional information. She simply said she might pop back later to see whether we had anything more we could tell her. In any case, the book won't be published before the autumn."

Jacqueline shrugged and turned away. "So, it´s nothing important. Well, that's it for tonight, Jo. Let's lock the gate and go for dinner."

He followed her down the hillside in the gathering evening gloom. The path had been cleared and graded and was now much more easy to negotiate. It took less than ten minutes to reach the car and they headed back to Quillan in companionable silence.

14

It was one evening several days later when Alain Hébert hurried to open the door in response to the urgent knocking. Standing outside in the pitch darkness was a breathless and somewhat dishevelled César.

"What's the matter?"

"Can I come in?"

"Of course." He stood aside to let her through.

"I need a drink." She ran her hands through her untidy hair. "A strong drink."

"Cognac?"

"That'll do for a start."

He went to the cabinet and took out two brandy glasses. It worried him to see such a strong and self-confident woman appearing to be so distressed. He poured a large drink for her and a smaller one for himself. He came back and gave her the glass.

"Sit down." He indicated the armchair he'd been occupying a few minutes before. She collapsed into the seat and took a gulp of the brandy. He bent over her and placed his hands on her shoulders. Despite their difference in age and background, he had grown fond of her in the last few days. During that time they had spent most of their evenings together and he had discovered a pleasure in personal contact which was completely different from his previously isolated life.

"Now, César – what on earth's the problem?"

She leaned back in the chair and took another slug of drink. She let out a shuddering sigh and began. "Well, as you know, following my chat with Jacqueline Blontard and her colleagues, when it became apparent that they were hoping to explore the whole castle and stay there for the summer, we agreed that our plans needed a re-think."

"Quite right."

"So, as we discussed the other night, I rang Marseilles to tell them about the problem with the archaeologists up at le Bézu. I tried to speak to papa, but the only one I could get hold of was that gruesome little Montluçon."

"I remember him." Alain let go her shoulders and sat on the arm of the chair.

"Well – I was astonished. The man went almost incandescent with rage. He's never spoken to me like that before. He seemed to blame us for the problem. He said it was up to us to get the archaeologists out of the place, and quickly. He said otherwise they would have to do something about it." She paused for another drink.

"I told him what we had discussed – that it was best if we left the archaeologists to do their work and came back again in the autumn."

She drank again and shook her head. "He said that was out of the question. Too much money had already been spent on preparations to wait that long. He seemed to be blaming me – blaming us for what had happened. He said everything had been arranged at their end and that we had let them down."

"He does seem to be getting a bit big for his boots," said Alain. "Did you tell him that I specifically didn't want any violence? If someone got hurt, it would only result in the police getting involved and a lot of unsuitable publicity. That would make it much more dangerous to continue here and would slow down progress to get the stuff out."

"I told him all that, but he didn't want to listen. He said he'd give us a week to sort things out. He said that if we failed, they would have to action at their end."

"That's just plain stupid." Hébert swore, then stopped himself. "What did your father say in all this?"

"He wasn't there. That is what's worrying me. I asked where he was and all Montluçon would say was that he was out and he didn't know when he would be back." She looked up at him. "I'm worried about him, Alain."

He put his arm round her shoulders. "What do you think may have happened?"

She shook her head. "I just don't know."

"Your father's the patron, isn't he?"

"Yes." She smiled weakly. "Well, he was. Suddenly I don't know any more."

The next second she was crying, racked by violent sobs. He hugged her to his chest, surprised at the sudden breakdown in her self-control. He felt the tears soaking his shirt. He mumbled something into her pine-scented hair. Nobody had ever asked him for comfort before, and it was a new experience to try to understand the feelings of another person.

"César – why should there be a problem?" He stroked her hair. "Here – have another swig of brandy."

She lifted her head and took another drink. She gulped it back and looked at him. "Oh, Alain! It seems to me as though everything is changing. I could feel the atmosphere over the phone. It was as though papa wasn't there anymore."

"It's just Montluçon mouthing off while your father's away. You've said yourself that the bloke is a heap of crap. He would never dare to act against your father."

"He wouldn't by himself." She shook her head. "But now there's all this money sloshing round, I wonder whether someone else has muscled in on the organisation now that papa is so much weaker than he used to be."

"What do you mean?"

"Oh, there will have been dozens of the vultures circling when the news got out about this Templar treasure. They will all want a chunk of the proceeds." She added bitterly. "You didn't realise what you were starting when you got in touch with *la Force*."

"You mean there's a fight going on between the various different factions in Marseilles?"

"That's right. And papa's right in the middle of it." She shook her head again, her expression miserable. "The trouble is that he's not the man he once was. He lost a lot of kudos when they tried to assassinate him."

Hébert's mouth fell open. "They tried what?"

"Didn't you realise? Someone from one of the other groups tried to take the quick way to the top. Papa's personal bodyguard was killed. He was a lovely great guy called Albert.

Papa was nearly done for as well but he was rescued by Montluçon and a bunch of my father's supporters. But papa was grievously wounded and was close to death for a long time. It gave Montluçon the opportunity to move himself up towards the top of the Force. I've been worried about that little bastard ever since. I've begged papa to give it all up and get away from Marseilles and find a quiet backwater for his retirement. I've offered to live with him and care for him." Her eyes were bleak. "But then this great new opportunity turned up."

"I suppose you blame me."

She gave him a brief hug. "No, I don't. It's what's likely to happen to anybody when a lot of money is involved. But I am afraid that Montluçon has seen the opportunity to bring someone in over the top of my father in return for a bigger slice of the rewards. And that would be very dangerous for papa."

"What do you want to do?" He was thinking rapidly. "I can go there and see them if you wish. I could drive to Marseilles in about four hours. I could be back tomorrow evening."

"Not likely! You would be putting yourself at serious risk."

Alain considered it carefully for a while. "I don't think I would be risking anything. I would take the same care as I did when I met Montluçon and your father for the first time. I would leave the appropriate information with my lawyers for public release if I didn't contact them by a certain time. And remember that nobody but me knows the exact location of the treasure. They can't afford to terminate *me* or even to upset me seriously, because they would lose the chance of being led to it."

"You would really do that?" She looked at him with a new appreciation. "Do you know, I think you may be a very brave as well as a clever man."

"I'll tell you one more thing," he said. "I don't believe in making snap judgements. I think we should spend this evening relaxing with some food and a good red wine. Then I'll decide what to do tomorrow."

She smiled for the first time that evening.

"I have a *cassoulet* simmering on the stove," he said, "and I think I'll open a bottle of Nuits St Georges. Will you join me?"

"That would be nice."
She took another deep slug of the cognac.

15

More than a month had passed since his meeting with the solicitor before Philip was able to arrange his fortnight's holiday in the Languedoc. He crossed the channel on a mid-morning ferry. Driving south in his little MG, he gave Paris a wide berth and stayed in a motel near Tours on the Saturday night. He was able to get away from there early next morning and, without hurrying, was in Carcassonne by tea-time.

His Michelin road atlas suggested le Bézu was somewhere south of there but it didn't show sufficient detail. So his first task was to find a bookshop where he could pick up a large-scale map. After a search of the town centre, he found a place where he was able to purchase a Carte de Randonée (footpath map) of the Quillan area. He took it back to his hotel and studied it carefully. He found that the map indicated a Chateau des Templiers on the Serre Calmette ridge near the village of le Bézu. He presumed that was the place he was looking for. He noted it was about fifty kilometres south of Carcassonne and at least two kilometres from the nearest road. It looked as though some cross-country walking would be required.

So the next morning he got himself some decent walking boots and spent the rest of the day exploring the town. Climbing up to the old city, he was able to absorb a lot of the local atmosphere connected with the Cathars. He didn't feel any particular need to hurry to le Bézu. He decided there was no reason why he shouldn't enjoy the benefits of his holiday in the South of France, as well as undertaking the task given to him by his grandmother.

He set off south the following day. It was a lovely spring morning. The car purred happily along the road as it wound through the deep valleys between the tree-clad mountain ranges. It certainly appeared that the Cathars had chosen a beautiful, if remote, location to establish their unusual society.

When he reached Couiza he stopped for a coffee and to consult the map. He worked out his route via Laval and St Julia de Bec, then he set off again. The roads were narrow and tortuous and the last twenty kilometres took him over half an hour. Arriving at le Bézu village, he parked in front of the church and set out to walk the final two kilometres along a farm track.

He strode out, enjoying the warm sunshine as he went. There seemed to be nobody about. The track climbed slowly, keeping to one side of a wide valley. There were meadows in the bottom and woods clad the slopes on both sides. As he got further up the valley, he became aware that the mountains were closing in upon the scenery, especially to his left, where a rough, irregular rocky peak poked up out of the trees. Pausing to look carefully at the ridge, Philip was almost sure he could make out a few vertical masonry walls, hardly differing in colour or character from the bedrock which formed their base. Checking on the map, he was almost sure this was le Bézu castle.

Feeling increasingly excited, he pushed on. As he rounded a bend, he came upon two four-wheel drive Land Cruisers parked at a place where the track widened out. From this point he could see that a narrow path led off up the hillside towards the castle. There was a patch of steeply sloping meadow and a small notice board. Philip went up to look at it.

This was certainly the place. The signboard described the chateau of le Bézu and gave a few details of its history. There was also a small, rather indistinct plan of the former layout of the castle which stretched along the precipitous, rocky ridge high above. Philip found it difficult to compare the plan with the terrain frowning down upon him, especially when there was so little of the actual castle remaining.

As he set off up the path he noticed that someone had recently cleared and widened it, even putting in timber pegs and supports to form steps in places where the going became difficult. Even so, the slope was sufficiently steep to get him breathing heavily and make the blood pump through his veins. When he reached the woods, he had to watch his footing to avoid tripping on tree roots. He kept his head down under the low-hanging branches.

Emerging near the top he found himself in front of a couple of stretches of low rough wall with a gap between them. He guessed this must be an old entrance to the castle. He noticed the ground in this location had been recently trampled more or less flat and that there was very little vegetation. There was a rough timber and wire-mesh gate across the opening which stood half open. Philip pushed it wide and entered the castle.

Which way now? He saw there was a small level terrace to his right at a slightly higher level. He scrambled up a low wall and went across the area to look at the splendid view.

"Hey!"

He spun round in surprise. He found he was confronting a young man of medium height with dark hair and eyes.

"*Qui êtes vous?*" The man's attitude was rather less than friendly.

"Oh!" Philip hesitated. "Er – *je suis* Philip Sinclair."

"Hah! *Anglische?*"

"English? Yes."

"OK. I am André Jolyon. I am arch-y-ol-o-giste." He indicated behind him. "This is arch-y-olo-giste site."

"Oh? Right."

The man gesticulated vaguely. "You not permit here."

"*Qu'est-ce que c'est*, Jo?"

A young woman appeared at the other side of the terrace. Her beauty had Philip's immediate attention. She was wearing jeans above short boots and her tight roll-neck sweater revealed an attractive figure. But it was her sparkling dark blue eyes which struck him most forcefully. Set in a beautiful face and framed by long dark red hair they seemed to hold his gaze.

"*C'est un anglais qui s'appelle Phillipe Saint Claire.*" He turned back to Philip. "Is correct?"

"More or less."

"This is Mademoiselle Jacqueline Blontard. She is director of site." He shook his head. "Sorry. You cannot come here."

"Yes he can." Jacqueline came forward. "We can't exclude the public, Jo. We haven't got an exclusive licence."

André Jolyon seemed not to take any notice of her. "But why you here?" he demanded. "We not allow any person who has not been checked."

Philip judged it was wise not to tell them too much at present. "I'm interested in the Cathars. I believe this was one of their strongholds." He held up a guide-book, which he had purchased in Carcassonne, but which he knew made no mention of le Bézu.

Jacqueline smiled and it seemed to Philip that the day became brighter. "You won't find much information here," she said. "Perhaps, if you come back at the end of the summer when we have finished our excavations, we might be able to tell you some more."

"Your English is excellent." Philip shook his head. "I'm afraid my French is very basic."

She smiled her beautiful smile again. "Thank you. I was a keen language student at school."

"And now you are an archaeologist."

"Jacqueline Blontard is most famous archaeologist in France," interrupted Jolyon. "Did you see the television films about her?"

"Were they shown on English television?"

She nodded. "The series on Egypt was translated into English. I did some of the translation myself."

"I'm sorry. I must have missed them. I'm afraid I don't watch a lot of television."

"I expect they were on at a strange time." She shrugged. "They wouldn't have seemed important to the English."

Philip indicated the castle in front of him. "Is this going to be another series?"

"It certainly is."

"Then I shall make sure I watch this one." He took a breath. "May I look around?"

"Of course," she said before Jolyon could refuse. "But I would ask you to be careful when you get close to any roped off areas - for your own safety. There may be holes in the ground and heaps of loose rubble to avoid."

"I promise to be careful."

105

"Don't go inside the restricted areas. You might damage or disturb some of our finds. In fact it might be best if I took you round the excavations and explained what we are doing."

"Yes please. I would appreciate that." Philip admitted to himself that he fancied the idea of spending some time with Jacqueline.

She put her head on one side. "I cannot do it today. I have promised Paris that I will telephone them to make some arrangements, but if you are here at ten o'clock tomorrow morning I will give you a guided tour."

"I look forward to it very much."

"Meanwhile you can explore the rest of the site – those are the areas which aren't roped off – at your own risk, of course. Remember to be careful. The terrain is very rough and steep."

"I will be careful. And I won't go into the roped-off areas."

Jolyon interrupted again. "I will still be here. I will check you go nowhere that is forbidden."

Philip noticed that Jacqueline gnawed her lower lip in vexation at her assistant's churlish attitude. But she said nothing. So he smiled at her and said, "Thank you. I will see you tomorrow morning." He started to cross the terrace towards the main part of the castle.

"Just remember, Monsieur Saint Claire, I will be watching you," Jolyon called after him as he went. "I am careful about security."

Philip ignored him. Jolyon seemed to be one of those men who liked to throw their weight around.

For the next hour he explored the rest of the site as well as he could. He soon realised that it would be almost impossible to carry out the task his grandmother had set him, at least on his own. As well as being very steep, the ridge on which the castle had originally been built was extremely rough and irregular. Rocks and heaps of rubble stuck up all over the place. These had been covered with soil and small stones which had been washed down from above over the centuries. And more than half a millennium of vegetation – bushes, trees and undergrowth – had grown up, died, collapsed, rotted and been replaced. So it was almost impossible to decide what had been located where.

A few surviving areas of walling projected through the greenery. The most obvious were standing on the tops of rocky cliffs where the creepers had been unable to cling to them. But these weren't much help to Philip. He knew from his reading of the journal that the room where the treasure had been secreted was in the depths of the castle. That meant it had either been found by the men who had robbed the fortress of its masonry in mediaeval times, or else it was buried under the rubble and completely obscured by centuries of vegetation and detritus which had fallen from further up the hill as the place fell into ruins.

Finding the hiding place of the treasure was obviously going to be a major problem. Philip was deep in thought as he scrambled back up the precipitous slope to the main site which had been roped off by the archaeologists. Up here he saw that there was an area where almost all the covering vegetation had been stripped away, revealing a chaotic tumble of rocks and masonry. Within the main area, a number of ropes had been stretched across the site in both directions about a metre above the ground. These divided the site into blocks about two metres square. Near one corner six men were working with pick-axes, crowbars and shovels to remove the loose rocks and chunks of masonry. A hand-operated swivel hoist could lift the heavier lumps and put them on a trolley which ran along a level scaffolding walkway to a spoil tip.

One of the men was André Jolyon. When he saw Philip he gestured to him to keep clear. "Go away," he shouted. "This is dangerous. You must not come here."

Obediently Philip moved round the roped-off area to a more remote spot, well above the excavated part of the site, where he could watch their work without any risk of getting in their way. However, apparently this was still not satisfactory to Jolyon. He left the others and came scrambling up to Philip's vantage point.

"You cannot stay here," he shouted. "It is dangerous."

107

"You needn't worry about me. I won't cause you any trouble."

"You may start a rock-slide."

"Rubbish." Philip indicated the solid area where he was standing. "There is no loose rock here. I will be very careful."

Jolyon shook his head. "It is not good. We do not know who you are or where you come from. We will be worried about you being above us."

"I tell you there is no need to worry."

"Look." He wagged a finger at Philip. "You do not understand. I do not want you here. You must go."

Philip gazed straight back at him.

"Very well. We will make you go." He turned and shouted down to the others, "*Gaston, Albert – ici.*"

There followed a string of instructions in French. Two of the other men stopped what they were doing and started up the slope. One carried a pickaxe and the other a large crow-bar.

Philip decided there was no point in prolonging the confrontation. "All right." He held up his hands with the palms showing. "I'll go and leave you alone. I'll wait until I meet your director here tomorrow morning."

Jolyon pointed towards the gate. "You keep away from us. We know how to deal with people like you."

"Don't threaten me." Philip pointed back at him. "We'll see what Jacqueline has to say about this tomorrow."

With as much dignity as he could muster, Philip turned and made his way back to the entrance to the castle and down the hillside. He decided he might as well find somewhere to have lunch and then return to Carcassonne. It would be wisest not to aggravate André Jolyon any further by returning to the castle that day.

16

"I have had great difficulty getting hold of you," grumbled Charles Robert. "Marcus must have slipped up and given me the wrong number for your mobile."

Armand Séjour decided he shouldn't confess that he had bought a smart new one. "There was no point in contacting you until I had something useful to report. I have been spending my time getting to know Jacqueline Blontard and her right-hand man – a chap called André Jolyon."

They were standing in the town square of Quillan surrounded by the bustle of the Tuesday market.

"Nevertheless you should have kept in touch. I am expected to send regular reports back to Paris. It has taken me nearly two weeks to find out which hotel you were staying at."

Armand doubted the truth of this statement. Quillan was the nearest decent-sized place to the chateau of le Bézu and there was only one proper hotel in the town. He thought this was the first place Robert should have tried. However, he said none of this to the stuffy old fellow. He was uncertain how much influence Monsieur Charles Robert wielded. And the "justice" which the Council visited on employees (even well-connected employees) who stepped out of line was well known.

"I apologise," he said with a small smile. "At least I responded quickly when I received your message."

Robert merely nodded.

"Why did you want to meet me here?" continued Séjour looking round at the activity on the market stalls. "Wouldn't somewhere private have been more appropriate?"

"No. This location is *very* appropriate. I want us to appear simply as a couple of innocent tourists." He drew himself up to his full one hundred and eighty-five centimetres. "It is important to our cause that nobody recognises who I am. Questions might be asked."

"Why? Have you been to Quillan before?"

"Certainly not. If I had, I should not have risked making this our rendezvous. I would have nominated a far more remote location." Robert paused. "Now – please walk with me. We will talk as we stroll." He turned and set off past a row of stalls on the east side of the square, taking no interest in any of the wares on offer.

Suppressing a grin, Armand followed.

"Now then," said Charles Robert. "What have you been doing for the last two weeks?"

"Well, as I told you, I have been concentrating on getting to know the archaeologists. I believe I have had some success. In fact, I have been enrolled as an unpaid helper in their excavations."

"Really?" The old man stopped and gazed at him. "What sort of things have you been excavating?"

Armand shrugged. "All sorts of things actually. Jacqueline and André have carried out a methodical survey of the castle to establish the areas where they wish to excavate. The le Bézu site is different from a lot of sites. For the last week we have been cutting away undergrowth and digging up roots of bushes and small trees to clear an area and to try to find out the ground plan of the place." He shook his head. "I can tell you it's not an easy task on a rugged site like le Bézu."

"Is that all you have done?"

"Well – there've been plenty of discussions about which is the best way to go and where to clear next. They seem to be taking the exploration step by step, working out their strategy as they find out more."

"So what have you found out about their final aims? Are they likely to be harmful to our cause?"

"I don't think so. They are mainly interested in establishing the history of the place and its links to the Cathar movement and the Albigensian Crusade. Later historical events don't interest them."

"No mention of the Council or our forebears?"

Armand shook his head. "Nothing like that. So far they have excavated a trench in the main entrance to the chateau, but that yielded very little of interest except establishing links to Roman

110

and Visigoth occupation. So they filled that in. Now we are starting to investigate the great hall. We've cleared the undergrowth and are lifting out chunks of fallen masonry."

"Will they continue exploring inside the perimeter walls of the castle?"

"I believe so – insofar as they can establish where that perimeter is. Why? Is what we're interested in located inside or outside the castle?"

Robert turned to face him. "That is not for you to know or to ask about. Please just answer my questions."

They had reached the northeast corner of the square and now he set out along the north side where the stalls were smaller and more spaced out. Here it was pleasantly warm. The sun, dappling through the freshly-leafed trees, highlighted the older man's pink scalp through his thin hair. Armand followed half a pace behind.

"Tell me," Robert asked, "What do the archaeologists hope to find in the area of the great hall?"

"I don't know exactly - presumably some information about the occupation of the castle in Cathar times. I believe they are hoping to find out something about the seneschal – this Pierre de Voisins – and his attitude towards the Cathars."

"Pierre de Voisins?" Robert's voice was suddenly sharp. "Has this woman archaeologist said anything about de Voisins?"

Armand was startled by the sudden change of tone. "No. Not very much. As far as I remember, his name was only mentioned in passing. He was simply the keeper of the castle in the period that they are interested in."

"What else has been said? How long are they expecting to continue this investigation?"

"I think they will be here all summer."

"All summer!" Robert spun round to look at him and Armand involuntarily stepped back a pace.

"I believe so. That is what they seem to be saying."

"I cannot stay here all summer," cried the old man. "There are many important things I have to do. I have to be back in Paris within the month."

Armand stared at him. "I am sorry, Monsieur Robert, but there is no hope of the archaeologists finishing their explorations in the next month. They will keep working until they find sufficient artefacts of interest, then the television cameras will move in."

"Television cameras?"

"That's right. They are doing a television series about the Albigensian Crusade."

"A series?" gasped Robert. "A series on the television?"

"Of course. Jacqueline Blontard is a star. Haven't you seen her previous series about the Louvre and Napoleon in Egypt?"

"Another series on the television!" Robert put his hand to his forehead. "And it will be set in le Bézu. Thousands of people will trek to see the location where the series is set. It will be an utter disaster. It cannot be allowed to happen."

Armand shook his head. "How can we stop it? These television people are very powerful. They deal in huge amounts of money. They cannot be bought off."

"Nevertheless, young Séjour, they must be stopped. You will have to stop them before they can get any further."

"And what do you suggest I do to stop them?" asked Armand coldly.

"*I* don't know. You must decide that for yourself. All I can tell you is that their activities at le Bézu must not be allowed to continue." He pointed a finger at Armand. "I will allow you one week to stop them. We will meet here in exactly one week from now." He checked his watch. "That is at precisely noon next Tuesday. And I will expect you to tell me that you have brought an end to this foolish and dangerous exploration."

Armand gazed at the enraged old man in front of him. "But I don't know what I must do to stop them."

"One week," repeated Robert. "If you tell me in a week's time that the archaeologists will be continuing their excavations, I will have no alternative but to refer the whole matter back to Paris. I need hardly remind you of what that will mean for your personal standing with the Council."

With that parting comment, Charles Robert turned on his heel and strode away without a backward glance.

17

The broken, twisted body of André Jolyon was found spread-eagled on the rocks at the foot of one of the cliffs of le Bézu at about nine o'clock on Wednesday morning. A search had been instigated when it was realised that he hadn't slept in his room that night. One of the men had spotted his dark blue anorak under the trees and Gaston had climbed down on a rope to investigate. He had found Jolyon's body was cold and very dead.

The police had been called and had instructed that the body should be swathed in a canvas stretcher bag and lifted up to the castle. Philip had seen the police Suzuki at the bottom of the path when he arrived and wondered about its purpose. He met the melancholy procession coming down the path and stepped aside to let it pass. First came Gaston and three other men, awkwardly carrying the misshapen canvas bundle. Gaston shot him a venomous glance as he passed.

Behind the four men came Jacqueline. She was clearly upset. Two gendarmes followed her, dressed in their kepis and short shoulder capes.

As she reached him, Philip asked, "Jacqueline? What has happened?"

She stopped and gazed at him with a tear-stained face. "It's André. He has had a dreadful accident. He – he is dead."

"Dead? What happened to him?"

"He fell from one of the cliffs. He – he wasn't wearing a safety harness. He must have lost his footing and slipped." She sniffed. "It seems that one of the anchors holding the rope had pulled out. That may have caused him to fall." She began to weep again.

"Oh, my God."

"I don't understand how he could have let it happen," she sobbed. "He promised me he would always wear his safety harness. I was most insistent about it. And he promised."

The younger gendarme gave Philip a reproving glance and shepherded her down the path after the others.

She turned briefly back to him as she passed. "Nothing will happen here today," she faltered. "The site is closed until further notice." Then she moved on.

The police sergeant, who was walking behind her, paused to address him in passable English. "Who are you, monsieur?"

"My name is Philip Sinclair. I have come from England. I only arrived here yesterday."

"Ah." The man looked at him with a calculating gaze before coming to a decision. "Please to follow me."

Philip decided that now was not the time to argue with such an order. So he tagged along at the rear of the desolate little group. He felt desperately sorry for Jacqueline, even though he had only just met her. He would have liked to be able to offer her some sort of comfort, but he couldn't think of any way that he might help at present.

The dejected little group went on down to the car park area. At the bottom of the path an ambulance was now waiting. It was squeezed into the small turning space beside the police vehicle, the two archaeologists' wagons and Philip's little car. The body bag was loaded into it. Instructions were given to the attendants – something about Toulouse – and, after an undignified shunting of vehicles to permit it to turn round, it set off

"Your car?" asked the sergeant, pointing.

"Yes."

"You will follow me to the *Mairie*," he instructed. He turned to the others and told them the same thing in French.

So a sad procession followed the police car into Quillan where, fortunately, there was sufficient parking space outside the town hall. They were shepherded into a waiting room. Jacqueline was immediately asked to accompany the sergeant into another office. So Philip was left alone with Gaston and the other men. Nobody spoke to him. The others talked among themselves in low tones and he felt their accusatory glances resting on him from time to time.

114

One by one the men were called in for questioning. Finally Philip's turn came. The junior gendarme came into the waiting room and beckoned him in a none-too-friendly manner. Philip followed the man down a short corridor and into a room with only two high-level barred windows. The sergeant was sitting at a desk near the centre of what was apparently his office and Jacqueline was seated to one side of him. Philip was told to sit on a chair on the opposite side of the desk and the other gendarme stood just inside the door as though to make sure that he didn't try to escape.

Jacqueline looked up at him. He noticed there was an empty coffee cup in front of her and, although her face was deathly pale and the brightness seemed to have gone from her eyes, she looked as though she had regained her self-control.

"The police sergeant has very little English. Because your French is not so good, I have been asked to act as interpreter for you," she said. "Is that agreeable to you?"

"Yes, of course."

"You can have a lawyer if you wish although it may be difficult to find one who can speak English sufficiently well in Quillan this morning."

"Am I accused of something?"

She smiled tightly. "No-one is accused of anything at present. The police are trying to find out what actually happened. That is the way they do things in France. Sergeant Leblanc here is making out a report to go to the examining magistrate, who will decide whether any crimes have been committed and who, if anybody, should be charged with the crimes. To do this, the sergeant has to interview anybody who might have been a witness or who might have been connected in any way with the events which occurred last night." She smiled again bleakly. "Unfortunately for you, the police have been told that you came to the site for the first time yesterday, and you spoke to André Jolyon. That means you may be able to provide the sergeant with useful information. Do you understand?"

Jacqueline explained to the sergeant what she had told him. The man nodded and directed her to ask a question. She turned back to him.

"He asks when you came to France and why."

Philip briefly explained his progress over the last few days. When it came to his reasons for choosing to come to the area, he felt he should give rather more information than he had the previous day.

"You know my name is Sinclair. I believe I am a direct descendent of a certain Phillipe de Saint Claire whose family lived in this area in the thirteenth century." He paused. "My grandmother died recently. She had spent a lot of time researching our family origins, but she died before she could come to Languedoc and continue her research. So she left me some money on the condition that I should come to this region to see what I could find out about our ancestors."

Jacqueline looked at him speculatively as she dictated to the policeman what she had been told. Her translation had to be slow enough for the man to write it all down.

After a pause Philip continued, "You can check this with the solicitor in London. His name is Mr James Baker of a partnership called Smythe and Baker. I will give you their phone number, but I think it would be best if I speak to James first to explain why you are contacting them. Otherwise, they may refuse to provide any information and insist on it being handled through the British Embassy."

She explained this to the sergeant who grunted and made a note.

"My grandmother found some old papers which suggested that my ancestor spent some time at le Bézu. That is why I came here. I wanted to see if I could find out anything about the castle and its owners in the Middle Ages. That is why I climbed up to look at the castle yesterday."

Jacqueline had raised her eyebrows at this additional disclosure. However, she translated it for the policeman to write down. When he had finished, the man had a further question to ask.

"Is that the only reason for your visit here? Did you know any of the people in this area before you arrived?"

"No. It was a surprise to me to find archaeologists working at the chateau."

"What was your opinion of André Jolyon?"

Philip considered. "I didn't really know him well enough to have an opinion."

She conferred with the sergeant and turned back to him. "Apparently Gaston Lesmoines has told the police that you had an argument with André yesterday and that he ordered you off the site. Is that correct?"

"No!" he exclaimed. Then he thought more carefully. "Well – yes, I suppose it is, in a way. Jolyon didn't seem to like me being there, although you had told him earlier that I had a complete right to look round." Philip looked straight at her. "You were there when I first arrived. I think, that if you hadn't over-ruled him, he wouldn't have let me on to the site in the first place. Do you agree?"

She explained his reply to the man. He asked her a couple of short questions and she seemed to agree. She turned back to Philip.

"What was your argument about?"

He took a deep breath and looked up at the ceiling. "What happened was this. After you left, I spent about an hour looking round the chateau. Then I went back to look at the roped-off area where Jolyon and the others were working. I didn't go inside the ropes because you'd asked me not to." He paused. "Well, as soon as he saw me, he told me to move away because he said I might have been in danger if one of the boulders had fallen while they were lifting it onto the trolley." He shook his head. "So I moved to a higher point on the other side of the site – but it was still outside the rope."

He continued, now looking straight at her. "However, he didn't seem to like me being up there either and he came to order me off. When I didn't immediately move, he called to Gaston and one of the others and they started to come up to where we were. I saw that Gaston was carrying a pick-axe and the other guy had a crow-bar. It looked to me as though they

117

intended to use them on me if I didn't go." He grinned sheepishly. "So I decided to leave, so as to avoid any further confrontation. I told Jolyon that I would come back this morning to meet you as we had arranged. Then I left."

She raised her eyebrows when she heard his explanation but she didn't respond. It took quite a long time for her to translate all his comments. Once again she was asked several questions and seemed to agree to the points put to her. Philip hoped she wasn't twisting his story. Finally she turned back to him.

"The sergeant will check these details with Gaston. Now he wants to know what you did after you left the site."

"I went back to my car which was parked in le Bézu village. By then it was nearly lunch-time, so I drove into Quillan, where I found a bar and got myself a glass of wine and a baguette. I believe the bar was called the Moulin Blanc. After that I drove back to Carcassonne where I am staying. My hotel is in the industrial area. It was still quite early in the afternoon and the day was pleasant so I walked into the town centre and strolled around for a while. Then I had a meal in a bistro – I'm afraid I can't remember the name, but I can take you there if necessary. After the meal I walked back to the hotel and I read a guide-book for a time until I went to bed."

All this was translated and written down.

"Can anyone confirm this?"

"Not really. I still had my room key so I didn't need to go to the hotel reception. I don't know if anybody in the bar or the bistro will remember my being there."

There was a long discussion between Jacqueline and the sergeant. At last she said, "I am told I must ask you this - did you come back to Quillan or go up to le Bézu chateau later yesterday or during last night?"

Philip couldn't prevent the ghost of a smile appearing on his face as he answered. "Certainly not. After Jolyon ordered me off the site – as Gaston put it – I didn't come back again until I saw you this morning."

There was further consultation between them.

"The sergeant has one more question. When you were looking round the site, did you interfere with any of the ropes which were fixed?"

"No. I didn't touch any of them."

"Did you hit or pull out any of the anchors?"

"As I said, I didn't touch any of the stuff which your men had fixed around the place."

There was further long discussion before she spoke to him again. "Usually, you would be asked to read what the sergeant has written and sign it to say you agree that it is a fair record of what was said. However, I have pointed out that your poor knowledge of French would mean that you can't honestly do that. So it will be left for now. The sergeant says that if anything results from the enquiry which might involve you, your lawyer would be able to have this part of the report translated independently and you could sign it then or change it if you wished. He will put a note to that effect on the report."

"Does that mean I can go?"

She addressed this question to the policeman. Philip detected a shake of the head in the middle of the loquacious exchange. There seemed to be a lot of discussion on this request. At last she looked back at him.

"The sergeant says that his enquiry will continue for several days. He needs first to be able to go and check the place where André's body was found. To do that he will need some special help which he may get later today, but it may not be until tomorrow. Also André's body has been sent to Toulouse to establish the exact cause of death." Her exhalation of breath was close to a sob. "That may take several days. Until he is able to finish his report, he wants to be able to get in touch with any of the witnesses. If you lived in France, you would be able to go home provided you left an address and telephone number so that you could be contacted if necessary. However, because you are a foreigner, he wants you to stay in the area – preferably in Quillan." She had the grace to look embarrassed. "I have told the sergeant that there are spare rooms at our hotel. He would be pleased if you would agree to stay there until the investigations are complete."

119

"What if I don't agree?"

She addressed the question to the sergeant. His reply was long and involved. She turned back to him. "He says that might cause a problem."

"What sort of a problem?"

"He says that an allegation has been made against you. Therefore he cannot let you leave France until the matter has been looked into."

"Is he saying I'll be stuck in prison?"

She spoke again to the policeman whose reply was once again convoluted.

"He says that decision would not be his to make. But the examining magistrate has the power to detain people who are refusing to co-operate with his enquiry."

"I see." Philip smiled ironically. "It looks as though I don't have any choice. But how will people treat me at the hotel if I stay there? Am I going to be treated like a murderer?"

She took a breath. "I'm sorry about it, Philip." He noticed it was the first time she had used his first name. "However, I will say to you that I do not agree with Gaston. I'm sure you are not responsible for André's death. So I promise you that I will personally do everything I can to make sure that you are not badly treated at the hotel." She looked at him appealingly. "Will that help?"

"Yes, I suppose so. Thank you."

"Now - the sergeant tells me that he wishes to accompany you to Carcassonne to pick up your luggage. He will drive you in the police car and you can collect your car from the parking place outside when you return. Can you wait outside until he's ready?"

That final request didn't make him feel any less like a suspect.

18

The gathering at dinner in the Hotel du Chateau in Quillan that evening was a restrained affair to say the least. Jacqueline was there, of course, closely attended by Gaston. One of the other archaeologists was present as well – a young fellow called Armand – together with his wife Jeanette, who was wearing a rather revealing dress and seemed to be doing her best to bring some brightness to the evening. The four of them made up a private quartet. The other three men who had been at the police station were absent.

Philip kept to himself, sitting alone at his table and trying to avoid watching the archaeologists. He was very interested in what he could make out from their conversation, but struggled to understand them with his limited French. Unsurprisingly, they seemed to be talking mainly about the events of that morning. Jacqueline was clearly very upset by the death of André Jolyon. Philip gathered that the dead man had been her second in command. He wasn't quite sure what the personal relationship had been between them.

The man who obviously intended to step into the vacancy left by Jolyon was a small but well-muscled character who Philip had discovered was called Gaston Lesmoines. The fellow seemed to regard the newly-arrived Englishman with a great deal of suspicion. This was the man who had alleged that Philip was responsible for Jolyon's accident.

For himself, Philip felt less than happy with the way things had developed since he arrived at le Bézu. Following the questioning at the police station, the sergeant had driven him back to Carcassonne to collect his baggage. The policeman had obviously decided to try and take the opportunity to talk to the person in reception at Philip's hotel, to see if they could add anything to his story. He doubted whether the man would have had much success.

They had then driven into the town centre to look at the bistro where Philip had his meal the previous night. However, the place was closed at that time, so there was nobody who was able to support his story. Throughout the journey there and during the return to Quillan the policeman scarcely spoke more than a dozen words to him, mainly asking directions. Philip had a distinct feeling of discomfort. He wasn't actually being treated as a criminal, but he was very obviously a suspect.

Arriving back at the hotel, Philip was allocated a room on the top floor under the eaves. Jacqueline was there to explain that this was provided to him at a special price at the request of the police. However there was no lift and no porter volunteered to help him, so he had to carry his bags up the four floors on his own. This made him feel even less welcome.

After completing a satisfactory meal, he decided to take a break from the disagreeable atmosphere in the dining room and have an exploratory walk round the town. There was apparently no restriction on his movements in the locality. It was a splendid evening following the beautiful spring day. Nevertheless the air was fresh and sparkling, with a hint of coolness and Philip was grateful for his padded jacket.

The town of Quillan was strung out along the banks of the river which threaded its way through the steep-sided valley. At one stage the road ran almost beside the river. There were seats beneath the plane trees that stood on the sloping grassy bank. Philip chose an empty one to sit and watch the sun gilding the castle and the houses beneath it on the opposite hillside. As the evening advanced, the bright sunshine gradually abandoned the lower buildings to the gloom of dusk until only the castle remained, lit up by the pink glow from the last of the setting sun.

There was now a decided chill in the air and Philip was considering returning to the hotel when he became aware of another person on the path close to him. He looked up and saw that it was Jacqueline Blontard. She looked surprisingly small and vulnerable, wrapped up in a light-coloured puffer jacket with the collar turned up and most of her long, dark red hair tucked away out of sight. Once again he noticed the startling deep blue of her eyes.

"Oh!" He stuttered. "Oh! *Bonsoir ma'moiselle.*" To his own ears the greeting sounded slightly foolish.

She didn't immediately respond but continued to stand and look at him for a few moments. Then she suddenly came out with, "I have challenged Gaston to say why he thinks you had something to do with André's fall from the cliffs."

"And what did he say?"

"He says that André told him that you were going to be trouble. But he admits he didn't know why André said that." She looked straight at him. "Did you have any previous contact with my assistant before you came le Bézu?"

"I promise you," he said solemnly, "that I had never seen him before yesterday."

She shook her head. "I thought you would say that."

She came and sat on the seat beside him, looking up at the last of the sunlight fading from the castle walls. However he noticed that she kept a space of a couple of feet between them.

"Don't you believe me?"

She remained quiet for a while, apparently deciding how to respond. Then she turned to face him, the renewed energy in those dark blue eyes flashing at him. "Of course I *want* to believe you. But I have questions in my mind. Please tell me exactly why you came here."

Philip was surprised by her sudden question. For a moment he felt an urge to tell her the whole story. Something made him want to make this remarkable woman trust him, to give him a sympathetic hearing. But the next moment he hesitated, aware that he was a foreigner invading the private space of the archaeologists. They would have a different attitude to his search for Phillipe de Saint Claire's treasure – if it existed.

After a brief mental struggle he said, "You heard what I told the police sergeant. Everything I said was the truth."

"Hmm." She appeared to chew over his comments. "But did you tell him everything?"

He was surprised by her perception. Had she somehow managed to guess that there was more to his story than he had revealed to them so far? Or was she just fishing for useful information? After a few moments´ thought, Philip decided it was too early in their relationship to tell her any more.

So he shrugged. "I told the police everything that was relevant to the accident." He looked back up at the castle, now darkly etched against the evening sky. "I want to be as helpful as possible."

"The story you told the sergeant interested me," she said. "That bit about your grandmother – was that all true?"

"Of course."

"She sounds a remarkable woman. Please tell me about her."

He shrugged. "What is there to tell? She was typical of the type of self-reliant English women who made Britain great in the Victorian age."

"That makes her sound a bit of a monster."

"I didn't think of her as being at all like that. She was always very affectionate towards me. But she was a very strong character. She'd had a very tough life. She was married to my grandfather just before the war and they had one son – my father, of course. Then grand-dad was killed in the war and she was left on her own to bring up my dad in the huge great house in Templecombe. That's a village in South West England."

"I've heard of it. I believe it used to be the main preceptory of the Knights Templar in England."

"Perhaps it was. Well, as a result of my grand-dad's early death, she didn't have much money and there weren't any close relatives to help her. But somehow she made a success of her life and built up the family fortunes and, at the same time, she managed to find out about the family history, going back to the time of the Cathars."

"Go on."

"Well – that's it really." Philip was being careful that he didn't give too much away. "As I told the sergeant, she found out that this guy, Phillipe de Saint Claire, escaped from the slaughter of the Cathars at the end of the Albigensian Crusade when he was a young man and came to England. He bought a piece of land in Templecombe and built a house on it which is still owned by the family. In fact, it's mine now."

"So do you think this ancestor of yours – this Phillipe de Saint Claire – was a Templar?"

Philip shook his head. "I don't know about that. All I was told was that he was a Cathar. Could he have been a Templar as well?"

"There's no reason why not." She paused. "What documentary evidence do you have to support your claim? You said that she had found some old papers. Have you got those papers?"

"Er – no. Not with me." He felt bad about not telling her the whole truth, but how did he know what she would do with it if he told her about the journal? "I haven't moved into the house yet."

"But she told you to go and look at le Bézu. Where did she get the name from?"

"I think it was in the papers she found." He pulled a face. "You must understand that I didn't know anything about this until I received a letter from her after she had died."

"And you came all the way down here as a result of what she said in her letter?"

"Well, she had left me a lot of money, and she especially asked that I came and looked at the place. I suppose she thought I would be able to find out more information locally." He shrugged. "So – I was able to take a couple of weeks' holiday, and here I am."

"I suppose that's fair enough." She turned away from regarding him and looked at the river. She sounded disappointed.

"Meanwhile, I'm trapped here while the sergeant completes his preliminary enquiry. I can't leave the area to do any research. I don't know what I'm allowed to do while I'm here." He leaned forward. "Am I allowed to go for walks and to explore the surrounding countryside?"

She shook her head irritably. "Don't be silly. All Sergeant Leblanc asks is that each one of us holds ourselves available in case he has any further questions. In the long run it will speed up the enquiry. There are no other restrictions on the movements of any of us."

"Am I allowed to go up to the castle and poke around up there?"

He was watching her closely and saw that she was a little startled.

"Why would you want to do that? You won't find any records of your forebears up there. It's just a ruin."

"Yes, but I only had a quick look round yesterday. I fancy the idea of getting a feel of what it was like for the occupants who were living in the place nearly eight hundred years ago. Who knows? – that may have included my ancestor. Besides which, I'm interested in seeing anything which you've found out about the place." He grinned mischievously. "Have you forgotten that you had promised to show me round and explain to me exactly what you are doing up there?"

Jacqueline had the grace to smile. Philip thought that it lit up her face with a rare beauty. "I think it would be unwise for any of us to go up there tomorrow. I understand the police forensic team are expected in the morning. They will be checking for clues of what may actually have happened to André last night." Her eyes turned sad again. "I don't somehow think that they would welcome members of the public being in attendance."

"And what about you?" asked Philip. "What are you going to do while you have to remain in the area? Will you continue your excavations?"

She shook her head and the tears in her eyes made him want to hug her. "It won't be easy. André wasn't only a very dear friend. He was an important assistant and organiser. What do you call it?"

"Your right hand man?"

"Right hand man - that's what I meant. I'd find it difficult to carry on without someone like him to organise things. However I will have to discuss what I must do with my principals."

"Who are your principals?"

She didn't answer him directly. "I rang my agent this afternoon. He will be here some time tomorrow. He will advise me what I should do next. I'm hoping he'll be able to arrange the right sort of support for me."

"But you won't simply give up and pull out?" It seemed important to him that she should continue with her exploration, even though it might make things more difficult for him personally.

She shook her head. "I don't think I would be allowed to do that. A lot of things depend on what we are doing here. There's a whole television series planned around the story of the Albigensian Crusade and the crushing of the Cathars."

"It's all sounds most interesting." Philip stood up. "So – will you keep your promise to show me round the excavations when they start up again?"

"Of course." She smiled up at him. At that moment he could easily understand how she had become the darling of the French television audiences.

He saw her shiver and he was suddenly aware that it was almost dark. This special little interval was at an end. He held out a hand to her and she accepted it to rise from her seat. Disappointingly, she immediately let go of it again.

Nevertheless, as they walked back to the hotel in a companionable silence, he felt that, as far as she was concerned, he was less of an outcast than he had been earlier.

19

It had been after midnight on the Tuesday when Alain Hébert got back to the cottage after his abortive visit to Marseilles. On the way back he had stopped near Montpellier for a meal and a rest. The cottage had been empty when he went in. It disappointed him a little. He had hoped that César might have been waiting for him, anxious to hear about her father. After all, she had a key to the back door. She could have lit the wood fire and might even have had a bottle of red wine warmed in preparation for their chat.

On consideration though, he acknowledged that it was really his own fault that she wasn't there to greet him. He had always refused to carry a mobile phone, holding the view that his contacts with other people would be when *he* wanted them to take place, rather than at any casual moment when they chose to phone him up and destroy his privacy. So he guessed she had probably been there earlier and had given up waiting for his return. As a result, it wasn't until the following evening that he was able to discuss his visit to Marseilles with her. By then he had heard about the death of the young archaeologist at le Bézu.

César arrived at her usual time of seven o'clock, carrying the bag of supplies which she habitually brought with her. Alain was in his usual seat on the terrace in front of the cottage. On the table beside him was a bottle of Bordeaux and two glasses, his own already half-empty. He rose and filled her glass as she drew near and he motioned her to the chair which he had put ready for her, set at ninety degrees to his own.

"I'm afraid the news is not good," he began. "I met your father and I *was* able to talk to him alone. He didn't appear to be under any obvious pressure from any other person. However he doesn't seem to be making the decisions any longer, and he absolutely refused to even consider leaving Marseilles."

She sat down heavily. "I knew he wouldn't come." She gazed down at the paving at her feet. "You don't get away from the Force that easily."

"What do you mean?" He had been prepared for her to be upset, perhaps tearful. He was surprised to hear this fatalistic acceptance of his failure.

She looked up at him, half-defiantly. "Once you are a member of the inner circle, you know too much to be set free. The only way out is death or, funnily enough, a long term of imprisonment."

"How is that?"

"Once you have been jailed you are a marked man. Your anonymity has gone. When you are released, the Force won't have anything more to do with you. They know the police have your number. You are the first person to be suspected when a crime is committed. You can never get away from that." She gave a short, bitter laugh. "You are an unacceptable risk."

"Don't they still care for members who have been jailed as a result of serving the Force?"

"Oh, yes. They will pension them off – as far away from Marseilles as possible. But none of their former colleagues will be permitted to have any contact with them."

"Wouldn't they be willing to pension off your father?"

"It's different for him." She looked down at her hands and appeared to be marshalling her thoughts before she spoke again. "I realised that he was in very serious danger as soon as he was disabled. He has lost his power in the Force. I'm very much afraid he will be eliminated unless I can stop it."

"What can *you* do about it?"

She didn't answer him directly. Instead she turned to him. "You did your best, Alain. It had to be tried." She shook her head slightly. "But I knew he wouldn't come back here. That's why I couldn't bear to go to Marseilles with you."

"I see."

"And what I didn't tell you, Alain - although I suppose I should have done - is that if, for some strange reason, they had allowed you to take him away, it would also have put both of us in dreadful danger. We would have had to flee from this place within a few days. He must have known that. It's probably one reason why he wouldn't come with you."

"Really?" It was the first time this thought had struck him. "Do you think we're *still* in danger?"

"No. I don't think so – at least not until they have found the treasure. They won't risk losing that."

She took a large gulp of her wine and looked down the valley into the distance. Alain also put his glass thoughtfully to his lips. For a long time neither of them spoke, contemplating what might have been. They were both digesting the unpalatable fact of being involved with *La Force Marseillaise*. After a while César put down her glass and rose.

"Let us prepare the meal," she suggested.

Alain followed her through the cottage to the back kitchen. This making of the evening meal together, before they ate it on the terrace as darkness fell, had become a regular routine. But this evening it was overshadowed by their earlier conversation. What Alain wanted to ask her was where she had been the previous night. However, he was aware that they had both been careful in the past not to presume on their developing relationship, and he did not feel able to change that now. So they both worked in silence.

At last he said, "I was horrified to hear of the death of that young fellow up at the chateau. Have you heard what happened?"

She looked sharply at him and, for the first time, he fancied that he detected a slight hesitation in her manner. "All I have been told," she said carefully, "is that he fell from one of the cliffs below the castle."

"And that was enough to kill him?"

"Well, it *was* more than thirty metres high. And I understand he fell on to rocks at the foot of the cliff. I was told that his body was dreadfully broken when it was recovered. That's all I know."

"You nevertheless seem to have picked up quite a bit about the accident."

She laughed, not altogether lightly. "I am a journalist. It is my job to be where the news is. I also found out that the dead man was quite important. He was the sort of second-in-command of the whole operation."

"How did the accident happen?"

"I don't know any more about it than I have told you. I believe the police are still investigating. Apparently one of the other archaeologists is alleging that the dead man had been in an argument with some Englishman who was visiting the site, but I don't know if that had anything to do with the accident."

Hébert was silent for a while as he worked out how to broach the next subject. "When I was in Marseilles I had a talk with Montluçon. As you and I had discussed, I told him that we wanted to delay uncovering the treasure until the archaeologists had finished at le Bézu because we felt the publicity surrounding the making of the television series would risk our secrecy."

"What did he say to that?"

"He was very angry. He said there was no question of a delay. The Force had invested a lot of money in preparing the operation and they weren't willing to put off getting a return on the investment."

"Well, I did warn you that they probably wouldn't be receptive to your suggestion."

"You did." He paused before continuing. "Do you think the death of this young man will make the archaeologists close down their exploration?"

She frowned. "I don't know. I think it is likely that they may be in trouble for not taking sufficient safety precautions and the authorities may at least insist that they don't continue without making the place much safer. Perhaps I ought to try and find out what their plans are now."

"I wasn't thinking about that. What I *was* thinking about was that it was suspicious that this important young fellow suddenly has a fatal accident almost immediately after I have told Montluçon that the archaeologists' activities were likely to delay our getting at the treasure."

"What are you suggesting – that somebody from the Force gave him a push?"

"Well," said Hébert defensively, "they could have done it, couldn't they? After all, they had enough time."

"Hardly." She turned away and concentrated on her cooking.

"It was at least twelve – maybe eighteen hours - after I'd spoken to Montluçon that this guy was killed. The Force can probably call on killers all over the place. You can't tell me that it's impossible."

"No," she said carefully. "It's not impossible."

What Alain really wanted to ask her was, "Where were you last night? Did you have anything to do with the young man's death?" but he couldn't quite bring himself to say it. He knew it would sound too much like an accusation. Besides, he was uncertain how she would reply, and he was not sure in any case that he wanted to hear it. Instead he changed the subject.

"Are you very upset about your father?"

She turned away and her voice was broken when she at last replied. "Well, I suppose I am upset. But I'm not surprised. I never expected that they would let him go. I just hoped that they could trust him enough after a lifetime of service." Her voice trailed off.

Alain moved to stand behind her. "César."

She turned and almost fell into his arms, now sobbing uncontrollably. He held her against his chest and gazed out of the window at the gathering darkness. Alain Hébert found he was experiencing a new set of feelings in his rather old and solitary life. He was suddenly feeling ridiculously happy.

132

20

Bernard Cambray, Jacqueline's agent and adviser, arrived at about midday the next day. He breezed in to the hotel lounge where Philip and several of the archaeologists were sitting having coffee. The man was a larger-than-life figure in his mid-fifties with thinning hair and a luxuriant ginger moustache. He was dressed in tweeds as though prepared for a day out shooting in the country.

Cambray was the perfect extrovert, seeming to embrace everyone in his welcoming bustle. The sombre atmosphere in the room brightened as soon as he arrived. Philip found himself smiling with the others at the fellow's bonhomie, even though he could not understand more than a quarter of what the man said.

"Oh, what a journey!" Bernard made the theatrical gesture of holding his hand to his forehead. "I can't tell you how dreadful it has been – three accidents and of course there were lorries everywhere."

Indeed, Philip calculated that he must have left Paris very early that morning to have arrived in the Pyrenees in time for a late coffee. It was a sure sign of the importance which he attached to his client. Or perhaps her contract with the television company was more onerous than he had understood.

"Jackie," Cambray called, catching sight of her. He advanced across the room with his arms held wide. "*Ma chérie.* How are you?"

She rose to meet him, tears suddenly glistening on her cheeks through her smile. "Oh, Bernard, yesterday was a dreadful day." Then she was enfolded in his bear-hug embrace.

"My dear," he announced to the room as he released her. "You must be strong. These awful things happen even to the famous – in fact, more often to the famous. I am sure you will rise above it, as you have risen above all the tests which have been set for you so far."

133

She smiled weakly and wiped her cheeks with the back of her hand. "Well, I don't know -"

"I must tell you, my dear, that I've been on the phone half the night – talking to all and sundry. I spoke to Alain of course – I believe it was five times in all. Between us we've got it all arranged for you."

"Alain Gisours?"

"That's right." He explained to the room, "You know he's the big boss at TV France." He turned back to her. "Alain made me assure him that I would pass on his deepest sympathy to you. He said he realised how much you relied on young Jolyon. He knew you would be devastated by his death. However, he also said that he knew what a fighter you are, and he knew you wouldn't let it set you back."

"That was good of him."

"My dear, he was back on the phone to me within twenty minutes to let me know that he had already sorted out the public safety side. You need have no fear that you will be investigated for any perceived failures in your safety organisation. All of those matters will be left to the local police."

"Goodness! I'd never even thought . . ."

"An hour later Alain was on again. He was already putting out feelers to find a suitable replacement. Of course I told him that the young feller who died had filled an essential role in your organisation – a sort of Mister Fixit combined with first lieutenant, if you know what I mean. I explained to him that somebody like that wouldn't be easy to replace."

Jackie's smile was strained. "Nobody will ever be able to replace Jo."

"They certainly *will*. Alain rang a third time soon after midnight to say he'd found just the right chap – *and* he'd made sure the fellow was available immediately."

"*Mon dieu*! He didn't waste much time."

"Of course not," retorted Bernard. "A man in his position doesn't hang about. You must realise, Jackie, that there's a lot riding on this one. In fact I'm not sure even now that you realise just *how* much. The whole series has been syndicated across Europe and North America. The translators are all lined up. There mustn't be any delays. We can't afford to waste time."

Philip noticed Jackie's face had set in a harder line. "So who is this wonder man who's going to solve all our problems?" she asked.

"Wait a minute. I've got his name somewhere." Cambray burrowed in his inside pocket and extracted a piece of paper. "Here we are. He's a guy called Jean-Luc Lerenard. Have you heard of him?"

"No, I have *not*. Who is he?" There was a hint of truculence in her tone and Philip guessed she might be a very strong-willed woman if she chose.

"Well, I can tell you that he comes very highly recommended – by no less an authority than Abbé Dugard. You'll have surely heard of *him*."

"Of course. Everyone in the archaeological world has heard of Bertrand Dugard. He's a marvellous old boy. I spent two seasons with him towards the end of my doctorate. I learned a lot from him."

"So you'll agree that this fellow must be something special."

"Well, I suppose so." She smiled suddenly. "Is the Abbé still working at Prouille?"

Cambray shook his head. "I wouldn't know, my dear. 'Fraid I didn't think to ask. Is that important?"

"I expect he's still there. He's been working his way through the site for more than a decade. Nobody has gone into a project in such depth as Bertrand."

"Then I'm sure he is."

"So – Alain's taken on this new guy without asking me first, has he? What's the fellow's name again?"

Cambray gave her shoulder as near to a gentle pat as he was able. "I'm sure he's not trying to foist an unwanted man on you, my dear. If you have any reasonable strong objections to the fellow then things can be changed. But, as I told you, time is of the essence. Alain doesn't want this hiccup to put things back more than a couple of days. He was going to contact the authorities this morning to ensure that this accident won't cause

135

any delay to your excavations. He told me he's got the cameras booked for next month."

"Next month!" The startled woman took a deep breath. "Oh, Bernard – I don't know whether I'm ready to go back up there just yet."

"Now then, Jackie, you know we can't hang about on this one. Programme time is already booked for late October. That's the peak viewing period. Your faithful public can't be let down."

"But what about André's death?"

"My dear, we can't let one tragic accident wreck the whole project."

Gaston suddenly interrupted. "How do we know it *was* an accident?"

"What?" For a few seconds Cambray's ebullience seemed to have been deflated. "Surely it was an accident. What else could it have been?"

Jackie gazed up into his face. "Who knows, Bernard? Why would André go up on to that exposed ridge at night? Why wasn't he wearing a safety harness? Why should the anchor have been pulled loose? Gaston says that he checked all the ropes and the anchors at the end of every day's work. Isn't that right, Gaston?"

"That's absolutely right." He stood up. "I checked every one of those anchors on Tuesday evening. Nothing was loose at that time. Nobody was working up where André was when he fell. There was no reason why the anchors should have worked loose by themselves." He looked straight at Philip. "I believe that somebody went up there and deliberately loosened an anchor."

"And why," she interrupted, "should André suddenly decide to go up into such an exposed area on his own at night when there was nobody else working on the site?" She shook her head. "He knew the risks. I'd especially emphasised to him that he shouldn't behave in a reckless manner and he'd promised me he wouldn't. If he'd had a reason to go up there, I'm sure he would have told someone else in the team and asked them to go with him."

136

"You think he was tricked up there?" gasped Cambray.

"And the person he would be most likely to contact if he suddenly decided to go up there would be Gaston. He's our expert on rock climbing. Did he say anything to you, Gaston?"

"Nope! I didn't see him at all that evening."

"None of us did." She took a breath. "We've discussed this among ourselves, Bernard, and we're all mystified. I wasn't here. I'd driven to Carcassonne that afternoon to do some research. I wanted to check up on some references in the Cathar museum. I didn't get back until late and then I went straight to bed. The rest of the guys have told me that they were in the bar or resting in their rooms most of the evening."

"That's right," agreed Gaston. "André said he had a bit of a headache after dinner. We assumed he'd gone up to his room early to rest or to do some paperwork. He always had a lot of paperwork to do."

"So what are you saying?" asked the agent.

Jacqueline shook her head. "We just don't know, Bernard. We've got to wait for the police to finish their initial investigations. Then we may get some idea of what actually happened. The forensic team is up at the chateau this morning."

Gaston looked truculently at Philip. "I think there's a good chance that it was murder. And I suspect it may be someone in this room."

"What?" Cambray's startled gaze swept the hotel lounge. "Somebody here? Surely not!"

"No," agreed Jackie. "That's just plain foolish, Gaston."

"Do you want me to leave you?" asked Philip, "So that you can discuss the evidence pointing to my guilt without my being able to deny it?"

"No we *don't*," said Jacqueline firmly, crossing to his side. She turned on the climber. "You're quite wrong, Gaston. You've blown up some minor disagreement beyond all proportion." She turned back to Cambray. "But you can see, Bernard, that we are going to have to pause for a few days while things are sorted out."

The agent held up his hand. "OK. OK, I accept that. In any case this new guy, Lerenard, won't arrive until Monday. Then it'll obviously take you a day or two to bring him up to speed on what's been happening so far."

"More than that, Bernard," she said. "I want to do a thorough check-up on the man."

"Check-up? Why?"

"Bernard," she insisted, "I've never taken on a person before without knowing all about him. I'm not going to start now."

"So how are you going to check him out?"

"You can get a report from our normal people. And I'll drive over to Prouille this afternoon and talk to Bertrand Dugard – that's if he's there and will see me. It's only fifty kilometres away." It was her turn to pat *his* arm. "Once I've had a chat with Bertrand I'll feel happier about the new man."

"All right." He shook his head. "But I'm afraid I can't come with you, my dear. I've got to be back in Paris this evening."

Gaston spoke. "Don't worry. I'll drive Jackie to this place."

"No thanks, Gaston." She turned back to Philip. "Will you accompany me?"

"Me?" His expression showed his surprise. "Why me?"

"Because I want the opinion of somebody who is unbiased." She touched his arm. "*Will* you come with me?"

"Well - yes. Of course I will."

"If that doesn't beat it all!" Gaston thumped his fist on the table. "I'm obviously not wanted around here." He stumped out of the room and slammed the door behind him.

"My dear," said Cambray, "Is this a good idea?" He turned to Philip. "I have nothing against you, young man, but you must realise how important Jacqueline is to all our futures. And none of us *know* you."

Philip noticed that the agent didn't point out that he was also English, though no doubt it had crossed his mind. "Well, if she really wants me to take her, I'll give you my promise that I'll be very careful with her," he said.

Cambray turned back to her. "Let me drive you, my dear. Paris can wait for a day. I'm sure this is important enough for me to spend a night here. We can discuss your plans as we go."

"I've made my decision, Bernard." Jackie stuck her chin out obstinately. "I'm sure I shall be perfectly safe with Philip and I

138

want him to come with me. Do you understand? It's much more important that you are sorting things out in Paris."

Philip watched with amusement as the agent's bubble of self-confidence was deflated. Suddenly, Jacqueline Blontard was very much the woman in charge. He began to see that she could be a very formidable lady.

"Let us have an early lunch and get off to Fanjeaux as soon as we can," she said, taking his arm. "I'll phone Bertrand Dugard to check that he can see us this afternoon, but I don't expect we'll have a problem."

As she swept from the room with Philip in tow she called out, "While we're gone, Bernard, will you speak to the police and find out when we're going to be allowed back on the site?"

21

As they left the Quillan sign behind, Philip changed up into top gear and eased his foot down on the throttle. However, he wasn't in a hurry. It was more than fifty kilometres to Prouille but there was plenty of time. He glanced sideways at his companion. Jacqueline was regarding the road ahead, apparently deep in thought.

"Why did you ask me to drive you to see this Abbé Dugard chap?"

She switched her gaze and smiled at him. He thought again how beautiful that smile of hers was. "Well, first of all, I wanted to stop this stupid idea of Gaston's. I don't want you to think that all French are biased against the English."

"Oh. Thank you for that."

"And secondly," she continued, "you intrigue me. I want to know the real reason why you suddenly turned up here, trailing this story about having ancient Cathar forebears. I know you've given me half an explanation, but I don't think you've told me everything. I suspect there may be something very interesting which has made you come to le Bézu."

"What I've told you is absolutely true."

"Ah, but it's not the whole truth, is it? I want to hear the rest of your story." She laughed lightly. "Perhaps I thought there would be no better chance of getting it out of you than on a long car journey."

"And your desire for a good story leads you to put yourself at risk from a man who may turn out to be a homicidal maniac."

"Do you think I believe that?"

"It seems to be what Gaston thought. He obviously doesn't think André Jolyon's death was an accident."

"Do you?"

Philip thought carefully about it. "I suppose there's a possibility it may not be. I agree that what happened certainly

140

needs some explaining. The question is, though, who would have wanted to kill him? *You* may know the answer to that. All I can promise you is that it wasn't me."

"Of course it wasn't. I know that. Even if I didn't believe your denial, I can't see André agreeing to go up to the chateau with you in the middle of the night."

"But your friend Gaston isn't at all happy with me. I think he would like to have thumped me when I accepted your invitation to drive you to Prouille."

"Oh, Gaston!" Now her laugh was ironic.

"Not only did he want to drive you to this meeting, it seems pretty clear he's hoping to take over André Jolyon's job."

She snorted. "Well, he has no chance of doing that. His experience is unsuitable. He's a good rock climber, but he's quite useless at organising anything. And he's also much too emotional and unreliable. I need somebody I can rely on, and I must be confident that the man won't let me down."

"Hopefully this new chap – what's his name? – Lerenard – hopefully he'll be able to take that job on."

"Maybe." She switched her gaze back to the road. "That's what I intend to find out when we talk to my old mentor, Bertrand Dugard."

"You have a lot of faith in the Abbé? I thought you didn't know him very well."

"Better than I admitted. I worked with him, on and off, for two or three years – firstly when I was at the Sorbonne. I spent the holidays digging with him at Prouille. He'd only just started then, but I realised immediately that his excavation methods were exemplary. I learned a lot of practical lessons from him which have stood me in good stead since."

"Yes. I can understand that," agreed Philip. "I've always maintained that a week's practical experience was worth a month in the classroom."

"That's absolutely right. And the good thing about Bertrand is that he only ever allows himself to have a small team working with him – never more than three or four people. That means he is able to spend more time working with each assistant."

"So you did your degree at the Sorbonne? I believe that's the equivalent of Oxbridge in the UK."

She smiled. "Actually, I also did my doctorate at Oxford after I'd had a year's experience with Bertrand. I enjoyed my time in the city of dreaming spires very much."

"That explains why your English is so good."

"You think it's good?"

"It's fantastic. It's much better than the English you hear spoken by most people in the UK." He gave her a quick glance. "I wish I could speak French half as well as you speak English."

She contrived to give him a little curtsey from her seat. "Thank you, kind sir."

"It's a pleasure."

An easy silence settled over them. Philip concentrated on his driving for the next few kilometres. He thought he was getting to like Mademoiselle Jacqueline Blontard more than was wise. He was aware that she was a star in her own world. She was also obviously extremely talented. It occurred to him, that if he wasn't careful, he might well become another of the band of devoted slaves who seemed to surround her.

After a while he said, "I'm quite looking forward to meeting this Abbé Dugard chap. Is he really an Abbé?"

"Certainly he is. He used to be an important figure in the French Catholic community – and that means he was really important in France." She chuckled. "But his first love was always archaeology. He is an authority on the Dominican Order. I don't know how he did it, but he managed to get the Church authorities to let him retire early from the priesthood and also to give permission for him to excavate at Prouille, which was the original headquarters of the Order."

"What age is he?"

"Oh, he must be close to seventy by now. However, he still seems to be healthy and in the prime of life. At least, he was when I saw him last. He's only a little man and is almost completely bald. But he's an absolute bundle of energy. He works a ten-hour day. Half of the time he's on his knees down in a hole. But he always seems to have time to talk to visitors or

142

helpers, and he's always willing to give a kindly word of encouragement to his staff or to discuss sensibly some probably-daft theory that his helpers have come up with."

"He certainly sounds like a nice guy."

"He's super." Her voice glowed with enthusiasm. "When I rang up to ask if I could discuss something important with him, he assented straight away. He sounded just as he always did when we spoke in the past. He immediately said I was welcome to drive over any time. This afternoon was as convenient as any other time. And," she added seriously, "I'm confident I'll get the truth from him."

"You sound a bit uncertain about this chap Lerenard."

She pulled a face. "Well, I've never heard of him before. Archaeology in France is quite a small world. I must admit I wonder why he has suddenly turned up so conveniently just when I've lost such an important member of my team."

"I see. Does that mean you think the man may have had something to do with André's accident?"

"Surely not!" Her surprise suggested she hadn't even considered it before. She went silent as she thought about it. After a long pause she said, "I suppose that's the logical conclusion of my suspicions." She looked at him seriously. "I think that you are a bit frightening, Philip Sinclair."

"Me? Why am I frightening?"

"Because you seem to say what other people have hardly started thinking. I suppose I would have come to the same conclusion in the end, but it would have taken me a lot longer to get to the point of admitting it."

He couldn't help grinning. "Well, I did promise to look after you, so I'll try not to frighten you any more before we talk to the Abbé. Let's discuss more mundane things. I do think this is a beautiful area of France – spectacular scenery, lots of history, and quite decent weather in the summer. Do you like it here?"

"I'll say I do. It's more or less my home territory."

"You mean you come from here?"

"Well, just down the road in Béziers, near the coast. Coincidentally that's where the Albigensian Crusade began. A large part of the population of that city was massacred by the

143

French at the start of the crusade. At that time the Languedoc was a more or less independent nation, although the Viscounts Trencavel, who ruled it, owed fealty to the King of Aragon."

"Were your family around in those days?"

"I don't know. I've never tried to trace my forebears. Why do you ask?"

Philip chuckled. "I was just thinking that our ancestors might have fought together against the French. I believe I told you that my ancient predecessor, Phillipe de Saint Claire, was a Cathar?"

"That's an interesting idea." She leaned forward enthusiastically. "My uncle would have been fascinated to talk to you. He was the historian in the family, and he was the one who encouraged me to start looking into the Albigensian Crusade. He always maintained that the French have tried to brush that part of their history under the carpet and it's time they faced up to what they did in the name of religion."

They continued to chat about the region and its history, and it seemed all too soon that an hour had passed and they had arrived at their destination. Philip parked in front of the Abbey, and they crossed a broad grass verge under the trees and entered the site through a small gate.

They walked across the sloping park, dotted with small trees at intervals. There seemed to be nobody about. Then they heard a scratching noise in one corner of the site. Philip followed Jackie as she hurried towards the sound. They arrived at a simple barrier beyond which was a deep pit from where the scratching sound emanated.

"*Est-ce Bertrand*?" she called.

The scratching stopped. "*Un moment!*" A few seconds later a bald head appeared climbing up a ladder out of the pit. "Who wants me?"

"It is Jacqueline – Jacqueline Blontard."

The remainder of a short, rotund figure emerged from the pit and hurried across to the barrier.

"Jacqueline!" He brushed off his hands on his already dirty black habit and gave her a hug. "How are you, my dear?"

144

"I'm fine, Bertrand." She stepped back. "This is Philip Sinclair – from England."

The Abbé leaned forward to shake his hand "Really. From England, eh? How nice to meet you." He turned back to her. "Is this the one then, Jackie?"

"What are you talking about, Bertrand?" She had turned delightfully pink. "Philip only agreed to drive me over to meet you. He's interested in what we're doing at le Bézu. You knew we were exploring the ruined chateau there, didn't you, Bertrand?"

"I had heard something."

"Had you also heard about the accident?"

"An accident? No. What has happened?"

"My number two – a lovely guy called André Jolyon – went up to the castle on his own the night before last. He fell from the top of the ridge and was killed."

"What! Oh, no!" Dugard staggered back as though he had been hit.

22

Philip stepped forward to catch the Abbé before he fell. He noticed how Dugard's ruddy complexion had suddenly gone pasty white. His frightened eyes stared from Jackie to him. His mouth had fallen slackly open. The old man seemed far more shocked than he would have expected.

"Did you know him?" asked Philip.

"No! I – oh, dear."

He seemed about to collapse and Philip moved to support him by the elbow.

Jackie hurried to his other side. "Are you all right, Bertrand?"

"Oh, my goodness," he gasped. "Oh dear, oh dear."

"Come out of the sun, Bertrand," she said. "Is there somewhere you can sit down for a few minutes?"

He took a deep breath. "The hut's just behind that wall."

They helped him round the corner to a modest wooden structure. The door stood open and there were a couple of simple chairs and a desk inside, plus a set of shelves on the end wall carrying trays of finds. They sat him down and Jackie fussed round him.

"Will you have something to drink?"

"Yes." He gestured to the canvas bag in the corner. "There's some water."

Jackie delved into the bag and came up with a large plastic bottle of Vichy water. She poured some into a cup which was standing on the desk and handed it to him.

He gulped it down and took a breath. "Thank you, my dear."

"Are you sure you're all right? You seem to have had a nasty turn."

"Yes, thank you." He took another drink and looked up at them with frightened eyes. "This assistant of yours - what exactly happened to him?"

"We don't really know yet. All we know is that yesterday morning his body was found on some rocks at the foot of the highest cliff at le Bézu. Nobody seems to know why he went up there or how he came to fall. The police are still investigating. We hope to find out more tomorrow."

He shook his head. "Oh, dear. What an awful thing to happen." He swallowed another mouthful of water. "What are you going to do now, my dear? Does it mean you'll have to close down the excavation?"

"There's no chance of that, Bertrand. My agent has been in touch with TV France and they're insisting that we carry on. You know what these television companies are like. Nothing must be allowed to interfere with the screening of the series. My contract won't allow me to back out once I've started. In fact some of the top names in Paris have got involved. That's why I've come to see you."

He shook his head. "Oh, I couldn't get involved, Jacqueline. I wouldn't be any good for you. Besides, I must continue with my work here.",

"No. That's not what I meant. The big boys in Paris say that they've found me a replacement. He's a chap called Lerenard. Apparently he gave your name as a reference. I thought I'd take the opportunity of the fact that we were only fifty kilometres from Prouille, to have a brief chat with you about him. I want to find out if you think he's up to the job."

Dugard was regarding her with wide, horrified eyes. "Oh dear," he said, "I was afraid this was going to happen."

"What do you mean?" asked Philip.

"Is the fellow a waste of time?" said Jackie. "I was wondering if it was a bit too convenient – him being available just like that."

"No." The Abbé gazed at her. "The man is a good assistant as far as I can tell. I only had him here for a few weeks, but he's very dedicated and very hard-working. I was very impressed with him. And he promised -" He paused. "I'm sure he will look after you very well."

"What's his background? Where did he train?"

147

"Oh, er -" He shook his head again. "I'm afraid I don't know. I never thought to ask."

She frowned. "That's not like you, Bertrand. You're usually so thorough about these things."

"Yes. Well, you see. . ." He seemed to be struggling to explain himself. "He came to me very highly recommended. I had no reason to question him about his earlier experience."

"Really? Who recommended him to you?"

"It was – let me see – the recommendation came from the Bishop's Palace in Narbonne. They obviously thought very highly of him."

"I see." She regarded him quizzically.

"Please don't ask any more, my dear. I'm afraid there's nothing I can really add to what I've already told you. The only thing that I'm quite sure about, is that you'll be perfectly safe if you do decide to take him on."

Jackie was quiet for some time before she said, "Well, that's something anyway. Thank you, Bertrand."

The old boy gave her a weak smile and nodded.

Philip noticed that she suddenly changed the subject, to the Abbé's obvious relief. For the next half an hour they discussed his progress on the site. She showed a lot of interest in his work and, after a few minutes, Bertrand began to respond. He seemed to have recovered sufficiently from his nasty turn to take them to the latest group grave which he was excavating, so that he could explain the interesting aspects of the original Dominican funeral rites.

By the time they left the site, after they had offered him refreshment in a local bar in Fanjeaux and he had refused, he seemed once more to be the relaxed and friendly old man they had first seen. He reminded Philip of a kind of favourite uncle.

When they were back in the car Jackie asked, "What did you think of that?"

"I wouldn't touch this bloke Lerenard with a barge-pole based on the Abbé's recommendation. It seems somebody has leaned heavily on Bertrand Dugard to make him support the man's application. The problem for them is that the old boy's a useless dissembler. He wouldn't know how to lie if his life depended on it."

She nodded, a slight smile curving her lips. "You've put your finger on it as usual."

"The question is - who is pressuring the good Abbé? Do you know anything about the bishop's palace in Narbonne?"

"Nothing special. I presume it's the seat of Catholic authority in this area."

"So why would they be interested in the excavations you are carrying out at le Bézu?"

"Well, I know the Church would like to forget all about the Cathars, but they're almost a local industry. So there's nothing they can do about that." She shook her head. "I don't know why on earth they should have a special interest in le Bézu. As far as I'm aware, they've never shown any interest in us before."

Philip thought for a few minutes. "Maybe it isn't le Bézu. Perhaps they're interested in the television series. Are they worried about what you'll turn up about their role in the Albigensian Crusade and the way they treated the Cathars?"

"I suppose they could be. The Catholic Church didn't behave very well at the time, but why would they still be worried about something like that nearly eight hundred years later?"

"Well, I don't know," he said. "And I guess you're not going to find out without speaking to Lerenard." He smiled weakly. "I'm afraid I'm not much help to you on this one."

"On the contrary, you've been very helpful. Your comments have helped me to make up my mind."

"You're not going to have anything to do with Monsieur Lerenard?"

"Oh, yes I am." Her eyes flashed as she looked at him. "I'm going to take the fellow on. I want to know why he's so keen to come and work for me. I also want to know who's put him up to it."

"Aren't you taking an awful risk? You don't know what sort of individual he is. He might be a killer."

"Maybe he is. But I don't think he's such a risk. Bertrand was careful to say that I would be safe if I took him on and I don't think he would have allowed himself to be a party to this business if he hadn't been certain about my safety."

Philip turned and looked straight at her. "Nevertheless, I don't think either Abbé Dugard or you fully realise what is going on behind the scenes. You don't understand the motives of the high-ups in places like the Bishop's Palace in Narbonne. I think you need to be very careful if you take this guy on, Jackie."

"Oh, I shall be." She smiled sweetly. "I intend to have my own special insurance policy."

"What do you mean?"

Her grin broadened. "I mean, Philip, that I'm going to take you on to the payroll as my special protector – if you agree, of course."

"A special protector? Do you mean a kind of weak bouncer? But you don't know anything about me."

"I think I know everything I need to know for the moment. You can tell me the rest over the next few days." Her eyes glinted. "Well? Do you accept my offer or are you going to abandon me, unprotected, to this man Lerenard?"

He couldn't help grinning. "What's the pay?"

"Not a lot. But you'll be able to put on your CV that you've worked close to one of the best known archaeologists in France."

"How can I refuse if you put it like that?"

They were both laughing as he started the car and began the journey back to Quillan.

23

Philip was in a quandary as they drove back. The conversation between them was casual, even light-hearted. He admitted to himself that he was looking forward to the next few days in Jackie's company. He wasn't worried about being unpopular with Gaston and the other archaeologists who he knew would regard him as an outsider with no appropriate experience. That consideration was outweighed by the prospect of spending a lot of time with the brilliant and beautiful TV star.

Nevertheless he had the problem that he had been less than completely honest with her about his real reasons for coming to the Languedoc. The question was, should he take her into his confidence and tell her all about the journal of Phillipe de Saint Claire? Would that destroy his chances of carrying out the task set for him by his grandmother if it once got out about his purpose for being here? More importantly, would Jackie feel bound to pass the information on to her wealthy backers or to the authorities?

On the other hand, if he kept the whole story from her, would she be upset by his apparent decision to take advantage of her kindness in offering him a position in her team and using it to his own advantage? One thing he was sure about – sooner or later he would be found out and that would terminate the help he got from Jacqueline Blontard and probably wreck their private relationship at the same time.

After a while he decided that the sooner he took her into his confidence the better. He would have to ask her to keep the information to herself, at least for the present, and hope her reaction would be favourable. He reasoned that if it meant losing the Cathar treasure to the French government or some other organisation – well, he had always known that was a risk.

Therefore, as they approached the town of Limoux, he asked her, "Do you fancy stopping somewhere for a meal?"

She looked at him carefully before she smiled. "All right. Since you're now in my employment, I'll pay."

"No you won't. My employment with you doesn't start until Monday. My grandmother left me a substantial sum to finance my visit to le Bézu. So we'll let her pay."

"I suppose I can't argue with that." But he was also aware that she had been watching him carefully while he was trying to work out what to tell her.

They parked near the town centre and took a gentle stroll round the little town. Within half an hour they had found the perfect place for their meal – a hotel on the banks of the river with a covered balcony restaurant jutting out over the water. It was still quite early, so they were the only couple sitting down to eat. However, the chef seemed to decide that they were worth a special effort. He announced he would start up the kitchen for them and serve them himself.

They discussed and accepted his recommendations from the menu. It didn't concern them that these were no doubt coloured by the ease with which he could prepare the food. Then he suggested the most suitable, and probably the most expensive, wine and left them to sample it with some cold canapés while he started to prepare their meal.

Philip and Jackie were seated opposite each other at a small table in the corner of the restaurant. Through the partly open window beside them, they could hear the chuckle of the river below. The lowering sun lit up the spring-leafed trees on the other bank of the river and dappled the restaurant with a gentle warmth.

"What a perfect setting," enthused Jackie. "Thank you for suggesting this, Philip."

"Thank *you* for agreeing to come."

His sense of justice wouldn't allow him to take advantage of the situation until he had told her of his decision. He looked seriously into the beautiful eyes, just a couple of feet from his.

"However, I have to tell you that I have another reason for wanting to talk face-to-face with you."

"Oh dear. What's that?" Suddenly her eyes were frosted with suspicion.

152

"Well, as you surmised earlier, there *is* more to my presence in le Bézu than I have told you so far."

"Really? Does that mean you're turning down my offer of employment?"

"No, of course not. However, when you've heard what I have to tell you, you may decide that it wasn't politic to offer me the job in the first place." He forced himself to smile. "In that case, I shall understand if you decide you want to withdraw the offer."

"Goodness," she exclaimed. "You make it sound as though you are in the pay of some foreign government."

Philip shook his head. "It's nothing like that, I promise you."

"Come on, then. Put me out of my misery."

"You say you want to know the real reason why I'm here."

"That's right."

"Well, I've told you most of it. I said that it's my grandmother who wanted me to come and find out about our ancestor. I feel guilty now that I didn't spend more time with her when she was getting old. I just didn't realise that she was so ill. Although she was over ninety, I sort of thought that she'd go on for ever. I suppose I was too tied up with my own problems to think about her."

"Problems? What were they?"

"Oh, you know – personal relationships." He waved a dismissive hand. "I thought I'd fallen in love when I was at university. She was a fellow student called Madeline. We got married as soon as we left Sheffield and moved back to London. It took us twelve years to recover from the mistake. It wasn't much fun, one way and another."

"You're married?"

"Divorced." He looked at the date on his watch. "For six weeks and two days."

"Do you have any children?"

"No. Madeline didn't have time for that - too much work and too active a social life."

She looked down at the table. "I'm sorry."

"Don't be. It's all over now and nobody else is suffering." He shook his head. "I'm not complaining. It's simply the explanation of why I didn't spend enough time with my gran. For almost her whole life she was on her own. You see, my dad was sent to boarding school when he was thirteen. They still do that sort of thing in England."

"I've heard about it."

"Then he went straight on to university. After Cambridge he got a job in London where he married. I was born and brought up in the suburbs. I occasionally visited gran in the school holidays when I was young, but I admit I found the big house in Templecombe rather oppressing. And she used to tell me all those stories about the Cathars and how I was related to them. I must say I didn't take them very seriously at the time. It all seemed so far away."

"Do you have a family tree?"

"No, although I suppose I could trace one fairly easily since the family always appear to have lived in the same place." He looked out briefly at the sparkling river, then back to her. "The interesting thing is that my grandmother was left all alone in that great big place for all those years. It seems that, while she was alone, she searched around and found an old document or series of documents which turned out to have been the journal of this man Phillipe de Saint Claire that I told you about. She was fascinated by the story, and it became her overwhelming obsession to translate the journal and research its background."

24

Philip paused for a minute before he continued. "When she had finished translating it, she found the journal was very interesting. It appears that our forebear had set down the story of his adventures, of his hiding the Cathar treasure and his subsequent escape from France."

Jackie was watching him very closely now. "How fascinating," she breathed.

"Apparently,, she couldn't understand anything in the journal at first. However she spent some time researching the language and she found that it had been written in Occitan. I understand that used to be the language of this area."

She smiled. "I know quite a lot of Occitan."

"Really? Is that another of your talents? Can you speak it?"

"Some, but please carry on with your story."

"OK." He leaned back in his chair. "Well, after a lot of study, she managed to translate it, although I believe it took her several years."

"So what does it say?"

"Well, Phillipe claims to have been one of the four *perfecti* who escaped from Montségur on the night when the Cathars finally gave up their defence of the castle and surrendered to the French. I presume you know the story."

"Yes, of course I do." Her eyes were glowing. "Go on."

"He says they escaped down the north cliff-face with the treasure of the Cathars strapped to their backs in sealed bamboo tubes. Phillipe had five tubes in his back-pack. He doesn't give any details about the others. And he didn't open the tubes so he doesn't know what was in them. He just says that, whatever the contents were, they were quite light. So it wasn't gold or jewels or anything like that. In fact, he was never told what it was. The journal gives us no details of the actual treasure itself."

"So what *does* it tell you?"

"The main part of the journal is about his escape hiding the treasure and his escape from France. He says that the four *perfecti* were told to separate and go in different directions in order to reduce the risk of being caught. Phillipe had been instructed to make for le Bézu where the local lord, Pierre de Voisins, was believed to be sympathetic to the Cathar cause."

"Ah," she breathed. "I begin to understand now why you are so interested in the place."

"Wait. There is more." He straightened up. "Just over a day after leaving Montségur, Phillipe reached le Bézu where he briefly met de Voisins. However, the lord was about to set off to Paris to make his obeisance to the French king. So he put Phillipe in touch with his kinsman, a young chap called Raymonde de Puyvert." He paused for a moment. "The journal goes on to tell how Phillipe and Raymonde hid the bamboo tubes behind a wall in a basement room in the castle and then how they escaped from France. Unfortunately Raymonde had an accident and died on the way across the Pyrenees, so Phillipe was then the only one to know where the treasure was hidden. That's why he wrote it all down in this journal."

He stopped and looked at her. "So now you know that I have come to le Bézu to try and find the location of this secret hideaway and see if the bamboo tubes are still there."

Jackie was quiet for a long time, thinking about the strange story. She was looking out at the river and the sun lit up her face in a golden glow, her hair appeared to be a dark bronze.

"Well?" he asked at last. "What's your reaction?"

Before she could reply, the first course of their meal was brought to the table. The chef chatted to them about the food while he topped up their glasses with wine. They began to eat as he retired to the kitchen. Philip ate the delicious food almost without tasting it as he waited for her to speak.

After a while she paused between mouthfuls. "I would like to see that journal."

"I have a copy of my grandmother's translation with me. You can have it to read when we get back to the hotel."

"And you believe this so-called lightweight treasure is buried somewhere in the basement of the castle? How do you know it's still there?"

"I don't. My grandmother put a note at the end of the journal saying she had tried to find out if the bamboo tubes had been discovered. She could find out almost nothing about le Bézu. The place seemed to have disappeared from the guide books."

"That's right," said Jackie. "It is only marked on some maps. And very few people seem to know about it in an area which has generated a lot of interest in the last few decades."

"My grandmother apparently wrote to the local papers in this area to see if there were any reports, especially about the time when Saunière, the priest from Rennes le Chateau, was fossicking about in the countryside around here. However she had no luck. Of course I appreciate that it doesn't mean that the treasure wasn't unearthed centuries ago before there were any records made."

Jackie was thoughtful. "There's not much of the castle left above ground – just a few walls - as you know. However the basement, if there *is* a basement, would be the most likely place to remain unexplored. As the good-quality stone was robbed from the upper walls to be used for newer buildings in the region, the mortar and fragments and useless rubble would gather in the lower levels filling up basement rooms until it built up to such a level that the masonry robbers couldn't be bothered to dig for it." She grinned. "It's the idleness of these people which we archaeologists benefit from."

Their conversation was interrupted by the chef arriving with the main course. For several minutes the food was discussed with him, sampled and enthusiastically commented on. Then he went off to prepare a surprise pudding for them.

"Now *there's* a man who enjoys his job," said Philip.

"We *are* getting very special treatment," she agreed. "I hope you're going to be able to afford it." Then she smiled. "Have you noticed the way he's looking at us?"

"What do you mean?"

"I think he believes we're celebrating some special event – the way we're talking so seriously to each other."

157

"What event?"

There was a sparkle in her eyes as she replied, "If you can't guess, I shan't help you."

Philip was silent as he thought about that, and as he consumed the delicious food. When he had finished, he laid his knife and fork tidily on the plate.

"Well," he said, "I have confessed to you my real purpose in coming here. I can tell you that I have taken a fortnight's holiday to do some research and to look around the place. I still have just over a week left to help you, if the offer is still open. But after that I shall have to return to London. Before I started speaking to you, I was planning to come back about once a month for a long weekend so that I could check up on your progress. I thought you might have found the hiding-place of the treasure by then. If you didn't have any luck, I thought I'd come back for a longer period in the autumn and make a serious attempt to uncover it."

She had a strange smile on her face as she listened to him. "Come and plunder my site?"

"Wait a minute." He put his head on one side. "What does French law say about my right to inherit something which was in the legal possession of my ancestor?"

"That's an interesting point." She nodded. "I think you might have the prior claim. But I'm afraid you wouldn't stand a chance of exercising it."

"What do you mean?"

"Once we have finished here and the camera crews have gone away, the contractors will move in."

"Contractors?"

"You don't understand, Philip." She shook her head. "After the TV series comes out in the autumn, le Bézu will become the next tourist destination for thousands of people who will want to view the sites which they have been watching on their television screens. The road to the site will be widened and re-surfaced. Reception offices and a car park and cafeteria will be built at the foot of the hill. A proper flight of steps will be constructed up the hill, with resting places at intervals to give access to the castle. Footpaths will be made around the ruins,

158

protected with handrails and fences. Notices will be put up all over the place explaining exactly what visitors are looking at. Public toilets and sales kiosks will be built. A whole new industry will be set up to make money out of a curious public who will want to sample the actual location of our discoveries." She paused. "And my agent has arranged for me to get a percentage of it all – and he gets his percentage of that."

"Good God!"

"When it comes to the modern world of the media and its attendant publicity," she reached across and patted his hand, "I'm afraid you're still an innocent, Philip."

He leaned back and looked at the ceiling. "I suppose I am," he said at last. He shook his head. "What am I going to do?"

"I tell you what *we're* going to do," she said brightly. "You tell me you have a week to find out whatever you can about the hiding-place of this treasure. In the morning I have to see the police about what they may have turned up in the forensic investigation, so we won't be able to do much tomorrow. But at eight o'clock on Saturday morning, I suggest you and I are going up to the chateau to have a hunt round for the most likely location for this hiding-place you have described."

"You should read the journal first."

"Oh, I will. After that we'll decide what to do next. I'll tell the guys they can have the weekend off to go back to their families because we will be returning to work at full effort from Monday."

"All right." He grinned at her. "You're on. My grandmother called the treasure my inheritance. I might even give you a share of this inheritance if you behave yourself."

She wagged a finger at him. "Watch out. Don't forget I'm the boss at le Bézu."

An argument was prevented by the arrival of the special pudding.

159

25

Jackie took Gaston with her to meet Sergeant Leblanc at ten o'clock on Friday morning. She would have preferred to have Philip beside her in the waiting room at the *Mairie*, but she realised that would have been interpreted by the rest of the archaeological team in a way which she wasn't willing to acknowledge at present.

Gaston's attitude was a little less truculent than it had been the previous day, but he was obviously consumed with questions about the new replacement for André Jolyon. At last he asked her, "Have you decided to take on this new guy, Lerenard?"

"Yes, I have. I've decided that I need as many people on the team as I can get, now that we have been told that the cameras are coming in next month."

"Are you satisfied that he has the right sort of experience?"

She avoided a direct answer to his question. Instead she said, "Abbé Dugard assures me that he will be a safe pair of hands."

There was a pause while he absorbed the meaning of her reply. Then he said, "So he'll be taking over the job of doing all the organisation and the back-up work?"

"And he'll be digging as well. As I said, I need as many hands as possible, with the imminent start of filming."

Gaston spent some time digesting this. After a while he said, "You were late back last night."

"Are you checking up on me, Gaston?" She felt a rising irritation with the man.

"Now that Jolyon's dead you need someone to look out for you."

"I can look out very well for myself, thank you, Gaston. I'm not a wet-behind-the-ears teenager."

"I don't know about that. But I think you're very unwise to get mixed up with that Englishman. I still think he had it in for André."

Her angry retort was stifled by the opening of the door to Sergeant Leblanc's office. The policeman gestured for them to enter. They followed him in, Gaston making way for Jackie to precede him, and closing the door behind them. The sergeant sat at his desk facing the door and the other two took the prepared chairs facing him.

Leblanc began by saying, "I must warn you that anything I say to you here is unofficial. It is not to be repeated outside this room as being official comment and must certainly not be communicated to any newspaper or other media organisation. You have to realise that the investigation into André Jolyon's death is still ongoing, and I am only talking to you because the authorities tell me they realise the importance of the matter to your organisation. Do you understand what I am saying?"

"Perfectly," she answered for both of them. "Thank you very much for agreeing to keep us informed of progress."

The policeman picked up a single sheet of paper from his desk. It was half-covered with typing. "This is a very brief preliminary report given to me by Monsieur Piedguard. He is the senior forensic scientist who inspected the site yesterday. I'm afraid it tells us very little, but it will be helpful to me if you will confirm a few points in it." He took a breath.

"First of all, forensics looked at the situation on the rocks above the point where the body was found. Piedguard says there are some signs of activity, scraping of boots on rocks, etc., but nothing that can be regarded as suspicious. He says a rough path had been cleared to get to the location in the last few days. However, he can find no evidence of any kind of a struggle occurring, or of a body being dragged in the area during the period when Jolyon's death occurred. In other words, there was no indication that he was pushed off the cliff."

He stopped and looked at Gaston. "I believe you were asked to accompany Monsieur Piedguard round the site yesterday afternoon. I understand you were unable to identify any locations where there had been obvious changes from how you left the site on Tuesday evening."

"That's correct," agreed Gaston. "We had already cleared a lot of the undergrowth and cut paths through what remained, so

161

it wouldn't have been necessary for anybody to clear any new areas to get to the top of the cliffs."

"Thank you. Now - to turn to the location where the body was found – that is, at the foot of the cliff – Monsieur Piedguard has some criticism of the fact that the body and its surroundings had been disturbed."

Gaston reacted strongly. "Now look here. As soon as we found where Jolyon's body was, I could see it was in a difficult spot to get to. We sent word to the *Mairie* that an accident had occurred. But I had to do something straight away. We couldn't just leave him lying there. For all we knew, the man might have still been alive. That's why I had myself let down on ropes to check the body."

The sergeant held up his hand. "I know that you did your best. In fact my department was also criticised for removing the body before the forensic team could inspect the area. However I had Maitre Amboisard's authority to do that, providing a full set of photographs were taken." He hesitated. "Er – Maitre Amboisard is the mayor and the examining magistrate."

"When I realised he was dead," said Gaston, "I had cutting gear thrown down to me so that I could clear an area round the body. I knew you would have to get people down there to recover André's corpse. But I only cut a narrow strip around the body. I didn't interfere with the actual place where he was lying. I was also careful to avoid making a lot of mess. I knew the place was a crime scene."

"Oh, I don't think it's that important," said Leblanc. "The summary of the forensic findings so far is that there is no conclusive evidence to be able to say exactly how the accident occurred."

"Will we ever know, do you think?" asked Jackie.

The policeman pulled a face. "I'm afraid it's too early to say. We may be able to find out more when the autopsy is carried out on the corpse."

"When will that be?"

"Jolyon's body has been sent to the forensic laboratories at Toulouse. They should be able to give us a detailed report within two weeks."

"Not for two weeks?" The shock showed on her face.

"I'm afraid not." The sergeant shook his head. "I understand that they are very busy at the moment."

"But what about the site? I have to tell you," Jackie continued, "that I am coming under pressure from Paris to continue with our excavations. They want to bring in the cameras in less than a month."

"I know all about that and it isn't a problem. Maitre Amboisard has also been in touch with the authorities in Paris. He has agreed with them that there is no reason why you can't continue straight away with your work up at the chateau. I am to tell you to that you must keep away from the area of the rocks at the foot of the cliff where Jolyon's body was found. That is in case the forensic team decides, before it completes its full report, that it wants to come back and check up on anything. I don't imagine that will present a problem for you. Otherwise the site is released for your activities."

"So we can start back as soon as we can get the team together again?"

Leblanc nodded. "That's correct."

"Thank you." She turned to Gaston. "The new guy, Lerenard, starts on Monday. There's no point in re-starting until he arrives, so I'll give the whole team the weekend off. That will let everybody have a chance to relax for a couple of days. He probably won't be here early on Monday so we'll meet up at ten o'clock in the hotel lounge to discuss plans before going up to the site. Can you go and tell them please, Gaston?" She turned back to the policeman. "Is there anything else you want to talk to us about, sergeant?"

He shook his head.

"OK, then." She stood up. "We'll all be available on Monday if you need to talk to us any further."

"What about the Englishman?"

"I'm afraid I don't know what his plans are," she lied. "Do you want to see him?"

"No. That won't be necessary today. But I will want him to be available on Monday." He looked at her quizzically. "Are you likely to see him?"

"I'm sure he'll be in the hotel bar this evening. I'll tell him that you expect him to be around on Monday." She didn't mention that Philip's plans were to return to England at the end of the following week.

With the interview completed Gaston and Jackie left the *Mairie*. She wanted to continue reading the journal of Phillipe de Saint Claire.

26

Philip and Jackie left the hotel before eight on Saturday morning. Nobody was around to see them go. Even the town seemed still to be sleeping in the early morning sunshine.

"I wanted to get away before Gaston appeared," she said. "He was the only one who didn't accept my offer of a weekend off to go home. He seems to have given himself the task of watching out for me."

Philip chuckled. "I expect he's trying to make sure you don't come under the evil influence of the foreigner."

"He was still going on about you when we met Sergeant Leblanc yesterday morning," she told him.

"What did you see Leblanc about?"

"It was to obtain clearance to continue working at le Bézu."

"And did you?"

"Oh yes." She smiled. "There was no problem. They'd already received instructions from Paris to let us continue. Obviously, Alain Gisours has been pulling a few strings."

They took Philip's car to minimise the man's suspicions and drove straight up to the castle. It was a trip of some fifteen kilometres on narrow, winding roads which took them nearly half an hour despite the lack of traffic. However, they were climbing the path to the site soon after eight-thirty.

Jackie had read the copy of the translated journal during the previous day and was as interested as Philip in its contents.

"Your ancestor says the tubes were hidden behind a wall which was built across a shallow cave in the lowest room of the castle," she said. "I get the impression in the journal that this room was some way from the entrance and also from the main accommodation area of the castle, which would have been centred round the great hall. That is the area where we are currently clearing the collapsed rubble and other detritus."

"OK. Let's go down and start from there."

They made their way to the roped-off section of the hillside where the archaeologists had been working for the last couple of weeks. Then they partly circumvented it to the bottom corner.

"I think it must be down in that direction." Jackie pointed down the hillside close to the foot of the sheer rocky cliffs on which the few remains of the castle still stood.

"The undergrowth looks pretty thick down there."

"It's an area we haven't cleared yet."

"Well, let's get started."

There was a bag of tools in the site shed containing secateurs to cut back the brambles and other scrub which crowded the site. Jackie began to cut a path as close to the rock face as possible. Philip used a mattock and a spade to cut steps on the steep slope. Cutting the path was slow work.

Jackie told him the office was equipped with a kettle and the materials for making coffee. So, after a couple of hours, she went back and brought them cups of steaming liquid. They sat on the rocks and looked at the view as they rested. The coffee tasted good.

"I'm enjoying this," he said.

She winked at him. "So am I. It's a change for me to get involved in mundane tasks like clearing the site. Once I've told them which areas need stripping, the others normally carry on while I'm working out locations for trenches, checking finds, etc. It's a change actually to be doing the physical work."

"Well, we've got a beautiful day for it. I must say I've been lucky with the weather since I arrived last Tuesday."

She smiled but said nothing. Philip discovered he was feeling happier than he had for a long time.

After a quarter of an hour's break, they restarted their work, cutting deeper into the undergrowth which was shoulder-high in places. By lunchtime they had got down to an area where the rubble under foot had formed a small dip in the hillside. When they cleared the scrub beyond the hollow, the land began to fall away very steeply and they seemed to have crossed a rock ridge where only fragments of masonry remained. Jackie stopped them going any further.

"I believe this is where the outside wall of the castle was located. The hillside is so steep here that I don't think they would have extended the construction beyond this point. This is such a good, naturally defendable boundary."

"So?" He looked at her hopefully. "Do you think we might have reached the location of the room that the journal talks about?"

She looked doubtful. "Could be. That's if we've chosen the right area of the castle. However, I can't think of a more likely location."

"But I've got to point out that there's no stone wall to our right as there should be. It's just sheer rock. Where do you think the hiding-place might be?"

For an answer she pointed between his feet.

"Straight down?"

"That's right. We're standing on rubble and earth and vegetation which has accumulated over centuries from the collapse of the castle walls above – the walls that aren't there anymore."

"You mean what's been left by the masonry robbers?"

She nodded. "I told you about that on Thursday."

"I know you did. How deep do you think the rubble might be?"

"I don't know." Jackie shrugged. "It might be five metres."

"Five metres! That's more than fifteen feet."

"It could easily be that deep – maybe even deeper."

"So we've got to dig out this whole area more than fifteen feet deep and we may still not be in the right place anyway?"

She thought for a moment. "Actually it's not as bad as it sounds. We can dig a metre-wide trench against the rock face and heap the spoil over the other side of the hollow. And, if you remember, the journal says the wall across the hollow in the rock face was high up in the room. So you won't have to dig all the way down to the original floor level."

"Thank you." Philip grinned. "You mean I may only have to dig down ten feet or so."

"Perhaps not even as far as that."

167

"But it's still going to take me several days," he pointed out. "I won't be able to finish it this weekend."

"I've been thinking about that." Jackie rested a hand against the rock wall. "I have decided that this work is a separate part of the main excavation which I will set up here. I can easily manufacture a reason which nobody will dispute. In that case, I will allocate one or two of the workers to start on this task and you can help them." She smiled mischievously. "It'll mean that I'll always know where you are and at the same time it'll keep you out of Gaston's way. He'll be less likely to create trouble for you if you're out of sight."

"I suppose that would suit me well enough as long as you promise not to forget that I'm here."

"Don't worry about that. I always make sure I keep an eye on what's going on in every part of my sites - even down here in the depths."

Philip thought for a moment. "What do I do if I find the wall across the cave?"

"You just record it. You wouldn't expect to be allowed to remove it without the approval of the site manager. That's me."

"Yes, ma'am."

"If we do find a wall we'll look for a later opportunity for you and me to explore behind it together." She pondered for a moment. "I think I'll allocate young Armand to take charge here. He's very enthusiastic and he's learned quite a lot in the few weeks he's been with me. He'll know how to look for finds and report on anything that you turn up."

"Can't I do it alone?"

"Certainly not." She shook her head. "Don't be silly. That would immediately make everybody suspicious. In addition to that, you haven't been trained to look for finds. You don't know how to strut a trench to make it safe. You don't know the correct form in which to make notes of progress. You'll have to learn all that from Armand, who's picked up quite a lot in the last few weeks. I'll tell everybody that he's the person doing the excavation to try and find the floor level of the lowest part of the castle. You will be his helper." She stepped back.

"Actually I think it will do Armand good. It'll give him a sense of responsibility."

"So I'll have to do whatever he tells me."

"You certainly will." She grinned. "I think I might also allocate his wife to sieve the soil and search for finds. That'll complete the team."

"So what do we do now?"

"I think we should leave everything just as it is for now. It would give the wrong message to the others if we had commenced work here before the site has officially re-started. You and Armand can begin digging this trench on Monday morning. I'll give you a list of kit and clothing you'll need."

"OK. So what happens next?"

She turned and faced him. "What about lunch? The other day I was taken to a lovely little place up the river near Cavirac."

"What a good idea." He grinned. "You do have some brilliant ideas."

"Come on then. Let's put the gear away and lock up." She preceded him up the steep, rough path which led back to the main part of the site.

As they approached the store shed they saw the door was open. "I'm sure I shut it when I got the coffee," Jackie said. "I think somebody's been here."

They had almost reached the timber building when a man stepped out. He was tall and well into his fifties and was dressed more as though for a walk in the city than on a wild, rocky outcrop in the foothills of the Pyrenees. However, Philip did notice that he wore smart new walking boots below his cavalry twills.

The man seemed not at all embarrassed by their arrival. He gave a little bow and said, "*Bonjour, ma'mselle. Quel beau jour.*"

"What are you doing in our shed?" demanded Jackie.

The fellow smiled in a superior way. "There was no sign to say it belonged to anybody. It was open and I was intrigued by the contents."

"It was *not* open."

"Well," he acknowledged. "It was unlocked at least. You can't blame me for being interested in what was going on in an out of the way place like this."

"Who are you?"

"My name," he said with another little bow, "is Alain Hébert. Before you ask, I am staying near Rennes-les-Bains and I enjoy walking in the area. May I ask who you are and what you are doing here?"

Her demeanour softened a little. "I am Jacqueline Blontard and this is Philip Sinclair. We are excavating at le Bézu for Cathar remains under licence from the Department of Ancient Monuments."

"I am very pleased to meet you." He stepped forward and shook them both firmly by the hand. "How nice to know that these old remains aren't being left to moulder away completely. Have you found anything interesting yet?"

"Not much. A few coins of low face value and some mediaeval detritus. Nothing to get excited about." She tossed her head. "But, so far, we have barely scratched the surface of the site."

"No secret caches of treasure?" He laughed a little falsely.

She smiled. "I'm afraid we don't place much reliance on the local tales of Templar treasure."

"What tales are those?" The man's eyes were suddenly watchful, a shade suspicious.

"If you spend any time in this area, Monsieur Hébert, you'll be sure to come across plenty of stories about treasure. The local guide books are full of tales about Cathar treasure hidden in caves, treasure left by the Templars everywhere, Visigoth remains – some stories even lay claims to this area being the hiding-place of the Holy Grail. Not that anybody has actually produced any genuine finds to support the theories."

"How droll." But his expression seemed to suggest that he wasn't very amused.

"You should go to Rennes-le-Chateau. That is the centre of the story-telling industry. You'll find that all the shops there are loaded down with books about the subject."

"Indeed I shall." He was smiling again, apparently reassured by her chatter. "Well, I'll wish you a good day and continue with my walk." He gave a little bow and touched the brim of his hat. Then he set off down the path towards the road far below.

Jackie hurried in to check the contents of the hut and Philip followed her.

"That was silly of me not to have locked it," she said.

"Never mind. No harm seems to have been done. I wouldn't have said that old boy was likely to be one of your archaeological thieves."

"You're right. Everything seems to be in order in here. Except that I'm pretty sure the site diary has been pulled to the front of the desk. He was probably having a snoop at it to see if we had found anything valuable."

"Does that matter?"

"Not really. He won't have seen anything significant in there, if for no other reason than the fact that we haven't found much yet." She turned to face him. "What did you think of him?"

Philip thought about it carefully. "Somehow he didn't look like a walker to me – he was too smartly dressed. And his walking boots were brand new."

"I think you're right. His clothing wasn't right for this sort of terrain."

"The other thing was that he seemed very interested when you were talking about the treasure. Do you think he might be some sort of treasure hunter?"

"Hah." She laughed. "I've never seen anybody look less like a treasure hunter than he does."

"In that case it's not worth wasting our time bothering about him."

They deposited their tools in the hut and carefully locked the door before setting off for their lunch.

171

27

"Is there a problem?" asked Charles Robert. "I was surprised when you asked to bring our meeting forward."

They had met this time in the cafeteria of a supermarket near Limoux which was conveniently open on a Sunday morning. Now they were seated facing each other and sipping their café solos.

Armand looked up from his cup. "Things have started to happen. Jacqueline Blontard's second-in-command, a chap called André Jolyon, was found dead on Wednesday morning."

"Ah." There was a long silence while Monsieur Robert absorbed the full meaning of this new development. At last he said, "How did he die?"

"He fell from the top of the highest cliff on which the castle stands. He fell thirty metres and landed on rocks at the foot of the cliff. He was found to be dead when they reached the body."

"Is there any evidence of foul play?"

"Gaston – the man who fixed the ropes which seem to have given way – says they were deliberately loosened by somebody, but I don't think the police are taking what he says very seriously."

"Well – congratulations to you. If there is no way that blame can be directed at the Council, it's the best thing that could have happened. That should put a spoke in their wheel."

The young man didn't respond to these comments. He dropped his eyes to the coffee which he was gently stirring.

"After all," continued Robert, "the archaeologists surely won't be permitted to continue their excavations after an accident like that has happened. The site obviously isn't safe. I'm certain the authorities won't allow further exploration until an enquiry has been held and the cause of the – er – accident established."

"You're wrong, Monsieur Robert. The police have already investigated the site. However, they say the archaeological dig can continue."

"What! Has Paris been consulted?"

"Yes. In fact the permission to carry on came from Paris." Armand looked up again. "It's obvious that TV France are a big organisation with enormous influence. They are making sure that the loss of one member of the team won't affect the whole operation."

"Hmm." Robert frowned. "We'll see about that. Was he an important member of the organisation – this André Jolyon?"

"I thought he was, but apparently they have already found a replacement. He is a man called Jean-Luc Lerenard. He seems to have been pulled straight out of a hat. So everybody's happy. The site exploration is going ahead again."

"Ah." Once again there was a long silence.

"There has been another development," said the Armand after an interval. "A young man has turned up from England. I don't know exactly what he has said to Jacqueline, but she has become quite friendly with him - very friendly in fact. She asked him to drive her to Fanjeaux, when she decided to go and talk to an old guy called Abbé Dugard about the new replacement for Jolyon. She obviously thinks this fellow is important."

"Really? What's the Englishman's name?"

"He's called Philip Sinclair."

"Sinclair? How interesting." Robert appeared to be thinking deeply. "Where does he come from in England?"

Armand shook his head. "That I don't know."

"OK. Leave it with me. I'll see what I can find out through my sources." Robert mused to himself. "Philip Sinclair, eh?"

"Jacqueline spoke to me on my mobile yesterday evening just after I had telephoned you. She says she wants me to take charge of a new area of the excavation. She has given me the Englishman – 'Philip' she called him – as an assistant. She wants me to train him up in the techniques I've learned from her." He shrugged. "But I gather the bloke's only here for another week. I don't know how much he'll learn in that time."

Armand became aware that Monsieur Robert was watching him very closely. "A new area?" asked the old man. "Now, where would that be?"

"I don't really know yet. All she said was that it was somewhere lower down the site."

"Lower down!" Armand was startled by the sharpness in the old man's tone. "How much lower down?"

"I'm sorry," he said. "I don't know the answer to that yet. I haven't seen this new location. Apparently it was only cleared yesterday. All she said was that she wanted to investigate the lowest point on the site because all kinds of detritus might have been washed down there over the centuries. She hopes we may come across some useful finds. I thought it was good that she was showing some interest in my work. It indicated that I had succeeded in gaining her confidence."

The older man ignored Armand's self-gratification. "Now look," he said after a pause for reflection, "I want you to go straight back and get Mademoiselle Blontard to show you the precise location of the new area where you are going to dig. You'll have to think up some excuse – say you need to plan what gear you will have to get – something like that. But it's very important that you come back to me later today to let me know exactly where this area is."

"I can't do that, Monsieur Robert. Jacqueline has sent us all away for the weekend. She says it'll be our last opportunity to have a couple of days off for some time. Jeanette and I are staying in a *Logis* near here but Jaqueline thinks we're back in Paris."

Robert gave an exasperated sigh, as though the delay was Armand's fault. "Oh, well. You say you're starting work in the new location tomorrow morning. I suppose it can't be helped. You'll have to telephone me tomorrow evening." He took a card from his breast pocket and a pen from inside his jacket. He scribbled down a number and handed it to the young man. "Here you are. This is the number where I'll be tomorrow evening. What time can I expect to hear from you?"

"It will probably be about seven – before dinner."

174

"Very well. I'll expect to receive your call earlier than seven-fifteen tomorrow evening. I'll wait until then to telephone Marcus Heilberg. Meanwhile I must tell you that I'm not happy about this Englishman turning up. I wonder what his game is."

"I heard it said that some ancient forebear of his is a Cathar."

"Is that so?" Robert's voice was sharp. "What exactly did he say?"

Armand racked his brain to try and remember. "I'm sorry. I'm not even sure I heard him say it himself. In fact I believe it was what Jacqueline told Gaston after he'd asked her about the Englishman." He shook his head. "Gaston doesn't like the chap at all. He even tried to suggest he pushed Jolyon off the cliff after they'd had an argument."

"Is that likely?"

"I don't think so. I was there when Sinclair first turned up on the site and started to look around. Jolyon ordered him off the site when he seemed to be watching what we were doing. Personally I thought it was an over-reaction, but the Englishman didn't really argue with him. He just left and said he'd come back the next day because Jacqueline had apparently promised to show him round."

Charles Robert sniffed. "That doesn't sound enough reason to kill a man."

"I think," said Armand, "that Jolyon was a bit jealous of the attention Blontard paid to Sinclair. André was very protective of his boss. He liked to wrap the lady in cotton wool, if you know what I mean."

"Nevertheless, I'd like you to try and find out what you can about this Sinclair fellow. That should be easy if you're going to be working with him."

"I'll do my best."

"And I don't think it's a good idea for him to be too friendly with our star archaeologist." The old man smiled and managed something near a wink. "Your own young woman – Jeanette is her name? – might decide to intervene in their friendship, if you understand my meaning."

Armand was genuinely astonished. "Are you suggesting she should seduce him?"

"Why not?" The smile had disappeared. "It's about time she earned her keep."

As he made his way back to the old inn on the outskirts of the town Armand couldn't suppress a grin at the suggestion made by Monsieur Robert. He wondered what Jeanette's reaction would be when he put it to her.

28

César had been away, apparently meeting her employers in Toulouse on the Saturday and she had stayed overnight in the big city. However she was back on the Sunday evening, and she came up the track to tell him about her weekend, as she had promised.

Alain could see that she wasn't wearing her usual jeans and open-necked shirt. Today she had on a loose sweater of some filmy material, and her knee-length skirt revealed her calves. Her hair was drawn back from her slightly perspiring forehead. He thought she looked rather sexy.

He was once again sitting outside the cottage with the bottle of warmed red wine and the two glasses ready for their evening drinks. He'd already been waiting more than half an hour and was slightly disappointed at her lateness. Furthermore, he sensed a tension in her as she picked up the glass that he had filled for her and drank thirstily before taking the prepared seat.

"Are you all right?" he asked, suddenly anxious.

She shook her head as though to banish the thoughts it contained and smiled at him. "Yes thanks. I'm fed up with this bloody Sunday afternoon traffic – the world and his wife seemed to be trundling home from the family lunch. If the police stopped them and breathalysed them, I'm sure at least half would fail."

"And how did the meeting go?"

"OK. The clients are happy with what I've done so far. They gave me a few more sites they'd like me to look at. It probably means some days away, possibly staying overnight – but the expenses they are giving me are good."

He wondered if she was trying to hold him at a distance. Perhaps she was regretting that their liaison had progressed so far. However, it had been agreed at the start of their relationship that each of them should have their own space and not make demands upon the other. So he didn't feel he could question her further about his impressions. Instead he said, "Wait till I tell you my news. I took a walk up to the site at le Bézu yesterday."

"Oh? Was that a good idea?" She sounded a shade resentful.

"I don't see why not. I had heard that the police had finished with the place. Besides those guys weren't working this weekend."

"But I thought you said you wanted to keep a low profile."

"Yes, I do. But I got fed up with sitting around waiting for something to happen. So I just took a stroll that way."

"A stroll?" She looked at him quizzically. "It must be at least ten kilometres."

"I tell you - it was a good job I did go. Anyway, it was a beautiful day, so I took some lunch with me. And don't worry – I kept an eye open for any notices or red and white tapes banning entrance. There was nothing."

"So the place was deserted?"

"Well – yes and no. There were no police." He leaned forward in his chair. "In fact it looked as though the whole site had been frozen in time and all the archaeologists had just moved out. There was a timber shed with a window which they appeared to have been using as a combined office and store. The door wasn't even locked."

The strain in her face seemed to be relaxing. "So what did you do?"

"I went in, of course. The place was pretty ordinary. There was a desk under the window with one of those large page-a-day diaries on it."

"I suppose you couldn't resist taking a look at it." She chuckled.

"Well I did give it a scan. It was a diary of progress since the site opened. I thought it was quite interesting. It recorded who was on site each day and what they were doing. There were comments on how they were getting on in each section of the dig. And there was a brief note of finds with a cross reference to a page in the finds catalogue."

"What did the catalogue of finds tell you?" Alain noticed she was showing real interest for the first time.

"I'm afraid it wasn't there. They must have taken it back to the hotel. Of course there was no entry for last Wednesday or the subsequent days. But, from taking a look around the site, it seems as if they intend to re-start soon. There has been no attempt to close anything down or fill in any of the trenches."

"You mean it doesn't look as though the death of the young man is going to put a stop to the excavations." César took a deep draught of her drink and he topped them both up, draining the bottle as he did so.

"You haven't heard it all yet. As I was looking through the diary a young couple emerged from among some trees further down the site. The woman was Jacqueline Blontard – you know, the archaeologist – the leader of the excavation."

"*Mon dieu!*"

"And she had a young chap with her – a bit older than she was, I would say. But what interested me was that they were talking in English."

"Could you understand what they were saying?"

He shook his head. "No. They were too far away in any case for me to hear their conversation in detail from inside the hut. On top of that, Mademoiselle Blontard had spotted that the door was open."

"My god! What did you do?"

"I just made the best of it. I closed the diary and stepped out of the hut to meet them."

"And?"

"Well – of course, she wanted to know what the hell I was doing in the shed. I pointed out that the door was open and I was just being nosey. Nothing more."

César pulled a face. "What did she say to that?"

"What could she say?" He took a breath. "She went on to ask who I was and I told her."

"So your anonymity is blown."

He shrugged. "I'm not worried about that. When I asked her, she confirmed who *she* was and she introduced the Englishman as a chap called Philip Sinclair." He shrugged again. "And that was all. We wished each other good day and I departed."

"You don't think she was suspicious about you?"

"Why should she be?" He smiled and spread his arms wide. "After all, I was acting perfectly naturally. I was out for a walk and having a nose around when I arrived at an interesting place. Anybody might do the same." He cleared his throat and leaned back in his chair. "However, the most interesting bit happened after that."

"What do you mean?"

He went to take another drink but found his glass was empty. "Hang on a minute. I need some more lubrication. I'll get another bottle."

He disappeared into the cottage and returned a few minutes later with a new, uncorked bottle of the same vintage. He poured himself a glass, topped up hers, took a large swig and settled himself back on his chair.

César meanwhile had been sitting on the edge of hers. "Alain, you bugger," she accused him with a smile, "You certainly know how to raise the tension."

"Really?" He smiled benevolently at her. "Now where was I? Aah – yes." He appeared to gaze into the distance. "Well, first of all – just in case they were watching me – I went all the way down the path to the roadway. I noticed their little car was parked there at the bottom. So I turned away from Quillan. I went a hundred metres or so up the track and entered a small copse of trees. I sat down where I had a view of the car and waited. I decided I would stay there all afternoon if necessary."

"Go on. What happened next?"

"Well, after a quarter of an hour or so, they came down the path. The car started up, turned round and set off in the direction of Quillan. I waited for another five minutes while I finished my lunch. Then I went back up to the castle. I kept a careful look-out as I went to make sure there was nobody else about, but the place was deserted."

He paused for a moment and looked back at her. "The thing is, César, I wanted to see where the other two had suddenly appeared from. So I decided to take a good look around the whole site. I checked the shed first, but of course that had been locked. That didn't bother me because I was pretty sure there was nothing of real interest in there. So I went and looked around the main area which had been roped off. They had cleared the whole of that part of the site and started digging two trenches across the area at right angles to each other. These had exposed the foundations of several old walls."

"Were they interesting?"

"I suppose they would be to someone who understood what they were looking at, but they didn't mean much to me." He sighed. "Anyway, I realised there wasn't anything to detain me there, so I decided to look further down the site. What I found next was *very* interesting – in fact, rather worrying."

César was on the edge of her seat again. "What do you mean?"

"I haven't told you the exact location of the Templar treasure, have I?" He took another mouthful of wine. "I wonder why you've never asked me."

She shrugged. "You'll tell me when you're ready."

"I've kept it to myself, you see, because it's the only hold I have over the Force. But I'm beginning to wonder whether somebody else has found out about it from another source – that Englishman, for example."

"You're talking in riddles, Alain."

"Well, I came by my information by a complex, almost unbelievable route." He explained again what he had already told Montluçon. "So you see, I'd assumed until now that I was the only one who knew about the exact location of the treasure. But when I went further down the site on Saturday morning, I found the archaeologists had recently cut a path to a location very close to where the treasure is. They seemed to be approaching it from the other side, so they may have different information from mine. But it seems too close to be a coincidence."

There was a long pause while they both considered the consequences of this new discovery. At last César asked him, "So what are you going to do about it?"

"That's what I've been worrying about since yesterday morning. If I tell the Force about it they are going to want to act immediately. I'm afraid they'll come blundering in here, resorting to violence again. As well as all the publicity that is

181

likely to generate, people may possibly be killed, or at least badly injured. It could wreck our chance of recovering any of the treasure." He faced her. "I must tell you that I abhor violence, my dear."

"Then why did you approach the Force? You know their reputation."

"I've been asking myself that same question for the last couple of weeks." He smiled bleakly. "The truth is that I needed a big organisation which would act outside the law but could cope with the logistics at the same time. That didn't give me many options. I thought that, if I kept the release of information in my hands, I would be able to keep them under control." He shook his head. "Now that I find the archaeologists are here and getting close, I fear that I am losing control."

"So," she said, "the alternative is not to tell the Force what you have found out."

"But if Jacqueline Blontard gets to the treasure first, we will lose it. The Force will be furious."

"You can say that again. You'll become their number one target. I don't fancy that. In that case I wouldn't give much for your chances." She reached over and patted his arm. "You're going to have to tell them, Alain. Perhaps you can control the release of information so that they won't over-react."

"That's right." He let out a big sigh. "I'd arrived at the same conclusion."

She leaned back in her chair and put her hands behind her head. "What we need to decide is how much to tell them and when."

"To start with, César, I think I'll wait a couple of days before I say anything. We need to keep the archaeologists' progress on site under careful observation and only tell Montluçon what's happening when they get too close. I hope that will prevent The Force from doing anything stupid."

"All right," she agreed. "The only thing is – don't leave it too long. How are you going to keep your check on the archaeologists?"

"Well, I thought you could possibly do that, at least to start with."

"What did you have in mind?"

"I thought that some time in the next few days you could turn up on site to write a report about the castle as part of your project for your clients in Toulouse. It's a suitable task and you've probably got some correspondence which would convince them that it's genuine, don't you think?"

"That sounds OK." She nodded. "Yes, I think I could carry that off."

"And you could probably spin it out for a few days. You could even ask them for some assistance with information about the place, don't you think? Of course, while you're there you could probably manage to find out what sort of progress they're making down at the bottom of the site. I could draw a sketch map showing you the area I'm interested in."

She smiled and took his hand. "You're quite a clever old stick, aren't you?"

He grinned. "I tell you what - I'm quite a hungry old stick." He stood up. "We can discuss the details as we eat."

He picked up his glass and the half-full bottle and made for the front door of the cottage. With a smile she accompanied him, carrying her own glass.

29

The archaeologists were at breakfast on the Monday morning and the dining room was alive with conversation when Jean-Luc Lerenard arrived. The big man walked in from reception and stood looking round at the scene. A single large bag swung lightly from his left hand. Maybe it was his arrogant expression which caused the conversation to die away.

His gaze alighted on Jacqueline sitting at a table with Gaston, Armand and Jeanette.

"Mademoiselle Blontard?"

She rose to greet him. "You must be Monsieur Lerenard. I hadn't expected you to be so early." Her manner was cool.

"I only had a short way to come. Early rising is no problem for me."

"Would you like some breakfast?"

"No thank you." There was no explanation.

Philip put him down as a man of very few words – not such a bad thing among these chattering Frenchmen.

"Very well. You'll excuse us while we finish ours. A bedroom has been reserved for you. Reception will give you directions. We'll meet in the lounge in half an hour to plan our day." She resumed her seat as he left.

Gradually the conversation started up again, but it was no longer quite so cheerful. Now there seemed to be a certain tension in the air. Philip was astonished at the way in which the arrival of this big man seemed to have changed the atmosphere.

After another five minutes, Jackie gave up and went up to her room, leaving a half-full plate behind her. Even she seemed to have been discomfited by the appearance of Monsieur Lerenard. Most of the others followed her example in a short while. Only Gaston remained, stolidly working his way through a large plate of croissants.

The meeting in the lounge after breakfast was a restrained affair. Jackie brought all the members of the team together.

Philip had almost been accepted by now within the group, although Gaston was still unwilling to address more than a few words to him.

She started by introducing the new arrival. "This is Jean-Luc Lerenard who has been head-hunted to replace André." She smiled sadly. "I'm afraid you are going to have your work cut out. My old friend won't be easy to replace."

The big man said nothing. There was no smile. He clearly took his new role seriously.

"The other thing to tell you all," she said, "is that I've decided to open up a second area of excavation. It is way down near the bottom of the site. It will only be a small operation – at least at the start." She switched her attention. "Armand, I'm going to put you in charge of it. I've been very pleased with the way you're coming on."

"Thank you." The young man nodded with pleasure.

"What's the purpose of this new area?" asked Lerenard.

"Well." She half-smiled at him. "Let's call it an insurance policy. So far, not much has turned up on the main site or near the main entrance. I'm hoping that we may get some finds near the bottom of the site – stuff that has gravitated from higher up."

"Stratification will be difficult."

"Yes it will." She was obviously impressed by his comment. "But I'm not looking to date the finds. We know most material down there will come from a restricted time zone. The castle hasn't been occupied for six hundred years. I'm just hoping we'll get some pointers about who might have used the site in its latter days."

"So you want us to be careful with sorting through our rubble?" asked Armand.

"Certainly I do. I've decided to put Philip, our new arrival from England, with you, to help you do the digging. And Jeanette can sort the finds." She nodded to the woman who was dressed as though about to go off on a shopping spree. "I think you've picked up enough from Marie to work on your own for a while. I've spoken to the scaffolders. They are already putting up a staging for you to use as a sorting platform. Of course you

185

will need to check your procedures with Marie before you start."

Philip was impressed with the smooth way Jackie had introduced the new area. Nobody seemed to object or question her motives. Perhaps they just accepted that she was the one who made the decisions.

"What about the rest of us?" Gaston wanted to know.

"Obviously the rest of the team will be working on the main site. Jean-Luc will be in charge of this site and you will be his number two, Gaston. We'll walk him round and explain everything to him as soon as we get up to the castle. Marie will continue with the classification of finds in that area. Any questions?"

There didn't seem to be any.

"OK. Please will everybody be at the vehicles in five minutes. We've lost the best part of a week. We might as well get on with the work without further delay."

Obediently, the meeting broke up and they all went to get their gear. The only problem was raised by Jeanette as she struggled down the path to the new location after Armand had rushed ahead to survey his new responsibility.

"I don't know why we have to come all the way down here," she complained to him in her charmingly accented English. "It is very difficult to get to this new place."

"I'll have to make a better job of clearing the path and put in some more steps to help you," said Philip as he helped her over one rough section.

She chuckled conspiratorially. "It is lucky I have you to hold my hand. Armand doesn't even think about me when Mademoiselle Blontard tells him to do something. He is too excited about his new job to show any interest in me."

Philip thought the lady was hardly dressed for an archaeological dig. Admittedly she had sensible new walking boots on her dainty feet but her skin-tight jeans restricted her movement and her loose blouse displayed a lot of her most obvious assets. He noticed her face was carefully made up and her golden hair was done up in a wispy scarf. She was wearing a strong perfume and he thought that her scarlet-painted nails were likely to suffer when she was sieving the soil. She was also carrying a shoulder bag which set her apart from the other archaeologists.

When they got to the area that he and Jackie had roughly cleared the previous Saturday, Armand was already photographing the site. A scaffold area about five metres by two had been erected at one side and a table was set up on it with a fixed sieve at the back, where the buckets of soil were to be emptied for Jeanette to sort through with a small trowel. A selection of boxes and trays were set out on the table waiting to be labelled as the finds were sorted. Philip noticed that the lady had had sufficient foresight to bring a pair of soft leather gloves which she was now putting on to protect her hands.

"Right," said Armand with Jeanette translating for him, "Mademoiselle Blontard says we've got to take out a trench a metre wide against the rock face here. It will be about six metres long and we'll take it down in half-metre steps. When we get down a metre we'll have to start strutting the side to make sure we don't have a collapse. But, for the first half metre, it'll mainly be vegetation and roots." He smiled. "Philip, I want you to take the end near the finds table. I'll take the far end. That means you'll have to lift up the buckets of soil and tip them in front of the sieve for Jeanette to sort through. Is that all right?"

"Yes, of course."

Philip was puzzled that Armand seemed to want him to spend so much time with his wife. Jeanette gave him a secret smile, which suggested she had no objection. Perhaps they were having some problems in their relationship.

This situation continued throughout the morning as they steadily dug downwards. Jeanette was cheerfully playing French pop music on the little radio which she had brought in her bag. She smiled at him gratefully as he lifted each container of soil on to the table for her to push through the sieve. She often patted his hand or his shoulder and sometimes rested an arm round his back. From time to time she would lean over the scaffold to show him something she had found. Then her blouse would fall open and he would be treated to a view down her

187

cleavage nearly to her navel – a panorama of bronzed flesh and white brassiere.

On these occasions Philip often looked at Armand to see what he made of his wife's flirting, but the fellow seemed totally unaware of what was going on, or else he was used to it and ignored it. If he made any comments they were normally about technical matters. His English was almost as poor as Philip's French, so conversation was stilted.

They stopped for lunch for half an hour at one o'clock and went up to the site shed where the food and drink were provided. Armand strode ahead leaving Philip to help Jeanette. She clung to him as he guided her over the rough sections. He reminded himself that he must bring a spade on their return to make a better job of cutting the access steps.

They continued digging throughout the afternoon and it was about four o'clock when Philip hit masonry under his feet. He did a little preparatory scraping with his spade before he alerted Armand. The young Frenchman immediately came over and crouched down beside him.

"It looks to be a flat stone surface," said Philip.

"*Vraiment.*" Armand called to Jeanette. "Can you give me my trowel?"

"Is this the one?" She stepped down from the scaffold platform and joined them, resting a hand on Philip's shoulder.

Armand took the trowel and began to scrape away the soil on the top of the stone. Jeanette stood beside Philip, watching her husband as he busily cleared the earth from the masonry. Within a few minutes he had uncovered the sharp edge of a slab, which seemed to be sloping down slightly in the centre.

"I think it is an old step," he announced. "We must tell the director. Jeanette, will you go and find her while Philip and I clear away more soil and take some photographs?"

She pouted. "I don't like climbing that rough path without help."

"Don't be silly."

"I'll go, if you like," said Philip. "Only one of us can work on the step at a time."

"I will go with you if you help me," she offered.

"That's not necessary."

"You might as well both go," said Armand. "Then you can separate to look for Jackie when you get up to the main site."

Philip shrugged. "OK."

With Jeanette hanging on to his hand, he set off up the rough path. Although she slowed him down a bit, she seemed to be doing all right at first. Then, on a particularly difficult section, she half-fell and sat down in a clump of brambles.

"Oh dear," she gasped. "Please can you help me?" She reached out both arms to him appealingly.

He took hold of her hands and tried to pull her up. But she stayed in the sitting position.

"I have prickles holding on to my clothes," she explained. "You will have to reach round me to release them."

He bent over her and she grasped him tightly round the neck. As he carefully released the prickly tendrils caught in her blouse and jeans, she pulled herself close to him and hung on like a limpet. When he had released her completely, he put his hands under her armpits and lifted her upright.

"Oh, thank you. You are my saviour." She hugged herself against him and kissed him full on his half-open lips. Her tongue darted into his mouth and explored it deliciously.

It took him a little while to extract himself from her embrace. At last he held her away. "Jeanette," he said "What about Armand . . ?"

"What on earth's going on?"

Startled, Philip looked round to find Jackie standing about six feet away, surveying them coldly.

"Oh." Philip felt himself go scarlet with embarrassment. "Jeanette had just fallen into some brambles. I was just releasing her."

"You seem to be making a very thorough job of it."

With an effort, he detached the grinning Jeanette's hands which were still clasped round his neck. "Actually we were just coming to look for you. We think we've uncovered a step."

"That doesn't seem to be the only thing that's been uncovered." Jacqueline gaze took in Jeanette's partly undone blouse.

189

Coolly, she stepped past him and preceded them down the path.

"Careful," said Philip. "It's a bit rough."

"I don't need any help from you," she called over her shoulder. "I'm obviously a bit more used to this sort of thing than Jeanette. You carry on keeping a hold on her."

Feeling a fool, he followed her down the path, trying to hold off the slipping and stumbling Jeanette with one hand.

When they reached the trench, Jackie went down on her knees beside Armand who had already cleared enough soil to show that the piece of masonry was certainly a step, worn down and cracked in the middle. He had even dug down the face of the stone at one end to reveal a second step, the leading edge of which was set at an angle to the one above.

"It looks like the start of a staircase," he said excitedly.

"I think you're right," she agreed. This lower step is what we call a winder. That's the sort of step you get when a staircase goes round a corner. It looks as though this flight of steps is turning away from the rock-face."

Armand was exultant. "This is my best find so far."

"Well done, Armand." She patted him on the shoulder. "Now then, I want you to take this staircase down as far as you can, still keeping within the width of the trench. If you find that it goes off to one side, send Philip to find me. I will then decide if it makes sense to put in another trench at right angles to this one. You'd better do this work by yourself, and I want you to be careful. We may come across some important finds in the corners as we go deeper."

She straightened up. "Jeanette will have to be especially careful sieving through the soil you get out, to make absolutely sure that nothing is missed. I'll come back again before we finish for the day to check up on your progress. OK?"

"Of course." Armand bent enthusiastically to his task.

"Philip can carry on clearing the trench behind you, so that you're not digging in a hole. The soil from that can be heaped further along the trench unless something else interesting comes to light. See you later."

She almost ignored Philip and set off back up the path, moving quickly.

30

"This latest news is most disturbing, Charles."

The president and Marcus Heilberg were sitting in the same chairs as they had four weeks earlier when Charles Robert had last been summoned to meet them. He suddenly had the ridiculous notion that they hadn't moved since that previous meeting.

There was no time wasted in asking about his health or his hurried overnight journey up the length of France; no apologies about requiring him to appear before them without having a wink of sleep in the last twenty-four hours or even having sufficient time to call at his home to freshen up.

Nevertheless he agreed with them, "It is indeed most worrying, monsieur le Président. I regret to inform you that, from the description given to me by young Séjour at seven o'clock last evening, it appears our worst fears may be about to be realised."

"Why do you think this situation has suddenly arisen," enquired Heilberg. "We had thought, from your previous reports, that the excavations were taking place further up the site. Why the sudden change of location?"

"I do not have the answer to that at present, Grand Treasurer. There have been two new arrivals at le Bézu in the last few days. Perhaps one of them has brought some new information which has led Mademoiselle Blontard to review her strategy. It is only a small additional area with three archaeologists working on it. Fortunately Séjour has been put in charge of the new area. So he is in a position to keep us right up-to-date with developments."

"Who are these new arrivals you refer to?"

Charles Robert took a breath. "You knew of course that Blontard's second in command – a chap called André Jolyon – had died in a fall from the castle cliffs?"

"Indeed we did. It was assumed that young Séjour might have had something to do with that. We wondered if it was an attempt to disrupt the exploration."

"Perhaps he did," agreed Robert, "although he does not admit it. I decided it was imprudent to question him closely about the matter."

"Very wise." The president nodded. "The council does not wish to be implicated in any way in that sort of activity."

"Exactly. Well, this André Jolyon has been replaced by a man sent from Paris – a fellow called Jean-Luc Lerenard. Apparently he is a great brute of a man."

The president and the treasurer exchanged glances.

"You need not worry about him," said the old man. "We know all about him."

Charles was surprised. "Really? What *do* you know about him?"

"Ah!" There was a pause. "I'm afraid that information is privileged, Charles."

"You mean it wouldn't affect any dealings which I or young Séjour might have with the fellow."

"Don't worry about it, Charles. Just accept my word that it will not have been Lerenard who directed Mademoiselle Blontard to look in the new location. If we decide that you need to know any more about the man, we will inform you when the time comes. The only thing I advise you to tell Séjour is that he should not attempt to confront Lerenard in any way."

Charles felt he had been firmly put in his place and made to look a bit of a fool at the same time. It seemed that he was having his information rationed. He was unable to decide why this was.

After a pause he continued. "Very well. The other new arrival is a young Englishman called. . ." He consulted his notebook. "He is called Philip Sinclair. I know very little about him but it has just this moment occurred to me that his name could be an Anglicisation of Saint Claire."

"How interesting," muttered Heilberg.

"While I think about it, Séjour told me that this Englishman seemed to be getting on very well with the Blontard woman.

Perhaps he brought some special information for her from England. I believe she did spend a year in Oxford a while ago. Who knows how far her contacts spread over there?"

There was a long silence while all three digested the possible importance of this new player on the scene. At last the president said, "Do we have any information about this Philip de Saint Claire, Marcus?"

"I will have him checked out this morning, *monsieur le Président*."

"Charles - tell me - what is this fellow's explanation for his sudden arrival in le Bézu?"

"I – I regret I do not know, *Président*." Robert was covered in confusion. "I did not think to question Séjour about him when I met him last night. It did not occur to me until today that the man might be important."

The silence which followed condemned his shortcomings more absolutely than any outburst of criticism which he might have received from another source. Charles Robert observed that his standing on the Council was beginning to shrink. This whole business connected with le Bézu seemed to have been a catalogue of errors on his part. He began to wonder whether he might even have his membership of this powerful central body terminated. He knew there was a number of rising stars in both government and industry who would give their right arm to step into his position.

"I have told Séjour that I do not regard it as healthy that this Philip Sinclair should get too close to Mademoiselle Blontard. He has agreed that the woman posing as his wife will attempt to find out what she can about the man's history and any links to the director."

The president steepled his fingers and studied them. "What do you think, Marcus?"

"I cannot see that will do any harm, *Président*." Heilberg swallowed. "However I think it is necessary for us to take far more positive action than that. I think we must ensure that the excavation at le Bézu is completely closed down as soon as possible."

"And how do you propose that this should be done?"

194

"I'm sorry, *Président*, but I see no alternative to making contact with the various important men in Paris. They must be persuaded – er - I mean encouraged, to change their support for the project. They must be helped to find new priorities for their funding."

"Really?" The president looked up at the ceiling and stroked his chin. "This sounds expensive, Marcus."

"It will be, *Président*. A lot of people and a number of big organisations may be involved. They will already have expended considerable sums which they may not be able to recover. There will also need to be a lot of personal persuasion."

"Just how much persuasion were you thinking of?"

"*Monsieur le Président* – it could amount to a hundred million euros."

Charles Robert was appalled. He had always believed that Marcus Heilberg, more than anybody else, was extremely careful with the organisation's substantial funds. Now they were talking of spending such a massive sum – no doubt much of it on personal bribes. It was all he could manage not to interrupt, when he heard these two leviathans discussing the colossal amounts of money involved as though they were mere baubles.

"What proportion of our capital does that represent?"

"It is something over twenty percent of the available liquid funds." Heilberg took a breath. "However, we must remember that it will be expended to protect a far greater amount of our long-term reserves. And, as you know, we are caring for far more here than mere money."

The president nodded sagely. "You are right. In that case we must do it. In fact I think we should add a fifty percent contingency to our withdrawals. We cannot afford to fail in this."

"Very well, *Président*."

"Do we need a full meeting to approve this?"

"I don't think that will be necessary," said Heilberg. "I can be in touch with at least half a dozen of the Council today to get their personal backing and I am confident I will get it. Of course Charles has heard the discussion. Can you give me your support, Charles?"

Robert swallowed his objections, realising it would be foolish to fall out with the decision-makers. "Of course, Treasurer."

"Call in to my office as you go to sign the voting slip."

"In that case you can start moving the funds very shortly," said the president. "As soon as you have majority approval you can commence approaching the individuals concerned. Will you let me have a list of those you intend to contact, for me to check?"

"Certainly, *monsieur le Président*."

"Many are likely to have direct contact with one or other of the members of the Council. I certainly expect that I shall know quite a few. We must use as many of our personal contacts as we can."

"I will obviously do that."

The president cleared his throat. "It is at times like this that I am grateful for the centralised method of running France which we enjoy."

"Truly, *Président*." Heilberg stood up. "Now, if you'll excuse me, I should be getting on with my tasks. There is a lot to do this morning." He gathered up his papers and left, with them clasped to his chest.

For a long time after he had gone, the president seemed almost to doze as he gazed into the distance. Charles Robert had to shuffle his feet to remind the old boy that he was still there.

The president looked at him. "Well, Charles, you must get back to your watching brief in Foix."

"Am I doing any good by being there, *Président*?"

"You certainly are. In fact I think you should instruct young Séjour to report progress to you on a daily basis in future. You should then contact me immediately by telephone if you have any changes to report."

He smiled gently at Robert's downcast expression. "Don't worry, Charles. It is only likely to be for a few more days. It is vital for us that we have a reliable man in place locally. And it

196

won't do your reputation any harm to have been involved in such a crisis – possibly the greatest in the Council's history for at least five hundred years."

Charles Robert breathed a sigh of relief. This was a most unusual softening of the president's attitude. He began to dare to believe that he might not be blamed for all the things which had gone wrong in recent weeks.

"One further thing, Charles." The old man leaned forward. "You have been given an insight this morning into the Council's most private affairs. I'm sure I do not need to remind you that not a word of this is to leave your lips."

"Certainly not, *Président*."

"Not even to your wife or family." The ghost of a smile crossed his face. "Or even to your mistress."

Charles Robert went slightly pink under his sun-tan. "My lips are sealed, *Président*."

To cover his embarrassment, Charles rose, picked up his notebook and left without further comment from either man.

31

By the next day the excavations had expanded considerably. Armand was working his way down the steps and he suggested that Philip clear the masonry wall which supported the side of the staircase.

It was a relief to Philip to be able to get on with some work away from the immediate attention of Jeanette. She seemed to have decided to flirt outrageously with him. Furthermore her husband appeared to be quite unconcerned about it. She had made sure that she sat next to him in the crowded cars going to and from the site, with her body pressed against him. Then she had invited him to join them at dinner the previous night. Seated beside him, she moved close and her hand was soon resting on his leg. She was wearing a short, frilly skirt and he suspected that, if he responded, he would find himself stroking her bare thigh.

She wasn't very subtle about her attentions, and he found the whole thing rather embarrassing. He wondered whether the other members of the team noticed what was going on. The problem was that his body had received no contact with females for some months. As a result, he found himself responding physically almost without his own volition. At the same time, he was very aware of the problems that would arise if he was challenged by Armand or by Jackie.

In fact, after the director came across them in that embarrassing position on the path the previous morning, her attitude to Philip had cooled distinctly. When she was talking to Armand she ignored the other two completely. She would take him on one side so that Philip and Jeanette couldn't hear what was being said. He had the feeling Jackie was deliberately avoiding him. This was disappointing, since they had seemed to be getting on so well over the weekend.

Armand had already cleared four steps the previous day. These turned a complete right-angle away from the rock face.

He had spoken to Jackie to obtain her authorisation to put in a second trench to follow the line of the staircase and she promised to come down later in the morning to make a decision. Meanwhile he had diverted Philip to digging down to clear the wall beside the steps.

Within an hour Philip had struck a further stone slab at a lower level. He pointed this out to Armand who gave him a trowel and told him to scrape away the soil from the surface carefully while he continued clearing the steps. Jeanette had less to sieve now that they were working with trowels, and she came down to join them and shovel soil into the buckets, but Philip was now working on his knees and that gave her no opportunity to make further contact with him.

After half an hour, Philip had cleared part of what appeared to be a large slab of masonry – far bigger than a step. As he scraped into the corner, it was clear that this flat stone had been put in place later and carefully cut to fit against the wall which supported the steps and against the natural rock cliff which the trench was following. Unfortunately, there seemed to be no interesting objects above the slab.

A little while after this, Armand's clearing of the steps reached down to a similar flat slab at the same level. When both men scraped towards each other, they met where the steps came to an end. It appeared that they had hit a flat paved area – but an area paved with massive slabs of stone.

"I think Jackie ought to be told about this," said Armand. "I had expected her to be here by now, but she hasn't turned up. You'd better go and find her."

So Philip set off – making sure he was on his own this time. When he reached the main excavation area, he was told that she had returned to Quillan to pick up some equipment which had just been delivered. He explained what they had found as best he could to Lerenard.

"I will come to inspect," said the big man.

When they got down to the trench, Jean-Luc looked at the expanding area of stone which Armand had uncovered. Philip was watching the man closely and saw his eyes narrow when he bent down to inspect the slabs, as if in recognition. However, when he straightened up again, he merely shrugged.

"Ah," he said. "It is only the floor of the room at the bottom of the steps. What finds have you made?"

"Not very much." Jeanette indicated the nearly empty trays.

"I think you are wasting your time here. I will tell the director and I think she will probably close down this area. We could use you more profitably up at the main site." He turned on his heel and left them looking disconsolately at each other.

After a bit of thought, Philip said, "Have you noticed that the stone slabs have been cut round the bottom of the steps as though they were laid down after the steps were there? I don't think this is the floor of the room as Jean-Luc suggests. Paving in a room gets worn smooth and is made dirty by the passage of feet. It would be especially dirty at the foot of the stairs where people entered. But this surface looks almost untouched."

Jeanette translated for him and Armand's eyes lit up when he thought about it.

"That is quite correct. I agree that this cannot be paving. But what is it?"

"I suggest we wait till Jackie sees it. She is much more experienced than Jean-Luc. She may come up with some ideas."

"But what do we do until she comes?" Armand seemed to have had his confidence shaken by Lerenard's dismissive attitude.

"While we're waiting for the director," said Philip, "I think we should clear as much of the paving slabs as we can. That will give her more to look at."

"Good idea," agreed Séjour. "I still believe this may be important."

"While you are finishing round the steps, I suggest that I dig a narrow trench along the foot of the cliff. That will tell us how big the slabs are and there may be a gap where we can try to see underneath. That might help us decide why they're here."

So they set to with a will to clear as much of the masonry as far as they could before Jackie arrived. It was nearly lunch-time when she finally turned up. By then, Armand had cleared an area nearly a metre wide around the foot of the steps and Philip had dug a trench about half a metre wide on top of the stone slabs and against the natural stone wall for about three metres. Neither of them had been able to reach an exposed edge of the paving but they had found some tight joints in the slabs which suggested they were huge pieces of stone approximately three metres by a metre and a half in size.

When Jackie turned up her attitude was different from Jean-Luc's. "Oh," she said. "This is interesting, Armand."

He put to her the thoughts which he and Philip had discussed about the paved area, but her reply was non-committal.

"It does seem to be a later addition," she agreed. "But how much later? You haven't had any luck with finds on top of the paving which might have dated it?"

"Nothing at all."

"Then it seems as though the paving may have been covered over with soil and detritus as soon as it was laid. And it is quite fine work. The joints are very narrow. That would suggest that it may be quite recent. But I can't shed any light on why it is here or when it was done."

Philip made his first comment. "If we could find an edge to a slab then we might get a better idea of what it is."

"But that is going to mean that we have to clear a lot of soil," she responded, "and Jean-Luc is right. We can't really afford to have three of the team involved in a job which doesn't seem to be advancing our knowledge of the Cathar occupation."

The other two looked disappointedly at each other.

"I tell you what," said Jackie. "You can have the rest of the day here. I suggest you continue the narrow trench against the wall as far as you can. But, if you've got nothing substantial to report by the end of the day, I'm afraid I'm going to have to pull you off and use you somewhere else. Is that all right?"

"OK. That sounds reasonable."

So they continued the narrow trench, taking it in turns to dig furiously while the other one cleared the soil and deposited it by the sieve. They worked through lunch, sending Jeanette to collect the food and drink from the main site, which Philip noticed she did without any apparent problem on this occasion.

They were still digging away energetically in mid-afternoon when a new woman turned up. Watching her approach down the path, Philip thought she was probably in her forties but still quite slim and fit. She obviously had no trouble in reaching them.

Jeanette greeted her brightly. "Hello. Are you a visitor?"

"I suppose I am." She stepped on to the scaffold and handed a visiting card to the girl. "My name is César Renoir. I am a journalist, but at present I am collecting information for a book about Cathar strongholds. I met your leader, Jacqueline Blontard, recently and she said I was welcome to walk round and take a look. What are you doing here?"

Armand climbed on to the scaffold and took the card from Jeanette and looked at it. He seemed to think it was genuine.

"We're just digging an exploratory trench."

"Why down here?"

He shrugged. "Archaeologists often do that sort of thing. They take a look at the land, decide the most likely place to yield information, and dig there, hoping to come up with some finds."

"What finds have you made?"

"Not much," he admitted. "In fact we're being pulled off this area tonight. We're just trying to uncover as much as we can before we finish."

She seemed genuinely interested. "So what part of the castle do you think this is?"

"Oh, nothing very special. We're right down in the basement of the building so it was probably just used as store-rooms or even a prison. But you often turn up interesting finds in the most unlikely places."

"It's a very grand floor for a prison, don't you think?"

"Yes," he admitted. "It is puzzling."

"And, correct me if I'm wrong, but this wall looks like the original rock of the mountain."

He nodded. "The original builders used the natural rock cliffs as a part of the structure. It meant that in the lower parts of the castle they only had to build the defensive walls on one side."

"Except for that area there." She pointed to an area of rough stone walling just above the paving about five metres along the narrow trench.

"That's right. We assume there was a recess there which they filled in to prevent seepage of water into the stores, or something like that."

The woman straightened up. "What will you do when you get to the end of the trench?"

"We won't today." Armand shook his head. "That's the frustrating thing about some of this work. Just when you think you may be about to find something interesting, a different priority arises. I sometimes wish we were like the old-fashioned archaeologists who employed large gangs of labourers and stood over them making decisions and peering at things they had unearthed."

"No chance of that here?"

He grinned. "Not with Jackie Blontard. Every trowel-full of soil has to be sieved. Every smallest find uncovered in location has to be photographed from at least four different angles, with scale markers and compass directions before it can be moved."

"I understand she is very well thought of in her profession."

"Oh, yes," he agreed. "I wouldn't want to work for anyone else."

"Very well." César took a breath. "Thank you for explaining it all to me so clearly. I'll go up and talk to the others now. Goodbye." With a lift of the hand and a smile, she was gone.

Philip and Jeanette had said nothing while she was there, leaving it to the senior man to give the explanations. Now Jeanette said, "You told her a lot, Armand."

"Well," he replied, "she was entitled to know for her book."

"What do you think, Philip?" she asked.

"I don't see a problem. None of the information was secret. Let's admit it – this area's a dead duck."

"A dead duck?" She giggled.

"It means it's useless."

"OK," interrupted Armand, "let's push on. I'd really like to get to the end of this last slab tonight, if we can."

So they continued right up to six o'clock when Gaston came down to warn them that the vehicles wouldn't wait for them any longer. By then, they had dug the narrow trench nearly ten metres along the top of the paving against the cliff. They had uncovered nothing except three long paving stones each three metres long with tight joints to each other and to the cliff face. It was obviously a substantial area of paving indicating a large room.

"This fourth slab is obviously the last," argued Armand. "If only Jackie would let us have another morning down here, I think we could get to the end. That would give us an edge to look at. Then we might be able to find out more about the reason for this unused floor slab. I think I'll try and get her permission to do that."

"It's worth a try," Philip agreed.

But in that hope they were to be disappointed. When it was put to her by Armand, she shook her head

"I'm afraid you're just wasting time and money. Jean-Luc has hit some interesting terrain on the main site. We need everybody up there. Maybe there will be a chance to carry on later if we find what we want in the great hall area."

And they had to be satisfied with that.

32

Philip was exhausted that evening. Recently he had had less experience of heavy physical work than the others and the rush to get as far as they could with the trench had tired him out. His muscles were protesting. So he decided to have a soak in the bath before dinner. He was luxuriating in the warm relaxing water when Jeanette walked into the bathroom.

He was astonished by her arrival. He was even more surprised to see that her long hair was loose, and she was wearing a skimpy white dress which revealed a lot of bosom and leg.

"What on earth are you doing here?"

She tossed her head. "You didn't lock your bedroom door."

"Even so, you should have knocked."

"I did." She grinned. "But only very quietly. I saw how tired you were in the car, Philip, and I thought I would come in to relax your muscles for you. I am quite a good masseuse, you know."

"Jeanette. You know you shouldn't be doing this."

"I promise that you'll enjoy it. Just sit up."

She sat on the edge of the bath and pushed him upright. Then she pressed on the back of his head and he felt her hair tickle his shoulder.

"Lean forward."

Philip found himself breathing in a lung-full of her rich perfume. He realised he was faced with a bit of a problem. If he ordered her out, he suspected she wouldn't go without physical persuasion. He would have to get out of the bath to push her out of the room. In order to do that he would need to stand up and expose the effect that her sudden arrival and sexy appearance had already had on his anatomy. So he obediently leaned his head forward and hoped she would go when she had finished massaging his back.

She began to rub his neck and shoulder muscles with the heels of her hands. He had to admit it was most stimulating. She gradually worked her hands down his back almost to his waist. Then the tips of her fingers crept up the knobs of his spine, circling in turn round each of his vertebrae, which made him shiver. She chuckled at his reaction and slid her enticing hands round his neck and began to stroke his chest. He felt her breasts cushioned against his back as she peered over his shoulder.

"My goodness," she exclaimed, "aren't you a big boy? Don't try to tell me you're not enjoying this, Philip."

His embarrassed reaction was to hunch further forward. "You must stop this, Jeanette."

As he moved forward her hands slipped off his body and her arms plunged up to the elbows in the bath with a splash. For a second she lost her balance and fell on top of his hunched back. Then she recovered and sat up again.

"I'm all wet," she complained. "Just look at me."

"I'm getting out," he said. "Can you pass me the towel?"

She stood up. "I said 'look at me'."

So he did. It was then he discovered that the water on the thin white fabric of her dress had made it almost transparent and revealed, as it moulded over her body, that she was wearing no underclothes. She didn't seem in the least bothered about him gazing at her nudity. In fact her appearance was incredibly provocative and she knew it.

"Please pass me my towel."

She looked down at his genitals. "I don't know why you've turned shy on me. Neither of us have any secrets from each other any more, have we?" She smiled, her tongue licking her upper lip as though in anticipation.

At that moment he nearly forgot himself and grabbed her and made love to her on the bathroom floor. For a short while he was too aware of the pleasure he would get from her luscious body to think of anything else. He knew it would be a great experience. But he also realised it would be likely to cause huge problems among the other members of the archaeological team if it got out. So he firmly pushed the urge away and took refuge in action. He climbed swiftly out of the bath, grabbed the towel from its rail on the wall and swathed it round his lower body.

To try and put her off he asked, "What would Armand say if he could see you now?"

She grinned. "If he saw me like this, he would drag me back to our bedroom and ravish me. I know exactly how to make Armand desire me."

"Not only Armand."

"He is a very good lover." She looked straight into his eyes. "Are you? You should show me."

Desperately Philip sought a way out of this situation. Underneath it all he had the suspicion that he was being manipulated – he wasn't sure of the reason. And he didn't understand precisely how Armand fitted in to the arrangement. But he knew that somehow, if he gave in to his desire to make love to her, he would regret it.

"I'm sorry, Jeanette. I would like nothing better than to show you what sort of a lover I am. But I'm afraid I'm not prepared to go to bed with someone else's wife."

Her eyes opened wide. "Oh, Armand and I are not married. We are just good friends."

"And lovers."

"Yes. Sometimes we are lovers."

"Well, I'm not prepared to share someone else's woman. I had enough of that when I was married."

"You are married?"

"I *was* married. Now I am divorced."

"What was your wife like?"

"In some ways she was remarkably like you." He couldn't tell her, that because she was better educated, Madeline should have known better. "That is why I'm not going to give way to my urge to make love to you."

She looked crestfallen. By now he had started to dry himself and had calmed down physically. He tucked the towel round his waist. Then he took his dressing-gown down from the hook on the back of the bathroom door and wrapped it round her damp, exposed body.

"Please, Jeanette, go back to Armand and enjoy your love-making with him."

"Do you hate me? Am I ugly?"

"You know very well that you're extremely pretty and sexy and, if circumstances were different, I would have accepted your invitation without hesitation."

He shepherded her reluctantly towards the bedroom door and opened it. Standing just outside, in the process of raising her hand to knock, was Jackie. Her mouth dropped open at the sight of them both half-dressed. Philip was struck speechless.

Jeanette recovered the most quickly of the three. "Ah – now I understand your reluctance," she said with a grin. She reached up and kissed him on the cheek. "You can collect the robe later, when you are free."

As she scuttled off, Philip was mortified to see that the dressing-gown had slipped off one shoulder and she was displaying a bare nipple.

Jackie was the first to recover the power of speech. "I appear to have interrupted something private."

"No you haven't. In fact I'm pleased you've come."

"Are you suggesting there's a mundane explanation for the two of you being semi-naked together in your bedroom?"

"Certainly I am. You may find it difficult to believe, but Jeanette came uninvited into my bathroom while I was having a soak. She said that she had come to give me a massage. However, when I asked her to leave, she slipped as I was getting out of the bath and got the front of her dress wet."

"Exposing a pair of bare boobs and her pubic hair."

Philip was slightly shocked by Jackie's knowledge of colloquial English and her willingness to use it. "Well, yes – as it happens. That's why I decided to give her my dressing-gown before I sent her back to her room."

She put her hands on her hips. "But this isn't the only similar exhibition which I have seen from you in the last couple of days. Let me tell you, Philip, I don't like members of my team having affairs with other members' wives."

"I can assure you that I am not having an affair with Jeanette."

"Well, she seems to think you are."

"The problem is that she is very flirtatious."

"I would say, Philip, that being found half-naked in a man's bedroom is a very extreme sort of flirting."

He decided that now was the time to eat humble pie. "Yes – I agree. In fact, after this happened, I was going to ask you what action I ought to take to avoid any further incidents like this."

"Hmm." Her expression softened a little. "Perhaps we had better discuss what to do about Jeanette later. I also wanted to talk to you about the things you've found in your trench during the last few days. I think it would be a good idea for us to sit down and have a chat this evening."

"Aren't you going to come in now?"

She looked down at the towel round his waist and shook her head. "I think that might be misconstrued, especially by Jeanette." Now she was smiling. "I think I'll leave you to clear up the mess from your relaxing bath. We'll meet after dinner in that place where we first met by the river – say about nine o'clock?"

"I'll be there."

"I was told that you also wanted to talk to me. Can that wait until then?"

Philip was suddenly suspicious. "What do you mean – I wanted to talk to you?"

"Armand said you wanted to speak to me. That's why I came all the way up to your room." She snorted. "You don't think I'm usually in the habit of snooping on my staff – even if their behaviour *has* slipped below the standards I would normally expect."

"Are you saying that Armand suggested that you came up to my room?"

"That's right." The look on her face made it clear that she was also beginning to wonder about him. "Do you think he was suspicious about his wife's behaviour?"

"Either that," said Philip, "or he deliberately sent you up here because he knew you would be likely to find Jeanette and me in a compromising situation. By the way – she's not his wife."

209

"Who told you that?"

"She did. She said they were just lovers and gave me to understand that he wouldn't object particularly if she went to bed with me."

Jackie's mouth fell open. "They told me they were a married couple taking a walking holiday in the area. What are you suggesting, Philip?"

"I'm not quite sure. Originally I was surprised that Jeanette was so obviously flirting with me in front of Armand, especially as he seemed to take no notice of her behaviour. In fact he actually pushed us together. He was the one, for example, who suggested that Jeanette and I went off together to look for you yesterday morning. Then she needed all that extra help going up the path and she fell into the bramble bush, where you came across us when I was extracting her. That was the start of the physical contact between us."

"Are you trying to suggest you didn't enjoy it?"

He couldn't help grinning. "I think that was the first physical contact I had had with a woman for at least six months. And she's a very sexy woman." He paused. "Yes – in a way I did enjoy it."

"Hmm." Jackie pondered. "I think we may need to re-assess our judgement of that couple. We'll talk about it later. Now, you'd better get some clothes on before you catch cold." She gave him a little wave and turned away.

Philip closed the door behind her and went back into the bathroom, deep in thought.

33

It was another beautiful, mild evening. Philip sat watching the river as it chuckled over the rocks below him and waited for Jackie to arrive. He was looking forward to the evening with pleasant anticipation. He hoped that, by now, she had realised that he had not encouraged Jeanette with her flirting.

Dinner had been a more subdued affair this evening. Jackie had chosen to join them and had sat beside Philip. Although Jeanette sat opposite him, she was now properly dressed in a pink dress with a pretty, frilly neckline which gave a full view of her curvaceous figure. However there was no attempt to "play footsie" with the director watching. Nor did any of them mention the events earlier in the evening in Philip's bathroom.

The conversation flowed satisfactorily about the day's work. Jackie filled them in on progress on the main site which they would be joining the following morning. She revealed that, to appease Armand for being taken away from the paved area, they were to be given a new trench to open on the opposite side of the great hall. She was able to tell them that finds on the main site during the last two days confirmed that the excavations had got down to the Cathar level.

Armand then told her exactly how far they had progressed with clearing the paving. He promised that one more day would get them to at least one exposed edge of the big slabs. Jackie confirmed that they might have a chance of tackling that later.

"We also told that journalist enough to send her away happy," said Philip.

"What journalist?"

"She said you'd told her she could look around and ask questions."

"I did nothing of the sort."

"Really? Well, she gave us her card and said she'd spoken to you. Have you still got her card, Armand?"

The young man fished in his pocket and brought out his wallet. He opened it, extracted a card, and peered at it. "Here we are. She's called César Renoir. This says she's a journalist.

"Let me see." Jackie took it from him and looked at it. "What did she look like?"

"About forty to forty-five," said Philip. "Quite tall, slim and fit, dressed in jeans and a shirt and with a small ruck-sack on her back."

"She was rather masculine and sexless," volunteered Jeanette.

Jacqueline looked a question at Philip, and he grinned. "Well – no make-up, fair hair tied back, well boned face." He nodded. "Yes, I would describe her as handsome."

"And what did she want to know?"

Armand broke in. "She asked us what we were doing and I told her it was just an exploratory trench."

"She asked which part of the castle we were in, didn't she, Armand," said Jeanette. "You told her it was probably a prison."

"And what did she say about that?"

"Oh, she said she thought the floor was too grand for a prison."

"She also asked what the bit of stone walling was infilling a hollow in the rock cliff," said Philip. "I thought she seemed quite observant for a visitor. But I suppose journalists are trained to look for things like that."

Armand shrugged. "She didn't stay long. I don't think she was very interested in what we were doing. I assumed that she went off up to the main site to get some real information. Didn't you see her?"

"No, I didn't. Of course I wasn't there all the time, but neither Gaston nor Jean-Luc mentioned her calling in." She pulled a face. "Normally Gaston especially makes sure that I know about things like that. I must ask him."

Philip shook his head. "That's strange, especially as she said she was writing a book about Cathar strongholds. You wouldn't have thought that she'd miss out on questioning the people on the main site."

212

"Well, I'll ask the others about it." Jackie sighed. "I don't expect it's anything important."

Soon after that Philip excused himself, went up to his room to freshen up and take a leisurely stroll to the meeting-place.

He looked up from watching the river to see Jackie coming towards him. He noticed that she had eschewed her normal blouse and jeans and had chosen a simple wrap-over dress. It seemed to cling to the curves of her shapely figure. She was also wearing more make-up than usual, especially accentuating the brightness of her eyes.

"Been here long?" she asked as she took the seat beside him, sitting quite close this time.

"Not long." He looked at her. "Am I forgiven for the scene with Jeanette?"

She shrugged. "There's no point in making too much of it. But I wanted to knock it on the head before it could go any further. That's why I joined you for dinner this evening. I think little Jeanette now has the picture and she won't trouble you again."

Philip thought about that. "You mean I'm to thank you for getting me off the hook?"

"Something like that." She grinned, taking the sting out of her comment.

"All right then – thank you very much."

"Tell me, Philip, have you thought any more about those two?"

"What, Armand and Jeanette?"

"Yes."

He sighed. "It's difficult to believe that they set out to make Jeanette seduce me. What would they gain by it?"

"If they suspected that you and I were getting on too well together, they might have decided they wanted to separate us."

"But why? We only met a week ago."

"And also," she pointed out, "they deliberately misled me about being married."

"I wonder why they should do that?"

213

"I don't really know. The only thing I can think of, is that by appearing to be a simple young married couple on holiday, they found it easier to become friends with us. You see," she explained, "Andre and I were becoming a bit suspicious of some of the people who were working for us. We were starting to wonder if they were spies from other organisations who wanted to find out what we were doing,"

"Why should they do that?"

"I don't exactly know. Of course it's always important to keep the information about a new television series under wraps until the bosses decide it's the right time to release it. Then there may be organisations who don't want some of the secrets about the Cathars to become public knowledge."

"What organisations are you talking about?"

"Well, the Catholic Church, for a start. They could be afraid that we might find evidence that the Cathar heresy was justified in some way or other. And their actions during the Albigensian Crusade don't appear in a good light."

"Anybody else?"

"I'm not sure. There have been rumours of a shadowy body close to government who may be interested in what's going on."

"Who are they?"

"Nobody knows. There are rumours about links to freemasonry and also to the Templars."

Philip laughed. "The Templars are ancient history. I ought to know. I believe my ancestors had links with the Templars, but they all disappeared long ago."

"Don't you be so sure." She tapped him on the chest. "Yes, they've gone deep under-ground, but they are rumoured to continue their existence in a different, secret form and to be all the stronger and wealthier for the secrecy."

"Good god! You make it sound as if we're being stalked by shadowy organisations waiting to spring on us, as soon as we find something."

She nodded. "Well, that may be the case. Why do you think that journalist woman suddenly turned up this afternoon?"

"Oh, she had a perfectly good explanation for her arrival. I don't see any reason not to believe her, even if she did invent the bit about speaking to you." He raised his head. "By the way, did she go up to the main site when she left us?"

"She did *not* – or if she did, she made sure that no-one saw her. I asked both Jean-Luc and Gaston and also a couple of other helpers whether they saw anybody matching the description you gave me, and nobody had. And I believe Gaston – I'm sure he's straight."

"That's a strange comment. You say you're sure Gaston's straight. Aren't you sure about Jean-Luc?"

"I suppose you think I'm becoming paranoid." She laughed, a little falsely. "You see, it was strange when he was suddenly available when we needed him. He was recruited in Paris, and he has no archaeological record."

"Hmm. You seem to be surrounded by dodgy characters. There's Armand and Jeanette, this journalist woman, Jean-Luc and the dodgiest of them all – me."

That really made her laugh. "You mean I may have put myself in mortal danger, just meeting you here?"

"That's right. Seriously though, you ought to carry out background checks on these guys – me included."

"Oh, I have." She shook her head. "The trouble is, I don't know how much to believe of the information I've received. You yourself saw how Bertrand Dugard more or less confirmed that I was right to be suspicious about Lerenard. And yet the background check on him was excellent. The only one I can believe is you."

"You've checked up on me?"

"Of course. And you came through with flying colours. There seem to be no hidden secrets about you. You're as transparent as," she grinned maliciously "as Jeanette's dress in your bedroom earlier this evening."

Philip had to smile at that. Jackie chuckled with him, and they ended up roaring their heads off with laughter.

"I don't think I'm ever going to live that down," he gasped.

"I should think not. It's not often that you get caught 'in flagrante delicto' by your . . ."

"By my what?"

She had turned delightfully pink. "By – er – by your director of excavations."

They both went silent, occupied by their own thoughts. At last Philip cleared his throat.

"All these dodgy characters make Gaston's comments seem less ridiculous."

"What comments?"

"Well, as you know, he was strongly of the opinion that André Jolyon's death wasn't an accident. Nobody took him seriously at the time – particularly me, who he was accusing of the murder. But *he* saw the body and the site before anybody else. Perhaps, with all these dodgy characters around, he was right, but he'd just chosen the wrong culprit."

"*Mon dieu!*" She put her hand over her mouth and Philip noticed her face had gone white. "André murdered! I thought that idea had been discounted."

"Has there been any news about the autopsy?"

"No. They said two weeks."

"I remember you telling me that it was very out of character for André to have gone up to the castle that night. So it seems possible to me that he could have been banged on the head, carried up to le Bézu, and thrown off the cliff at the top. I don't want to point a finger, but Jean-Luc *could* have done it. He's a big, strong man and I would guess that he's a real hard type under his educated exterior."

"Oh, god! Are you saying that he could have killed Andre in order to take his place? But Bertrand Dugard specifically said that I would be safe with him."

"Well, *you* may be, Jackie. But what about everyone else? Do you remember how shocked the good Abbé was when we told him about André's death? He had to sit down and have a drink of water before he could carry on and talk to us."

"Philip!" She clutched his hand. "This is awful. Do you really think Lerenard could have killed André? How can I continue to work with him with that suspicion at the back of my mind? I must have it out with him. I've got to clear the air before we continue."

216

"Steady on. You can't come straight out and accuse him. You haven't got any positive evidence. And, let's face it, a chap like that isn't going to put up his hands and say, 'All right – I confess'. No, Jackie. You'd be more likely to put *yourself* in danger by confronting him."

"But what else can I do?"

Philip shook his head. "Don't accept my suspicions. They're only theory. If you really believe he may be responsible for André's death, you'd better tell the sergeant. Give him all the details and let him decide what to do. My guess is that he'll just interview the guy and leave any further action until he has some solid evidence." He took a breath. "In any case, I may be barking up the wrong tree. What about Jeanette? Before she targeted me, did she show any interest in André?"

"I don't think so. Of course he made comments about her sexy appearance." She nudged him. "But he didn't get himself into the same problems as you."

"All right!"

"In any case *she's* not going to carry André up to le Bézu and throw him off the top."

"Not on her own perhaps. But she could be part of a team."

"Oh, my god!" Suddenly she burst into tears. Between sobs she said "This – sort of thing – has never – happened to me – before. – Always before – everyone – wanted to help. – We were a team. – Oh, - I do miss André. – He was the one – who dealt – with all these things. – I feel – so alone. – There's nobody – to help - to take away – the pressure –"

34

Philip had his arms round her and hugged her to him. "Here now. Don't take on so. I'm sorry. These are only silly theories of mine. They're probably a load of rubbish."

"No," she gasped. "I *must* take them seriously. But it's never been like this before. It was always fun up until now. If problems came up, André stepped in and solved them." She shook her head. "I'm only just beginning to realise how much I relied on him."

"I must admit I didn't fully understand before how important he was to you."

"Oh, yes. We were a team." She looked up at him. "Only a professional team, mind you. The relationship was never serious on a personal level."

"I only wish I could replace him. But I don't know enough about the business or the people involved to be any help professionally." He smiled. "Besides, I would want the personal relationship to be serious as well."

She was quiet for a moment, looking at him with those wonderful dark blue eyes filled with tears. "Is that an offer?"

"Call it more of an ultimatum."

She smiled, almost coyly. "Then I accept."

And then they were kissing, the salty taste of her tears still encrusting her soft, half-open lips. They continued for a long time, their bodies hugged tightly together, until they became aware of a giggling nearby. Philip looked up and saw two little girls standing about twenty feet away. They couldn't have been much older than five or six. They burst into applause when they saw his slightly embarrassed gaze.

He straightened up and looked at his watch. It was already nearly nine. "You should both be in your beds," he said firmly.

"Quite correct." Jackie emerged from his embrace long enough to give them a brief lecture in French and they both turned and ran off laughing. No doubt they would have a good story to tell their families.

The little interplay had restored their good humour. They still sat arm-in-arm but with smiles on their faces.

"Seriously," said Philip, "I promise to be there for you as long as you need me. I don't know much about archaeology or French society but I will always be willing to give my opinion and whatever support you want when you are dealing with the various people you come across. That's as long as you want me to, of course."

"Thank you, Philip. I think I may need that more than you expect. But what will happen when you go back to England?"

"I won't go until you release me. If you want me to stay for a long time, perhaps you can offer me a job on your staff."

She smiled. "Oh, I think *that* can be arranged all right."

"Now then," he said, suddenly businesslike. "We must decide what we're going to do about tomorrow. I suggest we leave everything as it is for now. But, without making it obvious, I think we should watch Jean-Luc, Armand and Jeanette like hawks. The latter two will be easy because I will be working with them. Now we're to be on the main site, I can also keep an eye on Lerenard during the day-time."

"I'll watch him as well."

"However, I guess the main time when they'll be likely to go off to do their own thing will be in the evenings. It's obviously too late tonight, but in future we need to try and keep some sort of tabs on them out of working hours."

"My!" Her eyes lit up with amusement. "This is my new man of action. I will put myself in your hands, my darling."

"Yes please."

"All right. That's a promise. But first I wanted to talk to you about what you've found down at the bottom of the site."

"I thought you weren't very impressed."

She shook her head. "That's quite wrong. What you've found poses a couple of very big questions. I didn't want to discuss them with you while Armand was around."

"Go on then. I'm listening. Do you know what this paving stuff is?"

"Well, it's not paving for a start. As you pointed out yourself, it's also obviously been installed later than the steps. I believe it's actually a roof – a lid put on top of something to cover it very securely. Then, as soon as it was laid, soil and rubble and vegetation were piled on top of it to disguise its true purpose."

"And what *is* its true purpose?"

"Who knows? We can only guess." She looked at him seriously. "This is really very exciting, Philip. Those slabs must weigh at least a tonne each. It would have taken a lot of men or some special equipment to haul them up to the castle and put them in place. They can't be easily man-handled out of the way. So whoever put them there must have wanted to cover up something very important."

"Of course," he breathed. "Why didn't I think of that? Do you have any idea what is hidden beneath them?"

"Not really. It's obviously something significant and it must be pretty big. We know it isn't your Cathar treasure. That was only a few light-weight bamboo tubes. *They* could have been hidden in a small hole under a single slab and still have been just as inaccessible."

"So we're looking in the wrong place?" he asked, feeling disappointed.

"Not necessarily. Your ancestor chose the most out-of-the-way corner of the castle because he rightly judged it was the last place anybody would come to look for the treasure of the Cathars. It's not unlikely that somebody else later decided on the same location to hide some secret hoard. Let's face it, le Bézu is very remote and off any main route. Because it's so difficult, even to find, it's not likely to be a first port of call for treasure hunters."

"I suppose that's correct."

"I think it is quite possible that somebody else decided the castle was a good place to hide something important. By chance, they may have chosen the same room as your ancestor."

"What damnably bad luck."

"On the other hand, your ancestor was even more careful, because, according to the journal, he found a little secret hiding-place which you wouldn't even guess about if you went into the room. This second group were obviously a much bigger organisation than Phillipe de Saint Claire and his friend. They probably didn't even consider unblocking the little cave which he found. But when they'd put away whatever it was they wanted to hide, they decided to seal the whole area up tight with those colossal stone slabs."

Philip shook his head. "We're not going to move those easily. We'd need to get in heavy lifting equipment. That would mean a special roadway up to the site. Even if we could get permission, that would create a hell of a lot of publicity."

"You're right." She agreed. "The only alternative is to get round the edge of those slabs, which is what Armand wanted to do. I was thinking of letting him do that at the weekend with us helping, but I don't think I can trust him any more."

"I agree. We've got to keep this to ourselves. But it's still going to be quite a big job. I don't think we can do it over a weekend, especially with the chance that one of the other members of the team may wonder what we're doing." Philip took a breath. "I think there's no alternative but to forget about it at the moment, and come back again at the end of the main excavation in the autumn."

She sighed. "It'll be frustrating to have to leave it for so long when we're so close. And in the autumn I will be very busy meeting people when the series is about to start, so I may not be a lot of help to you."

"But surely there will be a window of opportunity between finishing the hard work on the series and the start of the build-up to the television appearances. Whatever happens, we'll have to do it before the world and his wife start traipsing over the site, licking their ice-creams."

She smiled at his description. "I suppose it's possible. I will want a break before all the publicity starts. As for now, I can give Armand some other important jobs to take his mind off the paving. I'll have the scaffolding dismantled and the access path covered over. With a bit of luck that area down there will be forgotten."

"OK." He stood up. "Decision made. Anything else?"

"Nothing to do with the archaeological site."

"It's nearly dark. I think I'd better deliver you back to the hotel. Maybe we could have a drink in the bar before we say goodnight."

She rose and leaned against him. "The bar is a bit public. The concierge is always willing to do odd jobs for me. I can have him deliver a bottle of wine and two glasses to my room."

"Really?" Philip perked up. "In that case, let's make it champagne. Do you like champagne?"

"Two glasses of that and I'll be able to refuse you nothing."

"Are you sure your reputation will stand it?"

"Bugger my reputation. It's your body I want. It seems to be one thing that Jeanette and I share."

"How can I refuse when you put it so delicately."

"There's more than your body at stake." She put her arm round his waist and reached up to kiss him. "Jeanette will be sure to find out that you spent the night in my room. That'll make it absolutely clear to her that you're not available."

They set off to the hotel, walking as quickly as their frequent embraces would let them.

35

Jackie and Philip were awakened by a pounding on the bedroom door.

"What on earth? What's the time?"

Philip looked at his watch. "Nearly seven o'clock."

The pounding was repeated. Through the door they could hear, "Jackie, can I come in?"

"Goodness. I think that's Bernard's voice. What's he doing here at this time of the morning?"

"Jackie," he called, "it's most important that I speak to you. Are you awake?"

"Just a minute. I'll put on some clothes." She climbed out of bed and walked to the wardrobe to get her cream silk dressing-gown. She wrapped it around her and tied the belt as she went to the door, her tousled hair cascading over her shoulders.

"What do you want *me* to do?" Philip asked. "Do you want me to go into the bathroom?"

"Not likely." She looked back at him. "Perhaps you'd better pull the sheet over your private parts."

Obediently he leaned back against the bed-head and covered the lower half of his body.

Jackie unlocked the door and pulled it open. "Come in, Bernard. What are you doing here so early in the morning? You must have left Paris soon after midnight."

He burst into the room. "My dear, I have to speak to you before . . . Oh, my goodness," as he spotted the man in her bed.

"Morning, Bernard," said Philip sardonically.

"Morning, young man." He turned back to Jackie. "My dear, it's vital we have a private talk straight away. Can you throw on some clothes and meet me down in the lounge?"

She closed the door behind him. "That's all right, Bernard. We can talk here. It's much more private than the lounge." She indicated the chair in front of the dressing-table. "You can sit there and I'll sit on the bed with Philip."

"Jackie," said Bernard, "this really is *very* important. It's extremely sensitive and - er –." He nodded towards Philip. "I think you'll want to keep it to yourself, until we've decided exactly how we're going to play it."

"That's all right. Philip won't tell anybody else without my agreement, will you, darling?"

"Of course not."

"But, Jackie-."

"Look, Bernard." Philip noticed the slight frown which had furrowed her forehead and decided that Bernard would be in trouble if he objected much more. "Let me make it clear to you. This man is the direct descendent of Phillipe de Saint Claire, one of the four *perfecti* who escaped from Montségur in 1244. I have checked him out and I know he is telling the truth. You may draw the conclusion that he and I are closely involved and on the same side. Is it clear to you now?"

Her agent looked from one to the other of them and cleared his throat. "Yes," he mumbled. "Yes, perfectly clear."

"So what is this urgent matter you wish to discuss with me?"

"Well, in a word – it's simple really – there's no other way of putting it – not to beat about the bush –."

"Go on, Bernard."

"What? Oh, right. Well - I'm afraid, my dear, there's no way of making it less of a shock. TV France have decided to pull the plug."

"What!"

"That's right. I was telephoned at eleven last night by Alain Gisours himself. Apparently the man had been in meetings all day. He told me I was to get down here hot-foot and tell you that the whole project is off – cancelled lock, stock and barrel – knocked on the head with immediate effect. He said you are not to go back on the site. You are to pay everybody off as of today. Everyone is to leave the site. TV France will send contractors down in the next few days to clear and reinstate the whole area."

Jacqueline collapsed onto the bed. For a moment she said nothing, then, "Have I really heard you right?"

"Absolutely. There will be no television programme produced about le Bézu."

"What about the series?"

"The whole lot is cancelled. They want to talk to you about replacing it with some of the stuff you started five years ago regarding the remaining evidence of the First World War. Alain assured me that you wouldn't lose out as a result of this change of strategy."

"Change of strategy?" She thumped the bed violently close to Philip's foot. "The bloke's been got at. The gutless wimp has rolled over in front of the threat from the Catholic Church or some other influential bunch of characters."

"My dear, we can't possibly know that, and I do beg you not to make any allegations like that which might get back to Alain Gisours."

"I warned him right at the start that there would be parties trying to stop the story getting out. And what did he say? Oh, he told me he wouldn't let anything like that influence him. Now what do I hear? The bugger's been bought."

"Please don't talk like that outside this room, Jackie. It wouldn't do your standing in Paris any good at all."

"I expect that bloody, crawling weed has squirreled away several million in his Swiss bank account from some secret source. He's lost all sense of honour and integrity." She snorted. "My god, am I disappointed in Alain Gisours. I thought he had more guts than that. He said he knew it was going to be tough at times, but he promised me he wouldn't let me down. I believed him, stupid fool that I was. Huh! It's always the same. When the pressure comes on, he's as weak as the rest of them."

"The compensation for cancellation is extremely generous," Cambray hastened to assure her. "Everybody will be well looked after. All expenses up-to-date will be settled, with a reserve to cover unexpected items."

"How much?"

"Pardon?"

"How much are they going to give me for two years' part-time research and three months' full-time work here?"

Bernard's eyes strayed back to Philip. "My dear, do you think . . ."

"Out with it, Bernard. I want Philip to hear how good the wages of corruption can be in this lovely country of ours. How much are they giving me?"

He spluttered a little. "Er – it's one million."

"Euros or pounds?"

"Well, euros of course."

"I want a million pounds sterling in cash."

"Pounds? Why pounds?"

"Just to be bloody awkward! It'll be more difficult to get the banks to cough up the cash. Besides, I may decide to go and live in England after this." She tossed her head. "Oh, you can have your fifteen per cent in euros, if you want. The rest is to be in pounds."

"It won't be necessary for you to pay me anything, my dear. The million is for you alone. I have been separately looked after."

"Of course - they've got to reward their hatchet-man. How much are you getting then, Bernard?"

"My dear." He looked sideways away from her. "That information is private."

"Do you want to continue working for me?"

"You know I do."

"Let's leave it at that, Jackie." Philip was starting to feel sorry for her agent.

"Tell me – how much, Bernard?"

"Hmm. Well, all right, then. I'm getting a quarter of a million."

She exploded. "Bloody hell. That's not much, is it, for acting as their bully boy. I thought you were going to tell me that it was thirty pieces of silver."

"My dear." The man looked crestfallen, his normal bubble of self-importance completely burst. "In no way have I betrayed you to anybody. I wasn't consulted or warned about this decision at any time. When I received the phone call last night I was as shocked and surprised as you are now. I've just been sent down here as the messenger-boy. All the important

226

decisions were taken way above my head." He positively drooped with remorse.

"I'm sorry, Bernard." Jackie forgave him as quickly as she had censured him. "I shouldn't be attacking you. I realise that it's not your personal fault. I was just shocked to hear this awful news so suddenly. And I'm thinking about what will happen to all the members of the team who are really starting to gel together now." She stood up. "Right. That's it for now, Bernard. Now I want to discuss what this means with Philip. I want you to go downstairs and get everyone together to receive the bad news. I'll talk to them at eight o'clock."

"Very well, my dear." He picked up one of the empty champagne glasses from the dressing-table, twizzled it in his fingers and put it down again. "Am I to assume – er – that this new personal relationship . . ."

"You are to assume nothing, Bernard. We haven't discussed it." She shepherded him towards the door. "Now, off you go."

After he left, she closed and locked the door and turned slowly away. With a little cry, she threw herself on to the bed, face down, the hem of her dressing-gown riding up to her bottom and uncovering her legs. She didn't burst into tears. She didn't say anything.

36

After a moment's hesitation, Philip moved to Jackie's side and put an arm across her waist. She lay unmoving and, after a while, he started to massage the muscles of her back gently through the softness of the silk fabric. Slowly she began to relax and moved slightly against him. Still he said nothing and continued the massage.

At last she murmured, "I am lucky to have found you."

"Well, I do a good line in silent sympathy."

"Yes." She turned her head towards him. "That's one thing that André couldn't do at all. He would have been raging against the unfairness of the whole world and it would have been me who had to pacify *him*. At least I feel I can lean on you psychologically."

"You can lean on me any way you like."

"That's comforting."

"Of course, it's easy for me," he admitted. "I haven't been involved in all the work that went into planning this series. I can understand the frustration that you must feel about the research which seems to have been wasted. Can't you talk direct to this Alain Gisours chap and try to get him to change his mind?"

She shook her head. "It would be a waste of time."

"What about the people above him – his directors and shareholders?"

"I don't know who they are. I only know that I wouldn't be allowed anywhere near any of them. And if I tried too hard it would seriously damage the prospects for my future in television. Alain is the one who introduced me to television and has always supported me before. Mind you," she rolled on her side and supported herself on one elbow, "the way I feel at the moment, I don't think I want any prospects."

Philip had his own prospect where her robe had fallen open down the front. He pulled his mind back to attention. "With all

228

the effort you've put into this you could write a book about it. You're well-known. It would almost certainly be a best seller. They couldn't do anything about that."

"But it wouldn't have an ending, Philip. The work here at le Bézu was going to provide us with an ending."

"I don't know about that." He was thoughtful. "If we could find my ancestor's secret cache that would provide a hell of an ending."

"Yes, it would," she agreed. "But how are we going to find that?"

"Well, if everyone is paid off and leaves today, that will leave us with an empty site. I bet it'll be a week at least before this promised contractor appears to reinstate the place. I don't expect they've even appointed anybody yet. We could use that week to have a final search for the treasure."

"Of course we could." She sat up. "You – are - brilliant, Philip Sinclair – do you know that. How did I get through the rest of my life without you?" She hugged her bare front against him. "We could have a whole week here alone together." Suddenly she changed her thoughts. "Philip - make love to me again."

"You'll be late for your meeting."

"So what! They're going to be well paid for waiting. Bernard will have to keep them happy."

Philip didn't need any further urging. He pulled her dressing gown away from her half-naked body and entered her gently.

They were actually only a quarter of an hour late getting down for the meeting. Philip tried to make his entrance behind Jacqueline as unobtrusive as possible, but he guessed everyone knew how their relationship had progressed by now. He particularly noticed Gaston's scowl when he saw him appear.

Jackie was trembling slightly as she faced the crowd of silent faces. But she didn't delay in getting down to business.

"Have you told them the bad news, Bernard?"

"I thought I should leave that to you, my dear."

"Very well. This is it, folks, in a nutshell. Half an hour ago Bernard brought me the shocking news that we are all redundant; out of a job; laid off permanently. TV France has decided to close us down as from today. No reason is given. The whole thing is completely out of our hands." She paused. "Are there any questions?"

In reply to the chorus of "Oh, no's" and "Why's?" she shook her head. "I'm sorry," she said, "I can't give you any logical reason for the decision. The bosses won't talk to me. I think the reason is political – something outside our knowledge. The one thing I *can* say is that I'm sure it has nothing to do with any of you or your quality of work. I have been perfectly happy with all of you. This is the kind of thing I believe big companies do without consultation or explanation, although I must say it is the first time anything like this has happened to me." She glowered at Bernard. "And it will be the last."

He blanched under her gaze.

"So," she continued, "as from today we are all out of work. There will be no need for any of us to return to le Bézu unless we have personal possessions which we wish to pick up. If anyone needs to go back, let me know and I will run you up there in one of the Land Cruisers."

She paused for breath and there was a buzz of conversation, cut off by her next lot of comments.

"I understand all our hotel and bar bills will be paid by the company up to this morning. What is happening about wages, Bernard?"

He brought out a sheaf of five-hundred euro notes from his pocket. "I am authorised to pay everybody a thousand euros per week or part thereof. The two days you have worked this week will be treated as a whole week. I think you will all agree that the company is being generous."

There were a few mutters, a few cheerful acceptances.

"I believe that only Gaston has a formal contract. The rest of you are employed on a short-term, casual basis. Gaston - you will be entitled to the usual benefits of termination of employment for redundancy and, on top of that, I will pay you two thousand cash severance money, which won't appear on your contract documents." He handed the four bank notes over to him. "Now then, Jackie, if you will tell me how much to pay

230

to each person, I will need their receipt signatures on this sheet."

He sat at a table and went through the rigmarole of handing out cash to the helpers. Philip himself received two thousand euros, which he accepted, after a glance and a brief nod from Jackie. Following that, she spoke again. Philip noticed the tension in her which made her voice seem rather high-pitched.

"I just want to say thank you to everybody for what you've done. I appreciate it so much, even though my employers don't seem to. I thought we had the makings of a good team and I'm disappointed . . ." She broke down and turned to Philip who had a handkerchief ready. He saw that she was shaking violently almost as though she was in shock.

Gamely Bernard took over. "As Mademoiselle Blontard's agent, I would echo that and thank you personally for the support you have given her. You can see that she is finding it difficult at the moment to speak to you individually. But, if any one of you wishes to keep in touch with her, they may write to me and I will see that your letter or e-mail will get to her. I will leave a number of my business cards on the table, and you are all welcome to take one."

Philip noticed that most of them did so. There was now a generally sombre atmosphere in the room. Jackie was hanging on to his arm very tightly

"One final thing," said Bernard. "Jacqueline said that your personal accounts with the hotel will be paid up to date which I will do straight away. Of course, anybody who wishes may stay on here after today. However I must point out, that if you do so, it will be at your own expense."

Jackie turned back to face the room. She seemed to have recovered some of her composure. "I believe most of you who live away from here have your own transport. But what about you, Gaston?"

"No." He remained taciturn.

"Do you want a lift somewhere?"

"I would like to go to Toulouse."

"Please can you give him a lift on your way back to Paris, Bernard?"

Bernard spluttered a bit, but in the end he agreed that he could.

"What do we do about the police?" asked Gaston.

"Yes. Thank you for reminding me." Jackie´s face wore a worried frown. "If any of you were interviewed by the police in connection with André's death, and they thought they might want to speak to you again, they will have asked you to let them know before you leave town. So you will have to call in to the police station to tell them where you will be in the next week or two. Is that clear?"

It appeared that it was clear to everybody.

"Well," she gabbled, "I'll thank you again. I'm sure you'll understand that this has been an upsetting experience for me, as I guess it has for you too. I'm going up to my room to wind down a bit. If you have any more questions, I'm sure Bernard will be able to answer them. Goodbye."

She turned and bolted towards the door. As she passed Philip, she murmured, "Please will you come up in five minutes?"

Everybody was silent for a minute or two after she left. Then Bernard filled the vacuum by asking people whether they had any other expenses they wished to claim, and the room was once again filled with chatter.

37

When Philip got up to her room, he found Jackie once more lying face down on the bed. The shock she had received that morning seemed to have stripped away her aura of power and invincibility. She was no longer the famous television personality. She was just a beautiful, upset lady.

He started to massage her back again, trying to relax her and at least make her feel less overwhelmed by her problems. After a while he started to talk to her quietly.

"You mustn't let this defeat you. You're still the star that everybody wants to see on their television sets. All right, so somebody powerful and high up has been able to persuade or bribe TV France to change their mind about the Cathar series and that's very disappointing and frustrating after all the effort and commitment you've put into it. But it's not the end of the world."

"Isn't it?" she mumbled. "How can I get up in front of a set of cameras and talk to the watchers as though nothing has happened?"

"I'm sure you can do it. You're a professional. I bet there are a number of occasions when you haven't been totally happy with the words which have been put in your mouth. And yet you've been able to deliver them with real conviction."

"But that was only detail stuff. It was never like this."

"Perhaps it wasn't." He continued working the muscles of her shoulders. "I agree that this is more serious. But you're big enough to cope with it."

"I just don't want to do it any more."

"I don't believe that, Jackie. In a few days I'm sure you'll be raring to go again. You'll find some new project to get involved in. You'll find that you want to put your full effort – your very substantial effort – into making that project a success." He paused. "I've only known you for a week, but I have already realised what a fantastic talent you have."

She rolled over and looked up at him. "Kiss me, Philip."

So he did. It was a long time before she could draw breath again. "Do you know," she said, "I think you're very good for me."

"Well, you certainly do a lot for me."

She sat up with a sigh. "I feel much better already. I suppose you're going to tell me that I have to go back downstairs again and face all those people I've let down."

"You haven't let them down. You know that and they know that. They understand that it's out of your hands. I tell you what - why don't you have a shower to freshen up first? You'll feel better after that. We just dressed and rushed down to the lounge earlier. We didn't give ourselves a chance. I could do with one as well."

"All right then. I'll be ready in ten minutes."

"I'll pick you up,"

So they got back to the lounge about twenty minutes later. Philip thought Jackie looked devastating and the room burst into a round of applause when she entered.

"I don't deserve that," she said to them. "But Philip has persuaded me that I must put on a brave face and come down to say goodbye to you all."

Philip had the self-assurance to speak up. "But before we do that, does anybody want to go back up to the site to get anything?"

Suddenly it seemed that almost everybody did.

"Well, in that case we'd better take both Land Cruisers. Can Gaston and Armand drive them, please?"

They both said that they'd be pleased to do so.

"You can stay here if you want," Philip said to Jackie.

"No. I've got some sensible trainers in the car."

The trip up to le Bézu almost seemed like a friendly outing now that everybody had got over their shock and a substantial amount of cash was nestling in their pockets. Even Bernard came along to see what they had done on the site. When they got up to the Great Hall area, he was clearly disappointed.

"Not much to show for six weeks' work, is there?"

234

"We were just getting down to the Cathar level," said Gaston. "We had a lot of rubble and vegetation to remove before we got there. Everything had to be carefully sieved and searched."

"Oh, absolutely, old chap," Bernard hastened to assure him. "I know how careful all you archaeologists are not to miss anything."

When they got back to Quillan, Bernard took Jackie aside. "I believe I've settled all the hotel bills and anything else that I know about. Any contractors, such as the scaffolders, can send their invoices straight to TV France, where the orders came from. Now then," he patted her hand, "here's ten thousand for you to keep you going until your big cheque comes through in a week or so. Let me know if you need any more."

"Where does all this cash come from?" asked Philip.

"My dear chap, it comes straight out of the coffers of TV France."

"When did you get it?"

"Oh, I had to call round there before I set off to come here. They opened up especially for me. I can tell you, it was after midnight."

"It seems an awful lot of cash for a TV company to have lying around in their safe."

In reply Bernard just shrugged, before enfolding Jackie in his embrace.

"Keep your pecker up, old girl." He glanced at Philip. "Mind you, you seem to be in good hands. Goodbye. I'll see you soon. Now, where's that chap, Gaston?"

The man was waiting outside. Jackie saw them off. Philip kept out of the way. When she came back in, she announced, "Well, that's all of them gone now. Armand and Jeanette left half an hour ago. All the others had already gone. What about Jean-Luc?"

"He disappeared while the rest of us were up at le Bézu."

"He never even said goodbye."

"He's not exactly a social person," said Philip. "Oh, that reminds me. When you were walking round the ruins, I was in

235

the shed some of the time. If you remember I collected the record books for you. While I was there that journalist woman turned up again."

"I didn't see her."

"Well, I hope you won't mind." He cleared his throat. "She said that she wanted to interview you about progress and what you'd found about the Cathar occupation of the site. I'm afraid I told her that it was all over and that the whole place was being closed down. Did I do wrong?"

She shrugged. "It's not important any more. What did she say to that?"

"Oh, I think she just decided that she was obviously wasting her time and moved off again. I didn't see her after that."

Jackie smiled. "Forget it. So, we're all alone here now, are we?"

"I suppose we'd better check with reception."

When they did so, they were informed by a disappointed concierge that their two bedrooms were now the only two occupied rooms in the hotel.

"Are you going to move in with me?" she asked.

"Yes please." He grinned. "We might as well keep a tight rein on our money, even if we seem to be awash with the stuff at the moment."

"Well, we can at least make sure that we lunch well. I'm hungry and I expect the chef will be willing to get us a late lunch."

Over the meal Philip said to her, "I felt a fraud taking the two thousand euros. I've really only done two days' work."

"Rubbish, you've done more than most. If nothing else, you've kept the director sane." She pulled a face. "Besides, after the way Alain has treated me, I want to take TV France for every euro I can get."

After an excellent lunch they moved Philip's things into her room and took a restful siesta which turned into a love-making session from which they emerged at about six o'clock.

"It's a bit early for dinner," Philip observed.

"I couldn't eat another thing after that lunch. Why don't we just have a drink somewhere and come back here after that."

236

She smiled coquettishly. "I'm sure we could find a way of passing the rest of the evening."

Philip thought she seemed to have recovered well from her shock of the morning. "Well, actually, I've been thinking. This evening would be as good a time as any to go up to the site and do some poking around. I want to find out about this Cathar secret and it's likely to be very quiet up there at the moment."

"Are you sure about this? By the time we've got changed into work clothes and driven up to the castle, it will be nearly seven o'clock – not long before it gets dark."

"That's just the point. There won't be any visitors looking round at that time of day. You see, Jackie, I've been thinking about that bit of masonry walling while you were sleeping. I know it's partly above the new stone slabs. However, if you remember in the journal, the shallow cave where they hid the bamboo tubes was high up in the room. Why do you think they put this new paving over such a large area?"

"You're going to tell me." She was alert now.

"I think it's because the roof of this room, or the floor above it, had already been removed before they used it to store whatever they put there. Or perhaps the floor wasn't very strong and they decided to replace it with the new slabs. Anyway, I think it's possible that the new paving had been laid lower than the old floor and ended up being fixed across the stone rubble walling which my ancestor used to block up the cave."

"It's a possibility. How large was the cave?"

"As far as I remember – in modern measurements it was about two metres long by over a metre and a half high."

"And how big is the bit of stone walling?"

He rubbed his forehead. "Well, the length is about right. You can only see about half a metre of walling above the stone slabs, but I don't know how far down it goes below the slabs."

"Hmm." She looked up at the ceiling, trying to picture the area. "I suppose it's worth a try."

Philip leaned forward persuasively. "And this evening would be a good time to look. If anybody is still interested in what we're doing, they'll be less likely to watch us at night. I noticed

237

there was still a bag of tools in the shed – hammers, small cold chisels and crow-bars. We could use those."

"It might be a bit dodgy if we were stuck up there in the dark."

"Ahah," he said triumphantly, "I have acquired a torch."

She laughed. "You seem to have thought of everything. All right. I agree."

38

Although the evening was advancing, Jackie and Philip got dressed in working clothes – jeans, sweaters and safety boots – and went up to le Bézu in Philip's little car. It was about a quarter past seven by the time they'd picked up the bag of tools from the shed, carefully locking the door behind them, and made their way down to the trench. It obviously hadn't been touched since Armand and Philip were taken away from the area the previous day.

Jackie was worried. "Is it going to take a lot of work to demolish the wall?"

"Hopefully, it won't take long levering with that crow-bar. Luckily we've got better tools than my ancestor had."

However it took more than half an hour to get the first stone out. It had been very firmly hammered in by the people who built the wall. Philip had virtually to smash the stone into pieces to get it out. Finally it was done, and he cleared away the last of the rubble. Then he groaned because he found he was only looking at the face of the natural rock behind the wall, with a cavity only a few centimetres wide.

"Don't worry," said Jackie. "Phillipe de Saint Claire said the cave was quite shallow. It will get deeper as we remove more stone."

He realised she was right. So he concentrated on getting the next stone out, which was a much easier task. Gradually he enlarged the hole down to the paving level, handing her the stones when he pulled them out. As he did so, he found that the cavity was indeed getting deeper. Although they tried to remain calm, the atmosphere was getting more tense.

At last he decided the hole was big enough to get his head in.

"Can you see anything?" she asked.

"It's pitch black in here. Have you got the torch?"

He held out his hand and she gave it to him. He could just make room to squeeze it in beside his head. He switched it on and was momentarily blinded by the glare. However, he moved the torch away from his eyes and pointed it down into the darkness of the expanding cavity. It appeared to be just an empty black hole.

"There's nothing here," he said disappointedly. "This can't be the right place. There must be more than one little cave in this rock wall."

He waggled the torch around, trying to point it right down to the bottom of the void. Then suddenly he thought he saw something.

"Wait a minute. There *is* something here – right down at the bottom. But I can't see what it is."

There wasn't enough room to manoeuvre the torch into a position to light the far extremities of the cavity. Then he had the bright idea of turning the torch up to shine on the rock face so that the reflection would reach the bottom of the hole.

"Yes," he called excitedly, "I can see something. It's not very easy to tell what it is but it looks a bit like some sticks – straight sticks. They're right down at the bottom, close to the wall and partly obscured by stones projecting above them."

"Bamboo tubes would probably look like sticks," she reminded him. "Let me have a go."

He withdrew his head and let her look down, pointing the torch for her to try and give her enough light. After a minute or so, she pulled her head out again.

"I'm not sure," she admitted. "There are so many shadows. But I think there's definitely something there." She looked at him. "But how are we going to reach them? They seem to be an awful long way down."

Philip had been turning this over in his mind. The cavity seemed somewhat deeper than his ancestor had described. It did indeed seem a long way to the bottom.

"Well," he said, "I don't think it's much over a metre down from the top of the paving – perhaps a metre and a quarter. If we clear a decent-sized hole and remove the course of stonework below the edge of the stone slabs, I could lower myself head first into the cavity. You would have to hang on to my legs. Then, with my arms outstretched, I think I might be able to reach whatever it is."

So they set out to enlarge the hole. This took at least a further half hour. By the time they had made it large enough to get the whole of his upper body into the void, it was almost dark.

Jackie pointed this out. "Do you think we ought to give up for tonight and come back tomorrow morning?"

"Not likely. Not now we're this close. We've got the torch to light the path back." He took a breath. "Come on, Jackie. I'm ready to go in now."

Space was restricted in the narrow trench, but Philip lay down on his stomach and eased his way into the enlarged hole. With Jackie hanging on to his legs he was gradually able to wriggle down into the cavity. His progress was made more difficult by the back of one large stone which projected into the void and squeezed his chest. How was he going to get past this?

"Can you pass me the torch?"

He reached back one arm and she put it into the palm of his hand. He noticed she had the foresight to have already switched it on. He manoeuvred it past his body and pointed it down into the hole. Now it was much clearer.

"Yes, it's definitely the tubes. They're wrapped in some kind of material. That's what made them so difficult to see clearly before. The fabric seems to be sticking out in strange shapes but has gone almost transparent with age."

"If you can get hold of the tubes, you can pass them up to me," she called excitedly.

In response he tried to reach down to them, but he knew he wouldn't make it. The big projecting stone meant that the tips of his fingers were still at least a foot from the nearest tube.

"I just can't reach them."

"If you slide down further, I can still hold you."

"The problem is that one of the lower stones is very big. It projects into the cavity such a long way that I can't get my head past it and my arms aren't long enough to reach down to the tubes without getting part of my body past this large stone. I'll

241

have to break it off or knock it out of the way to reach to the bottom."

"That sounds like a long job," said Jackie. "It's almost completely dark now. I don't think we've got any choice but to abandon it for tonight and come back in the morning."

"Let me just have one more try. Then we'll pack it in."

"What are you going to do?"

"Give me the hammer. I think there may be a bit of movement in this big stone. If I can push it out of the way just a little, I may be able to get past it."

Philip transferred the torch to his left hand and reached back with his right. Still sitting on his legs, she put the hammer into it.

He pushed his body to one side to give space to swing the hammer a little. There wasn't room to get much momentum, but he gave the large stone as strong a knock as he could. He put the end of the torch in his mouth and used his left hand to try and wriggle it loose. There was a definite feeling of movement there. He took another swing at it and felt there was a clear loosening of the large stone. One more swing and he might push it out of the way.

He put all his strength into the next violent whack which he gave to it and the stone suddenly went. With a violent rush and rumble, the whole wall gave way below him and cascaded into the void. And with it, before his horrified gaze, the five bamboo tubes lifted on end and fell from his sight. As they went, he dropped the hammer and made a despairing grab at one as it upended and fell, and he triumphantly caught hold of the end of it. But, in the excitement, he opened his mouth to shout about his success. He let go of the end of the torch and it disappeared into the black hole and was immediately extinguished.

242

39

"What happened?" gasped Jackie as the rumble of the falling stones died away and darkness descended on them.

"Oh hell," swore Philip. "The whole wall has collapsed into the void below the slabs. I guess that must be the room which my ancestor was in when he hid the stuff."

"What about the bamboo tubes?"

"All the tubes but one have gone with the wall. I can't see what has happened to them. But I just managed to grab one."

"Can you hand it up to me? Then I'll pull you up."

"OK." With a bit of wriggling he managed to get the length of bamboo, which was swathed in some sort of greased fabric, past his body and Jackie took it.

"Can you help me out now?"

It took several minutes of pushing and heaving to extract his body from its bent position in the hole. At last he was able to stand up and brush some of the earth and dust from his clothes.

Jackie grinned at him. "You look like a scarecrow." She smoothed his tousled hair. "Actually, I think you'd make rather a sexy scarecrow."

"Blow that. I'm afraid I've also dropped the bloody torch. I put it in my mouth so that I could have both my hands free. Then, when the wall caved in and I grabbed at the tube, I let it go."

"Well, that certainly means we can't do any more tonight, without a light. We'll have to come back in the morning to see what we can find." She shrugged. "At least we've got one tube to look at."

Philip felt a new surge of hope after the heart-stopping moment of seeing everything disappear into a black hole from just beyond his reach. "Now we've got the problem of getting out of here carrying that one precious bamboo tube."

"I'll keep it close to my chest and hang on to you."

He looked back at what he could see of the opening in the rock. "Do you think that hole is too obvious?"

"Only if someone comes all the way down here. Who's going to do that tonight?"

"That's right. And we'll be back here first thing in the morning."

So they set off back up the rough track, slipping and stumbling in the dark. It took them a long time to get up to the main site. Jackie was carefully cradling the precious tube in her arms and Philip was trying to support her and prevent her from losing her balance on the rough ground. Yet twice she nearly dropped it and the second time she fell heavily and bruised her shoulder protecting the piece of bamboo.

When they reached the office, she said, "It's no good, Philip. We daren't risk damaging this as we go down the path."

"We're over the worst part now," he pointed out. "There's less risk of dropping it going to the car."

"But it's still rough-going in the dark. I don't think you realise, Philip, that this is a most valuable artefact. We don't know how fragile the contents are after nearly eight hundred years. I couldn't face my professional colleagues if I was responsible for damaging it or causing it to deteriorate in some way."

"What are you going to do with it?"

"I think we should leave it here in the office."

"Huh. We should have thought ahead and brought a padded bag to carry it. We must do that in the morning." He shook his head. "But will it be safe here?"

"The office is locked. I'll put the tube under the desk and pile some papers and equipment on top of it. That should keep it safe till morning. We'll come up here with a bag as soon as we can."

"I want to do that anyway. I've got to be able to let myself down into the void under the slabs to rescue the other tubes. I just hope they've not been seriously damaged. At least the stones went first and, because they're heavier, they should have hit the floor first and the tubes should have landed on top."

244

"I pray they're not smashed." She chuckled humourlessly. "I'm beginning to think of myself as the worst kind of treasure hunter – chasing after artefacts without a thought for what I'm destroying in my search. I've always hated that sort of person."

"Wait a minute, Jackie. We did agree that I probably have first right to these things, although I guess I'd have a problem trying to prove that in a French court of law. And it was me who blundered by knocking that big stone out of the way."

"But Philip, the information contained in these tubes may be vitally important to historical researchers. It's something we owe to posterity."

He put his arm round her. "Of course you're right. We must do everything we can to care for the tubes and their contents."

"The other thing we should do is photograph the cache and the circumstances in which we found the tubes. Even that information might be useful to researchers. We can't do that until the morning."

So they locked the length of bamboo away in the shed, well hidden from any prying eyes. Then they made their way carefully down the path to the car.

It was nearly eleven by the time they made it back to the hotel. They were filthy and exhausted. The place was in darkness but the concierge let them in, with a surprised look at their condition. After a quick shower, they collapsed into bed, too tired even to make love.

40

In fact they weren't able to go back up to the site first thing the next morning because a message was brought to them while they were having breakfast, that Sergeant Leblanc wanted to see them at nine o'clock. They agreed that there wasn't time to go up to le Bézu and return for the meeting. They could only hope that Leblanc didn't want to detain them for too long.

When they arrived at the police station, they were shown straight into the sergeant's office. He was standing at his desk with a grey-haired elderly gentleman.

"This is Maitre Amboisard," he explained. "He is the examining magistrate who is looking into the death of André Jolyon."

"Good morning, mademoiselle," began the old man. "I'm afraid I have to tell you that last night I received a telephone call from Toulouse. An initial inspection of Monsieur Jolyon's body leads the pathologist to the preliminary conclusion that he was struck on the back of the head and rendered unconscious before his body was thrown from the cliffs at le Bézu."

Jacqueline's hand went to her forehead and she reeled to clutch at Philip. He helped her to a chair.

"How can you tell that?" he asked.

The lawyer spared him a brief glance. "Apparently they are able to tell that the impact injuries which killed him when he hit the rocks occurred to an unconscious man." He turned back to Jackie. "Are you all right, mademoiselle?"

The sergeant passed her a glass of water, and she took a gulp before answering.

"Yes, thank you. It was just a bit of a shock, hearing it suddenly like that."

"Well. This means," continued Amboisard, "that I am now investigating a probable murder. You realise I must take this very seriously."

"Do you have any suspects?"

"Everyone who had an opportunity is a suspect until I can clear their name." He inclined his head towards the young Englishman. "You must understand that allegations have been made which makes you one of the possible suspects."

"Wait a minute," said Philip, "I realise that I was named by Gaston as a possible murderer, but have you considered how the murder was carried out? To make André unconscious and carry him up to the cliffs would either need at least two men or one very strong one."

Jackie was on her feet, suddenly recovered from the shock. "And Philip couldn't possibly have done that. Who would have helped him? He came to France on his own only the day before André was killed. Philip knew nobody here before he arrived. Are you suggesting that I fell instantly in love with him and helped him bump off my long-serving assistant?"

"No! No, mademoiselle." The Maitre held out his hand in a placatory gesture. "I am accusing nobody at this moment. I am just pointing out that everybody has to be investigated and cleared. That includes all the people who Sergeant Leblanc spoke to last week."

"Well," she said, "I had Philip checked out as soon as he arrived, before I offered him a job. I will let you have a copy of that report."

"Thank you very much. That will be helpful."

She raised a finger. "And I have a suspect who could have done it and who Sergeant Leblanc hasn't interviewed. The man who replaced Jolyon just suddenly appeared out of the woodwork the day after André's death. He's big. He's very strong, and I suspect that he has killed other men before."

"Really?" Amboisard looked startled. "Who is this man?"

"He is called Lerenard - Jean-Luc Lerenard. He could easily have done it, couldn't he, Philip?"

"Well. he's certainly a big, strong guy."

She jabbed her finger at the magistrate. "The man you need to question about him is Alain Gisours, the Chief Executive at TV France in Paris. Ask him where he conjured up this guy from later the same day that André was killed. We thought it was very suspicious at the time."

247

The magistrate's eyebrows had risen almost to his hairline. He opened his mouth to speak, but Jacqueline forestalled him.

"And then he went and disappeared yesterday without even saying goodbye."

"Disappeared?"

"That's right. TV France have closed down the excavation. Everybody seemed very upset about it. We all went up to the site yesterday morning to collect our things and say goodbye – everybody except Lerenard, who sloped off while we were gone."

"Do you know where this man Lerenard is?"

"No. But I know where you might be able to get directions to find him. Try the Bishop's Palace in Narbonne. Apparently, they recommended him to my old friend Bertrand Dugard. He worked with Bertrand at Prouille for a few weeks before he came to work for me."

"At Prouille? The monastery near Fanjeaux?"

"That's right. Well," she continued, her face betraying her anger. "Bertrand was instructed to take him on and train him by Narbonne. He told me this himself. And one thing you can be sure of is that the Abbé Dugard does not lie."

"Oh! – TV France – Bishop's Palace – all the others." The Maitre held his hand to his forehead. "I have a lot to do. Will you be rushing off somewhere before the weekend, mademoiselle?"

"No. We're staying here for a few days."

"You will give Sergeant Leblanc an address where you can be contacted before you leave?"

"Certainly I will. We both will."

After that he let them go without any further questions or instructions. Philip had been afraid that he might restrict them to the town of Quillan or tell them not to go back to the scene of the crime, but the thought didn't seem to occur to him. He obviously had too many other problems on his mind.

As they walked back to the hotel, Jackie had the grace to chuckle. "That should put a spoke in bloody Alain Gisours' wheel – and the Bishop's Palace at Narbonne."

248

"It has also given Maitre Amboisard a lot to think about. I was afraid he was going to tell us that le Bézu was out of bounds. We'd better get up there as soon as possible to recover those tubes."

"We'll have a coffee and go straight up there."

"First I must get a replacement torch."

She pointed an admonitory finger. "Two torches."

"Right you are," he grinned. "Two torches it is."

41

Alain Hébert insisted on going up to le Bézu in the morning.

César had told him about her visit to the site the previous day and her brief conversation with Philip.

"The Englishman told me, 'The plug had been pulled on the whole operation'. If I understood his English correctly, it meant the site was being closed down immediately. He said the archaeologists were up there collecting their personal possessions and they were all setting off back to Paris later in the day."

"How incredible," breathed Alain. "I wonder what brought that about?"

"Perhaps the police have at last woken up about the accident to the young man and have decided to close the site."

"Perhaps." He put his head on one side. "You don't think this Englishman was selling you a line?"

"Not in the least. I checked at the hotel in Quillan, and the concierge was very gloomy. He said all his rooms except one had been cancelled."

"So who's still there?"

"Ah." She grinned. "Apparently there's a love affair going on between the Blontard woman and the young Englishman. He's moved into her room. I don't think they'll be worrying about digging holes at le Bézu for the next few days."

Hébert was more cautious. "Maybe. But it seems a bit odd to me that those two should be getting on so well. I think we ought to keep an eye on them." He paused. "I also want to go up to the chateau and see what sort of a state they've left the place in."

So, immediately after breakfast, they set out for le Bézu in his car. They parked it in the empty parking area at the foot of the now well-trodden path up to the castle and climbed up to the site.

It was clear that the place was deserted. The roped-off areas with their warning signs had been left as they were before. But every tool and piece of equipment had been cleared away. Any areas which had obviously been worked on had been levelled off to avoid causing an obstruction. The shed was shut and locked. A peep through the window showed an empty desk and shelves. All the diaries, record books and plans had been taken away. It was so different from two days before.

"It's the lower site that I really want to see," said Alain. "I want to check that it's in the same state as it was when you saw it on Tuesday afternoon."

They scrambled down the rough path and steps to the bottom trench, cursing the brambles that tore at their clothes. The only things which seemed to be different were that the finds table and equipment and the scaffolding had been removed. Only the trench and a large heap of rubble and vegetation remained. At first sight there seemed to be no changes from Cesar's earlier visit.

"It doesn't seem to be any different to Tuesday," she said. "This appears to have simply been abandoned like the other areas."

Alain jumped down into the trench, landing on the solid paving slabs. He started walking along the trench, peering closely at the surface.

"No, it hasn't," he shouted. "There are tools down here. Come and take a look."

César got down into the trench and joined him. He was looking down at a small canvas bag lying at one side. It appeared to contain some mason's stone-working tools, and a short crow-bar lay nearby.

"What is this hole in the rock just above the paving?" he demanded.

She bent down to look. "I think that's where there was a low stone wall blocking off a damp hollow in the rock. I told you about it when I described the work they were doing."

"You mean that somebody's removed the wall since you were last here?"

251

"Yes, they have. That's puzzling because they seemed to be ignoring it before. And they said they were going to abandon this area."

Alain went down on his hands and knees and peered into the hole. "The whole of the wall which must have blocked off this hollow has been removed. That provides a way of getting round these slabs into the space below." He looked up at her with a horrified expression. "This is absolutely disastrous. This little cave must be blocked up straight away."

"Why? What's the problem?"

"The problem is this." He got up and pointed to the hole. "We must cover it up. Nobody must be able to see it looking like this."

"Do you think anybody's going to come down here and see it?"

"We daren't risk it. In any case I have a nasty feeling that Blontard and the Englishman have had something to do with this. I think they'll be back. And I want to prevent them from going down the hole at all costs."

"But Alain, we can't do anything to block it up now. We haven't got any materials. Of course we can drag some bushes and undergrowth across the trench to disguise the hole. But it won't take anybody who knows about it very long to remove them again. And it will also tell them that somebody's found out about it and wants to hide it."

"Hmm." He spent a few minutes ruminating. "We've certainly got to get this area filled in and that hole blocked up once and for all. I think we're going to have to bring the Force in to do that." He took a breath. "César, I want you to go back and contact them. Tell them to send some men and tools down here to move the earth back into the trench." He paused as he thought about it. "How long do you think they'll take to get here?"

"Well, you've probably got a better idea than I have. I guess it's about six hours' driving. But it'll take a further couple of hours to get the men together. How many do you think you're going to need?"

252

"At least four. And, as well as digging equipment, they'll need the stuff for cutting bushes and undergrowth. In addition, I'll want about four long planks to put across the hole to stop the earth falling down it when they fill the trench."

"It sounds as though they're going to need a large van to carry everything. That'll slow them down some more. I can't see them getting here much before nightfall."

Hébert pondered. "That's all right. I think that tonight might be the best time to do it. It would be wisest to do this work at night when we're unlikely to have visitors turning up to ask awkward questions." He wagged a finger at her. "That means we'll also need flashlights and screening to put up round the work area to make sure nobody reports seeing funny lights up here in the middle of the night."

"Careful. It's starting to sound complicated."

"I'm afraid it is," he admitted. "You'd better tell Montluçon to make sure he sends people who are capable of working quietly at night." He stopped for a minute, then suddenly clapped his hands. "Because I've decided to change the plan."

"What do you mean?"

"I think the time has come to act. I think we have to get the stuff out tonight. It means that altogether they'll need to send four three-tonne vans, including the one with the digging tools. Tell him the one with the men and the digging tools is to come here. He's to make sure that the other three are told to wait in three different locations so as not to alert the police. They must each have at least two mobile telephones that we know the numbers of, so that they can be called to the parking bay in sequence. We'll divert the diggers to clearing the path up to the outside door. Once the place is cleared out, it won't matter about filling in this trench. Is that all clear to you?"

She took a breath. "Yes. I think I've got all that."

"Tell him to make sure the group in each van has a competent leader with a detailed map of the area and a set of instructions telling them how to find the place. We don't want anyone getting lost and trundling round these mountain roads for hours. He'll need a back-up fast car to deal with any emergencies."

"You don't need to worry about that," she said. "They've been ready for this for weeks. Whatever else he may be, you can trust Montluçon to organise this sort of thing. He's done it enough times under my father's orders."

"OK. Well, you'd better be off, my dear. Here are the car keys." He handed them to her.

"What are you going to do?"

"I shall stay here and keep watch. We can't risk anyone turning up and finding this place in the state it's in at present."

"What will you do if somebody *does* turn up?"

"I'll have to play it by ear. I'll keep myself well hidden. If they just turn up, look round and go again, then no harm will have been done. It's if they try to go down the hole that I'll have to do something about it."

"But you haven't got any weapons."

He gave her a lop-sided grin. "I'll have to rely on my ability to talk them out of it."

"Best of luck." She sighed. "Well, I'm off." She pecked him on the cheek and turned away.

"Come back here as soon as you can to let me know what arrangements you have made with Montluçon. Oh, and can you bring some food and water with you when you return? Our watch may be a long one."

"Of course I will. See you soon."

With a half-wave she set off up the path.

42

When Jackie and Philip got to le Bézu they were surprised to see a little car parked in their usual place.

"Looks like we've got visitors," said Philip. "Let's hope they're not staying long."

Jackie was less casual about it. "Do you recognise the car?"

"I don't think I've ever seen it before."

"I've got a feeling I might have seen it here recently. And if it's just casual visitors, they're the first to visit this site in more than a month."

"What are you saying?"

She pulled a face. "I think it's too much of a coincidence to find visitors coming to the site just after the excavation has been closed down. I want us to go very carefully and see just who they are and what they're doing."

"What do we do with *our* car?"

"Drive on for another four hundred metres and pull in to the farmyard. That's the end of the track."

"Won't the farmer object?"

"It's not a working farm. They only usually come at weekends. I made my peace with them when we first started on the site."

They parked the car out of sight and Philip got the padded duffle bag out of the boot. Then they walked back down the track towards the site notice board. As they neared the path up to the castle, they heard a scrambling noise.

"There's somebody coming," she whispered. "Get into the hedge."

They heard the sound of a person pass along the path just above them, breathing heavily and obviously in a hurry. Philip peered after her.

"I think it's that journalist woman."

"César Renoir?"

The woman unlocked the car, jumped in and started the engine. She did a quick three-point turn with plenty of wheel-spin and sped off down the track.

"Blimey. She's in a bit of a hurry,"

"I don't like this," said Jackie. "I think we'd better get up to the site fast."

They started up the path at the best speed they could make over the steep, rough terrain. Jackie was moving quickly and Philip had to hurry to keep up with her.

"I wonder why that journalist should be in such a rush."

"I must say that I've been beginning to wonder about her nosing around," said Jackie, puffing a little from her energetic activity. "It seems odd that she's turned up to watch us several times since we started digging that trench down at the bottom of the site. I'd like to know who she's working for."

"Whoever it is, she obviously thinks she's found out something that they will urgently want to know."

"And we can guess what it is. Time is running out, Philip. We've got to climb down into that area under the paving slabs and get those other bamboo tubes out."

He took a deep breath to calm his pounding pulse. "OK. I'll go straight down there as soon as we get to the site."

"Have you worked out how you're going to get down through the hole? And, what's more, how you're going to get out again with the tubes?"

"I noticed there's still a coil of the safety rope left behind in the shed. I'll cut a length off that, drop it down the hole, and let myself down feet first. There should be plenty of room to get through now that the wall has collapsed."

"Please be very careful not to tread on any of the bamboo tubes when you land at the bottom. I don't want them to be damaged any more than they may be already."

"You could help me to see my way by pointing the torch down beside me to light up the floor where I'm landing. Then I can be careful to avoid treading on anything lying around."

"Also," she reminded him, "you must take the camera. We need to have flash photos of the cavern, taken from above and below and of the pile of rubble, hopefully with the tubes on top of the stones. While you're down there you could also take some shots of the room. Who knows, they may be useful later."

They soon reached the top of the site and, without pausing for breath, went straight to the office and unlocked the door. Jackie hastily checked that the first tube was where she had hidden it, while Philip got himself a decent length of rope.

"We'll pick this tube up on our return," she decided.

They locked the door and Philip led the way down the path. When he reached the trench he looked round quickly, but everything seemed to be as they had left it the previous night. The small bag of tools was still there and the short crow-bar lay where he had abandoned it in the dark. Of course the hammer was somewhere in the void below.

He set down the duffle bag, filled with its protective padding, and uncoiled the rope. He soon found a suitable trunk of a large bush to tie it to. There was enough rope to have a double length for safety. He then trailed the ends down the hole and straightened up, preparing to lower himself into the void.

"What on earth are you doing?" A man he vaguely recognised was standing on the bank of soil above the trench.

Jackie spun round. "Er –hello. Why, you're the man we discovered in the office the other day. It's Alain Hébert, isn't it?"

"Quite right. What are you doing here?"

"Er. We're carrying out archaeological investigations. What else?"

"I heard the site had been closed down."

"Where did you hear that?"

He waved a hand vaguely. "Oh, the news gets around."

"You wouldn't have heard it from a certain journalist by any chance?" She looked at him suspiciously. "Would your informant have been a Mademoiselle César Renoir who we saw leaving the site a quarter of an hour ago?"

"Maybe. But you haven't answered *my* question. What are you doing?"

"I don't know that it's any business of yours," she replied. "But, as I explained to you before, we're looking for Cathar remains. That's what we have a licence to do."

"You mean you're not looking for treasure?"

Jacqueline drew herself up to her full height. "What we are hoping to recover has no monetary worth but is more valuable to science. It is original material."

"You're doing this even though the site has been closed down?"

"The licence is still in existence. Only the funding has been withdrawn."

"Why was the site closed?"

She shrugged expressively. "The powers that be at TV France have been got at. Somebody was afraid we were finding out too much truth about the Cathars – information they didn't want to become public."

"What information is that?"

"That's exactly what we intend to find out in the next few hours."

"Are you going down into that room under the paving?"

"Philip is."

"He can't do that."

"Why not?"

"Well – he . . . He doesn't know what's there."

"Yes I do," said Philip, "because I caused it. There's a heap of stones and rubble and four precious lengths of bamboo. That's what I intend to pass up to Jackie. I just hope they're not damaged."

"Is that all?"

"That's all we're interested in. It's the whole purpose of our exploration."

"Those bamboo tubes are of Cathar origin," said Jacqueline coldly. "That's what my licence permits me to remove from the site."

"What about TV France?"

"I told you - they were providing the money. *I* have the licence."

"So what about you?" asked Philip. "Are you something to do with TV France?"

Hébert laughed. "Nothing at all."

"So – who *are* you?" Jacqueline was suspicious. "What are you doing here?"

He looked at her with his head slightly on one side. "Let's just say that I have a watching brief to ensure that you keep within the terms of your licence."

"From the Department of Ancient Monuments?"

"If you like to call it that."

She squared up to him. "Well, in that case you will know that I have a perfect right to remove those bamboo tubes. I will even give you a receipt, if you wish."

"That won't be necessary. It will be sufficient for me to look in that bag before you remove it from site."

There was a pause while they confronted each other like a pair of pugilists at the weigh-in. At last she turned to her partner.

"All right, Philip. You can go on down. Make sure that we take away nothing except the bamboo tubes. Remember to take photos showing their location."

"Very well. Can you use your torch to light my way down? I'll sling mine round my neck."

He took one out of the bag and handed it to her. Then he cut a short length of rope, threaded it through the steel loop on the end of his torch and tied it round his neck, leaving the torch to hang down on his chest.

"When I get down," he said to her, "you can pull up one of the lengths of rope and tie on the duffle bag and lower it down to me."

"Do you want me to help?" asked Hébert.

"No thank you," she said firmly. "I want you to remain on the bank where you are. I shall feel safer like that."

The man smiled but said nothing, remaining at his distance.

Philip took the two lengths of rope together and tied the ends round his waist. He then backed towards the rock-face. He started the descent by bending down and taking the weight on his hands at the edge of the paving slabs and lowering his legs into the hole. At a certain point he had to transfer the load onto the ropes and the result was some scuffed knuckles. Jackie helped him until his head disappeared, with his feet hanging in space.

"Can you give me some light?"

She switched on her torch and pointed it down into the void beside him. "Can you see anything?"

"Not yet." He continued lowering himself. "Yes I can. The hole isn't very deep – not much more than head-height. And there's only a narrow gap about half a metre wide between the rock-face and what looks like a rough timber wall."

"What was that?" asked Hébert.

She repeated Philip's comments for him.

"Can you see the tubes?" she asked.

He switched on his torch. "I can see one on top of the heap of rubble. I can't see the rest. Oh, yes – there they are against the wood wall – two of them."

"Don't stand on them please."

"I won't. There's enough room to avoid them. In fact I'm standing on the rubble now. I'll untie the ropes from my waist, and you can pull one up so that you can tie the handles of the duffle bag to it."

"Remember to take the photos."

"I'll do that now." Having released himself from the ropes, he made his way across the uneven heap of rubble to one side. Then he removed the camera from his pocket and took a number of shots of all the things he could see in the confined space.

As he did so, the padded bag landed on top of the stones. He abandoned photography to collect the three bamboo tubes that he could see, and he carefully packed them into the bag, pulling the padding round them to protect them.

"How are you getting on?" came floating down the hole from above.

"I've found three of the tubes and put them in the bag with the padding round them. The fourth one must have bounced further away. I'm just going to look for it."

With a certain amount of difficulty, Philip climbed over the heap and carefully worked his way along the narrowing corridor between the rock-face and the timber wall, probing his way with the torch. Within a metre there was a narrow break in the timber wall and here a big stone had hit the corner and smashed away a lump of wood. It was at that moment that Philip realised he was looking at the back of a couple of large wooden boxes which were almost as high as the room.

He pulled off a piece of broken timber and shone the torch into the hole which it left. What he saw took his breath away. In the torchlight there was the unmistakeable gleam of gold shining back at him. He swivelled the torch and peered as far as he could in all directions. Wherever he looked he could see golden shapes, although it was impossible to make out exactly what they were from his restricted viewpoint.

With a rising sense of excitement, he eased his way into the gap between the two boxes which could not have been much more than twenty centimetres wide. He could just squeeze his body through. In less than a metre his head came out into a larger space. When he raised his torch and shone it round, he realised he had reached the centre of the room. Here were stone columns and beams supporting the large stone slabs forming the roof which they had started to uncover earlier in the week.

Round all four walls stood a range of magnificent hardwood chests, each one with panelled full height doors with brass hinges, clasps and locks which glowed in the torchlight. In the central area stood a number of splendid brass-bound chests about a metre high with only narrow spaces to walk between them. Whatever was in these wonderful containers, somebody had obviously spent a lot of money and put a huge amount of work into storing the artefacts.

"What are you doing down there?" Jackie's anxious voice echoed down to him.

"I'm searching for the last tube," he shouted up to her.

Philip realised he couldn't stay here any longer without raising suspicions in the man watching them up on the surface. So he pointed the camera round the room and took several photos. Then he eased his way back between the chests into the passageway behind. Through the hole in the broken chest, he took a couple of shots of the golden contents. Then he turned away to start searching the narrowing gap in front of the rock wall with the torch.

There it was, right in the corner where it had bounced. He had to go down on his hands and knees and twist his body sideways to reach for the length of bamboo.

"I've got it," he shouted triumphantly, extracting himself carefully from the tight space and returning the tube to the padded bag.

"I'm afraid it's a bit damaged at one end," he called up as he packed it carefully into the duffle bag. "It must have bounced on its end and shot off into the corner."

"Has anything come out?"

"No. It's not that badly damaged." Philip straightened up from closing the zip. "OK. You can pull it up now."

He watched the bag disappear through the hole. Soon after, the rope was lowered again, and he tied them both round his waist again.

"Right. I'm coming up now."

Philip switched off the torch and started to climb out of the underground room. Now he knew where everything was, he was able to get additional support from pushing with his feet against the back of the heavy chests and the sloping back wall of the cave. Soon his head was above the slab and Jackie was able to grab his jacket and help him up. After a bit of frantic scrabbling with his feet, he was lying on his chest on the stone.

"Phew." He got to his feet. "Have you looked at the damaged tube?"

"Yes. I think it's only the end of the bamboo that's been split. The sealed fabric around the bamboo hasn't been torn. I hope the contents are undamaged."

"OK then. Let's get it back to the hotel and we can take a look at what's inside." He untied the rope from round his waist and began to coil it up. He wanted to tell Jackie about his discoveries in the room below but he had no intention of saying anything in front of Hébert.

The old fellow had approached. "Have you got them all?"

"Yes."

"What's it like down there?"

"It's very tight. The space between the rock-face and the timber wall is just about wide enough for me to get my shoulders through, but it narrows down towards the far end." Philip pointed. "The last tube had bounced right down there so I had to twist on my side to reach it."

"Can I see them?"

Jackie opened the duffle bag and he peered in.

"Not much to see, is there?"

"We hope they contain the secrets of the Cathar faith. History has failed to provide any details about their beliefs, except that the Catholic Church considered them to be heretical without really explaining why."

"I'm not into research into strange religions." Hébert raised his hands. "All right. I'm satisfied that you are only taking away what your licence entitles you to."

That seemed to be the end of his involvement. With a brief wave he turned and disappeared up the path.

"Well, what did you make of that?" asked Jackie.

"I don't know."

She pulled a face. "I've never heard of the Department of Ancient Monuments having inspectors before. I think it's more likely that he was sent to check up on us by some other body. And what about this journalist woman? They must have met up here. But, most importantly, why didn't he object to our taking the bamboo tubes away?"

"Perhaps because he couldn't have done anything to stop us on his own. Perhaps his job is just to observe us and report back, which," he pointed out, "he's done pretty well."

"All I can tell you is that I'm going to keep these tubes very safe." She shrugged. "Well, there's nothing more we can do here. Let's pick up the other one and get back to Quillan."

Philip put the crow-bar back in the tool bag and pushed it into the side of the trench. "We may need that later." He spoke quietly. "There's been a development I didn't want to mention in front of Hébert."

"What's that?"

"I'll tell you when we get back to the car. I don't want any flapping ears to hear it round here." He put the coil of rope over his shoulder, picked up the duffle bag and set off up the path.

43

They left the rope in the shed, transferred the other tube to the duffle bag and returned to the road. When they reached the car, carefully carrying their precious burden of five bamboo tubes, Philip unlocked the vehicle and placed the duffle bag on the back seat. They got in and shut all the doors and locked them from inside. Then he started the engine and set off down the track, driving gently.

"What's this mystery development you were talking about?" demanded Jackie.

"Ahah. When I was in the underground room, I discovered that the timber wall that I was telling you about wasn't a wall at all. It was actually the backs of several large packing chests pushed together. They were nearly as high as the room itself."

He paused for a response but she said nothing.

"I found a gap between two of the chests," he continued, "which was just wide enough to allow me to squeeze through into the middle of the room. Once there I found that the whole of the room was packed full of magnificent brass-bound chests. There must have been at least twenty of them."

"Were they locked?"

"Well, it was just at that time that you started calling down from above, asking where I was. So I didn't stay long enough to check. But I noticed that most of them seemed to have padlocks on the doors."

"How intriguing."

"More than that. I found that a large stone from the collapsing wall had crashed into the bottom back corner of one of the chests and had broken away some of the timber on the back. Now – are you ready for this? When I shone the torch into the interior of the chest, I couldn't see a lot. But what I could see looked like gold."

She put her head on one side and looked at him. "Gold what?"

"I couldn't really tell – gold furniture, gold items of equipment, gold funerary goods – something like that. I poked the camera into the hole and took a couple of photos . Perhaps we'll be able to make out some more when we inspect them."

She was quiet for a while before she asked, "So what do you make of that?"

"The evidence points to it being some sort of collection of valuable artefacts. Somebody has obviously spent a lot of time and effort and money having those chests made and then storing them away. The quality of the workmanship is impressive. I think it may be the storehouse for the wealth of some organisation."

"What organisation?"

"I don't know." He concentrated on steering through the little village of St Just. "Perhaps it's the fabled treasure of the Cathars."

She shook her head. "That's not likely. The Cathars didn't have the time or the manpower to create a proper store for their treasure. Besides, it must have been made after the bamboo tubes were hidden, which would be too late for the Cathars."

"What about the Templars? Didn't I hear you say that there are legends about the Templars hiding their wealth in this area?"

"Well, it's normally dismissed as pure fiction. But, yes. That's a possibility."

"The other thing," he pointed out, "did you notice that Monsieur Hébert asked if we were looking for treasure? I wonder if he was actually interested in the treasure, and that's why he had no objection to our removing the tubes. If he thought we had finished searching when we recovered the five pieces of bamboo, he would have been happy to see us go away with them. Did you notice whether he seemed to be relieved at our going?"

"If he was, he was careful not to show it. On the other hand, I must admit I was expecting more of an argument from him about us taking them."

Their conjecture continued all the way back to Quillan, until they parked the car and walked to the hotel, carefully carrying the duffle bag.

When they arrived at reception, Jackie said," I've been thinking about what to do with the tubes. I think we ought to put them in the hotel safe, if they can fit them in. That ought to keep them secure. I thought we would take the broken one up to the bedroom and open it at the damaged end after lunch. We can see what it contains and, based on that information, decide what to do about the other four. Are you happy with that?"

"I think it's a very good idea." He rang the bell for the concierge.

"Henri," began Jackie, "we have some pieces of bamboo which we want to keep in a secure place." She produced one from the bag, "Will these fit in the hotel safe?"

"I will try, mademoiselle."

He returned a minute later. "There is no problem."

"Thank you, Henri. Can you put these four pieces in? Please handle them very carefully because they're extremely precious." She smiled persuasively. "Oh, and Henri, it is most important that they are kept safe and only handed back to me or Monsieur Sinclair here."

"Certainly, mademoiselle." He nodded at Philip with his usual disapproving expression. It seemed he did not favour the idea of the young Englishman sweeping their beautiful French TV star off her feet.

Over lunch, Philip showed Jackie the photos he had taken. She was especially interested in the ones showing the interior of the room.

"Look at the columns and beams," she pointed out. "They are single pieces of stone. The material is granite because only granite is strong enough to carry the weight of the stone slabs forming the roof. The nearest granite quarries are two hundred kilometres away in the Massif Central. It must have been a major operation to build that room in such an out-of-the-way location."

"And look at the chests. The panelled doors are superb."

"They certainly are. I've seen less imposing ones in the Rue St Germain. And Philip," she peered more closely, "isn't that the entrance to the room, in the corner? There would have to be a proper entrance. The people who built the place wouldn't have got in by the method you used."

"Let me have a look." He inspected the little screen carefully. "I think you may be right. I didn't notice it when I was there because I suppose I was overwhelmed by all the other stuff. But I agree that looks like a corridor coming into the room. As you say, the entrance would have had to be big enough to get the contents into the room."

He clicked on a couple of further shots. "Here you are. Here are the ones taken when I was looking into the inside of the chest. I'm sure that's gold. There seems to be some carving on some of the pieces, but you can't see exactly what they are."

He handed the camera back to her to study.

After a while she said, "Yes. I think one of these items might be a tall candlestick like the ones they have beside the altar in churches. But I can't make out any other items from the small amount I can see of them."

"I reckon, with a hammer and that small crow-bar, I could have the back off that damaged chest in half an hour."

She looked at him, unsmiling. "You daren't do that, Philip. If nobody can prove legal ownership of that hoard, it becomes the property of the French Government. There are serious penalties for removing valuable articles to which you're not entitled, quite apart from the dreadful publicity which I'd get if you were charged."

"I'm not talking about removing them. I just want to expose them enough to know what they are. Then we can report the find to the police and hand the site over to them. Surely that's not illegal."

"No. I agree *that* isn't, as long as you can make it clear that you didn't take anything away. In fact you'd probably be entitled to a handsome reward. I think it's something like ten percent of the value."

"There you are then. Let's go back, expose a bit more, take plenty of photos. Then report it and claim the reward. I wouldn't say no to ten percent of a few million."

Jackie didn't respond. She had clicked back to the earlier photos of the room. She looked up. "As you say, Philip, someone has spent a lot of money in building that store. I wonder how long ago it was built."

"How could you find out?"

"Only by looking at the contents, I would guess."

"Well, if we report finding the treasure and the police take over protection of it, you could probably get permission, as an archaeologist, to lead the team investigating the finds."

"Mmm." An anticipatory gleam had come into her beautiful eyes. Then she shook her head. "Let's concentrate first on the job in hand – that bamboo tube. If you've finished lunch, we can go upstairs and start opening the tube."

44

When they returned to Jackie's room, she took the damaged bamboo tube out of the bag. She folded back the bedspread and laid the stick-like object on the pristine white sheet.

"I'm glad they changed the sheets today. Do you have your penknife?"

When he produced it she instructed him, "First take a photo of the tube as it is, looking at the broken end."

Next she carefully cut through the fabric surrounding the damage and folded back the bit covering the open end. She bent back and cut off three short pieces of bamboo which had been split off by the impact. Philip was then instructed to take another photo.

She lifted up the tube and peered into it. "There seems to be a coil of fabric in there. I think I can reach it with my fingers."

She laid the tube back on the bedspread and went to the dressing-table and opened a drawer. From it she took two clean pairs of fine fabric gloves and handed a pair to him.

"Please put these on to avoid any risk of contamination."

She did the same herself, then lifted the tube and handed it to him. "Can you hold this firmly? That will leave me with two hands to extract the material."

There followed a couple of minutes of careful manoeuvring of the contents before she began to extract them. A couple of centimetres were carefully pulled out before she stopped.

"See how flexible it is," she breathed. "I do believe this may be waxed silk."

"Does that mean it's old?"

"I should say it does – maybe more than two thousand years. I think it may be one of the first examples found outside India or China. The other great thing about it is that it means we can look at it here, as long as we're very careful. If it had been papyrus or parchment it would probably have begun to fall apart by now and the investigation would be a laboratory job."

She took the tube from him and laid it gently back on the sheet. "I want another photo – a close-up."

They then continued to extract the fabric from the tube, sliding it very gently. Jackie was so careful that it took nearly ten minutes before she finally laid the coil of material back on the sheet. Then Philip had to photograph it again.

"The great thing about waxed silk is that is retains its flexibility. It should unroll fairly easily, as long as we take our time. Now, if I gently open up the top edge of the coil, can you place that wooden ruler from my bag on it?"

She then proceeded, with Philip's help, to unroll the fabric slowly until they had a sheet of material lying on the bed. It must have taken nearly half an hour, checking the edges all the time to make sure that nothing got caught up. When they had finished, they could see a scroll which was approximately a foot wide by nearly three feet long. The edges were slightly ragged.

Philip looked at the sheet of material with interest. He noticed that there appeared to be four columns of signs on it, written in strange symbols. The rows of markings were so varied that they seemed to have been impressed on the fabric at different times by different people using different tools. Some of the signs near the top of the list had become so faint that they were barely decipherable.

"What on earth is it?" he asked, rather disappointed by the appearance of the scroll.

Jackie shook her head. "I'm afraid I don't know. It's obviously some sort of a list – but what of, I'm not quite sure. I can't read any of the words. They're in a language I don't know. I believe it may be ancient Hebrew. But I haven't studied that language, so I can't tell you anything about it."

"Oh heck!" Philip banged his knee despondently. "After all those hopes."

"Don't be too disappointed. I can find people to translate it for us. So we'll be able to find out what it means - but it'll take a week or two."

He smiled weakly. "I suppose you're right. Although, after all this effort, I was hoping for a more immediate outcome."

"Wait a minute." She put a hand to her forehead. "I believe Bertrand is a Hebrew scholar. You remember Abbé Dugard? I think he majored in ancient languages at university. A clever chap is our Bertrand. I'll ring him and see if we can take the tubes over to him this afternoon. I'm sure he'll be only too willing to help. He always likes to get involved in new mysteries."

Jackie picked up the phone by the bed and asked for Dugard's number. After a couple of minutes she was put through. There followed a quick-fire conversation in French which Philip couldn't understand. It concluded by Jackie saying, "*Oui, merci. Oui. Jusqu'a demain matin.*"

She hung up and turned to Philip. "I spoke to the nun who takes his messages. Apparently, he has gone to Narbonne today and won't be back until late. But he is working tomorrow. She says she's sure he'll see us if we go in the morning."

"Oh, well. What's one more day?"

"Exactly. We can use the time to open up all the other tubes and prepare them for Bertrand to look at – that's assuming they're all similar."

"How do we do that?"

"First, I want you to split this bamboo tube into two halves down its length. Now we'll roll up the scroll again and put it in one half. We lay the other half on top and tape the two halves together to protect the fabric. We also tape over the ends to make sure no foreign bodies get in. Tomorrow we can easily open it for Bertrand to look at."

"Full of bright ideas, you archaeologists."

"We do it all the time." She fished a roll of broad adhesive tape out of her site bag. "We carry the equipment for it."

It took them a further ten minutes to strap up the roll of fabric.

"OK. Now to collect the others. Where shall we put this?"

"It should be safe for now on top of the wardrobe," suggested Philip.

Having disposed of the first tube, they set off downstairs with the duffle bag to collect the other four. But, when they got to reception, they found Sergeant Leblanc was waiting for them.

45

"I was just coming to get you," said the sergeant curtly. "Can you come to the *Mairie* immediately." It was more of an order than a request.

They followed the man who was already striding across the square. When they got to the town hall, he took them straight to his office.

"Wait here a minute. Monsieur le Maire wants to see you." He went out and left them alone.

Jackie pulled a face. "What do you think that's all about?"

"Not very friendly, was he? Do you think they've discovered we've been back up to the site?"

"We've got a perfect right to be there. We're not breaking any laws."

"What about it being a crime scene?"

She shrugged. "It's some way from where André was killed. Besides, they had specifically told us we could return to the site as long as we kept away from the area where André died."

They waited in the office for more than half an hour before the sergeant returned and led them in to the mayor's palatial office.

"I apologise for keeping you waiting," said Maitre Amboisard, although his tone was far from apologetic. "I had some important telephone calls coming in." He paused, looking from one to the other, then he said, "The Bishop's Palace in Narbonne say they have never heard of Jean-Luc Lerenard."

"What?"

"Furthermore, Alain Gisours' secretary says that he knows nothing about a man of that name and didn't recommend him to you for employment."

"He what?" Jackie looked at Philip. "What is this?"

"Wait a minute," intervened Philip. "Have you spoken to Mam'selle Blontard's agent, Bernard Cambray? He was the one who brought the message about Lerenard."

"You didn't give me his telephone number." There was an almost accusatory tone to Amboisard's response.

"That's because I didn't know that you might want it." Jackie startling dark blue eyes flashed. "I hadn't realised then that I was getting embroiled in a conspiracy of lies."

"Perhaps," suggested Philip, trying to calm the atmosphere, "Jackie could use your phone to ring her agent now. She can explain the situation to him and hand the telephone over to you. Then you can ask him whatever questions you wish to ask."

"Very well." The mayor pointed to the phone and she picked it up and dialled the number.

"Please sit down." As a sign that he was unbending a little, he indicated a chair for Philip and placed another beside Jackie, before sitting back in the grand leather swivel seat behind his desk.

Jackie's fingers drummed on the edge of the desk while she waited. At last she got through. *"Oh, bonjour Pauline. Je veux Bernard, s'il vous plait."*

There was a pause while the woman at the other end spoke.

"Pourquoi?"

More explanation.

"Quand est-il départé?"

A reply. There came a rapid exchange of question and answer which Philip couldn't follow, before Jacqueline said, *"Oh, merçi. Oui. Au revoir."*

With a strange expression on her face, she hung up. "Bernard has gone on holiday to the Seychelles for two weeks. He flew from Charles de Gaulle airport at ten o'clock this morning. He won't be available to be contacted for several days. Apparently, he said he would telephone the office at the end of next week to take any messages."

There was silence while Amboisard digested this latest set-back.

"I asked Pauline why Bernard hadn't rung me to tell me before he went – he usually always does that. She said he only decided to go last night. He left a message for her to ring his clients later today to tell them." She passed a hand across her forehead and removed a stray lock of hair. "I feel as though I

275

am the victim of some kind of conspiracy. Wherever I turn, people are against me."

"What about Armand Séjour?" Philip asked the mayor. "Have you tried him?"

Amboisard bowed his head to look at the list in front of him. "We have. He hasn't yet arrived at the address in Paris which he gave us yesterday morning. They are expecting him but don't know exactly when he will arrive. They also say they do not know how to contact him. They have promised to ring me when he arrives or when they hear from him." He frowned. "Strictly speaking, he has broken the law by not going straight to his new address, but I can't do much about it for a few days."

"And," said Jackie, "I bet the same can be said for Gaston Lesmoins and everybody else on your list."

"So far we have been unable to contact anybody except you."

"I've just thought of something," said Philip. "A room was booked for Lerenard at the hotel and the concierge will be able to confirm that he took it. So you will then know that a man of that name was definitely here. Also, Jackie, you told me that you'd received an investigative report about Lerenard. What did you do with it?"

"It's in my brief-case." She stood up. "I'll get it for you. I can't remember who the agency was - Bernard organised it – but I expect their details will be on the report."

Amboisard had also risen. "Please be seated, mademoiselle. I shall send Leblanc to speak to the concierge and to collect your briefcase." He picked up the phone and called the sergeant to come to his office.

He put the phone down and leaned back in his chair. "Meanwhile perhaps you would like a coffee." He smiled at Philip. "I'm afraid my staff would not be able to prepare your English tea."

"Coffee will be fine." Philip sensed a gradual relaxing of tension in the room.

Leblanc arrived in haste. The situation was explained to him.

"Where can the sergeant find your briefcase, mademoiselle?"

"It's in the bottom of the wardrobe."

"Very well. Please can you write the sergeant a note for him to give to the concierge, authorising him to enter your room and remove your brief-case?"

"All right." Jackie was still a bit annoyed about not having her word trusted.

However, she relaxed as the conversation became friendlier. Amboisard had clearly now decide to be polite to them, after his brusque attitude when they first arrived.

"I must say," he admitted, "that at first I was annoyed to think that you might have invented a story to give to me, so as to prevent me from regarding you as suspects. That was especially so when such authoritative bodies as the Bishop's Palace and TV France denied it. However, I am now inclined to think that you truly believe that you are telling the truth and Leblanc should shortly be able to confirm this."

Jackie shook her head. "What I don't understand is why somebody seems to have gone out of their way to hinder your investigation by shielding this man."

"Neither do I. Of course it may be a genuine mistake. Perhaps I contacted the wrong departments at Narbonne and TV France. Once I have confirmed the truth of your story, I will go back to them and question them much more closely."

The mayor continued. "One other thought has occurred to me. Are you sure the name you gave to me for Lerenard was correct? It seems possibly to have been a made-up name. Could he have been known to his referees by some other name?"

"I was never given any other name. He was called Lerenard in the report, as you will see. And Abbé Dugard knew him by that name when he worked for him."

"Ah." His eyes lit up. "Perhaps I could ring the good Abbé."

She shook her head again. "I'm sorry. I tried to speak to him an hour ago about another matter. I was told he had gone to Narbonne and wouldn't be back until late tonight. You can get him at work tomorrow morning."

"It's the people in Narbonne again," said Philip. "They seem to be causing you a lot of problems, Monsieur Amboisard."

"Indeed." The gleam of battle was in the man's eyes. "I will have to sort out Narbonne. But first I will need the telephone number of Abbé Dugard."

"I have it here." She read it out to him and he made a note on his pad.

No sooner had he finished than the phone rang again. A considerable conversation ensued. Philip understood none of it but, when he glanced at Jackie, he saw she was biting her lip in vexation. At last the mayor hung up and he turned to them with a mirthless little smile.

"That was Sergeant Leblanc. Unfortunately Henri, the concierge, has gone out for an hour and there is a young girl on hotel reception. For some unknown reason, the hotel register doesn't seem to be there. Leblanc is just going up to your room to collect your briefcase." He shook his head. "I don't think I can recall a case where I have been led up so many blind alleys. It's almost unbelievable."

Later, as they returned to the hotel, Jackie said, "I think I understand the mayor's frustration. The only difference between us is that I believe somebody is setting up this plethora of disinformation to try to discredit me. I wonder who it can be?"

"The finger points at either Narbonne or TV France," said Philip. "And I can't really understand why it should be the latter. They are already losing too much by the cancellation of the series."

"I used to trust Alain. Now I don't think you can trust anybody in big business."

"Whoever it is, at least they couldn't suppress that report about Lerenard which was in your briefcase. It even mentioned Alain Gisours' office"

"No?" She turned to him furiously. "What do you bet? When they contact the agency, they will either say they know nothing about it, or else that the man who prepared it has just conveniently left for a job in Cambodia."

She was so angry that Philip couldn't help laughing at her. After a short pause she joined in and the tension eased out of her face.

"I do think that Maitre Amboisard believes us now." He grinned. "At least he hasn't stuck us in jail. I was beginning to wonder at one time whether he would let us out of police custody."

"And in a half-hour or so Henri should be back to produce the hotel register and support our story."

"And when he rings Abbé Dugard tomorrow morning, the mayor should get further corroboration." Philip had a sudden thought. "You don't think the Abbé can be bought, do you?"

"Who knows? I would have said 'no' until now. But these people seem to be able to wield a very big stick. He's got his pension to consider and his beloved excavations at Prouille. I'm not sure that I can even count on him anymore."

They arrived back at the hotel and went straight in to reception. Henri obviously hadn't returned and the young girl was still there. Jackie went up to her.

"You have four bamboo tubes in your safe. Can you let me have them now, or do you want to wait until Henri returns?"

"But, mademoiselle - that other gentleman took them, not ten minutes ago."

Jacqueline controlled herself. "I specifically told Henri that they were not to be given to anybody but me or Monsieur Sinclair here."

"I am sorry, mademoiselle." She shook her head. "I do not know anything about that. All I know is that the man gave me this note you had written which told me to let him have the bamboo tubes."

"Let me see it."

The girl handed it over.

Jackie read it. "It looks just like the note I gave to Sergeant Leblanc which authorised him to collect the briefcase." She turned back to the girl. "Who was this man? Was it Sergeant Leblanc?"

"Oh, no. I thought it was one of your helpers, but I had never seen him before."

"Right," said Jackie. "Give me that note. We're going to run this one to earth. First stop Sergeant Leblanc."

46

"You asked for this meeting as a matter of urgency. What have you to report?" asked Charles Robert of the young Armand seated on the bed opposite him in his hotel room.

"As instructed, monsieur, when the archaeological team dispersed yesterday afternoon, we took occupation of the top floor flat you had rented for us across the square from the hotel in Quillan. Jeanette and I took it in turns to watch. We saw that Sinclair and Mademoiselle Blontard went out at about seven o'clock. I was parked to the south of the town ready to follow them when Jeanette rang me. I collected her at our agreed pick-up point. She had tracked them to their own car and seen them set out towards Limoux."

He paused and Robert urged, "Go on."

"They were well ahead of us, so we couldn't follow them closely. But, from Jeanette's description of their clothes, I didn't think they were going for a celebratory meal. In any case, the place we most wanted to keep an eye on was le Bézu. So I decided to see if they had gone up there."

"And had they?"

"They had indeed. Sinclair's little red car was parked in its usual place. So I left Jeanette with our car and set off up the path after them." He took a breath. "The main site was deserted. So I decided to take a look at the lower trench and that's where they were."

"What were they doing?"

"Making a lot of noise for a start. They were hammering at some stones."

"Mon dieu. Were they trying to break through the roof into the room below?"

Séjour looked at him suspiciously. "What room is that? I know nothing of any room."

"Don't ask." Charles Robert pulled himself up to his full height. "That is none of your business. Just answer my question. Were they trying to break through the stone slabs you had found earlier?"

"No." Armand swallowed his resentment at the older man's attitude. "They were more clever than that. They were breaking out some stones from a wall which had been used to block up a hollow in the rock-face beside the stone roof. They had apparently decided that was the easiest way to get round the slabs."

Robert put his head in his hands. "My God!" He looked up. "What did they do next?"

"It took them a couple of hours to knock down the wall and by then it was getting dark. Philip carried on hammering by torchlight. Then suddenly there was a big noise of stone collapsing and the torch went out. He must have dropped it and broken it."

"What on earth had happened?"

"Of course, I couldn't see at that time. They talked for a couple of minutes then they obviously decided to give up for the night. I heard them start to come back up the path. So I had to move out of their way and lie low. When they went past my hiding-place, I could see that Jackie was carrying something very carefully. It looked like some sort of stick, but I couldn't be sure. They made their way slowly up to the main site. Of course, it was slow going for them in the dark." He paused again. "When they were out of earshot, I made my way down to the trench. It took me some time because I didn't have a torch."

"That was thoughtless of you."

His comment irritated Armand. "I didn't realise that I was likely to be scrambling around le Bézu in the dark. It's a fairly hazardous pastime."

"So what did you find when you got down there?"

"The big stone slabs were still in place and were undamaged. The whole of the rough stone wall across the hollow had gone. I lay on the slabs and reached down as far as I could into the hole, but it seemed to me that there was no wall left, at least for a metre below the slabs. I peered down, but of course I could see nothing."

"So what did you do then?" Monsieur Robert sounded vexed.

"What could I do? Firstly I phoned Jeanette and told her to move our car further along the track out of sight of Sinclair's MG. Then I set off back up the site, moving as quietly as I could to avoid alerting them to my presence, not that it was much of a problem. They were making enough noise themselves not to hear me. I just kept a comfortable distance behind them. Of course, when I got back to the parking area, they had already gone." He shrugged. "I walked along to where Jeanette was parked, and we drove back to Quillan. We checked that their car was parked back in its usual place, which it was, and then we went to bed."

"You should have contacted me then. I could have arranged for reinforcements. As it is we have lost a whole day."

Armand dared to argue. "What reinforcements? The Council hasn't got an army. When we got back to the flat it was nearly midnight and I wanted to be up at daylight to continue the surveillance."

"All right. Please continue."

"Well, first of all Jackie and Philip were delayed this morning by having to go to the *mairie*. Apparently it has been decided that André Jolyon, the chap who died, was banged on the head before he was chucked off the cliffs. So it was murder."

"Are they suspects?"

"I don't know. They came out of the *mairie* at about ten and went straight up to the site – obviously to see what they had uncovered the previous night. And they were carrying a large, blue canvas bag which seemed to be stuffed with something. When they got to the parking area at le Bézu, there was another car already parked there. So they went on and parked further along the lane out of sight. I told Jeanette to drop me, drive back to the village, and park where she wouldn't be seen. I hid just off the road under the trees. After a few minutes, the other two came back along the track and Philip was carrying the blue bag."

Robert snorted. "I'm not sure I want to hear the rest of this."

"The next thing was that a woman came hurrying down the path. It was the journalist who had shown an interest in us when we were digging the trench above the stone slabs. She is called César Renoir and she told us she was researching Cathar castles."

Charles Robert made a note of the name.

"The other two hid themselves so that she didn't see them. She drove off at some speed in her little car and I stayed in the bushes out of sight. When I saw Jackie and Philip next, they were going up the path to the site, so I followed at a safe distance." He took another breath. "When they got to the site office they unlocked it and Philip came out with some rope. Then they went down to the trench."

"I do not like the sound of this at all."

"When they got down to the bottom, Philip tied the rope to a small tree and dangled the end down the hole. He was obviously going to descend into the room."

"No! You couldn't let him. What did you do?"

"Ah. There was a surprise in store for them. Suddenly another man stepped out of a hiding-place just above the trench and accosted them."

"Another man? Who was this?"

Armand shook his head. "I did not know him. I wondered whether it might have been somebody who the council had sent. Of course there was nothing I could do with the three of them there. Some sort of argument took place, but I couldn't hear what was said." He pulled a face. "Anyway, after a few minutes, Philip went ahead and climbed down into the room on the rope. He was down there for about ten minutes. After a while Jackie lowered the bag down to him. A few minutes later she pulled it up again. Soon after that Philip climbed up and they opened the bag for the other man to look inside. He seemed satisfied with what he had seen and left them, coming up the path past my hiding-place. However, he only went a little further before he moved off the path and hid himself. Then Philip undid the rope and he and Jackie went back up to the site hut."

"So you don't know what he took away in the bag?"

284

"No. But it wasn't anything heavy. Although the bag was stuffed with something, I would say that was only padding. The path is steep and rough. I should know. I've been up and down it quite a few times. And he wasn't having any problems with carrying the bag."

"What did you do then?"

Armand sighed. "What could I do? I couldn't risk giving myself away to this other man, so I had to remain where I was until he had gone."

"So how long did you stay there?"

"For about another ten minutes. The old man came out of hiding when Jackie and Philip had gone and he went back up to the site hut. When he got there, he just sat down on a rock and seemed to wait for something else to happen. It was soon obvious he was going to stay there to see if any other visitors came. Or maybe he was waiting for César Renoir to come back."

"He didn't see you?"

"No." Armand allowed himself a brief smile. "I know my way pretty well round that site, so I was able to avoid going near the hut where he'd positioned himself. I decided there was no point in staying there any longer, so I set off back to the road. I rang Jeanette and she picked me up half an hour later. Then I got in touch with you."

Charles Robert scratched his head. "How can we find out what was in that bag?"

"I presume it is now in their bedroom at the hotel. But who is this man who seemed to be secretly guarding the place? He obviously didn't object to them taking away whatever it was they had found. He actually looked in the bag and Philip showed him what was there. Is this guy one of ours that they haven't told us about?"

"I will check," said Robert. "Meanwhile it is essential that you should immediately return to your watching brief."

"You mean spying."

"If you like. I have your phone number. If I get further instructions from Paris, I will contact you. Until then I want you to keep as close to Mademoiselle Blontard as you can." He paused. "Oh, and there is one further thing." He got up and went to the wardrobe. He lifted his suitcase down from the top shelf, opened it and extracted a soft leather bag which he handed to the young man. Armand opened the bag and looked inside. It contained an automatic pistol and several clips of ammunition.

"I am told that you know how to use these things." There was a hint of distaste in Robert's expression. "You are to do your best to prevent anybody from removing any part of the contents of the downstairs room until you receive further instructions."

"And what happens to me," asked Armand, "if I kill a man with this?"

"Provided you use it in defence of the Council's interest, I can inform you that you will be protected."

Armand stood up and slung the bag over his shoulder with a muffled clink. "I will report any developments to you," he said as he left the room.

47

In the hour after they discovered the theft of the bamboo tubes, Jackie and Philip had several meetings and interviews with the people at the town hall and elsewhere in Quillan. However, they got no nearer to recovering them.

They discovered Leblanc had left Jackie's note at reception. And, when they looked at the new note, they could see that somebody had cleverly altered the original to make it look authentic. It was a very frustrated and angry Jacqueline Blontard who ended up drinking another coffee with Philip outside the hotel.

"I'm sorry," she said, "but it looks as though I've lost you all your inheritance except for the one tube which is up in the bedroom." She clamped a hand over her mouth. "We haven't checked to see whether the one we opened is still up there."

They rushed upstairs, dreading that it might also have disappeared but, when Philip reached up on top of the wardrobe, he discovered it was still there. Jackie burst into tears of relief and Philip hugged her.

"Oh, my God," she said. "I wonder what else is going to go wrong today."

"Well," he said optimistically, "at least we've still got one tube. Perhaps we can use that to get back at whoever has the others."

"What do you mean?"

"We might arrange a swap."

"What!" She stared at him. "Give away the one we've got? That's a unique historical document."

"But what's most important is the information it contains – although we don't know what that is yet. What I suggest is that we photograph it in full and in close-up. Then we can make as good a written copy of the thing as we can. We must also copy the photos from the camera onto your lap-top. Can you then e-mail them to a safe recipient?"

"I don't know. I don't feel like trusting anyone anymore."

"Well, I can arrange for my colleagues in London to store them for you. I'm sure they'll be safe there. Then at least we'll be ready to negotiate if anybody contacts us."

For the next two hours they were busy carrying out Philip's plan. By the time they had finished, evening was already drawing in. They took dinner but neither of them had much appetite.

During the meal Philip said, "We haven't decided what to do about the treasure in the underground room."

"Let's leave that until tomorrow." Jackie smiled bleakly. "I've had enough excitement for one day. I feel tired and emotionally drained."

"I think it's our duty to do something about it, even if it's only to inform the police. I don't think we should let it drift for another day."

"All right. *You* go and tell the police about it. See what they want to do."

"OK." He patted her hand. "You go up to the bedroom and have a rest. I'll be back in half an hour."

However, getting hold of Leblanc was more difficult than he had expected. It was already after seven o'clock and there was only a youthful gendarme on duty at the police station below the town hall. The young man resisted Philip's request for a while, but finally agreed to ring the sergeant, clearly not happy about facing Leblanc's fury for disturbing him when he was off duty.

After a short introduction he handed the phone to Philip. The next five minutes were very difficult, with each man struggling to understand the other one with their limited knowledge of the other's language. It was clear the sergeant didn't believe that what Philip was trying to tell him was of any real importance. Finally he was told to come in to Leblanc's office at nine o'clock in the morning. Then the sergeant firmly hung up.

By the time he got back to the bedroom, it was fully dark and Jackie was almost asleep. But Philip was still worried about letting the matter wait overnight. He told her about his abortive conversation with Leblanc.

288

"If you'd been there, we might have got on better. He clearly doesn't believe me."

"I don't think I'd have done any better than you. Our credibility has been destroyed in the eyes of the police." She sighed. "Well, you can't do any more tonight. We'll have to leave it until the morning."

"I'm not prepared to do that." Philip was slightly surprised at his own perseverance. "I'm not happy about that chap Hébert. I've got a nasty feeling he may jump in there and try to make off with some of it. I'm going back up there to take the back off that cupboard and take enough photos to convince Leblanc that I'm telling the truth. Then, if Hébert tries to pinch some of the stuff, I'll have a record of what's gone. You stay here and catch up on your sleep."

Jackie was on her feet straight away. "Not likely! I'm not going to let you go up there on your own. We're a team and we'll stick together."

Despite his arguing with her, she would not change her mind. Half an hour later they were on their way, dressed in suitable dark clothing and equipped for the night-time task. After a short discussion, they decided the safest place for the last bamboo tube was in the boot of the car, wrapped in a spare blanket.

"Hopefully we'll only be an hour or so," said Philip. "I don't think I'll take long to prise the back off that chest. Then it'll be a few photos and return for an early night."

48

"There's a big van at the parking place," announced Philip as they rounded the last bend below le Bézu.

"I wonder who that is." Jackie decided, "Don't stop here to find out. Drive straight on past and down to the farm."

"Won't they wonder who *we* are?"

"I don't think so, as long as they see us disappearing into the distance. They'll probably think we're just locals on our way back to our isolated home."

As they drove past, Jackie peered in through the van windows. "There doesn't seem to be anyone in it anyway." She slapped her knee. "I've just had a thought. I hope they're not pinching stuff from the site, now it's been closed."

"Would it be the contractors who have been engaged by TV France to clear the place?"

"At this time of night?" She shook her head. "Besides it's too soon for them to have got here."

They parked the car and walked back down the track. A blustery wind had got up, swaying the newly-leafed trees and rustling the bushes. He could feel there was a threat of rain in the freshening breeze.

"This wind will mean that we're less likely to be heard or to hear others." He pointed at the van. "But since there may be some others about, we'd better be careful to use lights as little as possible when we're out in the open."

Jackie's hand went up to the torch, dangling on its lanyard round her neck, but she said nothing.

They walked carefully as they approached the van but, as far as they could tell, it was empty of people. So they started up the path. Philip was leading and occasionally switched on his torch briefly to light the rougher sections. When they got to the main site there was still no sign of life and, after picking up the rope from the office, they made their way down to the trench above the underground room.

Up at the castle the wind seemed much stronger. Philip suspected it was working itself up to a full gale. The bushes were lashing around and leaves and small branches were being torn from the trees and blown across their path. They had to make their way very carefully and use their torches more often. They stopped to listen frequently, but could hear nothing except the turmoil in the treetops.

Philip went ahead for the last twenty yards or so, but he found that the area around the trench was empty except for wind-tossed vegetation. He went back to collect Jackie. Then he tied the rope to the same tree he had used in the morning. Looking round the trench, he picked up the crow-bar which was still lying where he had left it, and put it in the tool-bag.

"I'll go down first," he said, handing her the bag. "When I give you a call, you can lower the bag of tools down to me. Then you can come down if you want to. It's quite easy and I'll have my torch on and will be able to guide you and put your feet in the right places."

Five minutes later they were standing by the back of the damaged chest and Jackie was peering in, her torch held above her head.

"I need to find the hammer," said Philip. "I think it must be under some of the rubble."

"While you're searching for that, I want to have a look at the room." She squeezed through the narrow gap between the chests somewhat more easily than Philip that morning and disappeared from sight.

He wedged the torch into a position to light the small space and started to move the rubble aside. Sure enough, within a few minutes he had found the hammer under a couple of stones.

"Got it," he called.

Then he opened the tool-bag and took out the small crow-bar and prepared to start work. As he did so, Jackie returned through the opening.

"Interesting, isn't it?"

"It is indeed," she agreed. "I had a look down the entrance corridor. It's about three metres long and seems to have been cut right through the old outside wall of the castle. The width and height has been made big enough to get the large chests through. At the end of the corridor is a wide, very strong door. There is no lock in the door, but when I tried to push it open it wouldn't move. I think there must be some sort of locking device on the outside."

"That's something to investigate." He prepared to start removing the planks from the back of the chest. "Can you hold the torch for me, please?"

It took a while for his careful blows to start to loosen the first plank. Philip was taking care because he didn't want to seriously damage the chest or its contents. He did rather more levering than hammering and it took a long time before they could see that progress was being made.

At last he managed to split the tongue off the first plank and ease it away from its neighbour. Then he broke the damaged piece of wood into two near the bottom. He pulled away the lower piece of timber and the square-cut iron nails came out with noises like creaking bed-springs. It required several heavy blows from the hammer to release it completely. Next he turned his attention to the top part of the plank. This was easier because he could get more leverage, working the crow-bar up nail by nail until he reached the top. Once he had got it free, he checked his watch. They had been there nearly half an hour already.

"I want to get some more pictures," said Jackie, so he laid the plank aside and waited.

After the photos, she turned back to him. "I've reached in and caught hold of a couple of the things in the chest. They are definitely large ornaments. They're pretty heavy. I think one is a lectern and I'm almost sure another is the statue of an angel. I can just make out one of the wings."

"Are they gold?"

"I believe so. But that's not important. If these ornaments are as old as I think they are, they will be absolutely priceless. Only a few museums have such ancient valuables. There would be tremendous competition to get hold of them."

"Well, let's carry on then."

For another half-hour Philip continued to ease the planks off the back of the chest. At intervals Jackie stopped him to take more photographs. There were only two planks left when she stopped him again.

"Can you hear something?"

He paused to listen. "I expect it's the trees thrashing about above us. That wind is really getting up."

"No. I can hear voices."

He listened again but shook his head. Then there was a sudden, louder noise – a kind of sharp crack followed by several bangs and the creak of a door opening.

"There! What on earth is that?"

"That came from the room. I think it must be somebody opening the door you found. Switch off your torch." He carefully put down the hammer and crow-bar.

Even with their lights extinguished, the space where they stood hadn't gone completely dark. There was a slight glow coming through the gap between the chests from the room beyond, which brightened even as they watched. Now there was also the increasing sound of voices.

"I'm going to take a look," he whispered to her.

"Be careful."

"I will be. Move over."

He edged past her and peered round the corner into the gap. There were at least two sources of light. One was almost in his line of vision. It seemed to be coming from a large lantern which had been set down on one of the low chests in the middle of the room. He could also detect several voices. They were speaking French. One was a rather gentlemanly tone which seemed to be explaining something. Another had a rougher twang which was barking out orders. He could also hear a woman's voice from time to time.

Philip tried to ease his way further along the narrow corridor between the chests to see if he could make out any faces. As he edged forward the men in the room broke into one of the brass-bound chests. There came a tremendous crash, and a cloud of dust came rushing down the corridor. There was a lot of spluttering and coughing.

The dust overwhelmed Philip and filled his nose and his lungs. He just managed to stifle the desperate urge to cough as he hastily withdrew from the gap and doubled up behind the damaged chest. His body was working with the desperate desire to clear his chest, despite the hand he had clamped over his mouth. Jackie was massaging his back, trying to relieve the tension. Then he had to take a breath and he could no longer resist letting out a strangled cough.

49

There was a sudden silence in the room, followed by the sound of several voices. Then the rough French patois shout of, "*venez ici.*"

Even Philip understood those words. But they both crouched there and held their breath. He was once more working up to a cough.

"Come out, or I will shoot."

Still they didn't move, although Philip knew that there was now little chance of his not being found. Then suddenly there was a tremendous crash as a shot was fired down the gap between the chests. The noise of the explosion was absolutely shattering in the confined space. The bullet slammed into the rock wall behind them with an immediate second eruption which showered them with chips of rock.

"Come out," said the voice, "or I will keep firing."

"OK," spluttered Philip. "All right, I'm coming."

"Come out now."

"I'm coming. Just a minute." He was overtaken by a further burst of coughing.

He made signals to Jackie to keep quiet and stay where she was. Then he switched on the torch and shone it up at his face as he struggled through the narrow gap, still spluttering as he tried to clear his lungs. He emerged into the room and held his hands out from the side of his body so that nobody would think he was about to use a weapon. He found himself confronted by a short, burly man with ginger hair. A gun was pointing at him and the man said something in French which Philip couldn't understand.

"He says to stand in front of that door and put your hands on top of your head."

Philip recognised the man who came forward as being the fellow who had accosted them that morning by the trench. He recalled the man's name was Alain Hébert.

The ginger-haired tough said something in his guttural tones.

"I am to check you for weapons," said Alain in a conversational voice. "I'm sure you have none, but I must show willing and make a thorough check." He patted Philip carefully all round his body and particularly in his pockets. "As I thought, you don't carry anything worth calling a weapon."

He turned back to ginger and said, "*Non.*"

Meanwhile, Philip had been looking round at the rest of the room. Besides Hébert and the ginger-haired thug, there were four others. One was a great, ignorant-looking brute of a man, and there was an evil little weaselly character, a man with a scar across his forehead and a woman. With a little surprise, Philip noted she was the journalist.

Hébert saw his eyes widen as he looked at her. "I believe you have already met César Renoir," he continued in his conversational tone. "This gentleman," a slight smile played about his features as he indicated the ginger-haired man, "is Henri Montluçon, who is the leader of our merry band. The others are Mickey, Gustav and Pierre," pointing to the weasel, the brute and scar-face in turn. "Tell me now, where is your partner, Jacqueline Blontard?"

Philip slowly lowered his hands. "She is back in her bed in the hotel, fast asleep. She has had a tough day, one way and another, so she decided not to accompany me this evening. She said I was nuts to come back up here. I'm afraid it looks as if the woman was right again."

"Nuts?" Hébert seemed amused. "You must think I am nuts if you expect me to believe you. Why don't you call to her to come out now and save us from wasting any more time?"

"I've told you . . ."

"Don't play around, Monsieur Sinclair. You don't want our friend Montluçon to fire another shot into that narrow corridor, do you? She could easily be killed this time."

"All right." Philip realised he was beaten and called out to her, "Jackie, they've guessed you're there. Come out through the gap into the room. Hold your hands up and shine the torch on your body so they can see that you haven't got any weapons."

"Very sensible." Hébert smiled as she emerged. "Hello, my dear. It's a pity we have to meet like this. I'm sure you will have realised by now that it was very foolish of you to come back here tonight. You are obstructing the arrangements we wish to make for removal of these items to a safe place. Now you have presented us with the problem of deciding what we are going to do with you."

He turned and began to speak to Montluçon.

Jackie moved close to Philip. "Hébert is suggesting they empty one of the large chests and lock us up in that," she muttered. "But Montluçon is afraid we will escape before they have finished removing the treasure."

An argument was starting to build up between the two men.

"Hébert says they can surround us with other chests to prevent us getting out. The ginger-haired thug wants to kill us now. He says we'll die anyway from suffocation or hunger. His actual words were 'dead witnesses don't tell tales'."

Alain Hébert was waving his arms around, trying to persuade the ginger-haired thug not to kill his two captives, but the other man appeared unwilling to take the risk of keeping them alive.

"Hébert says they'll be hundreds of kilometres away before we can escape. They can ring the police anonymously from Marseilles in a couple of days and we'll be released alive. but with no information that can help the police in finding *them*."

However, Montluçon was shaking his head, apparently immovable.

"Ginger says they don't have time to mess around. He wants to kill us straight away and get on with the job. He doesn't want us in the way." Jackie voice broke. "I don't like the look of this, Philip."

The ginger man pushed Hébert to one side and walked towards Philip. He raised his gun and pointed it at his face from about three feet away. Looking down the barrel at the intent, piggy eyes of the merciless killer, Philip went cold as he realised his life was about to end.

297

"No!" Alain Hébert stepped in front of the gun with his hand held up. "I will not let you kill him like this. I abhor unnecessary violence."

Without a word, Montluçon moved the muzzle of the gun a fraction and fired. There was a frightful explosion and the back of Hébert's head burst open and spattered Philip and Jackie with the revolting fragments of his blood and brains. Philip heard a shriek from across the room. He dropped the torch and went into a crouch as Hébert's dead torso toppled back towards him. His arms went round the man's waist and, using it as a battering ram, he rushed at Montluçon and knocked the murderer off his feet. The ginger-haired man fell on to his back on one of the brass-bound lower chests and the hand holding the gun swung outwards.

Philip was about to leap on the man and wrestle the gun away from him when a pair of muscular arms grabbed him round his upper body, trapping his own arms against his sides. He felt as though he had a broad band of steel across his chest. The great beast of a man, Gustav, lifted him off his feet and he was completely powerless. He drummed his heels against the brute's lower legs but it had no effect.

Montluçon climbed slowly to his feet, breathing heavily. He approached Philip slowly, an evil expression on his face. He slapped him violently on both cheeks, snapping his head from side to side. He snarled in English, "I kill you. But first I hurt you."

"No!" Jackie yelled and started forward, but the weasel ran towards her with a stiletto in his hand and she was forced back.

Philip's attempts to wriggle free of Gustav's grip were a waste of effort. Montluçon raised the gun slowly until it was no more than three inches from his mouth. An evil grin crossed his face and he moved the muzzle a fraction to one side. Philip realised the first bullet was going to be aimed so as to smash his right cheek and jaw, so that he wouldn't die instantly. He knew that would cause him agony.

Philip knew real fear then. He felt a weakening in the pit of his stomach and hoped he wouldn't suffer the additional shame of voiding his bowels. Although he was still held too tightly to struggle, he waggled his head violently to try to avoid the first bullet. Ginger frowned as he tried to place the shot to cause the most pain without killing him.

"No," moaned Jackie. "Please, no."

Then the shot exploded across the room. Philip felt no immediate pain as he watched Montluçon. A surprised expression had come over the man's face as he looked down at the red blotch which was spreading rapidly across his shirt-front. He leaned back and gazed at the pistol in César Renoir's hand, no more than six feet away from him.

"That is for killing my father," she said.

Then she fired again. This time the bullet hit him straight between the eyes, jerking his head backwards. He toppled gently onto the chest where Philip had earlier knocked him, the gun falling from his nerveless hand on to the floor.

"And that," said César expressionlessly, "is for killing my lover." She lowered the gun.

For a second, there was a complete frozen silence. The evil little Mickey recovered first. He spun round and hurled his knife with unerring accuracy at the journalist. With a sickening thud, six inches of razor-sharp steel plunged up to its hilt in her stomach. She dropped the gun and grasped her body round the knife. With a groan she sank to the floor.

Jackie started forward but Mickey pushed her back against the chest. Pierre also ran towards her, then halted as an authoritative voice rang out in French.

"Nobody move! I have an automatic pistol and I have the licence to use it on anybody who tries to resist."

Everybody looked towards the door. To Philip's astonishment it was Armand Séjour who walked into the room from the entrance corridor. He pointed the gun at Gustav.

"Release the Englishman." Then, when there was no immediate response. "Release him now, or I will shoot you in the knee."

The threat was spoken mildly as the young Frenchman advanced, but the brute promptly let Philip go.

"Now, lie on your face on the floor." He turned his gun on Mickey. "And you."

The two crooks hastened to do as they were told. Pierre had gone to care for César, wrapping his jacket round her middle. Armand seemed to trust him enough to half-ignore him.

"Can I help?" asked Jackie, for once apparently happy to take a supporting role.

Armand handed her his mobile phone. "Can you go outside and ring the police. Tell them there's been a double murder. That should bring them running. Also we need an ambulance for the journalist. Tell them as well that we have two Mafiosi to take into custody. Will you remember that?"

"Of course," her response held a little of the old acerbity which she might have shown to an assistant who got above himself.

However, Armand appeared unaware of it. "I see you have a torch. Good." He pointed to the entrance corridor. "If you go out through the main door, you'll find the path down to the road is rough and newly cut, but you shouldn't have any problems, using your torch. Will you go down there and wait for them to arrive and show them up here?"

She nodded and left without a further word.

Meanwhile Philip had been trying to wipe off the filthy remains of the contents of Alain Hébert's skull.

"Now," said Armand to him, "I will tell you how to truss up these two thugs to prepare to hand them over to the police."

Without questioning his authority, Philip found himself spending the next quarter of an hour strapping the men's wrists behind them with their belts. Then he had to cut some lengths off the rope and hogtie their ankles so that they would only be able to walk with short steps, making it impossible to escape.

"Will they be able to walk down the path like this?" asked Philip.

Armand shrugged. "They will fall down a lot, but will anybody worry about that?"

"I suppose not."

He grinned for the first time. "Now we wait for the police."

"What about César Renoir?"

"The journalist?" He seemed to remember her for the first time. "I don't know anything about repairing wounds, do you?"

300

"Not much."

"Well, you go and see what you can do to help the other guy. I'll keep watch on these two."

Philip went over and knelt down beside the woman. She still had the knife hilt protruding from her stomach. Her face was a ghastly white, but she was still conscious.

"We've gone to call for an ambulance. How are you feeling?"

She smiled wanly. "I seem to have gone numb down there. I think I'll just stay as still as I can."

"She has lost much blood," said the man.

"This is Pierre." She introduced him. "He was one of the men who stayed loyal to my father when Montluçon tried to take over. It was Pierre who told me, while we were cutting the path, that they killed my father two days ago."

"Are you sure you should be talking?"

"It's all right. Talking doesn't affect my stomach and there are some things I need to say to you in case I can't say them later." She paused for breath. "First, you must say sorry to Mademoiselle Blontard. I was responsible for the death of her assistant."

"André Jolyon?"

"That's right. I didn't do it myself, but I was the one who told Gustav and Mickey where his room was at the hotel."

"What happened?"

"They got into his room while he was at dinner. When he returned they knocked him unconscious. Then they waited until everyone was asleep and carried him up to the castle and threw him off the cliffs to make it look like an accident." She shook her head slightly. "But I never thought they'd fool the forensic scientists."

"Why did they do it?"

"It was one of Montluçon's clumsy schemes to try to get the excavations stopped. Alain had warned them that the dig was getting close to the treasure. Of course it didn't work."

Philip suddenly had an idea. "Did he then decide to put in Lerenard to take over and muck up everything?"

301

"Lerenard?" Her look was puzzled. "I know nothing about any Lerenard."

"Oh. So he's nothing to do with these guys."

"Not as far as I'm aware."

Philip got to his feet, confused by all the different people involved. He wanted to discuss it with Jackie, but he knew that would have to wait for an opportunity later.

Faintly floating through the corridor came the sound of the first police siren. Now somebody else would take over. Now there would be questions, interviews, hours of sitting waiting to be released from the cross-examination.

50

"At least Sergeant Leblanc had to take us seriously when you rang him that time," said Philip as they drove to Prouille the next morning.

Jackie laughed. "I don't think the good sergeant has ever had to cope with such a lot of problems at one time in his life before."

"That's right. Two more dead bodies; one seriously injured in hospital; three crooks in jail; and a room-full of priceless treasure to look after. The poor chap can't know which way to turn."

"On top of that," she pointed out, "there's apparently a big row building up over who actually *owns* the treasure in that underground room."

"Is that right?"

"That's what the mayor told me. Some shadowy organisation based in Paris is lobbying the government, telling them that they have recorded proof that the stuff belongs to them."

A full night's sleep and a late start had enabled them both to get over the shock of nearly being killed the night before. When they had got back to the hotel some time after midnight, they had immediately stripped off the clothes which still carried the smell and some of the remains of Alain Hébert's death and had stuffed them in a dustbin liner for burning. They had then showered carefully, washing every little last vestige from their bodies and their hair, before they had collapsed into bed.

Now they felt fit to face the world and get on with the business of understanding the little they had been left of the secret documents of the Cathar heresy. But of course their minds still dwelled on the horrific experiences of the previous evening.

"The real hero was Armand," said Philip. "I must admit I'd thought of him before as being a bit inexperienced, especially when he seemed grateful to be given a chance to dig trenches in out-of-the-way corners of the castle. Now he comes through like a mixture of James Bond and Inspector Maigret."

Jackie agreed. "We must both be very grateful to him. I don't know what would have happened if he hadn't turned up. There was the ginger-haired guy's gun lying on the floor and that little weasel was free to pick it up. I don't think we would have lasted long if he had."

"You're right of course. And then Armand took charge until the police turned up. I believe we were all too shocked to have been much use to anybody without him telling us what to do. It was as if he'd been doing things like that for years. And he said he had authority to use the gun. Do you think he's some kind of plain-clothes policeman?"

"I don't know. But I did notice, when the police turned up, that he went and had a quiet word with Leblanc, before the sergeant took over. I think there must be some sort of special role which he hasn't said anything about. But what I don't understand is why he should come and sign on with me as a trainee archaeologist, if he's got an undercover job."

"You seem to have surrounded yourself with personal mysteries. There's Armand and Lerenard." He grinned. "And, of course, there's me as well."

"At least we've cleared up the mystery about Alain Hébert and the journalist."

"I gather César was taken to the hospital in Carcassonne. Have you heard how she is?"

"I asked Maitre Amboisard this morning. He said she's in a bad way. They don't think the knife had completely destroyed any vital organs, but she'd lost a lot of blood and her body had gone into shock by the time they'd got her to hospital. As a result they couldn't operate on her. They gave her a local anaesthetic to enable the knife to be removed. And they've got to give her a few days´ intensive treatment before they can find out what sort of repair work they have to do on her. It sounds as though her chances are no better than fifty-fifty."

Philip shook his head. "I don't know whether she *wants* to survive now. She's lost her father. She seems to have been in love with the murdered Alain Hébert. Also I presume that, technically, she's at least committed manslaughter."

"That's right. And she's also been guilty of helping this criminal organisation which her father used to run and which has carried out I don't know how many crimes in Marseilles. Perhaps she can claim that she was coerced into it by threats of what would happen to her father if she didn't go along with them. But, if she recovers fully, I can't see how she can escape a long stay in jail."

"Not a very bright future."

"No." Jackie's face was set in a grim expression. "What I can't forgive her is showing those thugs where to capture André. He'd done nothing wrong. They just wanted to use his death to close down the excavations."

Philip reached out and grasped her hand. "I'm sorry, Jackie. There's nothing that can be done to bring him back."

"I know."

She was quiet for a long time. But when he looked at her she wasn't crying.

At last she spoke again, showing she had moved on emotionally. "On the plus side, I suppose that if she lives, she'll be able to provide the first-hand evidence to get Mickey and Gustav put away for pre-meditated murder. That should remove two of La Force Marsellaise's thugs for a long time."

"What's happened to them for now?"

"They've been taken to a high security prison near Toulouse."

Philip grinned. "Well, that's relieved Sergeant Leblanc of one problem. Now he's only got to look after Pierre."

"Why didn't that man go with the other two?"

"Well, he didn't actually do anything wrong yesterday," said Philip, "except that he was a part of Montluçon's gang who cut their way in to the treasure room. So I don't think Leblanc actually has anything to charge him with at the moment. No doubt he's sent the details off to Marseilles to see whether they have anything against him."

"It was what he told César about her father being killed which made her shoot Montluçon and saved you from a nasty, painful death."

"And you after me, I expect. We've both got to be grateful to them as well as Armand." He put his head on one side. "That reminds me – I'm sure Armand wasn't there just by chance."

"I agree with that. When I quizzed him about his role in all this, he wouldn't tell me anything. But when I asked why he had turned up at that very moment, he more or less had to admit that he'd been following us ever since the site closed down. Apparently they were just behind us when we drove past the empty van at the parking place. So he got Jeanette to drop him just round the corner before they reached the van. He saw us go up the path to the castle."

"But he didn't follow us?"

"No. Because apparently we'd only just disappeared out of sight when he saw two men come back to the van and collect some big crow-bars. This roused his suspicions so, instead of going up to the site behind us, he decided to follow them. It was then that he discovered they'd been cutting this new path through the undergrowth towards the lowest part of the castle walls." She paused.

"He told me that he was able to work out that they were getting quite close to the trench you and he had dug earlier in the week and he had a special interest in that trench. Of course, when they reached the wall, he found they had set up spotlights and screening round a large boulder which was leaning against the wall. They were working there, clearing an area of bushes and undergrowth. When that was completed he said they used the crow-bars to force the boulder away from the wall and revealed the outside door which led to the treasure room."

"That explains why you couldn't open it when you tried. They must have been making quite a lot of noise, but I suppose the wind stopped us from hearing them until they actually got into the room."

"And it also meant *we* weren't heard knocking the back off that chest."

306

"That's true." Philip was silent as he thought of how close they had come to disaster. After a while he said, "Have you found out anything about what's actually in those storage chests?"

"Only what's on the photos we took, and you've seen those as well. I took a look in the chest which they'd just broken open but it was full of a fine powdery packing stuff. It was that powder which made you cough. I tried feeling around a bit, but I couldn't find anything near the top of the chest and I didn't want to go too deep under uncontrolled conditions in case I damaged something."

"Ever the archaeologist."

She grinned. "There were also half a dozen policemen wandering round, in case you hadn't noticed. I particularly didn't want them poking around. That's why I put the top back on and kept guard near it."

"So what's going to happen now?"

"I asked Maitre Amboisard about that when I declared an interest in it. He said the information had been passed to Paris. Several high-ups are rushing down to take a look at it. Meanwhile, the door to the room has been padlocked and a permanent gendarme guard has been put on it. It's when these big noises from Paris turn up that the arguments will start."

"Will they break into the chests?"

"I sincerely hope not. I've reserved myself a place on the inspection party when we get back from Prouille. I'll be there first of all to see that they don't do anything destructive." She looked straight at him. "I can still pack quite a punch you know. I have a lot of influential supporters I can call on."

"Will they take you seriously?"

"They'd better. I've told Amboisard that it was us who found the stuff. I've also told him we removed the back from the first chest in order to provide positive photographic evidence, because Leblanc didn't believe us when we tried to report it to him yesterday evening."

"Will that get the sergeant into trouble?"

"I don't think so. I think he and Amboisard are hand-in-glove at the moment." She giggled. "But I'm going to hold that information over them to make sure they keep me up to date on developments."

"That means we're going to have to rush straight back after we've seen Abbé Dugard."

"I'm afraid so."

Philip was thoughtful. "Talking of that, are we going to let him look at the original of the scroll or only let him see the photos and the copies we've made?"

"I'm going to leave that decision to you, Philip." She leaned back in her seat and stretched. "It's your property, so you must decide."

"Would he treat the original with care?"

"Oh, there's no doubt about that. I'm sure he will appreciate its importance – probably more than me."

"And can you trust him to keep quiet about it? At least for now?"

"I hope so."

"All right. Then I think we'll risk showing him the original. I suppose it would be a bit of an insult to let him only see the photographs and copies."

She smiled. "I hoped you would say that."

So they continued the last few kilometres to Prouille and their hoped-for enlightenment.

51

Bertrand Dugard was expecting them. He was doing some cataloguing in his office when they arrived, so they were invited to go straight in. He treated Jackie to a kiss on the cheek. Philip set the bag down by the desk and found himself shaking a clean hand for a change.

Jackie launched straight into the reason for them being there. "We've brought you an old scroll, Bertrand. I think it may be written in Ancient Hebrew. What I hope is that you can give us an idea of what the document is about. Is that all right?"

"Of course it is my dear. How exciting. I'll be delighted to help."

"I'm sure you'll agree with me when I say that it is important to contaminate the scroll as little as possible. So I've brought a clean sheet to lay it out on. Can we clear your desk and spread the sheet over it?"

"That's absolutely correct, my dear. I'm pleased to see that you take so much trouble." He immediately set about clearing the desk of all its clutter, chatting away happily as he did so. "It's a long time since I was able to handle something like this. I seem to spend all my time these days down in the bowels of the earth."

When the table was cleared, she lifted the sheet from the bag and spread it over the top. "I've brought gloves for us all," she added.

"How thoughtful," said the Abbé. "I don't know where on earth mine are. And I'm afraid they'd probably be in a dreadful state if I could find them."

The men put on their thin fabric gloves and Philip lifted the bamboo tube out of the bag and set it on the sheet-covered table.

"We think this is at least seven hundred and fifty years old. But personally I believe the contents may be much older."

Jackie peeled back the tapes which held the two halves of the bamboo tube together and lifted the top half clear.

"My. Oh, my," Bertrand breathed.

Jackie put on her gloves. Then she lifted the scroll of fabric out of the container and laid it on the sheet. Philip removed the lengths of split bamboo and returned them to the bag, taking out the wooden rule as he did so.

"Can you hold the top as you did before?" she asked him as she peeled it back.

He placed the rule along the top edge.

"We think the material may be waxed silk, Bertrand."

He shook his head. "I'm afraid I would know less than you about that, but I have no reason to think your assumption is incorrect."

"You will see that it is still remarkably flexible. This is the third time we have unrolled it and it shows no sign of deterioration. Of course we won't do it again, once you have seen it, until we have it in controlled atmospheric conditions. However, I judged that it was more important to get some idea of what the document is, before we seal it away again."

She continued to unroll it very gently until it was laid out complete in front of him and lying almost flat on the sheet. The old Abbé watched in fascinated silence, his mouth slightly open. His eyes ranged down the columns of symbols. Then he sat down abruptly on his chair.

"Oh, my God," he said.

Philip looked at him, checking to see that he was all right. "What is it?"

His mouth opened a couple of times as he leaned against the back of the chair and he repeated, "Oh, my God."

"Do you know what it is?" asked Jackie.

He looked up at her with his rheumy eyes. "Oh, indeed I do."

"Have you seen something like this before?"

"Never! But I have heard rumours about the existence of this document."

"So what is it?" Philip entreated.

"It is the list of the kings of Judah."

"Oh. Is that all?" His face reflected his disappointment. "I thought all that stuff was in the bible."

"You don't understand." Bertrand pulled himself to his feet and looked down again on the scroll. "This is *the* list as actually recorded by the high priests in the temple as it happened. You see these circular impressions down the right hand side?"

"Yes."

"Those are the marks of the temple seal which have been applied against each entry and have been dusted with some sort of dye to make them legible. Only the one seal was ever made and it was never allowed to leave the inner chamber of the temple. Those marks completely authenticate this document as the original record of the kings of Judah."

"You mean this was originally in the temple in Jerusalem?"

"I do. If you have a small sample from this document carbon-dated, I am confident you will find it to have come from about a thousand years before Christ. In addition, you will note that each line is in a different hand and the seal marks are irregularly spaced. I am almost sure that this is not a forged copy."

"But how on earth did it get to France?"

The Abbé shook his head. "About that, I'm afraid I haven't a clue." He raised his head and looked straight at Philip. "You may know more about that than I do."

"All I know is that it was a part of the Cathar secret documents which were spirited away from Montségur the night after the castle surrendered."

"Indeed? How very interesting."

"This is a fantastic discovery," breathed Jackie. "The academic world will be set alight by it. Museums will compete to try to obtain it for their collections."

"That is certainly true," said Dugard.

"But what are the columns of information on the scroll?" asked Philip. "And why are there four columns?"

Bertrand leaned forward. "You may be aware that Hebrew is written from right to left across the document and down its length. The first column beside the seal is the name of the king. This third name down, for example, is David, whose name everybody knows. Those symbols, from right to left, spell out his name. The next column is the date of accession, using the Jewish calendar, which won't mean much to you." He paused as he read on. "Ah, yes. The third column is the parentage. For example the fourth king is Solomon, whom the Jews know as Jedediah. And the parentage is recorded as 'Son of David'. The final column is, I believe, the right to succeed. The set of symbols against Jedediah roughly means 'birthright'. The whole thing is very simple, but I believe it is absolutely authentic." He looked at Jackie. "How did you come by it?"

"Philip inherited it. He is a descendent of the last of the Cathars – a man called Phillipe de St Claire who escaped to England after the fall of Montségur. Philip found a journal written by his ancestor which described where this and four other bamboo tubes had been hidden. He unearthed and reclaimed these tubes yesterday with my help."

"Four other tubes?" asked the Abbé. "What is in the other tubes?"

"Unfortunately we don't know. They were stolen before we could open them." She sighed. "I am worried about them."

"Stolen? Who would do that?"

Philip had been watching Dugard's face closely. He was convinced the man had previously known nothing about the tubes. "We intend to find that out," he said.

Abbé Dugard turned his attention back to the sheet of fabric in front of him. His finger traced down beside the edge of the document.

"Yes," he said. "This is extremely interesting. You see this name. It is Zedekiah. He is generally taken to be the last king of the Jews because they were then overrun by the Babylonians and taken into captivity in Babylon. However the list continues, and still the entries are authorised by the temple seal. Somehow the Jews must have secretly taken this scroll and the seal with them to Babylon and continued to install their kings, even though the kings had no temporal power."

"Who are these unknown kings?"

Bertrand shook his head. "I'm afraid the names mean nothing to me at this stage. A lot of research will be required to trace the heritage. But it does mean that this is an absolutely unique document. Nobody has ever been presented with this information in the last two thousand years."

Jackie and Philip watched the old man as he continued to work his way down the list. "This is where the temple seal ceases to be used," he said. "After this the authority of the high priest no longer confirms the position of the king."

"That's strange," said Jackie. "Why would that happen? Who is the last king to receive the temple seal?"

"It's... Oh, my God." The Abbé collapsed with a thump into his chair. "Oh, my dear God."

"What's the matter?" asked Philip. "Are you all right?"

The old man regarded him for a while without seeming to register his question. At last he shook his head as if to clear it and looked up. "Yes. Yes, I am well, thank you. I've just had a great shock. You see the last official King of the Jews is named as Yeshua. That is Ancient Hebrew for Jesus."

The others were surprised into silence as he pulled himself to his feet and pored over the scroll again.

"Here it is, you see - Jesus the Nazarean - First son of Joseph - Acceded by birthright. The date is right. And on the line above is Joseph who also acceded by birthright."

He shook his head and sat down again. "That means the Jewish elders and high priests believed Jesus to be a normal human and not born of The Virgin Mary."

"My goodness," said Jackie, "that will be something for the Church to cope with."

The Abbé suddenly had another thought. He struggled to his feet once more and peered at the scroll. A strange expression came on to his face as he read the next line. "According to this document, the successor to Jesus is named as Sarah. It says she succeeds by birthright. The year of accession is the year usually accepted as the date of the death of Christ on the cross."

He looked at Jackie. "You may be aware that there is a legend in parts of Southern France that Mary Magdalen escaped from Judaea to France, bearing the child of Jesus. It would appear that the source of the legend by now had control of this scroll. Sarah is also the first woman on the list, which suggests

313

to me that the scroll has become a mere family tree, recording the succession of the bloodline."

He pointed back at the sheet of fabric. "You see, it carries on for centuries. After Sarah the names are no longer recorded in Hebrew. It looks like some sort of antique Latin but I can't understand it."

"Let me have a look." Jackie moved round the table beside him and bent over to study the scroll. After a while she shook her head. "No, I can't read that either. As you say, Bertrand, it's a sort of Latin script but the words aren't recognisable as Latin vocabulary."

She continued down the list. "But it's not Latin down here. In fact I think I can read it. It's something like old Occitan." She straightened up and looked at the other two. "Do you think the Cathars regarded themselves as some sort of successors to the Kings of Judah?"

"That's not very likely. They weren't Jewish. They didn't speak Hebrew."

"Of course that's correct. But if what Bertrand says about it being a record of the succession of the bloodline, it may have crossed national and religious boundaries."

"But surely," said Philip, "the Cathars were basically Christians – albeit heretical ones."

"Yes," she agreed, "but after reading this, can you tell me what a Christian is?"

There was a silence as they all absorbed the implications of her question. Philip, who regarded himself as a non-practicing Christian, was beginning to understand what a series of problems the scroll would raise for serious Christians of all denominations, when it was translated.

However Jackie had continued to read down the scroll to the bottom. "Here," she suddenly said. "Look at this. Oh no!" She looked up at him. "Philip – what was the name of the father of your ancient ancestor?"

"Um. I'm not quite sure I can remember. Wait a minute. Wasn't it something like Edmund?"

"Edmund de Saint Claire?"

"I think so."

314

She burst into peals of laughter. "I'm sorry." She patted him on the arm. "I'm sorry, my darling. If this scroll is what we think it is, it means you're a distant descendent of Jesus and King David." She shook her head. "This is unbelievable."

It was Philip's turn to look shocked. "That can't be. It's just too ridiculous."

"Well, somebody has to be his descendant. And it won't be just you. There are probably thousands of others who would be able to trace the same descent after looking at this document. You just happen to be the first-born." Jackie was still smiling. "This is a fantastic document. It will have to be very fully researched. I think it's going to blow the religious world into little pieces."

Philip looked at Bertrand who sadly nodded his head and said, "I think that is true."

"It must be placed somewhere very safe."

A voice came from the doorway. "Believe me, it is going to be."

52

They all spun round to see the man who had entered, dressed in a charcoal grey suit, wearing a black silk shirt with a white dog-collar. He was of middle height and looked to be in his fifties, with a round, pink face and thinning white hair.

"Oh, my God." The Abbé sat down again in his chair with a bump.

The man smiled broadly. "Not quite, my dear Bertrand. But I suppose I am moving in that direction. Let me introduce myself. I am Cardinal Clemente Galbaccino." He turned to the man who had followed him in. "And this is . . . ."

"We know who he is," said Philip, with loathing. "It is Jean-Luc Lerenard, wanted by the police for questioning in connection with the murder of André Jolyon who was Mademoiselle Blontard's assistant."

The cardinal raised his eyebrows. "Is this correct?"

"It is untrue." The big man said nothing more.

"I didn't say he murdered him," said Philip. "What the police want to know is how and why he inveigled himself so quickly into Jacqueline's employment after André's death. Maitre Amboisard, the examining magistrate, will be asking a lot of questions of the Bishop's Palace in Narbonne in the next few days."

"Ah, I understand." Galbaccino shook his head. "Unfortunately he will not be able to receive any answers."

"Why not?"

"Because nobody at the Bishop's Palace knows anything about Monsieur Lerenard. I am the only one who knows about him, and I will be returning to Rome later today."

"In that case they will be following you to ask some questions."

He shook his head again. "I am a papal emissary. I have diplomatic immunity. Nobody will even try to speak to me officially."

"They will certainly want to speak to Lerenard."

"But they will not be able to." The cardinal smiled gently. "Within an hour Jean-Luc Lerenard will no longer exist."

"What do you mean?"

"He will be another person. I'm afraid I'm unwilling to go into details but, when the police go looking for him, they will find no records of Lerenard's existence."

"What about the report I received," broke in Jackie, "when I had him investigated before taking him on to work for me?"

Galbaccino smiled at her in a fatherly way. "I'm sorry to have to tell you that the report will prove to have been prepared on unsubstantiated information. One of the agency's staff will be found to have slipped up and to have used data which he failed to check."

"So he'll lose his job," she said bitterly. "His career will be wrecked,"

"He will be taken care of." The cardinal shrugged. "However that is not what I have come here to discuss."

Jackie squared up to him. "So what *do* you want to discuss? I can guess, with that bully behind you."

"You want the scroll," accused Philip. "The scroll which exposes Rome as a sham. You have stolen the other four bamboo tubes, haven't you? But you have found out that this is the most important one."

"It is correct to say that the other tubes *have* come into my possession."

"So now you want to complete the set."

"You are afraid," accused Jackie, "of what its publication will do to the millions of peasants who slavishly follow all your dictates."

The cardinal refused to be ruffled. "I do intend to persuade you to let me leave here with this – er – document which will complete the set."

"Do you know," asked Philip, "that these five tubes are only one quarter of the number which left Montségur in 1245?"

"Ah, yes. I can tell you that all the remaining tubes were recovered within a very short time of the fall of the last Cathar stronghold."

"And you have them?"

"One set is in the secret archive at the Vatican."

"In the Tower of the Winds?" asked Jackie.

"You have heard of it. That is interesting."

"What about the other two sets?"

"They were destroyed. All three sets proved only to have been copies of the original set which you found yesterday. Now the third set of copies will be destroyed. We will only keep the originals."

Realisation dawned on Philip. "Of course, they wouldn't have wanted to risk the only set they had being lost forever. Tell me, what is in the other four tubes."

"Scrolls," said the cardinal. "Similar to this one but more recent."

"Are they also lists of kings?"

"One contains a list of the Merovingian heritage and the bloodline of the Cathars. One describes in detail the Cathar doctrine, together with condemnation of the Christian Church and justification of the Cathar heresy. Another one describes the Cathar festivals and other major events in the Cathar calendar and their meaning. The final one gave full details and the location of the Cathar treasure, the hope being that enough *perfecti* would survive after Montségur to rebuild the faith."

Jackie said acidly, "And of course all the Cathar treasure has been taken to the Vatican for safe keeping."

"I don't know exactly the location of all of it now," said the cardinal. "However, one must admit that it was a very valuable addition to Roman Catholic wealth in the middle ages."

"But none of the other scrolls is as important as this one," she pointed out. "Did you hear what Bertrand read in the scrolls?"

"We heard some of it when we were waiting outside the office."

"Then you will know that this scroll proves that Jesus was a mere mortal and that he sired a daughter to carry on the bloodline. This is the scroll, above all others, which you will not want to enter the public domain."

"Yes," said Philip, "you have come here to take it by force."

318

"I hope not," said Galbaccino. "I hope to persuade you that it would be in everybody's best interest to hand it over to me to take back to Rome for safe keeping."

"What do you mean?"

"Well, first of all you must appreciate that the Church – and I mean the whole of the Christian Church – not simply the Church of Rome – is a very important spiritual factor in many millions of people's lives. People deeply need to believe in something stable and permanent. And I include sophisticated people like yourselves in that, even though you may pretend that you are above such things."

"I can see the sense in that," said Philip.

"If you attempt to destroy or even diminish those beliefs, you will cause a great deal of evil to inflict itself upon the world. You will destroy one of the main props to the way of life we enjoy in the Western world and further erode the family unit, on which our personal security is based. You will increase the acceptance of criminality. You may even increase the tensions between states which at present are partly allied by their common beliefs."

"I think that's going a bit far."

"Is it?" The cardinal raised a cautionary finger. "Take a little time to think about religion – with all its faults – and decide how often the stabilising factors in people's lives can be traced back to the influence of religion. I'm not talking about extreme religious beliefs, which can often be destructive, but the honestly-held concepts of right and wrong."

Philip nodded, half-convinced, despite his personal views, by Galbaccino's arguments.

"I can understand that you are critical of Rome's behaviour over the centuries. It is easy to find fault in a huge organisation which has tried to arrange the spiritual lives of billions of people. Perhaps we have chosen to restrict too much the amount of information we have given to believers, in order to show Christ in the way we want him to be received by them. If his body was shown to follow the blood-line of the kings of Judah, it does not mean he could not have also been the son of

God. He could still have ascended back into heaven, even if he left his seed on earth."

"And that leads me to the personal aspect," continued the cardinal. "People are not going to be turned away from Christ by the fact that he had a daughter. Why should he not? Perhaps this is the little of God which is in all of us." He pointed a finger at Philip."Perhaps your discovery means that you are someone special. Perhaps you are even the son of God come again to us."

"What!"

Galbaccino laughed. "Have you thought, Philip Sinclair, what millions of innocent people in this world will think if you are exposed as the direct first-born descendent of Jesus Christ? They will come flocking to hear your words. They will want to raise you up on high above them. Who knows, the Vatican may even make it worth your while to be installed in Rome."

"Oh, my God!" Jackie's slightly hysterical laugh echoed round the shed.

"Do you want all that?"

Philip was speechless as the awful prospect opened up before him.

"Do you?"

"I most certainly do not."

"Then the way out is to permit me to take away the scroll and keep the other four. In that way life will keep to its old, unjust, incompetent but safe pattern. You can marry this good lady, settle down to a happy and wealthy life, and live, I hope, to a ripe old age."

"Wealthy?"

"Ah, yes. Of course, we do not wish simply to take away your property. We expect to pay a fair price for it. I even have the cheque with me, drawn on the Vatican bank."

He reached inside his breast pocket, drew it out and handed it to Philip. When he looked at it he saw it was made out for five million euros. He passed it to Jackie.

"What do you think?"

She looked straight at Galbaccino. "Will you destroy these tubes and their contents?"

"Certainly not. I promise you that they will be carefully stored under ideal conditions and will not deteriorate."

"So, some time in the future, the Vatican may decide to give this information back to the world."

The cardinal nodded. "You have my promise on that."

"Then I will suggest Philip accepts your offer." She turned to him with a smile on her face. "I couldn't have you turn into the New Messiah, darling. How could I go to bed with you again?"

She began to roll up the scroll, preparatory to returning it to its container.

Philip stayed silent for a long time. He didn't know what to say. At last he spoke. "Thank you." He breathed a deep sigh of relief. "Thank you for saving me from that prospect, cardinal."

"It is my pleasure."

He suddenly thought. "I also have a number of photos and a copy of this document which we made. I think I should give those to you as well."

"Where are they?"

"In the boot of the car."

"I will collect them as we go. I propose that now we should all leave the good Abbé to continue with his valuable work here without further interruption from us."

On their way back to Quillan Philip asked, "Do you think Abbé Dugard had betrayed us to the cardinal?"

"I don't know. He hardly said a word after the great man arrived."

"But he obviously knew him. He was shocked to see him. He was in Narbonne yesterday, presumably being interviewed by Galbaccino."

"Perhaps he was. But he didn't know then, that we were going to call in to see him this morning. And he didn't know what it was about."

"He could have phoned the cardinal this morning."

"Certainly he could. And I presume Galbaccino knew by then that we had the fifth bamboo tube, because Lerenard had already taken the other four to him."

Philip shrugged. "I suppose it's not important any more. I know that you've lost an important document which might have enhanced your reputation."

"But at what cost?" she interjected.

"And," Philip continued, "you can now concentrate on getting yourself onto the team which investigates the treasure in the underground room at le Bézu. That should be a reasonable compensation for you."

"But what will *you* do?" She asked. "That work is likely to take years. I don't like the idea of it keeping us apart."

"I've been thinking about that." He smiled at her. "I like this area. I think I'll spend some of my five million on buying a house somewhere near le Bézu. Then I'll be able to keep an eye on you. What do you think of that idea?"

She laughed at him. "Am I allowed to have an opinion, oh, my lord and master?"

"Watch it," he warned her. "If you're not careful I might drag you back to the hotel bedroom and beget a son of god on you."

"Oh, yes please."

He reconsidered. "On second thoughts, perhaps we ought to be married before I do that."

"Am I supposed to take that as a proposal?"

"Oh, no. I must do it properly. Let´s make a secret tryst for eight o'clock this evening at our meeting-place by the river. Then I'll get down on bended knee and beg for your hand."

"That sounds more like it," she agreed. "Maybe those two little girls will be there as witnesses. Then they'll certainly have a story to tell their families."

THE END ?

Do you want to know what happened to the treasure? What more do the archaeologists find? How are the Templars involved in this area? What will happen to the murderess, César Renoir, now near to death? How will Philip and Jackie's relationship cope with her star role on television? And how did the village priest come into a fortune in 1888? If you want answers to these questions, you will need to read the sequel -

The Legacy of the Templars (AMR No 5)

There is also a third novel in the trilogy - **The Treasure of the Visigoths (AMR No 9)**.

A message from the author

I hope you enjoyed this book. If you did you can help me by giving it a review. Reviews are my most powerful marketing device in getting my books noticed. I am unknown to the great majority of readers. I can't afford to pay for advertisements. But I have something more powerful, and that is a loyal group of readers.

Honest reviews of my books will help to bring them to the attention of other readers. So I would be grateful if you would spend five minutes giving **The Secret of the Cathars** a review on Amazon.

Thank you very much – Michael Hillier.

The Secret of the Cathars is the first book in the **Languedoc Trilogy** and the fourth in the **Adventure, Mystery, Romance Series** of novels created by **Michael Hillier**. To date the others are:-

The Eighth Child (AMR No 1) – Alan Brading witnesses the shooting of his French-born wife in a London street. The police seem to think it is a mistaken terrorist attack. When he recovers from the mental problems caused by the shock, he travels to her home-town in the Loire Valley to try to find the murderer, whom he has seen there. However the local people in Chalons are hostile to his enquiries. Only his wife's younger sister, Jeanette, is willing to help him uncover what happened forty years ago. Together they risk their lives in their pursuit of the truth.

The Mafia Emblem – The Wolf of Hades (AMR No 2) – When Ben Cartwright discovers the decapitated body of his Italian business partner, he finds out that he is in danger of losing his carefully built-up wine importing business. He flies to Naples to try to recover the company, but becomes caught up in the ancient vendetta between two of the oldest families in Southern Italy. His partner's sister, Francesca, doesn't like him. However she joins him in their fight for their lives in the erupting volcanic area of the *Campi Flegraei.*(This one is available free from the author's website.)

Dancing with Spies (AMR No 3) – Caroline Daley is travelling down the Adriatic on a ferry which breaks down and has to limp into the port of Dubrovnik. However the Yugoslav Civil War is in progress and the beautiful city is under siege from the Serb-led JNA. She becomes caught up in the seething web of violence and espionage among the ancient buildings. Her only hope of escape seems to be to put her trust the arrogant journalist, Ralph Henderson. And are they all in danger? Surely the JNA won't open fire on the World Heritage Site, will they?

The Templar Legacy (AMR No 5) – This is the sequel to **The Secret of the Cathars** and the second book in the **Languedoc Trilogy**. Philip returns from a short visit to England to find that Jackie has disappeared. His searches for her lead him, despite considerable personal danger, to Paris and the fascinating little town of Rennes le Chateau, near Carcassonne. He also inadvertently discovers the first clues about the remains left by the Templars when they were wiped out by King Philip II. When Jackie appears again they follow the route started by Philip until they come across the sensational legacy left to the world by the Templars. (To be published in the near future.)

The Discovery of Franco's Bankroll (AMR No 6) – Middle-aged former playboy Sebastian Bishop finds himself marooned on the Costa Blanca without any means of earning a living. His solution is to offer his services as an escort to rich single ladies. Of course he doesn't realise this is going to lead him into deep, deep trouble. After spending the night with a Spanish Condesa, he discovers her strangled body in the morning. He is sure to be charged with her murder. His desperate attempts to prove his innocence involve him with several groups of people trying to find the Nazi stolen hoard shipped to Spain in the last days of the war and threaten his life. (To be published in the next couple of months.)

Bank-cor-Rupt (AMR No 7) - Andrew Denbury is summoned to his bank one morning and told they are calling in the overdraft on which his business runs and they will appoint a receiver. What can he do? His wealthy father-in-law hates him and won't help. His wife is only interested in leading an enjoyable social life with her upper class friends. His suppliers are furious because the bank has bounced their cheques. The only person who believes in him is his secretary, Samantha. Somehow Andrew must try to find a way to confound the destroyers of his business. He conceives a plan which may save him, with Samantha's help. But will it work when he puts it into practice?

Network Virus (AMR No 8) - Charlotte Faraday is searching for twelve-year-old girl who has gone missing. Is she the victim of a paedophile gang led by a rich, dissolute local gentleman? To complicate matters, the girl's mother has been raped a few nights earlier in the car park behind the Red Garter Nightclub by a soldier who has escaped back to his regiment which is currently training in Germany. Meanwhile Stafford Paulson, is convinced that the death of Joanne de Billiere is suspicious. They are not helped in their enquiries by creeping corruption in the Devon and Cornwall police force.

The Treasure of the Visigoths (AMR No 9) – The third novel in the **Languedoc Trilogy** follows Philip when he inadvertently finds himself on the trail of the treasure of the Temple in Jerusalem, which was captured by the Visigoths when they sacked Rome in the fifth century. It is complicated by Jackie's concentration on launching her television series about the Cathars and by the two other women who are anxious for their own reasons to replace her. (Contains explicit sex scenes).

Other novels by **Michael Hillier:-**

The Gigabyte Detective
The Property People Series

Go to his website (http://mikehillier.com) for further details on all his published writing.

About the author

He has completed sixteen novels to date and there are several others which are partly written. Eleven of the novels have been published and are for sale on various sites, including Amazon, Apple, Barnes and Noble (Nook) and Kobo. The most popular novel to date is **The Secret of the Cathars** which has sold substantially more than ten thousand copies Two sequels have been published, forming **The Languedoc Trilogy**.

He has split his novels into three groups – detective novels, a four-volume historical saga, and the **Adventure/ Mystery/ Romance** series is explained on his website mikehillier.com.

Michael gets the inspiration for many of his books from family holidays to various beautiful locations in the world. Exploring historic towns and buildings has brought to light a host of untold stories which get his creative juices flowing.

Printed in Great Britain
by Amazon

81918524R00192